THE SCOUT

Fated Book 2   Legends of Pern Coen

Hannah E. Carey

Dedication

To ...

CONTENTS

CHARACTER LIST

Aengus: healer, village healer in Beag

Alannah: shapeshifter, servant of Fianna

Arwel: advisor to Cadfael

Awyr *(OW-air)*: Seren's wolf

Blaidd *(BLY-th)*: Wolf Spirit

Bran: shapeshifter, Seren's lover

Cadfael *(KAD-file)*: Ri of Blaidd, husband of Esyllt, father of Seren and Eamon

Cian *(KEE-an)*: healer, son of Sioned, cousin of Seren and Eamon

Cryfder *(CRUV-dair)*: Seren's wolf

Dara: mercenary leader

Domhnall *(DO-nahl)*: son of Muireann, advisor to Cadfael

Drystan: warrior chief of Blaidd

Eamon *(EH-man)*: son of Cadfael and Esyllt

Emer *(EE-mur)*: warrior of Blaidd, friend of Seren, wife of Lewella

Esyllt *(EH-sisht)*: Banrion of Blaidd, wife of Cadfael, mother of Seren and Eamon

Fflur: sister of Alannah

Fianna: Stag Spirit, Dark Spirit of Pern Coen

Fionn: brother of Cadfael

Gruffudd *(GRI-fidh)*: father of Bran, stablehand at Castle Clogwyn

Ithel: advisor to Cadfael

Laoise *(LEE-sha)*: advisor to Cadfael

Lewella: warrior of Blaidd, friend of Seren, wife of Emer

Lorcan *(LOR-kan)*: mind-speaker, servant of Fianna

Mair: healer at Castle Clogwyn, friend of Seren

Muireann: Ri of Seabhac

Seachnall *(SHAKH-nal)*: warrior of Blaidd, friend of Eamon

Seren *(SEH-rehn)*: seer, daughter of Cadfael and Esyllt, Bran's lover

Sioned *(SHO-nehd)*: sister of Esyllt, mother of Cian

THE ISLAND OUT OF THE SEA

The roar of Arth, the Bear Spirit, shook the earth and pushed the mountains up out of the water,

The powerful wings of Seabhac, the Hawk Spirit, created the wind that smoothed the jagged peaks,

Tyll the Owl Spirit flew over the land, pulling the trees out of the earth with his strong talons,

The hooves of Ceffyl, the Horse Spirit, pounded the valleys into being,

While the paws of Blaidd, the Wolf Spirit, dug the rivers and lakes,

Upon the completion of their work, the island of Pern Coen was created,

Gifted to the five clans to honor and care for.

But three Spirits remained, their offerings denied by the rest of those who resided in the Greater Spirit Realm,

Cigfran, the Raven Spirit, wished to bring death,

Fianna, the Stag Spirit, wished to allow decay,

Pysgod, the Fish Spirit, wished to allow for destruction,

And all wished for complete control over those who called the island home.

The Five Spirits were left to band together, diminishing the power of the Three.

Shunned by the Greater Spirits and their power reduced, the Three Spirits are forced to roam the Realm of the Mortals,

Sowing their darkness wherever they can and seeking to possess the souls of those who willingly give them.

CHAPTER 1

OUTSIDER

Bran

EVERY DAY, I WAS reminded that I did not belong at Castle Clog-wyn. I was only here because the Ri of Blaidd had decided I was worth more to him alive than dead. I was not welcome within the walls of the imposing granite keep, and the inhabitants of the castle made sure I knew it. Leaving, however, wasn't an option. Not only would Ri Cadfael have me hunted down and killed, leaving Clogwyn would mean leaving Seren. It would mean breaking my promise to help her rid the clan of the Stag Spirit, Fianna. It would mean letting Fianna and its servant, Lorcan, bring the land I called home to ruin. Seren needed me, the clan needed me, and that was why I stayed despite the continual injustices that I was forced to live with.

Sweat trickled down my back, rivulets of it running between my shoulder blades as the sun beat down on me. I made small, calculated movements, my gaze locked on Seachnall, the warrior in front of me. My fists were raised in front of my face in order to defend myself from his blows and the other man looked at me with a gleam in his eyes that left an uncomfortable feeling in the pit of my stomach. Like the rest of the war band, he was never pleased when he was ordered to train with me, and I had no doubt he would make sure I knew it before the end of our sparring.

A few feet away from us, the clan's warrior chief, Drystan, watched us with his arms crossed and a scowl twisting his face. Drystan hadn't liked me from the start. He'd made it clear that he didn't care for having a shifter in his war band, but as much as the warrior chief hated me, he wasn't going to defy his Ri.

Seachnall swung his fist at me and I barely blocked him, silently cursing myself for getting distracted. We danced around one another, getting in jabs here and there as the sun continued to beat down on us. The two of us had been sparring for almost an hour now, first with wooden swords and then with our fists. In the roughly two weeks since I'd started my training with Drystan, I'd spent almost every day like this, being thrust out onto the training grounds and matched with warrior after warrior, each of whom was more than willing to make me miserable any way they could. Drystan called it training. All I saw was the man who hated me making sure I knew my place.

I fought the urge to wipe the sweat off my brow as Seachnall lunged at me again, instead dodging away to keep his fist from connecting with my face. I swung back at him and he twisted away from me, but not before I landed a glancing blow to his shoulder. He narrowed his eyes and let out a growl, throwing his fist wildly at me. I managed to block him and jump out of reach, but that only angered him further. He deflected my next punch, but I didn't manage to fully stop his returning blow. His strikes were becoming harder and faster as his anger grew. He and the others hated when I bested them, and on more than one occasion, I'd experienced warriors going out of their way to make sure I always lost.

Drystan shouted something, his tone one of warning, but I was too busy trying to fend off Seachnall's rapidly increasing blows to pay attention. We were supposed to only be practicing our fighting skills, not pummeling each other, but it was clear that the latter was what Seachnall intended. I certainly wasn't going to sit there and take it without defending myself.

As the bout continued to devolve into a flat-out fistfight, I could feel the temptation to shift into my wolf form. Seachnall wouldn't stand a chance against me then, but doing so would only land me a trip to the dungeons. I'd been forbidden from shifting, unless Cadfael or Drystan specifically allowed it. It was just another one of the invisible chains the two men had wrapped me in since I'd bargained with my life.

The longer I fought to keep Seachnall at bay, the more I tired. I only dropped my defenses for a moment, my breathing hard and fast, and Seachnall took advantage. He kicked out with his right leg, catching me in the ankle. It was a low move and one he shouldn't have been using per the parameters Drystan had set around our fight, but that didn't stop him. I stumbled, losing my balance, and Seachnall took a swing at my face, catching the side of my jaw. My head snapped back and I went down to my knees, tasting blood.

My ears rang and I tried to lurch back up, but before I could get to my feet, Seachnall was behind me. He grabbed my left arm, wrenching it behind my back with enough force that I heard it pop. An excruciating pain erupted from my shoulder as the other man kneed me in the back, sending me face-first into the dirt.

"That's enough!"

Drystan's shout rang out across the open expanse of the training yard. Seachnall released his hold on me and I let out a gasp of pain, my arm now hanging at an awkward angle. Drystan stalked over to us, Seachnall stepping back out of his way. When Drystan reached us, Seachnall was quick to school his expression, but not before I caught a glimpse of his smirk. I gritted my teeth. Seachnall had dislocated my shoulder on purpose. I was sure of it.

"Get up," Drystan snapped, looming over me.

My jaw was clenched so tight, it was aching as I stumbled to my feet. The pain in my shoulder was almost unbearable.

"Seachnall," Drystan called, "go fetch someone to see the shifter to the infirmary."

"Yes, Pennathe Drystan." Seachnall gave the warrior chief a respectful incline of his head, the picture of an obedient warrior, before jogging off across the training yard toward the door that led into the armory.

"You're going to have to do better than that if you don't want to be killed the first time you're sent out on a scouting mission," Drystan said, not even bothering to hide the disgust in his voice as he glanced back over at me.

"That was hardly a fair fight," I retorted, my breathing shallow as pain continued to radiate through my body.

Resentment coursed through me at Drystan's words. As if I hadn't spent years acting as a scout for Lorcan. As if I couldn't kill someone faster than he could imagine if I were only able to use my gift. His ridiculous training was a waste. There was no one else in his war band more capable of hunting down Lorcan and killing him than me.

"Real fights won't be fair," Drystan said, his gaze hard. "I would think someone with your... history would know that."

I took a deep breath, fighting for calm. I knew about unfairness far better than he did. I was, after all, the one who had spent two years of my life being hunted by his warriors simply because of the gift that had been granted to me by the Spirits.

Not to mention all the unfairness I'd suffered since returning to these walls.

"What happened?" The sharp call broke through my bitter thoughts and some of the tightness in my chest eased as I looked up to see Drystan's second-in-command, Lewella, approaching us.

She was dressed in the black pants and dark blue shirt, embroidered with the wolf's head seal of Blaidd, that all the warriors wore. She kept her dark hair short and her brow was furrowed as she came to a stop beside Drystan, her gaze locked on me.

"You are supposed to be overseeing the archers right now," Drystan said, his scowl returning.

"No one else is currently willing to see the shifter to the infirmary. I don't believe he's of much use to Ri Cadfael if he's injured," she replied, raising her brows as she met Drystan's gaze.

He muttered something under his breath before motioning at me. "Take him then. But I want you back on the archery field once you've handed him off to Cian." He paused, turning to me. "I expect you back here for more sword work this evening, shifter. You obviously have some work to do."

I glowered at him and it took everything in me not to spew a string of curses. His continual insults were even more unbearable with the way he used the word *shifter*, as if I didn't have a damn name.

"Let's get you to Cian," Lewella said, motioning for me to follow her.

I squared my shoulders and limped off behind her, though I only made it a few steps before my ankle gave way and I ended up down on one knee. I cursed under my breath and squeezed my eyes shut against the pain. I could only imagine the taunting I was going to receive from the other warriors after this.

Seachnall and I had been far from alone in the sparring area and there were plenty of others who would have witnessed my humiliation.

"Here," Lewella said, bending down to help me.

"Thank you," I mumbled as she slipped an arm around my good shoulder to support my weight.

"Seachnall didn't exactly play fair, did he?" she asked, her disapproval evident in her tone as we slowly made our way toward the castle.

"Hardly," I muttered, letting out a low hiss when I stumbled over a rock and twisted the same ankle.

"I'll be having a discussion with him later," she replied. "Even if Drystan won't."

"Thank you."

Silence fell between us as we continued on and for not the first time, I wished Lewella was warrior chief instead of Drystan. She was certainly far more fair than he was. She was also one of the few at Clogwyn who had treated me decently and while I expected it probably had something to do with the close relationship of her fiancé, Emer, with Seren, I appreciated it all the same.

When we reached the door to the armory, Lewella ushered me through first. I waited for her just inside the door, trying to ignore the dark looks and hushed conversation of a handful of warriors who were polishing their blades a few feet away. None of them trusted me and most of them feared me, waiting for me to turn on them and slaughter them in their sleep.

Cadfael had done a thorough job of convincing the people of Clogwyn that shapeshifters were weak-minded monsters who would give their souls over to the Dark Spirits at a moment's notice, turning themselves into mindless killers. It wasn't true, but that hadn't stopped Cadfael from spreading such lies and people were all too willing to believe him instead of looking at the proof right in front of them.

Lewella came up and supported my good shoulder again, the two of us continuing on across the armory. My injured shoulder felt like it was on fire, but I forced myself to keep moving. As we stepped out of the armory and into one of the long castle hallways, I repeated the same words I had been telling myself for days now. *Kill Lorcan and destroy Fianna.* That was my purpose here. That was why I would endure the likes of Drystan and Seachnall. The moment Cadfael set me loose, no matter how hard it was, I would hunt down Lorcan and I would end him. That was the ultimate way I could aid Seren in stopping Fianna from turning the Clan of Blaidd into an uninhabitable wasteland, and I would see it through. No matter what.

CHAPTER 2

THE RI'S DAUGHTER

Seren

IT WAS DIFFICULT NOT to feel like the entire morning had been a waste. I'd spent two hours in the village of Gefell, talking to the village elder, Tesni, but it had been for nothing. She had not agreed to join me in pushing my father to do more to defeat Fianna. Tesni was content with my father's actions of sending small groups of warriors north to fight the band of rebels Fianna was using to carry out its attacks and deadly fires. But the forces Father was sending weren't enough. He'd been using the same tactics for months now and he was no closer to victory. He had built a significant war band in his years as Ri and yet most of his fighting forces remained at the castle. The warriors he had sent out paled in comparison to what he had at his disposal.

A sigh escaped my lips as my dun stallion, Ceol, followed the dirt path that led from the village to the castle. The bright sunshine and beautiful spring day felt at odds with the frustration and worry that swirled inside me. While the sky was clear and blue here, I knew the sky in the northern part of the clan was most likely covered in smoke and ash. The more recent reports had not been good. Lorcan and Fianna were growing bolder, attacking more villages and farms with their unnatural fires. The people were suffering and all the while, Father continued to sit in his hall and pretend that victory was near at hand.

"There are other villages," Domhnall said. He rode beside me on his own stallion, Gwynt. "Tesni is far from the only elder in Blaidd."

I glanced over at him and gave him a half-smile, which he returned. He'd been more supportive of me and my cause over the last few weeks than I had ever anticipated. Already he had enlisted the aid of one of his fellow advisory council members, Laoise, and the two of them were as committed as I was to seeing Fianna gone from this land.

"It would be harder for the two of you to go yourselves, but perhaps it would be wise to seek the aid of some of the elders in the north." The remark came from the rider on my other side, my close friend and warrior of Blaidd, Emer.

She had ridden with Domhnall and me down to Gefell, not only as protection for the two of us, but with the hopes of further convincing Tesni as well. Emer was a distant cousin to Tesni, but the family tie hadn't gone as far as we'd hoped.

"They haven't seen the same destruction here that they have in the north," Emer continued. "Not even during the Purge. Not to mention that it makes them feel safer, having most of the warriors remaining at Clogwyn and in the south. They're protected, insulated."

I nodded, knowing she was right. During the Purge, the last time Fianna had wreaked havoc across the land, much of the southern part of the clan had been spared, especially in comparison to the north. The fires themselves had never reached

Castle Clogwyn, something Father had long boasted about. Clogwyn and the villages closest to it had always been the safest places in the clan.

"I still think it wise to exhaust our closer options first," Domhnall said.

"We'll discuss it with Laoise this evening," I replied.

I still wasn't sure if I had complete trust in Laoise, having known her for most of my life and seeing how crafty and cunning she could be, but at the same time, if someone were to outsmart Father, it would be her. I'd gleaned that much over the last few weeks of secretive meetings and discussions, ones we had gone out of our way to keep hidden. Despite my misgivings regarding Laoise, I needed her, just like I needed Domhnall. The two of them wielded considerable influence at Clogwyn with their places on the advisory council. Far more influence than I did, despite being the Ri's daughter.

We rode the rest of the way in silence and before long, the imposing granite walls of Castle Clogwyn came into view. We were let through the castle gate without question and as soon as our horses trotted into the courtyard, we brought them to a halt and dismounted. A few warriors milled about, along with the occasional servant, but from the calm inside the castle, one would not know that a Dark Spirit was ravaging our land. It disturbed me. Father's lack of urgency was an insult to those who had already lost their homes and their lives.

I rubbed Ceol's neck as I pulled the reins over his head, noting that the warmth of the day on the ride back had caused my stallion to break into a slight sweat. The days were slowly growing warmer and soon, spring would fade on the island, making way for summer. Emer led the way to the stables, Domhnall and I falling in behind her, but we didn't make it far before I heard someone shouting my name. I stopped and allowed a castle runner to race toward me. He was young, like many of the messengers, barely sixteen from the looks of it, and by the time he reached me, he was slightly out of breath.

"Cian has need of you in the infirmary," the runner said.

My stomach clenched at the news, but I nodded. "I'll be on my way at once."

The runner dashed off and I tried to ignore the heaviness that was growing in the pit of my stomach. My cousin, Cian, was the castle healer and if he needed me in the infirmary, I doubted it was for anything good. He'd been working long hours over the last week with the return of a handful of warriors from the north. They'd all been sent back to the castle because of the extent of their injuries, many of them tainted with the poison of the Dark Spirits from Fianna's deadly shadow creatures. Father had done everything in his power to downplay the severity of the injuries, but Cian had requested my help more than once the last few days and I'd seen the truth for myself.

"Here," Domhnall said, holding out a hand. "I'll have a stablehand see to Ceol."

"Thank you," I told him, passing him the stallion's reins.

Once I had handed off my horse, I took off, drawing a few looks from warriors and servants as I rushed by them. Once I'd scaled the steps of the castle, I hurried through the front doors, into the large entryway. With my sole focus on getting to the infirmary, I didn't even pause to admire the beautiful wolf carvings that had been etched into the stone walls or the massive wrought iron chandelier above me. Instead, I hurried down the long, winding hallways to the castle's east wing.

The infirmary was on the far end of the east wing and I was more familiar with it than I would have liked to have been, having spent many long hours helping Cian tend to the wounded during the Purge. I let myself into the entry chamber, the smaller room where patients were first looked at by one of Cian's assistants and then separated out in order of need. The entry chamber at least didn't look particularly busy today; only a few servants were seated in the chairs along the wall, most of them looking as if they only had minor ailments. Still, I knew what lay inside the main chamber, despite Father's demands that the wounded warriors be hidden away.

As I closed the door behind me, I caught the attention of the assistant who was going from one patient to the next, talking quietly to them and making notes on a piece of parchment. I recognized her and though I didn't know her well, I at least knew her name, Aerona. She was considerably older than me, in her mid-fifties, and her mouth turned down as she looked over at me. Like most in the castle, she didn't much care for me, especially after the events of the Purge, when I had aided shifters in fleeing Blaidd.

"Cian sent for me?" I said, walking over to her.

"He did," Aerona replied, her tone flat. "I'll let someone know you're here."

She motioned for me to take a seat and I did so, trying to ignore the stares of the others in the room. Father had labeled me a traitor when he had learned of my actions aiding shifters after the Purge, and there were many inside Clogwyn who still held to such beliefs, even years later. My current relationship with Bran, not to mention how vocal I had been in expressing my displeasure over how Father was handling the situation with Fianna, hadn't helped matters. There were many who saw me as a troublemaker and my affections for a shifter an act of betrayal to our people.

They wrongly believed my father's lies that unlike the rest of the gifted, shapeshifters were weak and easily turned by the Dark Spirits. I was determined to change a great many things the day I became Ri of Blaidd, and making the clan a safe place for shifters was one of them.

The door to the main chamber of the infirmary opened and I couldn't hold back my quiet sigh of relief as Aerona returned with a healer trailing behind her. The healer, Mair, was twenty, the same age as me, and though she had come to Clogwyn a few months ago, I'd taken an immediate liking to her. Not only was she knowledgeable and skilled in the healing arts, she hadn't treated me with the same distrust that many others in the castle held.

I got to my feet as Mair strode over to me, Aerona wandering off to resume speaking to the patients waiting to see healers. A closer look at Mair revealed blood staining the sleeves of her shirt and her expression was weary.

"Cian is waiting for you in one of the private rooms," Mair said, motioning for me to follow her.

I did so, coming to walk side by side with her as we stepped into the main chamber. The dried blood splattering her clothes only made the knot in my belly grow. I hoped one of the warriors hidden away in the private rooms hadn't taken a turn for the worse.

"Bran arrived a short while ago," she said as we walked, "and Cian is going to need help seeing to his dislocation. I would do it myself, but I have a broken leg I have to set. And... I'm afraid no one else was willing to assist him."

My stomach clenched at the news of Bran and at the same time, an anger rushed through me with Mair's last statement. I hated the fear and vitriol that had been directed at Bran since he had come to Clogwyn. He had done nothing to deserve the ire of those around him.

Mair led me to one of the private rooms located along the far wall of the main chamber, usually reserved for the most severe of cases or people in the castle with high standing. Mair went to leave when we reached the door, but I placed a hand on her arm to stop her.

"Thank you," I told her, holding her gaze. "For being willing to help him."

"No one deserves to suffer," she said.

As she turned and left, I could feel a lump settle in the back of my throat. If only more people felt that way. If only my own father did. Shaking my head, I tried to clear my thoughts as I pushed open the door and stepped into the small room. Cian would need me to be focused. Even with his healing gift, fixing a dislocation wasn't the easiest of tasks.

Bran was seated on the small bed at the center of the room, hanging his head while Cian inspected his shoulder. I couldn't help but wince when I caught sight of the awkward angle of his arm. Both men looked over at me when they heard me enter, relief passing over their features.

"Spirits, Bran," I said as I came over to the bed. "What happened?"

There were streaks of dirt on his clothes and while it looked like Cian had cleaned up his face, he had the beginnings of a bruise along his jaw and a bit of dried blood at the corner of his mouth.

"I got a little too well acquainted with Seachnall's fists," Bran replied. He tried for a smile, but it was half-hearted and I could hear the bitterness in his voice.

"By accident?" I asked, raising my brows and trying to calm my own rising anger.

Bran shrugged his good shoulder, not meeting my gaze. I glanced over at Cian, his pressed-together lips and disapproving expression telling me everything I needed to know. Drystan needed to get better control of his warriors. There had been far too many training accidents lately that had ended in Bran getting injured.

"I've tended to his jaw and his ankle, but healing his shoulder will go more smoothly, and hopefully less painfully, with an extra set of hands," Cian said.

He walked over to a nearby table and grabbed a bottle of spirits that I knew was mixed with a few herbs that would give a sedative effect. He filled an empty mug.

"You're going to want this," he said, walking back over to Bran and handing him the mug.

Bran raised his brows as he took it with his good hand. "That bad, huh?"

"Better than if I had to force it back in with nothing but brute strength, but it's still going to hurt," Cian replied.

Bran let out a quiet sigh before throwing the drink back in three large gulps. Cian refilled the mug once more, getting Bran to down a bit more before instructing him to lie back on the bed. He then motioned me to join him next to Bran's awkwardly hanging arm.

"The spirits should knock him out enough," Cian said quietly. "What I'm going to need you to do is guide and support the arm as I push the bone back into place. It will go quickly, but the smoother it is, the less pain for him."

I nodded, the two of us waiting for the spirits to lull Bran into a state of semiconsciousness. At Cian's instructions, I placed my hands under Bran's arm, supporting the limb while Cian gently placed his hands on Bran's shoulder. It was an odd sight, watching as Bran's arm moved back into place simply under Cian's touch. As Bran's shoulder joint popped back into place, he let out a sigh of relief.

"Done," Cian said, releasing his hold on Bran before taking a step back. "Move it for me, just to be sure."

I too stepped back and Bran carefully rotated his arm, the pained expression leaving his face as he did so.

"Good as new," Bran said, his words slightly slurred.

"Good," Cian replied. "I still recommend you take the rest of the day to rest. You'll be back in the training yard tomorrow."

"Drystan wants me back tonight." Bran swayed slightly as he half sat up.

Cian frowned and steadied him. "I'll have a talk with Drystan."

"Okay," Bran said, rolling his shoulders. "Feels better but hurt like the blazes."

"Imagine if you hadn't had something to take the edge off," I told him wryly.

"I'm going to have you stay here for a bit, probably an hour or so, to let those spirits wear off," Cian said. "Mair and I will be in to check on you."

Bran nodded, getting comfortable on the bed once more. Cian walked back over to the table, cleaning up his work space, and I came around in front of Bran.

"I have to help with the wolves this afternoon," I said, taking one of his hands in mine and giving it a gentle squeeze. "But I'll come check on you as soon as I'm done."

"'Kay," he replied. "Love you."

"I love you," I murmured, brushing my lips across his forehead.

Though part of me was loathe to leave him, I knew he was in good hands with Cian and Mair. With Bran laid out on the bed, I helped Cian finish cleaning up before the two of us departed the room.

"We'll keep an eye on him," Cian said as I closed the door behind us. "And I'll send word to Drystan that he won't be going back to the training yard tonight, on my orders."

"Thank you," I replied, unable to hide a disgusted scoff as I shook my head. "If Drystan is so keen to use Bran as a weapon, it's beyond me why he continually allows him to get injured."

"Drystan has a tendency to let his personal feelings get the better of him. Much like Uncle Cadfael." Cian grimaced.

Which is why this clan is in the state it's in, I thought, a bitter taste filling my mouth as I thought of the roles Drystan and Father had played in the last few dark and deadly years. Cian bid me farewell, heading off to tend to other patients, and I saw myself out of the infirmary. Helping to care for my family's wolf pack this afternoon would at least offer me some distraction from worrying about Bran and my failure in Gefell.

I hoped that when Domhnall and I met with Laoise later tonight, she would have a better idea of what to do next. Enlisting the aid of the village elders and getting them to push back against Father's lack of action had seemed like a worthwhile idea, but it would do us no good if none of them were willing to speak out.

And we don't have time to wait for them to get bold enough to do so, I thought, my chest tight as I strode down the hallway, heading for the south tower. Each day that passed, Fianna's fires destroyed more land and the Dark Spirit became even further entrenched in Blaidd. What our people needed was urgency and Spirits be damned, I would get my father to understand that if it was the last thing I did.

CHAPTER 3

AN UNQUENCHABLE FLAME

Seren

"You did make beautiful children," I told the handsome male wolf, Taranau, as I brushed his sleek grey coat.

He flicked his ears back when he heard my voice, but otherwise, his gaze remained on the group of pups wrestling and yipping at one another a few feet away while their dam, Gylfym, napped in a sunbeam. The litter had been the most recent born this spring, the latest in the Ris of Blaidd's long line of cherished wolves. My family had raised wolves as both companions and hunting animals for generations. Most of the pack lived in the west tower that had been transformed into a large den centuries ago, though they were allowed to roam the castle at times, and some people, like myself, had cherished pack members we tended to keep close to us.

Seventeen wolves filled the den this afternoon and I'd spent the last few hours helping see to their needs with Nia, the Nead Maithair, or den mother. Nia had been in the well-respected position for as long as I could remember, and she took her care of the wolves seriously. Though I couldn't fault her on her care of the pack, she had never much cared for me when I was a child and her opinion of me hadn't improved over the years.

She cast wary glances at me as I continued to brush Taranau, as if she expected me to do something underhanded to the wolf at any moment. Her distrust had made for a trying afternoon and I continually had to remind myself I was doing this for the wolves, not Nia. Brushing Taranau was my last task for the day and once I was finished, I called my two wolves, Awyr and Cryfder, over to me before gathering my things. Nia watched me with continued skepticism.

"I'm heading out," I said when I walked over to her, Awyr and Cryfder at my heels. "Taranau has been taken care of and there's fresh water in the basins. I was wondering if I could take one of the pups with me to give them a bit more interaction."

"And where exactly would you be taking them?" Nia asked, narrowing her eyes at me.

"Not out of the castle," I replied. "Just to visit a friend."

"Make sure the pup is back before dinner." She let out a huff before grumbling under her breath, "Asking me things as I if can deny the Ri's daughter."

I forced myself to ignore the cutting remark and instead walked over to some of the older pups who were playing with a few deer antlers. It wasn't difficult to choose which pup to bring with me. Eofn was a troublemaker, just like my Cryfder, but the little pup was one of Bran's favorites.

I scooped him up, and we left the den behind. I cradled the pup in my arms as we walked down the hallway toward the warrior's quarters, noticing that he was looking more and more grey as he lost his puppy coat. Cryfder watched the young pup with interest as we walked, no doubt wishing to play with him.

"Easy, little one," I told Eofn as he wiggled in my arms. "Believe me: You don't want me dropping you on this stone floor."

I readjusted the pup, taking a firmer hold of him. The hallways were largely empty, but I passed the occasional servant, though they paid me little heed, going about their business for the day. When I reached Bran's room, I knocked and was pleased to see him looking a bit less haggard when he answered.

"I brought a few friends," I said. "I thought you might enjoy their company."

He grinned as he took in Eofn, Awyr, and Cryfder and ushered us in. I set Eofn down on the floor as Bran closed the door. Cryfder immediately swooped over to engage with the young pup, the two of them pawing at one another, while Awyr hung back and watched. Not only was she older than the other two wolves, she had always been more reserved and aloof by nature.

I glanced around Bran's small room while he got down on the floor with Cryfder and Eofn. It had a few more personal touches than the last time I had been in it a few days ago. And though it was one of the smallest rooms in the warrior's quarters, something I was sure had been intentional on Drystan's part, it at least had one small window that let in a little bit of light and looked out onto the distant Dail mountains.

"Thank you for bringing them," Bran said, coming up behind me and resting his hands on my shoulders.

His breath brushed the back of my neck as he spoke and I couldn't suppress a shiver of pleasure, my chest fluttering. The feelings he stirred up in me had been more thrilling than I had ever imagined.

"You're welcome," I replied.

He glanced back over at the wolves. "They're having so much fun, I'm almost tempted to join them."

I let out a soft laugh. "I don't think they would complain."

"Probably not," he said, gently spinning me around and letting one of his hands fall to my waist while the other cupped my face. "But then I wouldn't be able to do this."

He captured my lips in a kiss that left me breathless. I wrapped my arms around his neck, giving in to his touch. I could feel my blood heat, a warmth settling in my middle as he pulled me closer. I couldn't fathom how something that felt so right could be wrong. He had my heart and soul and I longed for him in ways that left me aching inside.

"You're supposed to be resting," I told him as we eased apart from one another.

"Mmm," he replied, resting his forehead against mine. "True, but this is making me feel much better."

I laughed before he pressed another kiss to my lips.

"Cian will have my head if I'm the reason you don't follow his instructions," I said when we parted once more. "And you need rest."

He released a long sigh before leaning back.

"Always the sensible one," he said, a teasing glint in his rich brown eyes.

"One of us has to be." I smiled, then made myself step away from him.

He did need to rest after his injuries today. Cian's gift had the power to speed up the healing process, but it still taxed the body. Cryfder, it seemed, had given up on his game with Eofn and wandered over to lie down near Bran's hearth with Awyr, though Eofn quite obviously wasn't done playing. He crawled over Cryfder, nibbling at his ears and causing Cryfder to let out a low grumble. Bran and I both chuckled before he called Eofn over to him. The pup trotted to him and as I watched Bran pick him up and cradle him in his arms, I swore my heart skipped a beat. How the rest of the castle couldn't see Bran's inherent gentleness and kindness was beyond me.

Bran walked over to his bed, grabbing an old-looking leather belt off a rickety table before flopping down onto the well-worn mattress. He set Eofn next to him, letting the pup gnaw on the gnarled old leather.

"Join us?" Bran asked, looking over at me. "Then you can report back to Cian that I did as I was told. Mostly."

I smiled, joining him on the bed. I stretched out beside him while Eofn curled up between the two of us, the pup fully occupied with biting the old leather belt. It was a tight fit on Bran's narrow bed, but we made it work. After a moment, Bran rolled over to face me, resting a hand under his head.

"We live in the same castle and yet I feel as if I never see enough of you," he said softly, taking my hand in his own and caressing the back of my palm with his thumb.

I briefly closed my eyes, reveling in the tingle of awareness his touch ignited in me.

"I know," I said with a quiet sigh.

"How did it go in Gefell?"

I grimaced. "Not as well as I'd hoped. Tesni believes Father is wise in not wanting to cause a panic. I think Emer is right. Tesni and those like her aren't in the north. They aren't seeing what's happening and Father is doing everything in his power to hide the evidence of how bad things truly are."

"You'll convince them," Bran said, giving my hand a squeeze. "I know you will. You've already convinced Laoise, and I can't say that's something I ever saw coming."

I leaned over and kissed him, careful not to squish Eofn between us. He had always shown me such support and I would forever be grateful for it.

"Careful," he teased when I eased away. "You might start something and then where will we be?"

I rolled my eyes at him, playfully shoving his arm, and he grinned before turning over onto his back and putting his un-injured arm behind his head. He tried to stifle a yawn, but he wasn't successful.

"Rest," I told him. "You've had quite the day."

"If you insist," he said, another yawn overtaking him.

"I do."

It didn't take long for his eyes to flutter shut and his breathing to deepen. Eofn soon tired as well and before long, the pup was also fast asleep. I felt a twinge in my chest as I watched the two of them. How I dreamed of a life full of peaceful moments like this one. And yet at the same time, I couldn't forget the looming threat of Fianna or the vow I had made to the Wolf Spirit. If I wanted the future I longed for, it was clear to me that I would have to fight for it. *But it will be worth it,* I reminded myself. I would bring about a new age in Blaidd, one of peace and acceptance. I wouldn't let Fianna and its darkness win.

CHAPTER 4

WHISPERS OF SMOKE

Alannah

FLYING WAS ONE OF the few times in my life that I felt truly free. The mountains beneath me grew taller as I soared through the air, the forest below becoming thicker the deeper I traveled into Ioliare. If I didn't want my charge to get lost in the maze of trees, I would need to change my altitude. I dove down, slipping between the branches of oak, poplar, and beech, slowing my speed now that I was forced to fly among the trees instead of soaring above them.

A lone horse and rider made their way through the forest, the rider shrouded in a cloak of dark green. With the light drizzle, he had his hood pulled over his head, obscuring his features, but I could easily imagine his narrowed eyes and the tight set of his jaw. Aengus hadn't wanted to drop everything to tend to Lorcan's injured fighters, but Lorcan had left him little choice and Aengus knew full well what the price was for defying him.

I let out a screech, letting Aengus know I was near and he turned his head toward me, guiding his horse so that he was following my lead. I continued on, dodging any low branches that sought to impede me. It had been my job to fetch him and bring him to our encampment, and it would be my job to lead him back to Beag when he was finished. Normally I would have griped about being forced to play the role of messenger, but I'd found such things didn't bother me as much when Aengus was involved. The healer intrigued me, despite his reluctance to be involved with Lorcan's band.

As we continued through the forest, I was forced to slow my speed even more as the ground became rockier and Aengus' mount began to struggle. Despite my frustration with the slower pace, it did give me time to admire the fine specimen of a man below me. Though the drizzle hadn't stopped, Aengus had pushed off the hood of his cloak, giving me a better view of his handsome face, golden blond hair, and forest green eyes. He was a prize of a man, that was for certain.

My current lover, Dara, was nowhere near as striking as Aengus, but at least he offered his own sort of comfort in the dead of night. He hadn't been my first choice for a lover, but my options were limited, and being with Dara was far better than the loneliness I'd spent so long trying to escape.

Especially now that Bran is gone. The thought of my fellow shifter made my chest tighten. Like a fool, Bran had betrayed Lorcan and run off with the Ri's daughter. There would be no coming back from what he had done. No one else could have told the war band of Blaidd exactly where our hideout in the caves of Ogof had been. If the Stag Spirit hadn't warned Lorcan, we all would have been slaughtered when Cadfael's warriors had come for us. We knew Bran was at Clogwyn; I'd seen him there myself, practically throwing himself at Cadfael's daughter.

I shook my head again, pushing away all thoughts of the traitorous man I'd once foolishly welcomed to my bed and forcing myself to focus on the task at hand. Aengus and I climbed higher up the craggy peaks of Ioliare, eventually coming to a small clearing that was well hidden in the rugged mountainside. A few crude huts had been fashioned in a small semicircle and a string of horses, not the finest mounts but serviceable enough, stood tied to a long picket line. Mercenaries milled about, most of them congregating around the few fires spread out in the center of the huts.

Aengus pulled his horse to a halt and I flew down beside him, changing into my human form as soon as my feet hit the ground. Aengus' mare shied at my sudden transformation, but he kept a firm hold on her. Three mercenaries stood guard at the edge of the camp and when they saw us, one of them headed toward the largest hut, which belonged to Lorcan.

One glance at Aengus showed me that he was no happier now than he'd been when we'd left Beag, his gaze still hard and his jaw clenched. The longer I studied him, the more I found myself hating the thought that he might blame me for forcing his hand. Aengus had made it clear that while he would aid Lorcan with his wounded, he'd not be drawn into our conflict. He was different from the sort of men I'd found myself drawn to over and over again; far different from a man like Dara. At times, I wondered if it was weak of me to be drawn to a man who showed such little aggressive and possessive tendencies, but I was drawn to him all the same.

"I didn't wish to force you here," I told Aengus, softening my tone as I stepped closer to him. "But I have my duties. I hope you can understand that."

He released a quiet sigh, giving me a slight nod. When his gaze lingered, I worked hard to hide the thrill that coursed through me. Maybe he wasn't as immune to me as I'd first believed. At twenty-three, I wasn't unaware of my beauty and I knew full well that it was usually one of the only reasons men were drawn to me. My auburn hair, piercing blue eyes, and the soft curves of my body had been the one power I had always been able to wield, and something that had driven my sister mad with jealousy.

The brief thoughts of Fflur made my stomach clench and I forced my memories away from my sister. She had betrayed me. She was the reason I'd been forced to survive in the wilderness. It was people like her that proved that Fianna and Lorcan were right. It was time for Blaidd to go through the fire so that a new era could rise. One day, when Lorcan was Ri, I would make Fflur pay for what she had done to me. Fflur and those like her would regret the day that they had supported Cadfael in his vengeful bloodshed.

"I assume you'll be the one seeing me back when I'm finished?" Aengus asked, pulling me from my dark thoughts.

"As always," I replied, allowing my arm to lightly brush against his.

The reaction I got in return pleased me. A slight flush tinged his cheeks and he cleared his throat before putting space between us once more. I didn't have much time to dwell on my pleasure, however, as commotion from the camp drew our attention.

Lorcan and Dara strode over to us with two burly mercenaries flanking them. Dara's gaze flitted between Aengus and me, a slight furrow marring his brow, but when I flashed him a smile, his expression smoothed. I forced myself to keep my smile on my face, resisting the urge to scowl instead. Dara had agreed to an open relationship, one with no strings attached. My attraction to Aengus was none of his business.

"Good of you to join us, Aengus," Lorcan said when he reached us, giving the healer a curt nod. "Never fear; you will be well compensated for your services."

I bit the inside of my cheek, part of me bristling at Lorcan's arrogant tone. Aengus *would* be well compensated, with the coin that I, and others, had stolen. Lorcan had promised us all a lifetime of lavishness and luxury, but not until Cadfael was dead, and I would be lying if I said that scraping out a living in the wilds of Ioliare while knowing the amount of coin that was being funneled into Lorcan's pockets wasn't starting to grate on me.

"If someone can show me to the wounded, I'll get to work straight away," Aengus said. "I have business awaiting me back in Beag."

"Of course." Lorcan motioned for Dara to go with Aengus and the two men walked off, but Lorcan lingered, turning his attention to me.

"After you see him back to Beag, you are to scout to the west, near Dearg and Isac. I want to know exactly how many warriors Drystan has clustered in that stretch of mountains."

"Understood," I replied.

"Good. Go get some rest. I'll need you at your best."

I gave him a respectful nod before making my own way into the camp. When I took my hawk form using my gift of shapeshifting, it drained me. I would need to recuperate before going out again, something Lorcan was well aware of.

Despite the growing tinges of frustration I felt toward him of late, I owed him. I'd been moments away from death when he had found me. My sister had turned me over to warriors of Blaidd who had planned my execution in the village square. To this day, I could still vividly remember how they had taunted and tormented me, calling me a monster simply for the power that flowed through my veins. But Lorcan had found me before they could hang me, freeing me from my captors with the help of Fianna.

I'd been with him ever since, devoting myself to the future he envisioned for Blaidd. The one where the Wolf Spirit's line of Ris was destroyed and a new line took its place; one that would be forged by Fianna itself. What Lorcan was doing was necessary. Cadfael had poisoned Blaidd and its people. He and his son had hunted my kind until we had almost ceased to exist. Fianna had to purge the land of Cadfael's poison. When the era of the Stag Spirit came to Blaidd, shifters like me would finally be free.

I skirted the small fires dotting the camp, along with the mercenaries gathered around them, heading for the hut I shared with Dara. Though we had to share the space, we at least each had our separate quarters, the benefits of Dara being the leader of the mercenaries and me being Lorcan's prized shifter. The rest of the mercenaries weren't so lucky, crammed into other huts practically piled on top of one another.

Once I reached the hut, I ducked through the hide flap that created the front door. The shared space in the front of the hut was small and narrow, boasting only one crudely put together chair and a small hearth for cooking, but it was more than what the others had. The doors that led into the two separate sleeping rooms were nothing more than flimsy pieces of canvas, stolen from a tentmaker a few weeks ago. Still, they were better than nothing.

I ducked through the canvas flap that led into my room and shed my boots before lying down on my sleeping pallet. Once I'd settled into the blankets, I rolled over onto my back to stare up at the ceiling, a wave of exhaustion washing over me. I'd just let my eyes flutter shut when I felt another presence enter the room, one that carried with it a familiar darkness.

The smell of smoke filled my nostrils and my eyes flew open. I sat up on my elbows, my heart beating rapidly as I looked toward the door and saw a shadow creature standing just inside my room. The grotesque being stared back at me with flickering ember eyes. Its body was made of smoke and ash, its form similar to that of a small deer, but that was where any similarities ended. Sharp claws grew from its legs instead of hooves and long fangs protruded from its mouth. Smoke drifted from its nostrils as it breathed, and the presence of Fianna filled my room.

The creature belonged to the Stag Spirit, though it and four others had been granted to Lorcan to help him defeat Cadfael. The shadow creatures were how we started Fianna's fires, though they were fickle, difficult beings. With my gifting, I was able to exert some control over them, and Lorcan would often put me in charge of one of the creatures during our attacks, but I'd never had one seek me out. As far as I knew, the beings only truly answered to Fianna and Lorcan. A tingling in my wrist caused me to look down at it. A quiver settled in my stomach as I noticed the small burn mark on the side of my wrist, the one that had formed when I had sworn my blood bond to Lorcan, had taken on an odd, fiery glow.

"What do you want?" I asked the shadow creature, slightly unnerved by the fact that it continued to stand and stare at me, filling my room with smoke as it breathed.

The creature gave a low sound that was something akin to a snort, a few glowing embers leaping from its mouth before dying out after they hit the dirt floor.

Lorcan is losing focus. He cannot get me what I seek, nor is he proving himself capable of destroying the threats to my future line.

The voice that infiltrated my thoughts made me tense. Fianna had been speaking to me with far too much regularity of late. I still wasn't entirely certain what to make of its sudden interest in me.

What do you want from me? I asked, swallowing hard.

Your loyalty.

You already have it. I have no loyalty to the Wolf Spirit and its line. What is it you really want?

I heard something that sounded like a wheezing laugh in return and the shadow creature's eyes blazed.

Always so to the point, Fianna said. *I like that in a mortal. It isn't so much what I want from you; it is what I need. There are threats in Castle Clogwyn and there is a mortal who carries blood that has the power to destroy the Wolf Spirit's claim on the Clan of Blaidd.*

And what do I have to do with this?

Lorcan has shown me over and over again that he will not deal with the threats at Clogwyn and he has continually failed to ensnare the mortal I need. But you...

I shook my head, letting out a shuddering breath. I wasn't foolish enough to go behind Lorcan's back. Not even for Fianna. He would have me killed if he even caught a hint of such treachery. I would do my part to bring about Blaidd's new era, but I wasn't going to slit my own throat.

You have the wrong person, I said.

So certain are you? Tell me, how long will you believe your sister's lies? You could be so much more than what you are.

I took in a sharp breath, hating how the quiver in my stomach grew. Memories came back to me: memories of my parents dying, of Fflur's taunts and the way she would always make sure I knew my place in her home. I had been only fourteen when our parents had died and Fflur, newly married and living in Blaidd, had taken me in. At first, I'd thought my tragic story might have a happy ending, but Fflur had made my life misery from the moment I'd stepped through her door.

None of her hatred for me had waned in the years we'd been apart and she used her aid of me to make herself a martyr to those around her. And then the Purge had come. Fflur had sold me to Cadfael's warriors to save her own skin, her last words to me ones that had told me that I was nothing. But how had Fianna known of that old, unhealed wound? It was Lorcan I had sworn myself to in blood and given the power to infiltrate my thoughts, not the Stag Spirit itself.

Oh, you will find that I know a great many things, little mortal, it said, its rasping laugh once more ringing in my ears.

You would be better served with someone else, I replied, averting my gaze from the creature.

I will keep my own counsel on how I will be best served. There was a hard edge to the Spirit's tone and the shadow creature's eyes blazed once more. *But there is time yet. I have waited over a thousand years to claim the land of Blaidd. I can be patient.*

The dark presence faded and the shadow creature turned into a ball of smoke, materializing through the canvas flap and taking with it the smoky haze that had filled the room. I slumped back down on my pallet, squeezing my eyes shut as a shiver coursed down my spine. I was committed to a new Blaidd, to seeing the end of Cadfael and all who shared his blood, but bargaining with Fianna meant bargaining with my soul. And that was a bargain I was not certain I was ready to make.

CHAPTER 5

THE BLOOD OF BLAIDD

Seren

WATER CASCADED DOWN THE *falls in front of me, the moonlight reflecting off the rushing river below. I stood alone on the rocky riverbank. The Spirits had guided me to this place, leading me over the grassy green hills and through the starlit forest. There had been an urgency to their call, an urgency I could still feel even now.*

I smelled the smoke before I felt the suffocating darkness fill the air. When I turned, I saw that Fianna stood behind me. A human figure was beside it, hooded and cloaked, but neither the stranger, nor the Stag Spirit, seemed to pay me any heed. Their focus was on the distant wood line.

The shrill cry of a hawk broke through the still night air. Above me, I saw the creature's shadowy form as it streaked across the sky. It dove down to the ground between Fianna and the stranger, but before its talons hit the grass, it transformed into a ball of smoke and then took the shape of another cloaked, shrouded figure.

Fianna turned its attention to me, its antlers blazing. "Do you still wish for death, little Daughter of Blaidd? Or do you wish to join the others who see the wisdom of a new order?"

I could only assume it spoke of its shadowy companions. They were obscured by the darkness, preventing me from making out their features.

"I have made my vow," I told Fianna, lifting my chin. "I will not side with you."

"Then you will learn what happens to those who are foolish enough to stand in my way," Fianna snarled, sparks spraying from its mouth and antlers. "And you will see what power I can wield when I have the blood of the line of Blaidd at my disposal."

I was thrust out of the vision, Fianna's words still ringing in my ears. As my body shook, I forced myself to focus on the things I could hear, taste, and smell. I always struggled with my soul's sudden return from the Spirit Realm. The pungent scent of the lavender and vervain, the herbs still burning strongly in the brazier, gave me something to focus on and I forced myself to take slow, even breaths.

When I finally opened my eyes, I was no longer disoriented. Fianna was strong, but I had prepared the small room I used for my visions with herbs that would keep my soul grounded, even with an interaction with the Dark Spirit. After remaining sitting cross-legged on the floor for a few moments more, I got to my feet.

There was a smoky haze in the air from the brazier, and a bit of daylight peeked around the edges of the closed curtains. The room was attached to my personal chambers and had once been used as a nursery many years ago, but my former mentor, Anwen, had helped me transform it into a sacred space where I could harness the power of my gift.

I walked over to the table near the room's one small window and put out the brazier. Next to the ceramic pot were a few vials of restorative tinctures that Cian always concocted for me to help lessen the fatigue that followed my visions. His mixtures did not completely take away the toll it took on my body to venture from one realm into the next, but they helped. I uncorked one of the vials and put a few drops of the liquid on my tongue, my thoughts returning to what I had seen in the Spirit Realm.

Fianna was growing in power, of that much I was sure, and I knew the hawk I had seen. It had to be Lorcan's other shifter, Alannah. Bran had known her during his time with Lorcan's band, and she had hunted us after we fled Ogof. I knew she wasn't to be underestimated, but it was the last words that Fianna had spoken to me that stayed with me and made my stomach churn.

What had the Stag Spirit meant by the line of Blaidd? As far as I knew, I was the only one left who bore that blood. Eamon was dead, as were my uncle and his children. None of my cousins had survived the burning of their home, and all their bodies had been accounted for. So who had Fianna been referring to?

I shook my head, letting out a deep breath before making my way to my common room. I might not understand Fianna's warning, but it had been there all the same. It would be unwise to discount it. Once in my common room, I peeked into my bedchamber to check on Awyr and Cryfder. The two of them were sound asleep on my bed, taking a late afternoon nap. Earlier this morning, I had taken them on a ride with me, knowing I would be preoccupied for a better part of the afternoon, and the exercise appeared to have done its job of tuckering them out.

Leaving my chambers, I made my way across the castle to Domhnall's rooms. I was to meet with him and Laoise again this afternoon to discuss what our next course of action would be. *And now I must tell them of what I've seen,* I thought, pressing my lips together as I passed a few servants carrying loads of dirty linens. Laoise and Domhnall at least would listen to my words, unlike my father, who would discount whatever I said outright.

When I reached Domhnall's chambers, he answered the door and ushered me in. Laoise was already present, seated near the table that Domhnall used as a desk. I joined her in another chair, putting my back to the bright sun that shone in through the windows, while Domhnall settled across from us. Like the rest of the advisors, Domhnall had one of the more spacious chambers in the castle, and he'd made it his home after almost five years of living at Clogwyn. There was a shelf of leather-bound books, a beautifully woven rug that bore the scene of a lively hunt, and tapestries with hawks and mountains that spoke of his homeland of Seabhac.

"I think," Laoise said as I settled in my chair, "that it is time to express to others that Ri Cadfael intends to break the hymddeol. Cadfael knows the importance of such tradition. He knows he must step down. In all of Blaidd's history, no Ri has ever defied it. I haven't wanted to spread such rumors without more proof than just my word, but the elders need something to spur them to act. We can't afford for them to waste time hemming and hawing over what to do."

"What about traveling north?" I asked. "I believe Emer made a valid argument that those here in the south were somewhat insulated during the Purge and even now, they do not see what is happening outside of their own homes."

"Traveling means leaving the castle." Domhnall shook his head. "It's one thing to come up with excuses for why we might be gone for a day, another to make up believable excuses for a multiday journey."

Laoise held up a hand. "Under other circumstances, I would be in agreement, but we have Ri Cadfael to contend with. The less of his notice we draw, the better, and I don't see how venturing north could be done without drawing his attention. And

I, for one, do not trust any messenger in this castle to deliver any sort of message that would be kept from Cadfael's prying eyes."

"If only we could utilize Bran," I said with a sigh. He was the ideal discreet messenger, with his shapeshifting abilities, but Father had kept him under lock and key ever since sparing his life.

Domhnall tensed slightly at the mention of Bran, but the moment passed, and my attention once more returned to Laoise as she spoke again.

"Cadfael's intentions regarding the hymddeol should be more than enough," she said. "Even the rumor of him planning to disregard it will be unthinkable to the elders." She paused, focusing directly on me. "Have you seen anything more of late?"

"I have," I replied, worrying my lower lip. "I fear Fianna is only growing stronger, drawing others to its side, including quite possibly another shifter. A woman who is known to Bran and has aided Lorcan for some time now. And... there is another possible threat, one that I do not entirely yet understand."

Domhnall's shoulders bunched and he leaned forward in his seat.

Laoise motioned for me to continue. "Let's hear it."

"Fianna spoke of someone," I said, "of having the blood of the line of Blaidd under its control."

Domhnall frowned, his brow furrowing. "A threat toward you, perhaps. Nothing more."

I shook my head. "I don't think it meant me. I have rebuffed it repeatedly, in this last vision and every interaction before it. I fear it referred to someone else."

"There is no one else," Laoise said, her tone firm. "Not any longer. Domhnall is right; it is most likely nothing more than a threat against you. A sinister one, yes, but one that has no basis so long as you resist it."

I wet my lips, rubbing my palm along my pant leg as I searched for my next words, hoping they wouldn't sound entirely crazy. I had spoken very little of Aengus since I had returned to the castle, largely because there had been an odd, strong feeling in my gut that perhaps those at Clogwyn did not need to know of the healer who reminded me of my brother—a feeling that felt like it had come from the Spirits themselves.

"There was a man," I said. "In Beag. A healer. He aided Bran and me when we escaped Lorcan and... there was a resemblance between him and Eamon. At first I thought it was wishful thinking on my part, but Cian has confessed to me that he noticed it as well."

"A coincidence, nothing more." Domhnall waved his hand. "I met this man as well and outside of hair a similar shade to Eamon's, I saw little evidence to suggest any sort of blood relation."

"You didn't grow up with Eamon in the same way that Cian and I did." He hadn't known Eamon half as well as Cian and even though my brother and I had never been close, we'd still spent our entire lives in the same home.

"We cannot go around making such weighty accusations and assumptions off of a resemblance," Laoise said. "No matter how close. Unless there is some proof that this man is somehow kin to Ri Cadfael or Fionn, it is wisest to assume the Stag Spirit was making a threat against you, Seren."

I didn't agree with them, but I didn't have any sort of real proof to convince them otherwise. And, in all fairness, it *was* a bit far-fetched that Aengus could be any sort of blood kin. Father was a hard man, but I'd never heard even rumors of him being unfaithful to my mother, and Fionn had been devoted to his own wife. It still niggled at me, but I could see the wisdom in Laoise's caution.

"I think it wisest if I am the one to start broaching the subject of the hymddeol with others," Laoise said, smoothly shifting the topic of conversation. "We will meet again in three days, unless something pressing reveals itself between now and then."

Domhnall and I voiced our agreement and Laoise got to her feet, taking her leave. As she slipped out the common room door, I tried to ignore the unsettled feeling that remained in the pit of my stomach. I couldn't seem to shake it since my vision. When I got up, Domhnall did as well, catching my hand in his before I could leave.

"Are you alright?" he asked, his tone gentle as he looked down at me.

"Just... worried I suppose," I replied, not quite meeting his gaze. "I can't help but feel like time is running out and that we aren't acting fast enough. And yet Father ties our hands at every turn and spends his time pretending that Fianna is defeated and Lorcan is no more than some proverbial bump in the road."

"I know it seems slow, but we *will* defeat this." He lightly stroked the back of my hand with his thumb. "I promise you that."

I looked up at him, offering a faint smile. "I do appreciate all that you've done. You and Laoise both."

"We only want what is best for Blaidd." He paused, dropping his chin before meeting my gaze again. "I don't mean to upset you, but I'm worried. With as much as Fianna has visited you and its focus on you, are you so sure that this shifter can be trusted?"

Despite the lack of hostility in his tone, his insinuation still frustrated me and I removed my hand from his, lifting my chin. "Yes. I won't deny that he had a tie to Fianna once, but he does not have it now. He bears no mark and he vowed to defeat Fianna and Lorcan. He wants the Stag Spirit stopped as much as you and me."

Domhnall pressed his lips tightly together. "Dark Spirits and their servants are masters at deception."

"Believe me, Domhnall, I am very well aware of the Dark Spirits and what they can do," I replied, unable to keep a hard edge from coming to my tone. "I've been seeing into the Spirit Realm since I was five years of age. I saw Bran's tie to Fianna severed myself. He is no servant of the Stag Spirit."

"You saw it severed yourself?" Domhnall's brow wrinkled.

"Yes," I answered. I hadn't confessed the entire truth of what I had done, the vow I had made, to Domhnall or Laoise, part of me still leery of trusting Laoise completely, but I needed Domhnall to trust Bran. He was a key to defeating Lorcan. "I promise you I am in no danger from him."

The set of his jaw left me suspecting that he still wasn't entirely in agreement with me, but he gave a slight nod followed by a heavy sigh.

"I just want you to be safe," he said.

"I will be," I replied, giving him what I hoped was an encouraging smile.

I bid him farewell, some of my irritation with him fading as I did so. Domhnall could be difficult at times—he had always been so—but his heart was usually in the right place. Not to mention that after the Purge, he was one of the few people in Clogwyn who hadn't looked at me with complete disgust and disdain after the truth had come out that I had aided shifters in escaping my father's vengeful wrath.

Upon leaving Domhnall's chambers, I headed in the direction of the castle library. Fianna's words still nagged at me and though I had been visited by the Spirits since I was a child, I had enough sense to know that I did not know everything.

Years of history and lore had been archived within the walls of Clogwyn for centuries and I hoped that something there might shed more light on what Fianna could have possibly meant. Domhnall had been right when he spoke of the Dark Spirit's skills at deception. With every day that passed, more of Blaidd burned. There was no time to waste.

Chapter 6

The Stag's Bargain

Alannah

THREE SHADOW CREATURES WERE gathered around Lorcan, their eyes blazing with raging flames. They let out disgruntled eldritch hisses, sparks flying from their mouths and giving light to the darkness. The creatures seemed more agitated than usual, but Lorcan barely acknowledged them, focusing intently on me instead as we stood at the edge of the wood line with our backs to the distant camp.

"I want you to pay close attention to where the warriors are headed," Lorcan said. "Especially if they split off into smaller groups."

"Understood," I replied, unable to keep the irritation from my tone.

He'd already given me the same instructions three times today, treating me as if I'd never been on a scouting mission before. I'd been with him for two years now, acting as his eyes and ears across the Clan of Blaidd, and the way he had spoken to me today was insulting.

"Be sure to be on the lookout for Drystan," Lorcan continued. "If he has left Clogwyn, I want to know at once."

"I will," I replied. The blood bond that had been created between us allowed Lorcan and me to communicate over vast distances, thanks to his gift as a mind-speaker. He'd be keeping a close watch on me, as always.

"I will see you in three days." He gave me a stiff nod before turning and striding back off toward the camp.

The shadow creatures followed behind him, but not before one of them looked back at me, studying me intently enough to cause a shiver to pass down my spine. Lorcan called something to the creature in Old Pernish and it let out a yelp of pain before hurrying to catch up with him.

I shook my head as I watched Lorcan and the creatures disappear into the darkness. I had work to do; there was no time to waste on dwelling on the creatures' odd interest in me of late. Taking a few deep breaths, I focused on envisioning the form of the red-tailed hawk that had become a second skin to me, calling on the power of the Spirits deep within me. The transformation was quick, as always, and in moments, I was flapping my wings and soaring up into the air.

Rising above the treetops, I relished the freedom that came with flight and began to chart my course south. I would need to fly to the edge of the Dail mountains to reach the main road that led north from Castle Clogwyn. There would be no other route that Drystan would send his warriors on; the main road was the only easy path through the Dail. To the warriors of Blaidd, I would be just another hawk in the wilderness, if they even saw me at all, but I would be watching their every move.

You will cross the Dail.

The rasping voice of Fianna infiltrated my thoughts and a cold blast of wind ruffled my feathers. I jerked my head back, my belly tightening. I was not Fianna's chosen; I was not bound to do its will, and yet there was a threat in the way it spoke to me, its tone implying that I would do its bidding, or else.

You will cross the Dail, Fianna repeated, *and when I usher in my new era, you will be rewarded beyond your wildest dreams.*

A stiff wind blew again and I tensed, struggling to maintain the course of my flight. Fianna's instructions were a direct contradiction to Lorcan's, and while I had no bond with the Stag Spirit, I did have one with him. I knew all too well the power he could wield, especially over another person's mind. I'd seen him drive others to insanity, and I wanted no part of that.

You think I cannot handle a mortal like Lorcan? Fianna let out a harsh laugh. *His power is nothing compared to mine.*

His instructions were to watch the main road and follow the warriors, I replied, half-holding my breath. I could guess how Fianna felt about impudence, but I was also aware of Lorcan's lack of tolerance for disobedience.

There are more pressing threats than the warriors of Blaidd. There is something I seek inside of Castle Clogwyn, something that could put an end to the future I have planned if it falls into the wrong hands.

It spoke in riddles that I did not understand. I let out a frustrated breath. The castle was the last place Lorcan had been interested in over the last few weeks, his attention once again more focused on drawing Cadfael away from the protective walls of Clogwyn, and for good reason. Slipping a force inside the granite walls of Castle Clogwyn was an impossible task unless one had massive numbers. It made more sense to draw Cadfael out into the wilderness, where we could have the advantage. Unfortunately, the man was as stubborn as he was vengeful and heartless. He seemed perfectly content to hide in his precious castle while his warriors perished and his people suffered.

What is this thing you seek? I asked, the cold wind that carried Fianna's presence still blowing hard against me.

A weapon, it answered. *One that has lain dormant all these years, but one that could give the line of Blaidd strength if the Wolf Spirit should allow it.*

It was an ominous warning, but still, I hesitated. Lorcan's punishment would be swift and with our connection, it would be difficult to hide from him that I was not where I was supposed to be.

I will handle Lorcan, Fianna said, *but this obstacle must be eliminated, and it must be done by someone with the skills to slip in and out of Cadfael's fortress without notice. Lorcan will not harm you while you are doing my bidding and once my Ri is seated in Castle Clogwyn, I will grant you a life you can only dream of. Fionn's son will need a Banrion, after all.*

Its last words caught me so off guard that I almost plummeted into the forest below. Over the last few weeks, Lorcan had been insistent that once Cadfael was dead, *he* would become Ri of Blaidd. And everyone knew that Fionn's children had all perished in the fire that had killed Fionn himself. Lorcan had been there; he had borne witness. No one had survived.

Fionn's sons are dead, I said.

You think it wise to accuse me of falsehoods? There was a sinister edge to Fianna's tone that left me swallowing hard. *Fionn's bastard son was no victim that night and Lorcan was not the only being who was there. Do my bidding and I will make certain you become Banrion of Blaidd when I establish my new order.*

I wavered, hating how tempting its words were. Me, as a Banrion? It was one of the highest roles in the clan, only second to the Ri. In a million years, I would have never dreamed of such a place belonging to me. I was the lowly daughter of a simple herder and a weaver who'd been seen as different since the age of six, when my gift had first appeared. And then, during the Purge, I had become the enemy, the very thing that the people of Blaidd hated and feared.

And yet here such a thing is, I thought, *seemingly within my grasp.* Even if Fionn's bastard was far from an ideal spouse, I would have luxury beyond my wildest dreams as Blaidd's Banrion. With such power, I could bring Fflur to justice for what she had done to me. I could make certain that those who had spent the last few years hunting shifters paid the price for their actions, and more than that, I could ensure that Blaidd was a safe place for my kind for years to come.

Fianna laughed, the noise bitter and grating. *Oh, I assure you that you will be quite pleased with the man who carries Fionn's blood. And I can give him to you. Just as I can make you Banrion. All I ask for in return is your obedience.*

And you will handle Lorcan?

Lorcan will be none of your concern.

I will do it, I said before I could think too hard on the implications of what I agreed to. The allure of what Fianna offered was too strong to resist.

Never fear, Fianna replied. *I always reward my servants.*

The Stag Spirit's dark presence disappeared on the wind and I released a shaky breath. It would not be easy to sneak into Clogwyn, but I would be damned if I got captured doing so. I'd snooped around its grounds for Lorcan plenty of times in the past, not once having been caught. Whatever weapon the Stag Spirit wanted, I would get it.

CHAPTER 7

LOST TO HER

Bran

AFTER A RELENTLESS DAY of Drystan's training, everything ached, and while I had wanted to take the evening meal back to my room, Father had pressed me to eat with him in the Great Hall. I hadn't had the heart to deny him. Throughout the meal, much of my attention had been on the table at the head of the hall where Cadfael, his family, and his advisors ate. During the other daily meals taken in the hall, Seren and I always sat together, but at the evening meal, we were forcibly separated by the clan's traditions.

If I were anyone else, it was possible that Seren would be allowed to invite me to dine with them, but Cadfael would never allow it. Not with what I was. So every night when I ventured to the hall for the evening meal, I was made to watch her from a distance. And every night that I was present, it seemed Domhnall was glued to her side. I knew she trusted him, and I knew he had been helping her try to influence the council to push Cadfael to act more strongly against Fianna, but still, I didn't trust him. I had yet to see anything that had proven to me, at least, that he was different from the self-serving man I'd known years ago.

"Grip that knife any tighter and you're liable to break it," Father said, casting me a sidelong glance.

I let out a long, low breath and loosened my grip on the knife I'd been using to cut into my roasted chicken. It wasn't Father's fault I was bone weary after being pushed around by Drystan all day and having to watch Domhnall try to cozy up to Seren, but I hadn't been able to shake my disgruntled mood. I wouldn't necessarily admit it to Father out loud, but truth be told, I hated coming to dinner in the hall.

Father and I were always left to sit alone, separated from the rest of the castle's inhabitants. Some nights, Emer and Lewella would sit with us, but tonight they were spending the night in Gefell with Emer's family. The rest of the warriors and servants routinely went out of their way to avoid us. *Avoid me, really,* I thought as I took another bite of my chicken. It wasn't a surprise, per se, how much the people of Clogwyn feared and loathed me, but I despised how their feelings extended to Father. He tried to hide the poor treatment he'd received at the hands of others because of me, but I was aware of it and I hated causing him pain, directly or indirectly.

"I know you care about her," Father said, drawing my attention and inclining his head toward Seren. "But she doesn't inhabit the same world as you do. Not while her father is still Ri."

My jaw tightened in response. I'd hoped Father's misgivings over my relationship with Seren would lessen with time, but so far, that hadn't been the case. If anything, he seemed even more worried. I knew his concern stemmed from his worries for my well-being, but I found that it frustrated me all the same.

"Cadfael will not be Ri forever," I replied, unable to keep the bite out of my tone.

"I just don't want to lose you," Father said, staring hard at his plate. "Again."

My frustration vanished, instead replaced by a sense of guilt that left a knot in my body. Since returning to the castle, I'd seen just how hard the years of not knowing if I was alive or dead had worn on him.

"I'll be careful," I told him. "I promise."

He gave a slight nod, his expression tight as he continued eating his meal.

"Drystan still hasn't said when he intends to send you out?" Father asked after a few moments.

"No," I answered with a shake of my head. "He claims I'm not ready yet."

I couldn't hide the bitterness in my tone. Drystan's excuses were lies. I was more than ready and every moment I wasted here prevented me from hunting down Lorcan and doing my part to put an end to all of this.

"Well," Father said slowly, "I can understand how that would hurt your pride, but I won't lie and say I'm not glad you're still here. Clogwyn is a safer place than the rest of the clan."

"For now. Every moment that passes allows Lorcan and Fianna to get stronger."

"No Dark Spirit has ever gotten inside these walls, not since Ri Rhonwen built them five hundred years ago."

I pressed my lips together but bit my tongue to keep from arguing with him further. I didn't want our night to end in a fight. And perhaps if I had not experienced Fianna's darkness for myself, I would have agreed with him, but I knew all too well the Stag Spirit's power. It was unwise to underestimate it. Just because it had never breached Clogwyn before didn't mean it was impossible.

Out of the corner of my eye, I noticed Seren getting to her feet. She called to Awyr and Cryfder, the two wolves lounging with the rest of the pack near the large firepit. They scampered over to her and she crossed the hall with her canine companions at her side. I shoveled down the rest of my chicken and steamed vegetables as quickly as I could before draining the last of my drink.

"Can you see that this gets back to the kitchen for me?" I asked Father, motioning to my empty plate and mug as I got to my feet.

Father's brow was furrowed, but he nodded. I thanked him and bid him farewell, then departed the hall myself. Seren was waiting for me in the entryway, the wolves sitting at her feet. When Cryfder saw me, he let out an impatient whine, his whole body wiggling with excitement as he looked up at Seren. She gave him a rueful smile before giving him permission to come greet me.

Cryfder bounded over to me and I gave him an affectionate rub on the head before continuing on, the wolf keeping pace at my side. When I reached Seren, I brushed a light kiss over her lips. The soft smile that graced her features as I eased away from her filled me with warmth.

"I need to take them out one more time for the night," she said, nodding at the wolves. "It shouldn't take long."

"Do you want me to come with you?" I asked.

A steady rain had moved in around midday, and though I wasn't keen on being out in the elements again after spending all day in the training yard, I'd go with her if she wanted.

"You've already had a long day," she said, shaking her head. "We won't be long."

I kissed her forehead, telling her I would wait for her, and she walked off with the wolves. I leaned against a nearby wall, watching her disappear from view as she stepped through the front doors. The continual din of noise from the Great Hall drift-ed out into the entryway, muffled by the stone walls, as I waited for her to return. Cadfael had been working hard to distract those at Clogwyn from what was truly happening in the north, and I was disappointed to say that it was working. Even my own father at times didn't seem to grasp the true devastation of what the Stag Spirit had unleashed. I worried that it would be only a matter of time before the Stag Spirit's darkness spread here.

The opening of the hall doors caused me to start, pulling me out of my dark thoughts. I stiffened at the sight of Domhnall. He strode over to me and I straightened, forcing myself to give him a respectful nod of acknowledgement. I didn't care for him, but he was one of Cadfael's advisors. He held far more power in this place than I did.

"Where has Seren run off to?" he asked.

"She took the wolves out," I answered. "Is there something you wished to tell her? I can pass it on for you."

"Or," he said, a slight hardness coming to his expression, "I could simply tell her myself. Tell me, shifter, why do you insist on following the Ri's daughter around like a pathetic pup?"

I stiffened. He'd been like this more and more of late. Civil in front of others, but quick to show a different, more aggressive side when he thought no one else was looking.

"I don't think that's any of your business," I said.

"Isn't it? I think anything regarding the future of the Clan of Blaidd is entirely my business. What happens when she be-comes Ri one day? You truly think the people of Blaidd would accept a shifter as their Tiarna?"

I gritted my teeth, trying to control my temper. I knew the road before Seren and me would be difficult, but once she be-came Ri, things would change. She would make sure of that.

"Again," I told Domhnall, my tone sharp, "none of your business."

"Your presence is *never* going to be accepted within these walls," he retorted. "The sooner you figure that out, the better."

One of my hands curled into a fist and it took everything in me not to let it connect with his face. The way things were right now, I'd only land myself in the dungeons, no matter that Domhnall had provoked me.

Domhnall smirked as he glanced down at my hand. "So easily baited. Perhaps you're as unstable as people fear, after all."

Before I could snap back at him, Seren stepped in through the front doors with the wolves in tow. She looked between the two of us, her brow furrowing as Domhnall quickly schooled his expression and greeted her with a welcoming smile.

"Is something wrong?" she asked as she came to stand beside me.

"Just a bit of conversation with our resident shifter," Domhnall replied. "Have a good evening, Seren."

He gave her a low, respectful nod before walking past us down one of the long, dimly lit hallways.

Seren laid a hand on my arm and I forced myself to uncurl my fist. "Is everything alright?"

"I don't like him," I said, rolling my shoulders as I tried to rid myself of the tension that had taken over my body. "And I don't trust him."

She let out a sigh, briefly rubbing her forehead. "I know he can be difficult to get along with at times, but he is doing his part to help bring an end to Fianna. I need his aid, and Laoise's."

"I know," I replied, pressing my lips together.

We'd had this conversation multiple times over the last few weeks and I knew there was little use in arguing with her about it. She hadn't seen the side of him that I'd seen. The worst part was that I knew she wasn't entirely wrong in her insistence that she needed Domhnall's help. He did hold power and sway in the castle with his place as an advisor. He certainly had more power and influence than I could ever hope to amass. I could do my part to stop Fianna by killing Lorcan, but I was of little help to Seren when it came to matters of politics and influencing her father.

"Shall we head upstairs?" she asked.

I nodded and she led the way to the staircase. We climbed the granite steps to the castle's second level and I forced myself to push aside all thoughts of Domhnall. I wasn't going to let him ruin the precious private moments Seren and I were able to spend together.

She took my hand in hers and I laced our fingers together. When we reached the top of the landing, we walked the hallways to her chambers in the Ri's wing of the castle. The wolves trotted in ahead of us when Seren opened the door, Awyr going to curl up by the fire while Cryfder grabbed a well-gnawed sheep's bone to entertain himself with.

"I'm going to get out of this dress," Seren said as we stepped into her common room and I closed the door behind us.

We exchanged a brief kiss and she walked off into her bedchamber. The evening meal was a more formal affair at Clogwyn and Seren was dressed in some of her finer clothes, a dark green gown that was particularly becoming on her. My own attire wasn't nearly as extensive as hers, and as such, I'd had to choose from my less worn shirts and pants.

After Seren left, Cryfder brought me his bone, dropping it at my feet. The wolf looked up at me with an expectant expression, wagging his tail. I chuckled softly, picking the bone up and walking over to an open spot on the large rug in front of the fire. As I settled down on the floor, I called Cryfder to me and the young wolf trotted over.

Awyr dozed while I played with Cryfder, occasionally cracking open an eye and watching us. At almost eight years old, she didn't quite have Cryfder's energy. Seren soon rejoined us. She'd unpinned her hair and changed into an older, but comfortable-looking, pair of pants along with an oversized shirt. She joined Cryfder and me on the floor, sitting down behind me and wrapping her arms around my waist as she rested her chin on my shoulder.

"Some days, I think Cryfder likes you better than he likes me," she said, a hint of teasing in her tone.

"He only likes me because I'll roughhouse with him," I replied, giving the wolf an affectionate rub.

He'd given up on our game now and had wedged the bone between his front paws so that he could chew on it with his back teeth. I turned in Seren's arms, but I noticed that her gaze had drifted to the fire that burned in the hearth. The night was chilly with the rain and despite the shadows, I could see the strain in her features. I knew the burdens she carried, especially with her gifting. I could only imagine how heavily it weighed on her to not only see glimpses of the future, but to see the Spirits themselves, including Fianna.

"What is it?" I asked, cupping the side of her face and running my thumb along her jaw.

She released a soft sigh, her chin dropping as she looked down at her lap. "I saw something today and I can't seem to get it out of my thoughts."

"Something with Fianna?"

She nodded, worrying her lower lip. "Does it make me a bad person to say that I'm weary of this? I know what I must do, but it's been so much death and suffering, it's hard not to feel like there's no end in sight."

"It makes you human," I told her, tipping her chin up to hold her gaze. "We're going to put a stop to all of this, Ren. Together. I promise you that."

She brought her lips to mine, wrapping her arms around my neck. As I deepened the kiss, I slid one arm around her waist and the other under her knees to pull her into my lap. Her kisses left me breathless and I held her even closer, feeling the heat of her body pressed up against my own. For a few moments, all of the darkness and fears that had haunted both of our steps for years seemed to vanish and I was content to let it be so, at least for a little while.

Her hands crept under my shirt and the feeling of them skimming over my bare skin made my heart race. I eased back from her, desire coursing through me. Up until now, we'd both shown a level of restraint, and I hadn't pushed her. I'd known she would tell me when she was ready for more. Her breathing was as ragged as mine as we stared back at each other, her eyes dark and her lips slightly parted.

"Do you want to take this further tonight?" I asked, searching her face.

"Yes," she said, holding my gaze. "I need something other than this darkness. I trust you."

I was lost to her at those words, covering her lips with mine. Somehow, I got the two of us to our feet between kisses and tantalizing touches, lifting her into my arms and making my way back to her bedchamber. The moon drifted in through the windows, illuminating the room as I stepped inside and pushed the door shut with my heel. She was mine and I was hers. Tonight wouldn't be about Fianna. The Stag Spirit wouldn't be what was consuming her thoughts. Tonight would be about the two of us. There would be nothing that separated us and she would know just how much I loved and needed her.

CHAPTER 8

OF WOLVES AND BLOOD

Seren

I KNEW BRAN HADN'T meant to stay all night in my bed, but when I woke up the following morning with my back pressed up against his firm chest, our legs tangled together, and one of his arms loosely holding my waist, I couldn't deny my happiness that he had stayed after all.

The wolves were asleep at our feet, having joined us at some point in the night. Awyr was curled up closest to me while Cryfder had wedged himself next to Bran. An unexpected thickness came to my throat as I lay there, the room bathed in early morning light. By the Spirits, this was what I wanted. In this one, peaceful moment, it didn't feel as if Fianna and its darkness was hanging over me. I could pretend that things were as they should be. That Blaidd was a peaceful place once more. A place where Bran and his kind could live freely and where the tattoo on his back would make no difference to how the world saw him.

I took his hand, lacing our fingers together. I was more than content to stay tangled in the blankets a little while longer. All too soon, however, he stirred.

"I think I should be giving some apology for not leaving last night like I'd intended," he murmured, pressing a light kiss to the top of my shoulder. "But I can't seem to find it in myself to regret staying."

"Don't," I said, rolling over to face him.

I kissed him, cupping the side of his face and feeling the slight stubble underneath my fingers as his arm around me tightened. I regretted nothing about last night and I didn't want him to either. There were no secrets in a place like Clogwyn and there would, most likely, be inevitable gossip once he was seen leaving my chambers this morning, but I wouldn't let that cheapen what we had shared. I loved him. Nothing would change that.

Our kisses continued and for one brief moment, I thought that perhaps we would find ourselves having a repeat of the previous night, but Cryfder let out a loud whine, stretching out and pushing his front paws into our legs. I quietly groaned, breaking away from Bran and bringing my forehead to rest on his chest while we both caught our breath. Cryfder whined again, even louder this time, jostling into us once more as he impatiently wiggled on the bed.

"I'm assuming he has needs that need tending to?" Bran asked, a hint of humor lacing his tone.

"Yes," I said with a sigh. "It's like having children already."

He laughed and Awyr began to stir, letting out her own whines and grumbles to express that she too, needed to venture outside, and sooner rather than later. Bran brushed one last lingering kiss over my lips before sitting up in the bed and pushing the blankets down to his waist. I couldn't help but take a moment to admire the broad expanse of his shoulders and the muscle he'd put on in recent weeks. Though I was sorely tempted to pull him back down onto the bed with me, Cryfder stood all the way up and threw his head back to let out a mournful howl.

"Alright, alright," I chuckled. "We're getting up. We promise."

Bran affectionately rubbed Cryfder behind the ears before rolling out of bed and throwing on his pants. I gave a brief stretch before getting out from under the warm blankets myself, settling for simply pulling on my large shirt from the night before, which had been thrown on the floor, along with a dark blue dressing robe that I kept in a chair near my bed. We'd at least woken early enough that we had a bit of time to get ready for the day and see to the wolves before going down to the hall to get breakfast. Bran pulled on his own shirt while I belted my robe in place. Cryfder and Awyr danced around our feet, as if to make sure we got the message that they needed someone to get them outside to relieve themselves as soon as possible.

"Do you want me to take them out?" Bran asked. He paused, not quite meeting my gaze and fidgeting with one of his sleeves. "I can be discreet."

I closed the distance between us, taking one of his hands and resting my other hand on his cheek, gently encouraging him to look at me.

"I'm not ashamed of what we did," I said, holding his gaze. "People will talk. Let them. The sooner they realize that I am not going to be my father, the better."

He covered my hand with his own. "I love you."

"And I love you." I leaned up and lightly kissed him. "Though if you would take the wolves out now, I might love you just a touch more."

"Well, in that case..." He grinned, capturing my lips in another, longer kiss before stepping back from me and calling the wolves to his side.

"We'll go to breakfast together?" I asked as he walked to the door with Awyr and Cryfder at his side.

"I'll get them out and then stop by my room and get changed," he said with a nod. "Then I'll meet you back here."

After he left, I turned my attention to getting ready for the day. I had another morning of helping with the wolf pack ahead of me and then I intended to spend the afternoon in the castle library. I hadn't found anything useful the day before regarding Fianna and its threat, but there were still plenty of older texts to go through. With a morning with the wolves in mind, I chose a flattering but practical pair of pants and a dark grey shirt. Taking a seat in front of the mirror in my room, I set to brushing my hair and then pulled it back into a series of braids that I could pin up out of my way. I'd just pinned the last braid in place when the world around me spiraled to darkness—

The undergrowth in the forest was dense, ferns and clusters of wood sorrel closing me in on every side. Somewhere nearby, I could hear the distinct noise of another creature crashing through the brush. Smoke was in the air and a shiver passed down my spine as I felt the unmistakable presence of Fianna.

The crashing grew louder and my gaze was soon drawn to a flash of gold racing toward me. The smoke in the air grew thicker and I heard the grating shriek of a shadow creature. A large wolf burst through the trees in front of me, its coat an unusual tawny gold color.

The wolf was panting, its sides heaving as it continued to run in a seemingly blind panic. The shadow creature shrieked again and the wolf flinched. I felt an odd wetness on the inside of my wrist and I looked down to see a trickle of blood running from my wrist to the inside of my hand. I looked back up at the wolf to see a thin trail of blood running from its shoulder down one of its front legs—

I almost fell out of my seat when I was forced back into the Mortal Realm. I gripped the sides of my chair, the smell of smoke still strong in my nostrils. Frantically, I glanced down at my wrist, but there was no blood marring my skin like what I had seen in the Spirit Realm. *But what in the blazes did I just see?* I worked to calm my breathing, waiting for the tremors that always accompanied my visions to subside.

When the door opened, I started, still not feeling completely grounded in the Mortal Realm. Bran took one look at me and rushed over to my side, his brow wrinkled as he crouched down next to my chair. Awyr and Cryfder followed him, both of my wolves gazing at me with worried expressions.

"What is it?" Bran asked, taking my still trembling hand. "What did you see?"

"I don't know." I squeezed my eyes shut. "Can you get me my tinctures?"

He retrieved them from the nearby table, bringing them over to me. I put a few drops on my tongue, knowing they would ease the lingering fatigue, before handing them back to him.

As he put them away, I slumped in my seat, letting my head fall back against the chair. "It doesn't make any sense and yet I *know* I need to know what it means."

"Can you tell me?" he asked, soothingly stroking the back of my hand with his thumb.

He'd known me long enough to know that I couldn't always share what I saw, or that at times I could only share parts of it. With as uncertain and complex as the future was, what I saw did not always come to pass, nor did it always come to pass in the ways I had seen. It was a potentially far-reaching, and dangerous, power that I carried. But I had yet to figure out the answers to the current riddles the Spirits were showing me on my own. If my old mentor, Anwen, were here, I would confide in her, but she had long since left this realm behind. *I trust Bran,* I reminded myself. He would hold what I told him in confidence.

"Fianna has spoken to me," I said, wetting my lips and opening my eyes. "Of the blood of the line of Blaidd. And just now it showed me a golden wolf, one that seemed tied to me some-how. But I do not know who, or what, it refers to."

"Could it be speaking of you?" Bran replied. "Or perhaps even your father?"

"I'm not sure."

The vision of the golden wolf left me wondering if that *were* indeed the case. If the wolf had been meant to symbolize me in some way and that had been why I had seen blood spilling from both my body and the animal's. But something about that theory didn't sit right. And in the previous vision I'd seen, it had seemed clear to me that the hooded figure with Fianna had been someone else other than me. *Golden hair.* My thoughts flitted to Aengus, again.

"Has Aengus always lived in Beag?" I asked, angling myself toward Bran.

He jerked his head back slightly at the abrupt change in con-versation, but he knew the healer better than I did.

"No," Bran answered, his brow furrowing. "He grew up just south of here, in Cnoc. Why?"

My chest tightened, part of me having hoped that Bran would have answered yes. The village of Cnoc was close to the castle. My own mother had hailed from there.

"What do you know of his parents?"

"A thatcher and a healer, though not a gifted one, from what I recall him mentioning in passing. I can't say we ever had long conversations about our personal lives. Have you seen him in your visions?"

"Not exactly, no." I worried my lower lip. "But... did you ever notice the similarities between him and Eamon."

"I can't say that I did." Bran gave a light shrug. "I can see it somewhat, now that you mention it, but as far as I know, he lived his whole life in the village with his parents until he got the opportunity to strike out on his own and make his way north."

I let out a sigh, my shoulders slumping as I rubbed my forehead. Maybe I was imagining things. So desperate for an answer that I was willing to entertain any idea, even unlikely ones. Odds were high that Aengus' resemblance to my brother was only coincidence and that he bore no ties to the Ri's line. Even if he did, he would have had to have been a bastard. And Laoise was right: Those weren't accusations I could make without some sort of proof.

"What is it, Ren?" Bran said, his tone gentle.

"I'd wondered if the Stag Spirit was referring to him," I replied. "Far-fetched as that is."

"We'll figure this out." He gave my hand a squeeze and I let him pull me to my feet. "All of it. I promise you that."

I wrapped my arms around his waist as he embraced me, laying my head on his chest. I didn't know what I would have done these last few weeks without him and his unwavering support.

"It won't win," Bran said softly, kissing the top of my head. "And neither will Lorcan."

"No," I replied, taking in a deep breath. "They won't."

I wouldn't let them. *We* wouldn't let them.

"Let's go get breakfast while we still can," Bran said, stepping back from me.

I kept a hold of his hand, letting him lead the way out of my bedroom. The wolves trailed behind us and I tried to shake the sense of unease that had settled over me in the wake of my vision. I'd find the answer to the golden wolf and Fianna's cryptic words. It would have none of the blood of the line of Blaidd at its disposal. I would see to that.

Despite spending a better part of the afternoon in the archives, I found nothing of any real use. I was able to find census records that contained the names of Aengus and his family, but it only proved what Bran had told me. Aengus was the son of a thatcher and a healer, born in the village of Cnoc twenty-five years ago. He had no ties to the Ris of Blaidd.

That knowledge, however, had done little to ease my constant sense of unease, and there was still a quiver in my stomach as the wolves and I walked down the long hallways of Clogwyn to my parents' chambers. Olwen, the castle servant who usually tended to my mother had come down with a cold and I'd offered to chip in and help with Mother's daily needs. She had an illness she'd been born with that affected her joints and made it difficult for her to get around and care for herself. Today, I knew, had been a particularly difficult day for her. She'd been absent from all of the meals in the Great Hall, including the evening meal, and had barely come out of her chambers.

I had left the hall early tonight, in part due to helping Mother but also because of my own worries. Bran hadn't been present at the meal either, though Emer had passed on to me that the reason for his absence was a late night of training with Drystan. I didn't know how far rumors of Bran leaving my chambers this morning had spread, but Father had spent the night fixing me with a particularly stony expression and I'd heard whispers here and there among warriors and servants when I'd passed them.

We did nothing wrong, I reminded myself. I'd meant what I had told Bran about refusing to feel shame about what had passed between us. I was almost one and twenty. I was old enough to decide to bring a man to my bed if I wished.

When I reached the door to the Ri's chambers, the two warriors standing guard let me in without question. Mother called to me from the bedchamber when I stepped into the common room. I joined her, telling the wolves to go lie down on the rug in front of the hearth. They obeyed, both of them tuckered after spending most of the day with the rest of the pack.

Judging by the almost empty tray that had been placed on a table near the bed, Mother had at least eaten most of the food that had been sent up from the kitchens. She was already in her nightgown and seated in front of her vanity, struggling with the pins in her hair. I couldn't help but wince when I got a look at her hands. They were noticeably swollen.

"Here," I said, coming up behind her. "I'll get it."

"Thank you." She slumped in her seat as I began to undo the twisted braids that had been piled up on top of her head. Her weariness was evident in her features, but she mustered up a smile while I worked.

"Do you want me to send for Cian before you turn in for the night?" I asked.

She shook her head, pressing her lips together. "No. He already came up before dinner and did what he could. He needs his rest anyway. He's more exhausted than he will admit these days."

I bit my own lower lip, knowing she was right. At dinner tonight, he'd seemed particularly fatigued. More badly wounded warriors had arrived from the north late this morning and the infirmary had already been strained as it was, especially with Father's ridiculous demands that the most severely wounded be cloistered away, lest the castle know the truth of the depths of his lies.

"I told him I would help where I could in the infirmary tomorrow," I said.

"I'm sure he will appreciate it. Sioned as well. She's worried about how hard he's pushing himself."

"It's all the more reason for Father to put an end to all of this," I replied, unable to keep the bitterness out of my voice.

Mother released a heavy sigh, her gaze focused on her folded hands resting in her lap. "Doing the right thing has never been your father's strength."

"And the people pay for it every time. Right now, once again, they're paying for it with their lives." She winced at my harsh tone and I sighed, softening my voice. "I'm sorry. I don't mean to take that frustration out on you. I know you and Sioned have tried speaking to him as well, countless times."

"You care," Mother said, reaching around and placing a hand on my arm. "That is a strength that one day will serve you well."

I nodded, my throat tight as I finished with the last of the pins. Grabbing a bone comb off the vanity, I began to untangle her hair, the once bright red strands now closer to a pale blond.

"I just fear that he will wait too long to do the right thing," I said. "And I feel like I'm running out of ways to force his hand."

"You will find a way. You always have." She paused and our gazes caught as we both stared into the mirror at one another. "I haven't told you like I should have, but I've always been proud of you for that. You found a way to do what was right during the Purge. I know you'll find a way again."

I blinked rapidly, moisture stinging my eyes. She had been so absent for so much of my life. For the longest time, I'd wondered if she'd ever even loved me. And then something had changed when I had been kidnapped by Lorcan. Since I'd returned home, Mother had become a woman who, many days, I almost didn't recognize, but in the best of ways. She'd seemed to be slowly shedding the shell she'd worn for so long. Sioned had hinted at it for years, but something had to have happened after Mother had married Father, something that had changed her irrevocably and turned her into the indifferent ghost of a woman I'd known for most of my life. But that was changing.

"Your father spoke of rumors that have been circulating the castle today," Mother said. "About you and Bran."

I almost dropped the comb, the back of my neck heating.

"What sort of rumors?" I asked, clearing my throat.

Mother didn't answer immediately, instead turning in her chair. I let go of the few strands of her hair I'd been combing, stepping back slightly.

"You love him, don't you?" she asked.

"Yes," I answered, holding her gaze. "I know what others say of him, but they don't know him. Not really."

Mother's gaze drifted to the hearth where the wolves lay, a pained expression briefly flitting across her face. "There was once a time where I made the mistake of listening to others instead of the man who held my heart. Jealousy and fear can make people do and say all manner of things." She took in a deep breath before looking back at me. "Do not make that same mistake."

My chest hitched at her unexpected words. I knew the man she was speaking of wasn't Father. There had to have been someone else in Mother's life, someone no one had ever spoken of before—not in my presence, at least. *The blood of the line of Blaidd.* My stomach tightened as my thoughts raced, and yet it didn't entirely make sense. Mother didn't carry the blood of the Wolf Spirit's line of Ris. That blood could only come from Father or his brother, Fionn. And as far as I knew, my uncle had only had eyes for his wife, having known her since they were children.

"I know I haven't given you much motherly advice," Mother said, putting her back to me once more. "But do be careful. There are certain things that can have unintended consequences... such as children."

I could feel my face heat and I noticed Mother looked slightly uncomfortable herself. She hadn't given me much in the way of motherly advice, but Sioned had and I'd made a point to discuss such things with Bran last night. I wasn't opposed to children one day, but not any time soon.

"I can promise you that I am being as careful as possible about such matters," I told her, gathering her hair again and working it into a simple plait for the night.

A more comfortable silence fell between us as I finished with her hair and then helped her into bed.

"Do you need anything else?" I asked as she got settled under the blankets.

"No," she replied. "Thank you. Have a good night, Seren. I haven't told you like I should have, but I love you."

"I love you," I said, my throat tight with emotion. I'd waited so long to hear those words from her.

I stepped back from the bed, calling Awyr and Cryfder to me. When I let myself out of the bedchamber and into the common room, I came to an abrupt halt as I found myself face to face with Father. We both tensed at the sight of one another and I could feel my jaw tighten. He'd been going out of his way to avoid me these last few weeks and what interactions we'd had hadn't been particularly pleasant ones.

Though night had fallen outside, torches on the wall lit the room and despite Father's fine clothes and gold and silver jewelry, I could see the strain in his features. On some level, I suspected he knew the depths of the danger we faced. His pride, however, wouldn't let him admit it.

"What in the blazes are you doing here?" he asked gruffly.

"Helping Mother to bed," I answered. "Since Olwen is ill."

Father muttered a curse under his breath, disgust in his voice. "As if that woman is some child who can't even care for her own needs."

"She's been in pain today."

"You're as weak as she is," Father snapped. "Though arguably more of a disgrace than her. I do not want to hear any more rumors of you inviting a shifter to your bed. What you did during the Purge was insult enough. Sleeping with one of them is inexcusable."

"I am twenty years old," I retorted, my body heating at his callous words. "That is my decision. Not yours."

I brushed past him, fixing my gaze on the door, though I heard him whirl around after me.

"Keep this ridiculous defiance up and I will make certain that you are *never* Ri," he yelled after me. "I will not leave this clan in the hands of someone who will bring it to ruin!"

I stopped with a hand on the door, my shoulders taut as I looked back at him, forcing myself to meet his gaze. "You have already brought this clan to ruin. I am only seeking to make sure it doesn't pass away into nothing more than memory at Fianna's hands."

His face scrunched in anger and his hands clenched into fists, but I turned away and let myself out. I could hear him bellowing but I ignored him, letting the door slam shut behind me with a bang before stepping past the warriors standing guard.

As I strode down the hallway, the wolves keeping pace with me, I rolled my shoulders, trying to release some of the tension in them. Father's threats were empty ones. When I had made my vow to the Wolf Spirit, that I would cleanse the clan from Fianna and protect the shifters, it had told me I would become Ri one day. I believed the word of a Spirit far more than I did the word of my father. He was not as powerful as he deluded himself that he was.

Don't lose sight of the real enemy, I reminded myself, letting out a long, low breath. As much damage as Father had caused, he was nothing compared to Fianna. I had to discover the mystery behind the blood of the line of Blaidd. Mother's strange confession had only added to my confusion around that mystery. I'd always been told my father had been the only man she'd ever cared for. Some had even gone as far as to hint that she'd tried to trap him in some way, a castle servant bent on catching herself a Ri. And yet what she'd said tonight cast doubt on such stories. Clearly, there were things in our family history that had been omitted.

Sioned, I thought, nodding as I walked the dimly lit hallways. I would speak to her and see what I could get her to tell me of not only Mother, but Fionn as well. There were secrets in this castle, ones that I was beginning to suspect had been hidden for some time now, but the clan couldn't afford for them not to be uncovered. Not with Fianna on the loose.

Chapter 9

Darkness Brewing

Bran

As always, the warriors of Blaidd were frustratingly slow when it came to navigating the forest behind Clogwyn. Like I had done for a better part of the night, I forced myself to slow my pace as we made our way through the underbrush, heading back toward the walls of the granite keep. I was in my wolf form, having spent the evening tracking a goat and two chickens through the dense forest. It was yet another one of Drystan's insulting training exercises, treating me like I didn't know how to use my highly attuned senses of smell and hearing.

The night's activities had been child's play for me and by the time I'd tracked down the last chicken, it was taking everything within me to keep a tight lid on my mounting frustration. These tasks were a waste of time when I could be out hunting Lorcan and putting an end to him. I'd been a key part of Lorcan getting the upper hand on Drystan and his warriors multiple times and the warrior chief knew it, but still he insisted on making me practice these ridiculous games.

The warriors trailing behind me were in no better mood than I was. Led by Seachnall, they grumbled and cursed under their breath about getting dragged out after dark to go traipsing through the forest. Drystan had instructed them to assist me, but really, they were with me to make sure I didn't step a paw out of line. *Really, they've been a nuisance,* I thought. None of them seemed to have mastered traversing the forest without being noticed. I swore they'd made enough noise that every creature in the forest must have known of our presence tonight.

Moonlight lit our way as we stepped out of the trees. I trotted over to the dirt path that led up to one of the castle gates, eager to get back inside and be done for the night. I'd promised Seren that I'd join her in her chambers, something that had become a habit of ours over the last few days, and tonight's ridiculous display of training had taken longer than I expected.

"Slow down, shifter," Seachnall snapped.

I growled but did as I was told, slowing my steps and waiting for the three men to catch up with me. The guards at the gate on the back side of the castle let us in without question upon seeing Seachnall. Cool air ruffled my fur as we crossed the courtyard, a gentle breeze keeping the night comfortable. We walked to the training grounds and then entered the castle through the armory.

Once we were inside the large room, I shifted back into my human form. The warriors eyed me with distrust as I did so and I resisted the urge to roll my eyes. I was weary of them all acting like I would attack them at any moment.

"I'll get the report on how the shifter did tonight to Pennathe Drystan in the morning," Seachnall said. "You're all dismissed."

The other two men told him goodnight, both of them pointedly ignoring me before leaving the armory.

"After you, shifter," Seachnall said, nodding his head toward the door. "Pennathe Drystan doesn't want me locking things up for the night until you're safely on your way."

I snorted. Safely. That was a joke. More than likely, the warrior chief didn't want me stealing a blade or a dagger and coming and stabbing him in his sleep. Not that I would, but I hadn't exactly hidden my dislike for the man who made my life living misery. Ignoring Seachnall's dark looks, I strode out of the armory with him following behind me.

Once in the hallway, I left Seachnall to lock up and strolled off toward the opposite wing of the castle. I was more than ready to see Seren. Drystan had kept me busy today, and outside of sharing the midday meal together, we'd barely seen each other. I yawned as I reached the bottom of the castle steps, fatigue setting in after my long day. I had just taken the last step when a voice stopped me cold.

The servants' door, Son of Blaidd. By the Ri's study.

I jerked my head back at the Wolf Spirit's words, my muscles tensing.

Go, it said. *Trouble is brewing.*

The Spirit's presence faded and though I didn't entirely understand what all was transpiring, I turned on my heel and bolted back down the stairs. My heart pounded as I ran down the hallway. I saw no signs of danger, but I knew the Wolf Spirit didn't pass on warnings for no reason.

When I reached the servants' door closest to the Ri's study, I skidded to a stop. The hallway was empty and I heard nothing save for my own loud breathing. Still, my body was tense as I pushed open the door and stepped outside, moving as cautiously and as quietly as possible.

I lingered just outside the doorway, scanning my surroundings. The moon had been hidden behind clouds, but the torches on the castle wall kept me from being completely blinded by darkness. I could see warriors standing guard on top of the wall in the distance, though they showed no signs of any alarm. My gaze flitted to a row of bushes a few feet away. The clouds rolled past and the moon revealed itself once more. That was when I saw her.

Even in the dark, I recognized Alannah's shadowed form. She was hidden among the bushes, pressed up against the wall, but the darkness wasn't cloaking her any longer. I shifted into my wolf form at once. Teeth bared, I took off to the bushes, lunging at her just as she shifted into her own hawk form.

I silently cursed as she flapped her wings and darted out of my reach. Barreling through the bushes, I leapt up at her, but my teeth snapped at nothing but air. A growl ripped from my throat as I landed back on all fours. She swooped down at me, striking out with her talons and attempting to blind me by flapping her broad wings at my face, but I darted out of her reach. I let out a bark, hoping to draw the attention of the guards on the wall, but in our dueling, we had moved even farther away from the servants' entrance and the noise wasn't loud enough.

Alannah swooped at me again, clearly intent on either running me off or killing me. I jumped again, twisting in midair. For a moment, I thought I had her by the wing, but she fought me and I came away with only a mouthful of feathers. I spat them out, shaking my head. My bite had at least done some damage. Alannah was awkwardly flapping her right wing, not quite as high in the air as she'd been moments ago. I rocked back on my haunches, preparing to leap up at her again, but a loud bang distracted us both.

Harried voices filled the air, causing Alannah to give a frustrated shriek before taking off into the sky out of my reach. I curled my lips back and snarled, anger and frustration filling me as I watched her disappear into the star-filled sky. I shifted back into my human form, cursing under my breath the moment speech was once again granted to me. Not only had she gotten away, I didn't know what in the blazes she'd even been here for. But the sheer fact that she had evaded all of Clogwyn's defenses spelled trouble.

"Bran!"

I whirled around at Seren's voice to see three figures scrambling through the bushes toward me. Seren was in the lead with Emer and Lewella flanking her, all three of them breathing hard as they skidded to a stop in front of me. Seren's eyes widened as she focused on the few feathers still stuck to my clothing.

"She was here?" Seren asked, pressing her lips into a thin line.

I nodded. I didn't need to tell her more. She was well acquainted with Alannah after our escape from Ogof.

"What happened?" Lewella asked, her brow furrowing as she looked between the two of us.

"Lorcan's shifter was here," I answered. "I don't know what she was after, but she got inside the castle walls without anyone knowing."

Lewella let out a curse, both she and Emer tensing at my news.

"She's gone now?" Emer asked.

"Unfortunately." I grimaced. "She takes the form of a hawk. She's not an easy foe to contain."

"Drystan will need to know about this," Lewella said. "And the guards will need to be on high alert." She paused, her gaze flicking to me. "Drystan will need a full report in the morning."

"I will give it," I replied.

"We'll see to alerting him and the guards," Lewella said with a slight nod.

Seren and I thanked them and she came to stand beside me while Lewella and Emer strode off into the castle.

"You're unharmed?" Seren gently took hold of my arm, scanning my body.

"Yes," I replied. "How did you know she was here?"

"The Wolf Spirit. It came to me in a vision. I got to Lewella and Emer as soon as I could. Did she give any indication as to why she was here?"

I shook my head. "She was skulking outside the door here, I assume to try and get inside. But I don't know what her end game was."

"I don't like any of this." She let out a long, low breath. "Fianna never had one of her kind at its disposal during the Purge. Not that I'm aware of, at least. I only recall reports of wolf shifters, nothing else. It's far easier for a bird to slip in unnoticed than a wolf."

"I've warned Drystan that he and Cadfael need to strengthen their defenses, including here at the castle, but I can't say they've heeded that advice."

"Maybe this will get them to listen." She glanced up at the sky before releasing a shaky breath.

"We can only hope." I slipped an arm around her shoulders, pulling her to me and lightly kissing her head. "Are you still up for company tonight?"

"I will never not be up for your company," she replied, leaning up and brushing a soft kiss over my lips. "Especially not on a night like this one."

I took her hand in mine and the two of us pushed our way back through the bushes before re-entering the castle. As we walked back toward the main staircase, I couldn't rid myself of my unease. It was extremely concerning that Alannah had gotten inside the keep so easily. I didn't want to think what all could have happened if the Wolf Spirit hadn't warned us. If this wouldn't make Cadfael take the threat of Fianna and its darkness seriously, I didn't know what would.

CHAPTER 10

RECKLESS DANGER

Bran

NEITHER SEREN NOR I slept well that night, both of us on edge after Alannah's appearance. The following morning, Emer came to Seren's chambers while the two of us were readying for the day, informing me that Drystan had sent for me. My chest was tight as I closed the door behind Emer and I rolled my shoulders, trying to relieve some of the tension in my body as I walked back into Seren's bedchamber.

She was finishing braiding her hair, Cryfder and Awyr lying at her feet. A few days ago, I had taken to keeping a stash of fresh clothing in her room and like her, I was already dressed for the day. I'd tried my best not to be bothered by it, but it was hard not to notice just how worn and threadbare my clothing was compared to hers. I knew the way the rest of the castle judged such things; her the Ri's daughter and me, the worthless and dangerous son of a stablehand with no clear place within these walls.

With a slight shake of my head, I pushed aside the unpleasant thoughts, instead allowing myself a brief moment to simply take in the woman who had so completely captured my heart. The early morning sun bathed her in soft light as she worked her hair, but when I closed the bedroom door behind me, she looked up at me, a slight wrinkle in her brow.

"Drystan has sent for you?" she asked, tying off the thin piece of leather that would hold her braid in place.

I nodded. "He wants to see me before breakfast, it seems."

"Hopefully that means he's taking this situation with the gravity that he should," she replied, getting to her feet.

"One can hope."

She walked over to me, taking my hands in hers and giving them a squeeze. "I wanted to try and talk to Sioned this morning before breakfast myself. I'll see you in the Great Hall?"

"Of course."

I was curious as to what exactly it was she wished to speak to her aunt about, especially with the way she briefly averted her gaze when she said it, but I chose not to press her.

Bending down, I gave her a brief kiss before leaving the room. After I had descended the staircase and was once more on the first level, I strode past the hall and off to the castle's east wing, where Drystan's small meeting room was located. I was presentable this morning at least, dressed in a pair of brown pants, brown boots, and midnight blue shirt, with the wolf's head seal of Blaidd stitched into the chest. Drystan wouldn't be able to complain about that. I looked every inch a warrior of Blaidd today; even if Drystan would be quick to remind me that I was no permanent member of his war band.

The castle was already starting to bustle with activity as I walked, with warriors and servants on their way to the Great Hall to partake in the morning meal or starting their day's work. I silently rehearsed what I would say to Drystan. I knew Alannah better than most. We'd been more than merely shifters in the same band of rebels; at one time, we'd been lovers. She was cunning and she was not above doing whatever it took to get what she wanted. On top of that, she was driven by the same bitterness and hatred that drove Lorcan, and, like him, had a personal stake in all of this. Cadfael had ruined her life just as he had ruined mine. Like Lorcan, she was driven by revenge and I knew she would stop at nothing to get it.

When I reached the meeting room, the warrior standing guard let me in. Drystan stood over a wooden table near one of the windows, his back to me, as he pored over what appeared to be a map of Blaidd. Out the window, I could see a clear view of the training grounds, including a handful of warriors who apparently were partaking in an early morning archery practice.

"Pennathe Drystan," I said, clearing my throat and giving him a respectful nod as he faced me. "You wished to see me?"

He looked up at me with a slight scowl before motioning to another table and chairs a few feet away.

"Have a seat," he said.

I did as he bade and he settled in a seat across from me. Drystan's ill temper was clear, but I met his gaze and pulled my shoulders back, sitting straight in my chair. Much like Cadfael, Drystan almost always seemed to be in a foul mood. I refused to be intimidated by it, especially after years of dealing with Lorcan. Cadfael and Drystan weren't nearly as threatening as the man who sought to destroy them, no matter how much they thought otherwise.

"Lewella has reported that you claim to have seen another shifter last night," Drystan said.

His tone and his raised brows told me how much he doubted my words and I clenched my jaw. Drystan and Cadfael's foolish pride would be their undoing and at this rate, they would ruin the clan along with themselves.

"I did see another shifter," I replied. "The one I have told you of, the hawk shifter, Alannah."

"And yet according to Lewella and Emer both, neither they, nor Seren, saw this intruder. Nor did any of the guards."

"She took off before Seren and the others reached me. A hawk could have easily slipped past the guards, especially if they weren't looking for it."

"Don't get impertinent with me, shifter," Drystan snapped. "I highly doubt the possibility of any shifter getting within these walls undetected. It never happened during the Purge. I fail to see why one would be successful now."

"You only dealt with wolf shifters during the Purge. A hawk shifter is another matter entirely. I don't know what she was here for, but the fact of the matter is that she breached your defenses. Quite easily from the looks of it, I might add."

Drystan frowned and he shifted in his seat, showing the first hint of discomfort since I'd entered the room. "Or you told a convenient lie to cover up for the fact that you were perhaps up to things you shouldn't have been. You were seen in your wolf form last night, when you have been given specific instructions that you are only allowed to shift under the supervision of myself or a warrior I have deemed skilled enough to handle such situations."

I let out a sharp breath through my nose, my jaw aching. "Perhaps I should have saved the feathers I pulled off of Alannah's wings last night, since you're so determined to doubt me."

"Unless you have some sort of proof other than your word, I have no choice but to treat these allegations with suspicion."

"Alannah knows she can breach this fortress now. She will be certain to pass that information on to Lorcan. You need to strengthen your defenses. Lorcan and Fianna aren't going to ignore such an opportunity."

Drystan slammed a hand down on the table. "*I* will make any and all decisions regarding this war band and the defenses of this castle. I will look into these accusations of yours, but until there is some solid evidence behind them, you will keep them to yourself. I will not have you spreading fear and causing trouble within these walls. Are we clear?"

I wanted to continue to argue with him, to force him to have some manner of sense, but his hard gaze and stiff spine told me his mind was made up. He didn't want to believe me, didn't want to believe he had failed. Like Cadfael, he was caught in his own delusions. *And it's the people who will pay the price,* I thought with disgust.

"Perfectly," I said, my tone clipped.

"I expect you in the training yard ready to get to work in an hour." Drystan gave me a dismissive wave.

Somehow, I managed the respectful nod he was due as warrior chief, though I didn't bother to try and school the irritation from my expression. If Fianna destroyed the line of Ris as it planned and laid claim to the clan, the land would fall into complete ruin. There would be nothing left, only decay and darkness. There was no room for the pride of men like Cadfael and Drystan with that sort of darkness running loose, and yet every day it felt like more and more of a losing battle.

As I made my way back to the Great Hall, I tried to tamp down my rising fury, but I was hardly successful. The long walk did at least help me burn off some of my frustration. When I entered the hall, servants and warriors were milling about and food had been laid out on long tables along one wall. I walked over and grabbed a plate, helping myself to an assortment of meat, eggs, bread, and berries.

Once I'd filled my plate, I got myself a drink and searched the room for Seren, but I didn't find her. Her conversation with Sioned must not have been a short one. Avoiding the warriors and servants who shot me dark, fearful looks and muttered unkind words when I passed them, I found myself a secluded spot at one of the long rectangular tables spaced out around the hall. Putting my back to the sun, I took a seat and dug into my meal.

As much as I wouldn't want to admit it out loud, the disdain and fear those at Clogwyn treated me with hurt. I wasn't a monster who went around turning on people and harming them, but Cadfael's lies and the memories of the Purge had been so ingrained into the castle's inhabitants, they couldn't see anything else when they looked at me. It was likely that some of them had lost friends or family to shifters who had turned to Fianna years ago, or they knew someone who had. At the very least, they remembered the death of Eamon at a shifter's hands, and now it seemed my kind was destined to be painted with the same broad brush, no matter how unfair that was.

I wasn't far into my meal when one of Cadfael's advisors, Laoise, approached my table. She was in her mid-fifties and I could remember her being on the council back when I was a boy. Though she hadn't had much to do with me since I had returned to Clogwyn, I knew she had been doing her part to aid Seren.

"Laoise," I said, respectfully inclining my head as she settled in the seat across from me.

"Bran," she replied, taking a sip of the drink she'd brought with her.

Her use of my name, instead of the usual insulting *shifter*, didn't go unnoticed by me. It was odd how such a simple act of being treated with some manner of dignity eased some of my ever-present resentment and hurt.

Laoise took another sip of her drink, her gaze briefly flitting around the room before she focused on me once more. "I've heard rumors that you stumbled across a bit of excitement last night."

I raised my brows. That news had traveled surprisingly fast. And at the same time, a place like Clogwyn was ripe for gossip. It always had been.

"I'm surprised you've heard already," I replied.

"There are no secrets for those who know where to listen," she said, lightly shrugging one shoulder. "According to what I heard, you seem to think this particular development was a considerable threat."

I pressed my lips together, fidgeting with my fork as Drystan's warning rang in my ears. Seren trusted Laoise, though, and I knew she was on our side. More than that, Laoise had far more sway and power within Clogwyn's walls than I could ever hope to have. Someone needed to act before Alannah grew even bolder. Who knew what Fianna and Lorcan's purpose for infiltrating the castle was? Especially in light of Seren's words regarding the Stag Spirit speaking of the blood of the line of Blaidd.

"I do see it as a considerable threat," I said, trying to be careful to hedge my words. We were in the middle of the Great Hall after all, and though we were seated off on our own, anyone could walk by and hear our conversation. "I think it would be extremely unwise if the castle defenses were not heightened because of it."

Laoise gave a slow nod, a slight wrinkle settling in her brow. "If you have anything else you would wish to share regarding the matter, Seren knows where to find me. And I am always willing to listen."

"I'll keep that in mind," I told her.

It was tempting to tell her everything here and now, but this was a dangerous game we were all playing, a game that Cadfael would see as a betrayal and usurping of his authority. Laoise got to her feet just as I noticed Seren walking up behind her.

"I'm afraid Ithel is waiting to speak with me this morning," Laoise said, inclining her head to Seren and me. "Good day to the both of you."

She wandered off out of the hall and Seren took her seat.

"What did she want?" Seren asked, setting her food and drink down on the table.

"She wanted to talk about last night," I answered, keeping my voice low.

"You can trust her," she said, "at least as far as the clan goes. How did things go with Drystan?"

"Not well." I grimaced. "He accused me of lying about the whole thing."

She cursed under her breath, stabbing into her cooked eggs with her fork. "Perhaps it *would* be wise for you to speak with Laoise then. Drystan ignoring what happened last night is reckless and dangerous. If he's going to do so, the council needs to be made aware of it."

"If you think it will help, I'll speak with her."

"I do."

"Were you able to speak with Sioned?"

She dropped her chin, staring hard at her plate. "I was."

Her tone left me with the feeling that particular conversation perhaps hadn't gone as she had hoped, but her obvious discomfort made me hold back from pressing her further.

"I want it out of this clan and banished back to the shadows from which it came," she said, an edge coming to her voice and her gaze hardening as she continued to stare at her plate.

"I know," I said, knowing full well the *it* she spoke of was Fianna. I reached across the table and took her hand. "It will happen. We won't give it any other choice."

She looked back up at me, giving me a tentative smile when I gave her hand a squeeze. We both resumed eating our meals, though I couldn't help but feel like a cloud of darkness had settled over Clogwyn since last night. It disturbed me deeply that Alannah had gotten as far as she had so easily, and it disturbed me even more than Drystan wasn't acting with the force I knew he was capable of. *But I will not let her go unchecked,* I thought as I took a long sip of my drink. Drystan might not be watching for Alannah, but I would be.

CHAPTER 11

ANCIENT SECRETS

Seren

I HAD NEVER SUSPECTED Sioned of lying to me until this morning. When I had asked my aunt about the man Mother had obviously cared for prior to marrying Father, she had been unusually tight-lipped, telling me that it was in the past and hardly any matter of importance. I wasn't sure I believed her. I had pressed her further about Fionn, telling her what the Stag Spirit had told me of the blood of the line of Blaidd, but she had been insistent that my only cousins had perished in the fire that had killed my uncle and my aunt.

I had no real reason to doubt that she was telling the truth, at least as far as Fionn was concerned, and yet I did. I was missing something here, something important, and I was running out of time to figure it out. My uneasy, worried thoughts still swirled around in my head as I reached the door to Father's study, and I fought to clear them. I was to speak with him this afternoon, along with Laoise and Domhnall. Laoise had found me during the midday meal and told me of the arrangement she and Domhnall had apparently made with Father earlier this morning. The four of us were to speak in his study this afternoon regarding my most recent visions. I hoped Father would listen.

No warriors stood guard outside the Ri's study when I reached it. I took a deep breath before pushing open the door and stepping inside. I'd gotten here early, hoping to have a few moments to clear my thoughts and organize what I wanted to say after a stressful night and morning. I had a feeling Laoise would bring up what had transpired with Alannah as well, judging by the discussion we'd had an hour ago. She, at least, was taking last night's threat seriously.

I walked over to one of the windows that looked out onto the stable yard, resting my hands on the windowsill as I tried to think of what would have the most impact on Father. Laoise, I had begun to notice, tended to stroke his ego, as if she were trying to make her ideas his. I couldn't say that it didn't work, but that sort of thing didn't come naturally to me. I was far more inclined to demand he do the right thing, insistent that it should be enough to make him to act. The problem was that Father had little care for such things as right and wrong. I sighed in frustration, tapping my fingers on the windowsill.

Daughter of Blaidd...

I jumped at the strange voice, stepping back from the window and searching the room. That hadn't been the Wolf Spirit I had heard, or even Fianna. The voice itself had been oddly neutral in tone and timbre, and yet there had been something about it that seemed old and ancient. I waited, my shoulders tense, but nothing around me looked out of place and the room was as silent as it had been when I'd first entered it. I took a tentative step back toward the window, though I put my back to it this time, my brow furrowing.

They have forgotten me...

I turned my head to the right, where it had sounded like the voice had come from, and my gaze fell on the beautifully carved longbow that hung on the wall. Running wolves and crashing waves had been carved into the ancient wood, marking the bow's uniqueness. It was an old weapon, from a time when the island had been young. I knew its story; every child in Blaidd did. The story of Ri Rhonwen, who had built the very walls of Castle Clogwyn. She had battled all three of the Dark Spirits and had almost been defeated, until the Wolf Spirit had given her the very bow that now hung on the wall as a reminder of where our people had come from and the power that sustained our land.

The bow was said to have held the power of life and death, that a single arrow from it would instantly kill. The legends told that the bow had lost that power after Rhonwen's death, and as far as I knew, no one had actually even used the weapon in over a hundred years, but I still knew its story. Rhonwen's tale had been one of my favorites when I was a child. I'd often begged Sioned and Anwen to tell it to me and on occasion, Bran had been with me to hear it as well.

And he'd loved hearing that tale as much as I did, I thought, the memories coming back to me. Rhonwen's husband had been a shapeshifter, an owl shifter from the Clan of Tyll. Rhonwen would have never saved the Clan of Blaidd without his aid and support. *And how things have changed,* I thought, biting my lip. How had the clan gone from a time where a shifter could be seen as Tiarna of Blaidd to a time where they were seen as dangerous monsters who threatened the clan's very future and blamed for Fianna's darkness when it was the Stag Spirit itself who had created it.

The door creaked open, pulling me out of my thoughts, and I tore my gaze away from the bow as Laoise strode into the room. She looked agitated, moving stiffly as she approached me. I glanced behind her for Father and Domhnall, but saw no sign of anyone else with her.

"I'm afraid Ri Cadfael has declined to speak with us," she told me, her brow creased.

"Does he at least plan to do something about last night?" I asked, frustration erupting within me at her news.

"He apparently plans to leave that in Drystan's capable hands."

"And Drystan has no interest in protecting the castle."

"Drystan is as blind as your father." Laoise gave a disgusted wave of her hand, propping her other onto her hip. "He'd rather delude himself into thinking his defenses are adequate than admit a shifter got the better of him. I've at least spoken with Lewella, as has Domhnall. She intends to do what she can to make sure Clogwyn's walls are more closely watched."

I bit my lower lip. It was something, though Lewella would be limited in what she could do. She was Drystan's second in command, not warrior chief herself.

"In the meantime," Laoise continued, taking in a deep breath and letting it out slowly, "I suggest you do whatever you must to figure out these riddles the Spirits have shown you."

"Believe me," I replied, some of my irritation channeling to her instead of my father. "I'm trying."

"You are next in line to be Ri of Blaidd. People will be watching to see how you handle this threat. Remember that."

She turned and left without another word. As the door shut hard behind her, I let out a shaky breath, bringing a palm to my forehead. I needed answers and solutions and it felt like all I had were more questions and uncertainties. My gaze drifted back to the bow, but the weapon stayed silent and I was left wondering if I'd imagined the strange voice and odd interaction from the start.

I didn't, though. I heard it. I know I did, I told myself. Perhaps there was some clue somewhere, something in Rhonwen's story that would help guide me to answers. She had battled Fianna herself, after all. *Which means another afternoon in the archives.* Squaring my shoulders, I left the study and headed for the library a short walk away. I knew the eyes of others were on me, but I would not fail. Fianna wouldn't take this clan.

CHAPTER 12

TEMPTING DREAMS

Alannah

DARA SNORED AWAY BESIDE me, but I couldn't sleep. Every time I closed my eyes, I saw it: flaming antlers, eyes like embers, and billows of smoke rolling out of its nostrils. Fianna haunted me and I could not get rid of it.

My attempt at fetching the weapon it desired from Castle Clogwyn had been a failure and I knew it was displeased with me. It had made that clear on my flight back to Ioliare. I had at least gotten away from my scuffle with Bran with minimal injuries, ones that I had blamed on an encounter with a territorial owl while spying on the warriors of Blaidd. Thus far, Lorcan had seemed none the wiser that I had ventured to the castle, and I intended to keep it that way.

I readjusted in Dara's bed, trying to ignore the tingle I felt in my right arm. When the light irritation continued, I lifted my arm out from under the blanket, the burn mark on the inside of my wrist glinting with an odd, fiery glow. I'd received the mark after making my blood bond with Lorcan and though I'd never seen it take an odd glow before, it had started doing so after I had agreed to aid Fianna. I shoved my arm back under the blanket, closing my eyes and desperately trying to fall back to sleep. I'd failed the Stag Spirit and I had seen how it felt about things such as failure.

I am not done with you yet, little mortal.

The sinister voice made my eyes snap open. I turned my head to look at Dara, only to find him still sound asleep. Fianna's words had been meant for me alone. Letting out a shaky breath, I squeezed my eyes shut once more. Fianna had not spoken to me since my failure. I had thought perhaps it was done with me. After all, I had not kept up my end of our bargain. I hadn't gotten what it wanted and the castle had been on far too high alert for me to attempt getting inside it again so soon after my initial try.

And yet as I lay there in the darkness, I saw it again: the great stag made of flames and ash. I let out a frustrated growl, throwing the blanket back. I'd slipped into bed with Dara hours earlier, hoping the physical release I found with him would grant me sleep instead of Fianna's torment, but tonight, not even that was enough. With a heavy sigh, I rolled out of bed.

"Where are you going?" Dara mumbled, turning toward me.

"I need to relieve myself," I told him. "I'll be back."

He grunted some unintelligible response before putting his back to me once more. I grabbed a thin robe that I'd stolen months ago, then pushed aside the piece of canvas that served as a door. The front room was dark, no fire burning in the hearth with the latest spell of warmer weather, but I was comfortable with the darkness.

I settled in a chair in front of the empty hearth, my shoulders slumping as I hugged myself around my middle. My future with Lorcan had begun to feel more uncertain in recent days, something I was loathe to admit after years of pinning my hopes on him. We'd been trying to draw Cadfael out from the castle for months now, with no success. The Ri of Blaidd always sent his minions to do his bidding, even when we'd held his only remaining child captive. Not even Lorcan's attempts at capturing or killing Drystan had been successful. For all the warrior chief's arrogance, he was certain to always surround himself with his finest warriors. Lorcan swore that at some point, Drystan would make a mistake and we would be there to take advantage of it, but the more time that passed, the more my doubts grew. Even with Fianna's aid, attacking the castle itself was folly with our small numbers. Especially with the massive war band Cadfael had amassed during the Purge and continued to maintain.

Somehow, even after failing it, I still felt the allure of Fianna's offer. Wherever Fionn's bastard was, it seemed as if we needed him now more than ever. Lorcan only seemed to be leading us in circles, gaining the upper hand on Drystan here and there, only to have the warrior chief once more come out the victor. Morale was low and a future without Cadfael and his line was starting to feel more and more impossible.

Cadfael of Blaidd's fate will be sealed. I will see to that, and a life as Banrion is still within reach. I am not an unreasonable being, after all.

Fianna's voice made me shiver. Out of the corner of my eye, I saw the canvas that served as the front door to the crude hut flutter. The smell of smoke filled my nostrils and I sat up straighter in my seat, my gaze fixed on the doorway. A ball of smoke materialized through the battered canvas, transforming into one of Fianna's creatures. It walked over to me, its ember eyes glowing brightly.

"What do you want this time?" I asked, my body tense.

It said nothing, only cocking its head before awkwardly sitting down on its rump. The creature let out an odd hiss, showing me its fangs. I snuck a glance at Dara's room, practically willing the oaf to wake up. The shadow creature was entirely too close for comfort, but there was no sign of the damn man. I'd grown more accustomed to the strange beings during my time with Lorcan, but I still didn't trust them. I'd seen them rip mortal beings to shreds and sever souls from bodies.

"I am not your master," I told the creature, leaning as far away from it in my chair as I could. "What do you want from me?"

They know the future when they see it, Fianna said. *I still have need of the weapon that hides inside Castle Clogwyn, but there are other obstacles that need to be eliminated first. Namely, the Ri's daughter.*

I couldn't say I would be unhappy to see Cadfael's wretched daughter dead, but the Stag Spirit had a servant, and that servant was Lorcan. Not me.

Lorcan is unwilling to do what needs to be done, Fianna said, an edge to its rasping voice. *He is unwilling to change. I cannot wait for him to come to his senses.*

And what exactly am I to do? I asked. *I am not your servant.*

Not yet. I heard what sounded like a strangled, bitter laugh and the shadow creature's eyes blazed. *Help me in this. Help me bring an end to the Wolf Spirit's line of Ris and I will reward you, just as I promised before.*

The shadow creature got to its feet, a puff of smoke billowing from its nostrils. It drifted in front of my face and I froze as I watched the smoke morph before me into flashes of images. I saw myself in my hawk form, soaring over the mountains before diving back down to the earth and landing on a man's gloved hand, the cloaked and hooded stranger stroking the top of my head. The image then morphed into the Great Hall of Clogwyn and my breath caught as I saw Aengus seated at the head of the hall, with me at his side. On his right hand, the golden clan ring of Blaidd glimmered, the mark of the clan's rightful Ri. The image changed yet again, this time showing Aengus and me wrapped in a passionate embrace. My mouth went dry and a yearning filled me. Then the images vanished as quickly as they'd appeared, leaving my heart pounding and my chest aching.

I can give you the objects of your heart's desire, Fianna said. *All I ask for in return is your obedience. One day your soul, perhaps, but not yet. Just your aid in cleansing this land so that a new future can come to pass.*

My thoughts raced with what I had seen. Aengus. It had shown me Aengus. Aengus seated in the Great Hall like he was the Ri of Blaidd. *Like he is Fionn's blood kin.*

Is it him? I asked, my breathing shallow as a thrill coursed through me. *Is he Fionn's bastard?*

There was no answer. Instead, the shadow creature dissolved back into a ball of smoke.

Is it him? I repeated, stiffening as a sense of panic set over me. The possible truth Fianna had thrown at me was far more tempting than I had ever imagined. *You must tell me!*

I cannot tell you what I know until you give me what I want.

I let out a frustrated hiss, the ball of smoke drifting back toward the doorway. I wanted what it had teased me with. It was the same goal, the same thing I had been fighting for since Lorcan had rescued me. For those who had risen against my kind to pay, for Cadfael and his line to meet their doom, and for a new era to begin in Blaidd. It was all of that and more. All of that and a life as Aengus' Banrion.

I'll aid you, I said, swallowing hard. *I'll aid you, so long as I get him and the place of Banrion in return. And that you do not demand my soul.*

Oh, if I want your soul, little mortal, I will not have to demand it, it replied, letting out a harsh laugh. *But, yes. It is your precious Aengus who bears the blood of Blaidd. And it is him who I will sit in Castle Clogwyn as my Ri.*

My heart raced as the smoke disappeared. I half fell back into my chair, letting out a quiet noise of disbelief. For so long, I had envisioned Lorcan taking the place of Ri. He had spoken of it like it was a certainty from the time I had met him. But Aengus? Unassuming Aengus who had long expressed a desire to live his quiet little life in Beag?

I let my eyes flutter shut, trying not to let my imagination run wild, but I wasn't exactly successful. I could see it, the future Fianna had displayed before me. Aengus choosing me as his Banrion, living a life of ease and pleasure inside Castle Clogwyn, sharing his bed. Oh, how I could make Fflur pay for what she had done if I were Banrion of Blaidd. How I could make them all pay.

I heard shuffling somewhere behind me and I started, half-turning in my chair. Dara stood in the doorway to his room, the canvas flap partially pushed back. He looked at me with a frown, his brow furrowed.

"What are you doing out here in the middle of the night?" he asked.

I ducked my chin, biting the inside of my cheek. The last thing I needed was for him to know of my recent dealings with Fianna. I didn't trust him not to go running to Lorcan.

"I couldn't sleep," I said, shrugging one shoulder.

"I can fix that. Come back to bed."

Arrogance oozed from his words and I couldn't stop my thoughts from flashing back to Aengus. I shook my head, getting to my feet. Aengus was not mine yet and I didn't need Dara to be suspicious. I crossed the room and joined him in the doorway, letting him snake an arm around my waist before pulling me back into bed with him. One day, it would be Aengus' lips covering mine, not his. One day, I would be Banrion of Blaidd.

CHAPTER 13

ANGER'S POISON
Seren

THE ECHO OF POUNDING on the door made me jolt awake. Awyr and Cryfder had already been roused by the noise, the two of them leaping off the bed with their hackles raised. I clutched the sheets to my chest as Bran stirred next to me. He blearily sat up as well, running a hand down his face. He'd been spending almost every night in my bed of late, to the point where it felt wrong to not have him near. The banging echoed into my bedchamber again and we both tensed.

"There's a dagger on the table next to you," I told Bran quietly.

I wanted to think Clogwyn was safe, but after the incident with Alannah, I didn't see the point in taking any chances. Bran nodded, fetching the dagger as the two of us cautiously got out of bed. Bran grabbed a shirt and I wrapped myself up in my dark blue robe. Whoever was knocking at the door was doing so without ceasing and my stomach tied itself into more knots with each loud bang.

Coming around the bed to my side, Bran passed me the dagger. "Here," he said. "I already had one in my boot."

I nodded, taking hold of the blade's hilt, finding some comfort at having the weapon in hand. Cryfder and Awyr were on full alert, their bodies rigid and a low growl rumbling from Awyr's throat as the pounding continued. It wasn't exactly normal for people to be storming into my chambers in the dead of night.

I called the wolves to me and they obeyed, though they were alert for trouble as Bran pushed open the bedroom door. The common room was dark and the banging got louder. My heart pounded in my ears and I was moments from unsheathing my dagger when a muffled voice shouted through the door, "Seren!" It was Domhnall. "I must speak with you! It's urgent."

I hurried over to the door, hating how my hands shook as I fumbled to unlock it. I was relieved it wasn't an intruder, but I couldn't think of many good reasons for Domhnall to come banging on my door in the dead of night. Half the castle was probably awake with his racket. Bran came up behind me, standing right at my shoulder as I flung the door open.

Domhnall looked more put together than either of us, but it was clear to me that he'd been roused from sleep as well. Though he was fully dressed, his brown hair was slightly rumpled and there were heavy circles under his eyes. His gaze flitted from me to Bran, his brow furrowing and his head jerking back slightly before he schooled his expression. I'd hoped he would eventually learn to let go of his distrust of Bran, but apparently, he was not entirely there yet.

"Refugees just arrived from Cawl and Traeth. Large swaths of the villages were burned," Domhnall said, his tone grim.

"Many of them are wounded and Cian is in need of help in the infirmary."

My grip on the door tightened, the churning in my stomach returning as Bran placed a reassuring hand on my shoulder.

"How many?" I asked.

"More than thirty, from what I've been told," Domhnall answered. "I know Cian will have need of you, but Laoise feels it is important that we speak with Ri Cadfael at once. Your father has to release the full power of the war band against this threat, and he has to do it now."

I nodded, swallowing hard. "Of course. Just let me get dressed."

"The refugees have been moved to the infirmary?" Bran asked.

"The wounded ones," Domhnall answered. "Cian is seeing to them while Lewella is seeing to the rest and trying to find them accommodations within the castle for the time being."

"I'll see who can use my help," Bran said, giving my shoulder a squeeze.

"I'm not sure if that's the best idea." Domhnall's jaw tightened as his gaze flitted to Bran. "Especially since it sounds as if a shifter is rumored to have been seen at the site of both of these fires."

"Cian and Lewella both are going to need all the help they can get," I said, allowing a bit of sharpness to come into my tone. "And that will be for them to decide."

Domhnall pressed his lips together into a thin line but stayed silent.

"Give me a moment to get changed and I'll be right with you," I told Domhnall before pushing the door closed.

The second it clicked shut, my shoulders slumped and I blinked rapidly, fighting back the moisture that stung my eyes.

Yet more of our people suffering because Father would rather save his pride than deal with the real threat.

"It will be harder for him to ignore this now that it's right at his front door," Bran said, gently tipping my chin up and holding my gaze.

"I pray to the Spirits that you're right," I said, swallowing hard.

He pressed a kiss to my lips, his touch somehow filling me with a sense of hope that I desperately needed. He knew what was at stake, he was willing to do what needed to be done, and he was there to support me. I wasn't alone in all of this. We had each other. We held each other's gazes for a brief moment before returning to my bedchamber to get dressed.

I threw on a clean pair of pants and shirt before pulling on a pair of ankle-height leather boots. A quick comb of my hair was followed by braiding it into a simple plait. Bran changed into fresh clothes as well, the two of us leaving my chambers behind, with Bran agreeing to take the wolves to the tower to be with the rest of the pack on his way to find Lewella. Domhnall was waiting for me in the hallway, leaning against the wall. I gave Bran a brief kiss and out of the corner of my eye, I noticed Domhnall's intense gaze on us.

"I'll find you later," I told Bran.

"I love you," he murmured.

"And I love you."

After one more short kiss, he turned and went his own way.

Domhnall cleared his throat, drawing my attention as he straightened from his place on the wall. "Shall we?"

I nodded, letting him lead the way down the dark hallways. We met Laoise at the bottom of the main staircase, and I could hear a loud din coming from the Great Hall. Five grim-faced warriors stood outside the tall oak doors and my stomach twisted at the realization that the refugees were most likely being held in there for now. My heart broke over the terror that they would have experienced watching their homes burn and their loved ones perish.

"Come," Laoise said, motioning for me to follow her.

I swallowed hard, tearing my gaze away from the hall doors and doing as she bade. As I walked next to Domhnall, he laid a hand on my arm, giving it a gentle squeeze. The touch was brief, so quick I almost thought I had imagined it, but it did something to bolster my confidence as I followed Laoise to Father's study. I wasn't on my own. I had allies. When we reached the study, four warriors stood guard outside it, blocking our entrance.

"Ri Cadfael is meeting with his warriors and is not to be disturbed," one of them said.

"You will tell Ri Cadfael that two members of his council demand an audience with him," Laoise replied.

They exchanged uneasy glances before one gave a subtle nod and slipped into the study. I briefly heard raised voices, one of which was clearly Father's, before the warrior returned.

"Ri Cadfael has said that he will meet with his council once the sun rises," the man told Laoise.

"Then we will wait," Laoise said, folding her arms. "As I'm afraid that is not good enough for at least two of his advisors."

The warriors glowered at Laoise, but she was unmoved. One of them grumbled something under his breath but they made no move to force us to leave. The shouting inside the study had ceased, but I was on edge the longer we waited. Odds were high that Father was already going to be in a recalcitrant mood, and that would only make things more difficult for us.

When the door to the study finally banged open, I tensed. Drystan and Lewella strode out, the former wearing a particularly menacing scowl. Before the warriors could close the door behind them, Laoise had shoved her foot in it, forcing her way forward.

"You cannot go in there!" one of the warriors shouted at her, but she paid him no heed.

The sharp look she shot Domhnall and me made it clear we were supposed to come with her. Domhnall moved forward, pushing the warriors out of the way and motioning me to go ahead of him. I hurried after Laoise, Domhnall stepping inside as the door slammed behind him with an audible click. I glanced over my shoulder to see that he had wisely latched the lock.

Father stood over the main table in the middle of the room, his spine rigid and his shoulders taut as he whirled around to face us. Candles had been lit, dimly lighting the space, and on the table, I could make out a large map of Blaidd.

"What in the blazes do you think you're doing here?" Father said, narrowing his eyes at us.

"The current turn of events cannot wait until morning," Laoise replied, her cool tone a sharp contrast to Father's snarl.

"It will wait if I say so." Father widened his stance.

"Do not think that I do not have my own leverage," Laoise said, holding his gaze. "And I would think you have known me long enough to know that I will use it."

The door behind us burst open, the lock breaking. I started, bumping into Domhnall, who steadied me with his hands on my shoulders as the warriors barged in.

"We tried to keep them out, Ri Cadfael," one of them said, slightly out of breath. "They wouldn't heed us."

Father's jaw was tightly clenched and he folded his arms as he and Laoise stood locked in a deadly silent stare. Finally, he jerked his head at the warriors.

"Leave us," he told them.

They looked perplexed but did as instructed, stepping back out of the room.

"Why is my wayward daughter with you?" Father asked, still focused on Laoise as the door shut.

"Because she is the seer of Castle Clogwyn," Laoise answered, "and because she has something to add to this conversation. There is darkness looming in this realm and in the Spirit Realm. Fianna has made considerable threats of late, ones as impactful as the terror its servants are ravaging this clan with. Threats that are directly tied to the line of Blaidd."

"There are other seers," Father retorted, cutting his eyes at me. "Certainly ones more reliable than her."

"And yet she is the seer right in front of you. A seer who has been hearing from Fianna itself, no less."

Father muttered under his breath and I gritted my teeth. Every year that passed, he seemed more and more determined to ignore the Spirits. He hadn't wanted to listen to Anwen and he didn't want to listen to me. *And he has the power to doom us all because of it,* I thought, clenching my jaw so tightly it ached.

"Ri Cadfael," Domhnall said, clearing his throat as he stepped forward. "You must send out the full force of the war band with these latest attacks. It is clear that Lorcan is feeling brazen enough to continue moving south."

"Last I checked," Father replied, his words clipped, "it is not your place to decide where the war band goes, and when."

"It is his place to offer advice," Laoise said, moving closer to Domhnall. "Advice that you would be wise to heed in a time like this one. You cannot wait until Lorcan and the Stag Spirit are on your doorstep."

"This castle was never breached during the Purge," Father retorted. "It will not be breached now."

"It was breached less than a week ago," I said. "By one of Lorcan's scouts, no less."

"Stay out of this, Seren!" Father snarled. "And count yourself lucky that I do not have you thrown from this room."

"Your hymddeol is coming, Ri Cadfael," Laoise said. Father's gaze darted back to her. "You cannot ignore what is built into the very fabric of this clan. What do you wish your legacy to be?"

Father's face reddened. He was nearing the age where he would be expected to step down from his place as Ri, following the ancient practice of passing the role from one generation to the next. He should have been preparing his successor, should have been preparing me, but he had made no move to do so.

Father's hands clenched into fists, the veins in his neck throbbing as he bared his teeth. "Do not think that your years on this council will spare you from my wrath, Laoise. You should be more careful when you threaten me. And you." His gaze cut to Domhnall. "I do not fear going against the deal I struck with your mother. You would be wise to watch your step unless you wish to get sent back to Castle Ciall in disgrace. I will make any and all decisions regarding the war band, along with Drystan. None of you have any power of the warriors of Blaidd. Not now, not ever. Now, get out."

Laoise's expression only grew colder but she gave a subtle nod to Domhnall and me, motioning us toward the door. I didn't want to leave. I wanted to stay and fight him until he did what he should, but the odds would be poor indeed on my own. Father had never been inclined to listen to me, and he was already in a rage. *This isn't over,* I reminded myself as I reluctantly turned to follow Domhnall out.

Father, however, stopped me. "I am not done with you yet, daughter," he growled.

I came to an immediate halt. Domhnall stopped just inside the doorway, his gaze flitting between Father and me with something akin to worry in his eyes. He started to move toward me but Laoise grabbed onto his wrist, hissing something at him before tugging him out of the room with her. The door clanged shut behind them and I turned to face Father, lifting my chin.

"Are you finally ready to see sense?" I asked. "To listen to the guidance that the Spirits have given?"

"I have had enough of you and your disloyalty!" he shouted. "And I will not tolerate it any longer. You have no respect for what I have done for this clan."

"What have you done for it, Father? It lies in ruin! Your people are at your doorstep after fleeing for their lives. Their crops do not grow, their forests are bare. Come winter, they will starve. Holding onto this vengeance and pride of yours will not bring them back. Not Uncle and not Eamon. It is time to let this go. Send the full strength of the war band out and defeat Lorcan and Fianna. Let the shifters live in peace so this land can heal."

"I did defeat it!" he roared, slamming one of his fists down onto the table so hard that I heard the wood crack, his face beet red and his muscles quivering. He let out a string of curses, cradling his hand, and I wondered if he'd broken it with the force of his blow. "*I* won! Not it!"

"You did not defeat it then and you have not defeated it now! Will it take this clan becoming a wasteland for you to act? Fianna is not going to wait for you to come to your senses. It wants the clan for itself and it has given every indication that it wants the blood of the line of Blaidd as well."

"I am the victor that saved this land then and I am that victor now!" His chest heaved, his eyes burning bright with anger, reminding me far too much of the rage that had taken him after both Fionn and Eamon had died.

"You delude yourself," I said, feeling my own hands beginning to shake with my mounting anger.

He growled, the noise low and menacing before he pointed a finger at my chest.

"I did not punish you the way I should have after the Purge," he said, his gaze like ice as he curled his lip. "I listened to your mother when she begged me to spare you after finding out the truth of what you had done. I see now what a mistake that was."

My breath caught. That, I had never heard. A flicker of guilt rushed through me. How much had I misjudged Mother all these years?

"This time," Father continued, "I will not spare you. You have continued your disobedience, flaunted both it and your betrayal of our people openly. I know that mongrel shares your bed every night and I see what deceptions you have been getting Laoise and Domhnall to sow. Continue this and you will find yourself locked in the dungeons until you finally learn to see the error of your ways. Are we clear?"

A lead weight settled on my chest, a sickly feeling pooling in my stomach. In all my twenty years, he had never used that threat and yet looking into his hate-filled eyes, I feared he would follow through with his words. But Blaidd would cease to exist if I did not fight for it. I could not let that happen and I had my own vows to keep.

"I have my own promises I have made, to beings far more powerful than you," I said, making myself hold his gaze. "I will do what I must for the Clan of Blaidd."

"As will I," he replied, his tone colder and harsher than I had ever heard it.

The resentment in his eyes left a shiver running down my spine. My feet felt as if they were weighed down with a thousand stones as I turned and left the study. He had reminded me too much of how he'd been during the darkest days of the Purge, when he had been beyond reason. The hatred and grief he carried were killing what little heart he had left like a poison.

Despite the late hour, I made my way toward the Great Hall instead of my chambers. My people needed me. Lewella would need help getting them settled and Cian would need help tending to the wounded. I would not be Father. I would not sit in Clogwyn and ignore the plight of those around me. Even if he threw me in the dungeons, I would come out of them fighting.

CHAPTER 14

THE POWER TO CHANGE FATE

Alannah

AFTER SCOUTING OUT A small band of warriors camped on the western border of Ioliare, I found myself escorted to Lorcan's hut when I returned to our encampment. Dara had been waiting for me at the camp's outskirts, seeing me to Lorcan, though he'd left me on my own after we'd reached the rickety wooden door that led into Lorcan's lair.

Night had already fallen and I was exhausted after the day's flight, but there would be no rest for me until I saw to whatever it was Lorcan wanted. Grumbling under my breath, I pulled open the door and stepped inside. While Lorcan's hut was still little more than a hovel, it was in far better shape, not to mention much larger, than any of the others. He had an actual bed of sorts, a sleeping pallet raised off the ground by an awkwardly made wood frame. Precious candles that had been stolen from a band of traveling merchants lit the dark space, casting the hut in shadows.

Lorcan himself stood by the unlit hearth, the warmth of the night replacing the need for a fire, with three of his shadow creatures around him. When I shut the creaking door behind me, he didn't even glance my way, though the shadow creatures did. All three of them watched me intently as I strode across to the hut to join him.

"You have need of me?" I asked.

He started, causing me to frown. As long as I'd known him, he'd been unflappable, and yet over the last few weeks, there had been something different about him. An uneasiness and paranoia that hadn't been there before. He quickly regained his composure before angling himself toward me.

"You will not go on the raid tomorrow night," he said. "I have need of you elsewhere."

I stiffened, my brow wrinkling. The last time I had stayed back on a raid had been back when we'd had Bran at our disposal.

"Who will handle the creatures?" I asked.

The shadow creatures were not beings that were easily managed or controlled. Only someone with a gifting could even hope to try. Lorcan had always given the task to Bran or me, though despite our giftings we had often struggled to keep control of the difficult beings, even with Lorcan doing his part to control them from afar.

"I will." He rubbed the inside of his wrist with a slight wince. As he did so, I caught a glimmer of his own mark from Fianna glowing in the dark.

Even though I kept my mouth shut at his surprising words, I had a feeling my surprise showed in my features. Lorcan rarely led raids; that was one of the many reasons he'd hired Dara. He claimed that if he was to be Ri one day, his life must be guarded.

He was too important to be caught up in the fighting and with his mind-speaking abilities, he could easily communicate with and control others from a distance.

"I have another task for you," he continued. "You will travel south, back to Castle Clogwyn."

My jaw tightened, memories of my last failure at Clogwyn returning to me. The only venture I wanted to take back to Clogwyn and its wretched inhabitants was one that involved murder.

Oh, there will murder on this venture, Fianna said with a rasping laugh. *Never fear, little mortal. You will get to sate your bloodlust.*

Despite having heard the Stag Spirit many times over the last few weeks, its voice overtaking my thoughts still startled me. I worked to school my expression, unsure if Lorcan had heard it speak or if the words had been for me alone. He gave no indication of it, only rubbing at his wrist again.

"You will take one of the creatures with you," he said, still not meeting my gaze. "It has been given its instructions and it will obey you, so long as you do not contradict what it has been told."

"And what are those instructions?" I asked, raising my brow. He was being unusually vague and it was starting to irk me.

"To kill Cadfael's daughter. You will make sure it achieves this."

"Gladly," I said with a smug smile, a thrill of excitement coursing through my veins. That was a death I would be more than happy to ensure came about.

"And if you have the chance, you will kill Bran as well." Lorcan paused, grimacing as he clutched at his wrist. "But only if that does not interfere with the killing of Cadfael's brat."

"Understood." My blood practically sang for Bran's. If I could bring his death to pass as well as Seren's, I wouldn't hesitate.

He had betrayed us all and continued to do so with his foolish decision to be Cadfael's lackey.

"You will leave tonight." Lorcan let out a low hiss, his knuckles growing white as he continued to clutch at his wrist. "Fianna will... Fianna will oversee your task."

A hint of uneasiness settled over me as I took in his contorted features. His obvious pain was a subtle reminder of Fianna's power. No matter how powerful any of us thought we were, we were nothing compared to it. Lorcan spat out a muttered oath, a sheen of sweat sitting on his brow as Fianna's darkness swirled in the air. The shadow creatures let out a series of growling and clicking noises, puffs of smoke billowing from their nostrils as all three focused on me with almost expectant expressions.

"I will see it done," I said.

Lorcan nodded, dismissing me with a wave as he ground his teeth, his gaze fixed on his arm. I backed away from him and one of the shadow creatures got to its feet. It began to follow me back to the door, leaving me to assume that it would be the creature to accompany me on my journey to Clogwyn. I'd commanded it before and while it was often intractable, it was also a particularly bloodthirsty and deadly beast. Seren and Bran would be hard pressed to stand against it.

Remember what I have promised you, Fianna whispered as I stepped back out into the dark night with the shadow creature at my side. *Remember that I can change your fate.* I wanted a future as Banrion. I wanted Aengus and wanted both more and more with each passing day. Fianna had asked for my obedience and I would give it.

CHAPTER 15

FLAMES AND SHADOWS

Seren

THINGS HAD BEEN SOMBER at Castle Clogwyn since the arrival of the refugees; their plight had been much harder for Father to hide. I'd spent much of my time helping them get settled and helping Cian tend to the wounded. To my surprise, Father had sent a larger group of warriors to Cawl and Traeth in the wake of the destruction. I still feared the numbers he'd sent weren't enough, but Laoise was insistent that it was a step in the right direction on Father's part.

Days had passed, my thoughts and dreams haunted by the haggard faces of the refugees and Fianna's threatening words. It still haunted me with the threats of the blood of the line of Blaidd and I was no closer to discerning its meaning. Still, the slight change in Father, along with no word of any new fires, gave me some hope. Especially with the arrival of the Gwanwyn festival.

Every spring, the clan gathered together and celebrated the season of growth and paid its respects to the Wolf Spirit. In spite of the ever-present darkness this year, the festival itself offered a reprieve for the people, no matter how short. But even with the festivities, as I walked the streets of Gefell, I couldn't help but worry about what Fianna's next move would be. Bran shared my concerns, as did Lewella, and as such, Bran had accompanied me down to Gefell, despite Father and Drystan's continued rules that he wasn't to leave Castle Clogwyn without their permission.

Lewella had agreed to Bran's scheme of guarding me in his wolf form, especially in light of Alannah's recent break-in. While I knew she would keep our secret, I'd been worrying since we'd left the castle a few hours ago that someone would recognize Bran. Thankfully, so far, he'd blended in seamlessly with Awyr and Cryfder and no one had questioned his presence. The only person outside of Lewella who knew the actual identity of the large grey wolf at my side was Cian and he hadn't spoken a word of the truth to anyone.

I took in a deep breath as Cian, Mair, and I walked the crowded village streets, taking in the tantalizing smells of cooking meat and fragrant herbs, along with the heavy scent of wood smoke. I'd always enjoyed Gwanwyn. The festival would start early with a massive market in Gefell and all manner of culinary creations. Throughout the day, there would be a large horse sale along with competitive games that warriors and villagers alike could participate in. Once night fell, the village would be left behind for the castle, where more food and drink would be supplied and a large bonfire with music and dancing would take place just outside the castle walls.

"Do you want to look at the vendors on the far side?" Mair asked, breaking my focus away from a pair of traveling jugglers as she took a bite of her apple pastry.

Cian had invited her to join us in Gefell for the day and I'd been happy to have her for company. This was Mair's first Gwanwyn at Clogwyn and her enjoyment of the festival had helped distract me from my worries. We were planning on meeting up with Lewella and Emer back at the castle tonight, the two of them spending the day in Gefell with Emer's family.

"I'm up for it." Cian glanced over at me. "Seren?"

"Sure," I replied. We hadn't been over on that side of the square yet today except once, passing by on our way to watch the horse sale.

We pushed through the crowds that filled the large village square, the wolves and Bran sticking close to me. A band of traveling musicians played merry tunes in the center of the square and my thoughts flitted to the dancing that was sure to take place tonight. It had always been one of my favorite parts of the festival and I hoped to enjoy a few dances with Bran.

As we reached the long rows of vendors, many of whom had traveled to Gefell for the festival, I glanced down at Bran, noticing his pricked ears and lifted tail. He'd always enjoyed feasts and festivities. I was glad he seemed to be getting some enjoyment out of today, especially with his difficult return to Clogwyn.

"Don't tell Rhodri," Mair said as she took the last bite of her pastry, "but I think that might have been better than what comes out of the castle kitchens."

Cian and I both chuckled at the mention of the castle cook.

"Your secret is safe with us," I told Mair with a smile.

When we strolled by a vendor with a handful of lovely hairpins on display, I slowed my steps and paused to peruse them. My thoughts flitted to Mother as I looked over the beautifully carved pieces. She hadn't been feeling well enough today to come down to Gefell, but Sioned had passed on that she had every intention of joining the festivities at the castle tonight.

It would be the first Gwanwyn festival event Mother had participated in in almost ten years and I sincerely hoped Father wouldn't make the night completely unbearable for her.

I lightly brushed a hand over a set of hair pins displaying beautifully carved howling wolves. I'd wanted to pick something up for Mother, with her illness confining her to the castle today, and I felt like they suited her. Pulling out a bit of coin, I purchased the pair from the older woman behind the table and she wrapped them in a thin hide, tying them off with a beautiful piece of dyed yarn.

"For Aunt Esyllt?" Cian asked as we walked away the table, moving on to the next row of vendors.

I nodded. "Hopefully she'll like them."

"I'm sure she will," he replied.

We hadn't gone much farther when I felt the hair on the back of my neck rise, the uncomfortable sensation of being watched coming over me. My gaze darted through the crowd, my body instinctively tensing. Bran had gone rigid as well, his hackles rising. It was impossible to get a good view of anything with the masses of people around us, and the uneasy feeling stayed with me. To my right, I could have sworn I heard the flap of wings, but when I looked, nothing was there.

"Seren?" Cian placed a hand on my shoulder, his expression wary as he looked down at me.

I shook my head, the uneasy feeling that had come over me fading. Bran, I noticed, had given himself a slight shake and relaxed as well.

"I thought I saw something," I said with a light shrug.

"It would be tempting for Fianna and Lorcan, I'm sure, what with the chaos of the festival," he said, keeping his voice low. "But a day like this one also means a great number of witnesses."

I pressed my lips together, giving him a slight nod as we continued to wander through the crowd. Nothing had happened all day and it wasn't as if Gefell was absent of warriors. There were more of them in the village today than there ever were under normal circumstances. *And Clogwyn will be teeming with them later,* I reminded myself.

We wandered a bit farther, the sun falling lower in the sky, before we were stopped by two warriors. They were seeking Cian and though they spoke quickly, I gleaned the gist of the conversation. Apparently, someone had suffered a minor injury in one of the games and was in need of a healer.

"I can go," Mair said.

"I appreciate that, but I'll see to this," Cian replied. "It will be an easy fix with my gifting. And you two don't have to wait for me to head back to the castle. It'll probably be better to do so now before the road gets busy."

"Probably wise," I said. "Good luck."

Mair and I bid him farewell and he strode off with the warriors.

"Are you ready to head back?" I asked Mair.

"I think I've seen everything I wanted to see here," she replied.

"I know a shortcut we can take through the forest," I said. "The road won't be too bad yet, but it will still be crowded."

She nodded and we made our way across the square to our horses, who had been tethered along with other mounts from Castle Clogwyn, most of them belonging to warriors. It was always a chore getting from Gefell to Clogwyn on the evening of Gwanwyn. People came from all over the clan for the celebration, and the dirt road between the village and the castle hadn't been built to handle that much foot traffic. The shortcut I knew of was one I'd been taking since I was a girl. It cut through the forest that connected Gefell and Clogwyn, letting out on the back side of the keep.

I untied Ceol, and Mair did the same with Copar. I'd arranged for her to be able to ride the gelding, who was mostly being used as an extra mount for the warriors or for any castle visitors, and he'd been as well-mannered for her as I'd hoped. We swung up onto our horses and Mair brought Copar alongside Ceol and me as we made our way out of the village. Bran, Awyr, and Cryfder all stayed close to the horses without getting underfoot. Soon, we reached the village outskirts, the noises and crowds fading away behind us. The forest loomed ahead and as we passed under the boughs of oak, pine, and poplar, we moved the horses into a trot.

I expected we would make good time back to the castle, which would give me time to wash up and change. For the festivities down in the village, I'd worn a finer pair of pants and a dark green shirt embroidered with wolf heads, but a dark red gown awaited me back in my bedchamber for the bonfire tonight. I was to sing the tale of Rhonwen with Cian, a tradition the two of us had been performing together since I was thirteen. I'd picked the dress out with that in mind, but also with Bran. I suspected with the way it left my shoulders and a large part of my back bare, he would be appreciative of it.

The thoughts put a smile on my face as the horses picked their way along the deer trail we were following. Though it was darker under the trees with the fading sun, beams of light still broke through the tree canopy above, shining down in golden streams. Mair and I rode in comfortable silence as we traversed deeper into the forest with the wolves at our side.

A light crashing noise drew my attention and when I looked to my left, I saw the white flick of a deer's tail as the creature bolted away from us through the underbrush. At first, I thought little of the intrusion. The wild creatures of the forest were usually understandably startled by the appearance of people, horses, and wolves, but as we pressed on down the path, I could feel a change in the air.

The temperature plummeted, the sunlight fading as heavy dark clouds moved overhead. Both horses tensed, arching their necks and slowing their steps, hesitant to keep moving forward. The wolves had all slowed as well, including Bran, each of them raising their hackles. Bran stepped closer to Ceol, letting out a low, threatening growl. My chest hitched as Fianna's presence swirled through the air, dark and bitter. Ceol threw his head up, letting out a loud, sharp snort as his body quivered.

"Seren?" Mair called from behind me. "What is it?"

I twisted in the saddle, trying to get a better look at her. Copar was equally alarmed and she was doing her best to calm the nervous horse.

"We need to—"

I didn't get the chance to finish, cut off by the sharp shriek of a hawk. The bird plummeted down from the sky right in front of Ceol. The stallion reared, just barely missing the hawk as he struck out with his front hooves, almost unseating me in the process. I grabbed the hilt of my sword, unsheathing the blade, though I silently cursed not bringing my bow.

The hawk took back off into the sky and one look at her brilliant red feathers told me exactly who she was. Alannah had returned. She flapped her wings loudly, letting out another piercing shriek. Bran gave a ferocious growl, his teeth bared as he leapt up and snapped at her. Awyr and Cryfder bared their teeth as well, picking up on Bran's tension.

I tried to push Ceol forward, but he balked, refusing to do so, and Mair was having no better luck with Copar, from the look of it. Suddenly, a ball of smoke snaked up from the forest floor. Ceol shied again and my stomach twisted as I watched the smoke take the form of one of the most grotesque beings I'd ever laid eyes on.

Fianna's shadow creature came up to the horses' bellies and Ceol and Copar were terrified of it. The creature hissed and wailed, smoke billowing from its nostrils as its eyes gleamed like twin flames. It pawed the ground, sending sparks flying from its clawed feet. My grip on my sword tightened, but my stomach clenched. My weapon would be of little use against such a being.

Alannah's cry drew my attention away from the creature and I just managed to shield my face as she swooped down at me. Her talons raked across my arm and I could feel the rush of wind from her wings as she flapped them in my face. I swung at her with my blade but an eldritch wail came from the shadow creature, making Ceol rear again.

I grappled for balance as my stallion's feet hit the ground and the shadow creature lunged at us. Bran sprang at the creature. I screamed his name, my heart in my throat as he latched onto the side of the creature's neck with his powerful jaws. The shadow creature let out a bloodcurdling cry, snapping at Bran with its sharp, elongated fangs. Awyr and Cryfder went to run to Bran's defense, their instinct to protect their pack taking over, but I yelled at them to come back. My precious mortal wolves wouldn't stand a chance against such a beast. Even Bran had only the slimmest one.

A shout from Mair made me whirl around in my saddle, my heart racing. Alannah had moved on to attacking her, striking at Mair with her beak and talons. Mair was trying to fend Alannah off with fists, but the shifter was hardly deterred. I wheeled Ceol around, racing toward Mair with my sword drawn. My steel was useless against the shadow creature, but Alannah bled the same as any other mortal.

I swung my sword at Alannah when I reached her, only to have her dart away from my blows. The more she evaded me, the more my frustration built. Awyr and Cryfder did their part to try and bring Alannah down, jumping and snapping at her if she made the mistake of getting too close to them. Cryfder even pulled a few feathers from one of her wings, but it wasn't enough. Behind us, I could hear Bran's fierce snarls and the shadow creature's screeches, their battle still raging.

Alannah finally made a mistake, flying too close to my blade, and I sliced across her side, under her right wing. She jerked back and let out a sharp cry as she flapped back up into the tree canopy, blood dripping from her feathers. Bran let out a frenzied bark and Mair a yell of warning, but not before I felt something slam into Ceol and teeth sink into my skin. The pain of the shadow creature's bite left me gasping and my body erupted with fiery pain. I swung my sword at the creature, trying to force it to release its hold on me, but my blade went right through its body like it was passing through smoke.

Ceol plunged sideways in his haste to get away from it, but it held fast. Bran once again launched himself at the creature, a blur of grey fur and gleaming white teeth, and he sprang onto the creature's back and sank his teeth into the back of its neck. The creature let go of me, wailing with rage as it bucked and ran backward. Bran clung to it as it twisted and contorted, trying to throw him. Fiery spasms radiated up and down my leg, leaving me hissing and gritting my teeth. All too soon, the creature got the upper hand on Bran, throwing him off, and he hit the ground with a sickening thud. He scrambled to his feet, panting heavily, just as the shadow creature went to move toward me again.

To my astonishment, however, its movements faltered. It stumbled, letting out low grunts. I took in the gashes that marred its body and the odd black blood that oozed from it.

Bran had damaged its neck, a bloody black hole evident as the creature wheezed. Its sides heaved, the fire seeming to leave its eyes. Bran barked, drawing my focus, and our gazes locked. A heartbeat passed before he took off down the deer trail in the direction of the castle.

This was our chance to escape. I called back to Mair and urged Ceol forward past the disoriented creature. The stallion was fractious, but did as I bade. I followed after Bran, Mair and the wolves right behind us. My leg felt like it was on fire and I fought to ignore the pain as our horses plunged down the trail. There wasn't time to stop, not with the chance that the shadow creature might give chase.

With every step that Ceol took, however, the burning in my leg increased. I felt too hot, a cold sweat breaking out over my skin. An excruciating wave of pain caused me to slump forward onto Ceol's neck and out of the corner of my eye, I saw that Mair had come up beside us. She grabbed onto one of Ceol's reins, pulling him and Copar both to a halt. Tremors had begun to wrack my body and my breath was coming short and fast.

"Easy, Ren, I've got you." Bran's touch startled me but I felt him place a hand on my waist from my other side, steadying me in the saddle.

I swayed where I sat, black spots dancing in my vision.

"She can't ride back like this," Mair said.

"I'll ride with her," Bran replied.

"I think I'm going to be sick," I muttered, heat flushing my body as my stomach churned.

"The poison from the bite." Mair touched my leg, the pain that followed making me cry out and the edges of my vision blacken.

"She needs Cian, but we need her to make it that far."

Mair's voice was oddly muffled to my ears and Bran's response was almost intelligible. My whole body was wracked with stinging, burning pain and I collapsed onto Ceol's neck, letting the blackness overtake me.

CHAPTER 16

BITTER ENDS

Bran

THUS FAR, I HAD to give it to Mair that she had taken our current ordeal shockingly well. She'd stayed calm, despite being attacked by Alannah and a shadow creature, having me shift from wolf to man right in front of her, and Seren looking as if death would sweep her from this realm to the next at any moment. I could certainly see exactly why Cian had found her to be a valuable addition to the infirmary.

I cradled Seren in my arms, trying to get control of my own panic, as Mair inspected the ghastly bite wounds on her leg. Seren had fallen off Ceol when she'd lost consciousness and I'd barely managed to catch her before she'd hit the ground. Cryfder and Awyr were pressed up against my legs, letting out low whines as they gazed up at their mistress.

Where Alannah and the shadow creature were, I didn't know, but I hoped they'd both been wounded badly enough that they would be incapable of giving immediate chase. While I had injured the shadow creature significantly, I hadn't killed it. I couldn't. My gift allowed me to inflict damage on the creatures, but I did not have the power to end them.

"We need to get her to Cian, but we need to stop this bleeding," Mair said, taking a step back.

The wounds were deep and had already begun to fester with the poison from Fianna's creatures that had begun to seep into Seren's blood. My own right arm burned and stung, bearing a few scratches from my tangle with the creature, but those injuries were nothing like the deep, ragged punctures that marred Seren's leg.

"Wait here," Mair said, her lips pressed together as she scanned the forest that surrounded us.

My heartbeat tripled when she left, my shoulders tensing. We were too vulnerable out here for any of us to be wandering off on our own.

"What are you doing?" I called to her.

"We need to not lose Seren before we get back to the castle. Or you," Mair called back, continuing her strange search.

I let out a muttered oath. I could feel the heat radiating from Seren's body as I held her, could see the cold sweat that slicked her skin, and my stomach clenched. I'd seen what Fianna's creatures could do and the sort of death they could bring. That was not the ending I wanted for the woman I loved.

Mair let out a small noise of triumph, drawing my attention back to her. She unsheathed Seren's sword, which she'd taken from Ceol's saddle, and carefully began to cut off the leaves of some sort of plant. Once she'd gathered a bundle of it, she hurried back over.

"What in the blazes is that?" I asked as Mair began to press the leaves inside Seren's wounds.

"Yarrow," she replied. "It should slow the poison and help stop the bleeding."

"Where did you learn that?" I asked, raising my brows as I eyed the handful of green leaves that now covered Seren's wounds.

Lorcan had never spoken of such a thing and I'd never even seen Aengus resort to such measures. Only his gifting had ever had any effect on a wound from a shadow creature. A few of Dara's fighters had been stupid enough to taunt and tangle with Fianna's beings when they'd first arrived, and only Aengus had kept them from dying.

Mair bit her lip. "I read about it, in a book. I've never actually used it, but it's the best option we have, as far as I can see."

She grabbed the hem of her shirt, her face slightly paling as she carefully cut off a long strip of fabric, somehow managing not to cut herself in the process. Letting out a sigh of relief, she wrapped it around Seren's leg and then tied it securely in place.

"Here," she said, coming around to me. "Let me see your arm."

I held still as she applied the leaves before ripping off another strip of cloth from her shirt to tie around my wounds. To my astonishment, I could feel the burning sensation leaving my arm, replaced by a soothing cool.

"Can you ride back with her?" Mair asked.

"I'll manage."

Mair helped me get up on Ceol with Seren. Once the two of us were settled on the stallion's back, I wrapped an arm around Seren's waist and picked up the reins. Ceol was tense underneath me, but I held him back until Mair was mounted on Copar. We urged our horses into a gallop, Awyr and Cryfder following us at my call.

My throat was tight as our horses raced through the trees, every moment that passed one moment closer to losing Seren. My anger at Alannah, Lorcan, and Fianna burned hot, keeping the adrenaline from the fight coursing through me. That shadow creature had been after Seren and it wouldn't have stopped until she was dead. If this would not convince Cadfael that he needed to secure his fortress, I didn't know what would.

By the time we reached the gate at the back of the castle wall, dusk had fallen and my stomach had tied itself into knots with fear and worry. Seren was still unconscious in my arms, though her breathing seemed less labored. As Mair and I pulled our horses to an abrupt halt, the warriors standing guard at the gate rushed over to us. I grimaced when I recognized Seachnall by torchlight. He narrowed his eyes at me, his gaze flitting between me and Seren.

"Seren has been injured," Mair said to them. "Cian must be sent for at once."

"And you have a shadow creature and a shifter running loose in the forest behind the castle," I added. "Probably wise to send out warriors."

Seachnall jerked his head back at my words. "This isn't the time for your delusions, shifter."

"It's not a delusion," Mair said, thrusting out an arm that bore long jagged scrapes from what I assumed had been Alannah's talons. "I was attacked by them as well."

A murmur broke out from among the warriors and Seachnall shifted, as if uncomfortable where he stood.

"Gerallt," Seachnall said, gesturing to one of the warriors, "alert Pennathe Drystan of what has happened."

The warrior nodded before hurrying off through the gate, back toward the castle, and Seachnall stepped closer to Ceol.

"We will take it from here regarding the Ri's daughter," he said, reaching for Seren.

My hold on her tightened. "I can take her to the infirmary. Cian will need to know exactly what happened regarding her injuries."

"And I suppose you would know all about that, wouldn't you? Rather convenient that the one night you slip out of the castle, Seren gets attacked by one of your kind." Seachnall's tone was mocking and his accusation left a wave of anger coursing through me. As if I would *ever* seek to harm Seren in such a way.

"Bran needs to be seen by Cian as well." Mair had swung off Copar, squaring her shoulders as she came to stand in front of Seachnall. "We will see Seren to the infirmary. Send one of your warriors for Cian. You're wasting precious time with your pettiness."

"Last I checked," Seachnall said, his gaze hard, "you're not the one in charge here."

"And last I checked, I'm the only one standing here who has any knowledge in the skill of healing," Mair replied, refusing to step out of his way as he went to maneuver around her.

"Fine," Seachnall growled, casting me another dark look. "You can be the one to explain to Ri Cadfael why the shifter was allowed to go free under such circumstances when he's been barred from stepping foot outside these walls without an escort."

I swallowed hard, clenching my jaw. Technically, he was correct, but if I hadn't gone with Seren tonight, she and Mair would have both died. I'd known what rules I'd been breaking, but with all of the threats of late, I hadn't wanted Seren going down to Gefell without someone there to watch out for her. Lewella had even agreed with me. Though I might pay for the ridiculous rules I'd broken, I'd never regret it.

"Someone needs to see to Awyr and Cryfder," I said, nodding at the wolves.

Seachnall muttered under his breath but instructed one of the other warriors to see the wolves to the Nead Mathair before barking at another warrior to go find Cian and bring him to the infirmary at once. Mair and the remaining warrior helped me get Seren out of the saddle before I swung off Ceol's back myself. Once I was dismounted, I took Seren back into my arms, despite the disapproving looks from Seachnall and his companion.

Seachnall led the way through the gate, but once we were inside the keep, Mair took the lead. I only halfway noticed the gasps and alarmed looks from warriors and servants as we hurried through the castle to the infirmary, my attention solely focused on getting Seren to Cian as quickly as possible. I knew there was no time to waste with Fianna's poison. I could feel her skin growing clammier and my chest was tight as we jogged down the hallways.

Once we reached the infirmary, Mair had me bring Seren back to one of the private treatment rooms, quick to shut out, in the name of privacy, Seachnall and the other warrior who had come with us. I laid Seren down on the small bed while Mair lit a few candles before beginning to pull various items from shelves. When I placed the back of my wrist on Seren's forehead, heat radiated from her skin and her face was flushed.

"You, sit," Mair said, gesturing to a chair in a corner of the room. "The yarrow is only a short-term fix. As soon as Cian has seen to Seren, he's going to need to draw whatever poison is left from your body as well."

Mair's commanding tone, along with my growing fatigue and the pain in my arm, left me doing as she instructed. As I sank down into the chair, my shoulders slumped and I rested my elbows on my knees. If Cadfael's pride and refusal to listen cost Seren her life, I didn't know if I would be able to control the rage that would follow.

After cutting off the leg of Seren's pants, Mair began cleaning the hideous bite wounds. The moments waiting for Cian passed with an agonizing slowness and I fought the urge to go hunt him down myself. Spirits only knew where he was with the festival going on. He could still be down in Gefell, for all we knew. Though Mair worked quickly and efficiently, I could see the unease in her expression. Once she was done tending to Seren, she walked over to me.

"Take this," she said, passing me a tincture. "Four drops on your tongue. It should help with the pain."

I uncorked the amber vial, trying not to make a face as I tasted the bitter contents. Mair set to work assessing my wounds, and all things considered, I'd come out of my fight fairly unscathed. I was far from unfamiliar with Lorcan's creatures, and I'd used that to my advantage. The worst of it had been when the shadow creature had thrown me from its back. My ribs ached and I was fairly confident that at the very least, I'd bruised them. I'd been lucky tonight that we'd only had one creature to contend with. If there'd been any more, we all would have ended up dead.

After she finished cleaning the wounds on my arm, Mair turned her attention to my back and ribs, poking and prodding as she inspected me. When she hit the lower part of my ribs on my left side, I hissed, pulling away from her.

"Hopefully you didn't break those," she said, stepping back with a frown, "but I'll let Cian determine that."

"Hopefully." I paused, clearing my throat and briefly ducking my chin. "Thank you, by the way."

So far tonight, she'd treated me with far more kindness and far less suspicion that I would have expected.

"You're welcome," she replied. "Anyone who is willing to risk their own life to protect someone else against a creature like that one is no bloodthirsty monster."

My throat thickened, but before I could respond, the door to the room burst open. Cian strode in looking slightly out of breath, as if perhaps he'd run the entire way here. Two warriors, one of whom was Seachnall, went to enter the room behind them but Cian turned and ushered them out before firmly closing the door.

"What happened?" Cian asked as he hurried over to Seren's bedside.

"She was attacked by a shadow creature," I answered, getting to my feet and joining him, along with Mair. "We were ambushed in the forest behind the castle."

"I put yarrow on the wounds," Mair said, "to try and slow the poison. It was dry, though; there was no way to combine it with bentonite and make a paste."

"A shadow creature?" Cian jerked his head back, his eyes wide. "Here?"

"Yes," I replied, holding his gaze.

"I bore witness to it as well," Mair said. "There was also a hawk. One that didn't act like an ordinary bird."

"It was Lorcan's shifter," I said. "The same one that invaded these walls a week ago."

Cian's jaw tightened. "Uncle Cadfael and Pennathe Drystan will need to hear all of this."

"Bran was injured by the shadow creature as well," Mair said.

"My wounds are minor." I shook my head. "See to Seren first."

"Take a seat for now," Cian said, eying my injured arm. "Mair, start making that paste. That was good thinking, finding yarrow and using it. There should be some dried leaves in with the rest of the herbs. And once I'm done with Seren and Bran, I'm taking a look at you as well."

I returned to my chair at Cian's instructions, taking a few deep breaths. Cian and Mair knew what they were doing, Seren couldn't be in better hands, but still, as I watched Cian begin to use his gifting on Seren's leg, I couldn't help but hold my breath. The longer he worked, the more the puncture wounds from the bite lost their angry, red, inflamed appearance and Seren's breathing noticeably deepened. There was a shake in

Cian's hands when he finally stepped back from her and he used the back of one to wipe the sweat from his brow.

"The poison is out," he said. "Mair, apply that paste to the wounds and then wrap her leg."

She nodded, taking Cian's place at the bed with the herb and clay mixture she'd created.

"Let's have a look at you." There was weariness in Cian's expression and a definite slump in his shoulders as he turned toward me.

"It's minor," I said. "I'll probably be fine. I think that yarrow helped."

"A wound from a shadow creature isn't something to take lightly, no matter how minor it is," he said, beginning to inspect my arm. "I saw too many die from such wounds during the Purge."

An uncomfortable feeling settled in the pit of my stomach and I couldn't quite meet his gaze. There had been far more creatures than just Lorcan's current ones roaming the clan at the height of the Purge, and I had no doubt I'd played a role in some of the deaths Cian had borne witness to. The more time passed, the more it became a past I wasn't particularly proud of, and part of me hoped that maybe bringing about Lorcan's death would assuage some of that guilt.

"His ribs were injured as well," Mair threw over her shoulder as she worked on Seren's leg. "His left side."

Cian nodded in acknowledgement before taking a firm grip on the wounds on my arm. He closed his eyes and I felt a tingling heat pass from his hands to my arm. It stung for the briefest of moments, but then became soothing, and I watched as the injuries began to slowly close. When he was finished, fresh new skin covered the gashes and scrapes. He released his hold on my arm and then made a further inspection of my ribs.

"Just bruised," he said after poking around for a few moments and making me grimace. "I'm too drained right now to use my gift on them tonight, but let's put a salve on for now to help with the swelling."

He stepped back from me, but swayed as he did so. I shot to my feet to steady him, drawing Mair's attention.

"Sit down, Cian," she said. "I'll see to the rest."

He grimaced but nodded.

"Here," I said, guiding him toward the chair I'd been using. "I'm feeling a lot better now."

He slumped down into it while Mair finished bandaging Seren's leg. He looked bone weary and I silently hoped he hadn't overextended himself. The door to the room slammed open again, causing all three of us to start and I tensed as Cadfael stormed in with Sioned right on his heels. Cadfael's face was marred with a particularly unbecoming scowl while Sioned was deathly pale. When her gaze fell on Seren, she covered her mouth with one hand to muffle her shocked gasp, wrapping her other arm around herself.

"What in the blazes happened?" Cadfael snapped.

"Seren was attacked by a shadow creature," Cian answered, straightening some in his seat, though it looked like the motion took considerable effort. "In the forest behind the castle. I have seen to—"

"You expect me to believe that?" Cadfael scoffed, shaking his head. "You truly believe that a shadow creature would be so close to Castle Clogwyn and none of my warriors would be aware of it?"

"A shifter slipped into your fortress a little over a week ago and you hadn't a clue," I said, raising my brows.

Cadfael let out a snarl, cutting his angry gaze toward me. "I will deal with you shortly, shifter. Keep that mouth of yours shut unless you'd like to ensure a longer punishment for your-self."

"I witnessed the attack," Mair said, clearing her throat, "along with Bran. He came to our defense. If he hadn't been there to fend off the shadow creature, none of us would have made it back to the castle alive."

I shot her a grateful look. It was a risk she was taking, speaking up so. Cadfael had punished and dismissed castle servants for less.

"Heroic actions from a shifter are as unbelievable as a shadow creature lurking in the woods," Cadfael retorted before looking back at me. "Of course, I suppose this whole wild tale would make perfect sense if your intent had been to lead the last of my remaining blood kin to her doom. That is something I certainly wouldn't put past your kind."

One of my hands clenched into a fist, my face heating. "I would *never* do such a thing. Not to the woman I love."

"Your kind knows nothing of love." Cadfael curled his lip.

"Your daughter has almost lost her life, Cadfael," Sioned said, now at Seren's bedside and clasping her niece's hand. "I do not think this is the time or the place for your outbursts."

"My daughter has almost lost her life thanks to the likes of *him*!" Cadfael pointed a finger at me, his face beet red. "He could have ended my very line tonight with his treachery."

"I saved her life!" I gritted my teeth, my own body hot with anger. "And while you sit here bellowing, a shifter and a shadow creature are roaming the forest."

Cadfael abruptly turned on his heel, facing the door. "Seach-nall!"

The door opened and the warrior strode in.

"Yes, Ri Cadfael," he said, giving him a respectful nod.

"Take the shifter to the dungeons," Cadfael said. "He will stay there until we can ascertain his role in this attack and as punishment for leaving the castle grounds. I also want Pennathe Drystan to make certain that every inch of that forest is scoured."

"The dungeons?" I knew I shouldn't have been surprised by his cruelty, but it still flooded me with a fresh wave of anger. "If I hadn't left the castle grounds, Seren would be dead! Every living being there would have been killed by the creature."

"I truly think it best if Bran stays in the infirmary," Cian said. "With his wounds from the shadow creature—"

"That is enough!" Cadfael roared. "From all of you. See to him, Seachnall."

Seachnall called more warriors into the room. Three of them strode over to me, wrenching my arms behind my back. At first, I fought them, but one of them landed a punch to my ribs that left me doubling over and gasping in pain. It took everything within me not to shift and make them pay for following Cadfael's deranged orders, for taking me away from Seren when she needed me the most.

"Get him out of my sight," Cadfael said, motioning to the door.

The warriors were far from gentle as they hauled me out of the room. I tried valiantly to get one last look at Seren, but one of them shoved my head forward. As I was marched out into the main part of the infirmary, I could hear Sioned and Cadfael's raised voices echoing from Seren's room, but whatever Sioned was saying was too late for me. Cadfael's orders had already been given and the loyalists of Clogwyn would follow them to the bitter end.

I gritted my teeth as I was shoved out into the hallway. I needed to be with Seren, not locked away in the dungeons. I needed to know she was okay and that Fianna would not steal her from me. Someone had to make certain Drystan acted; Alannah and a shadow creature couldn't be allowed to roam free, especially on a night like this one. There were far too many terrors they could unleash on far too many lives with the ongoing festival. *Damn him,* I thought as one of the warriors gave me a hard shove, pushing me to move faster. *Damn him and his ridiculous arrogance.*

If he remained Ri, it would doom us all. It was past time for new blood in the halls of Clogwyn, if only Lorcan and Fianna didn't destroy us all first.

CHAPTER 17

UNFORESEEN

Bran

MY HOPE OF NEVER again finding myself locked away in the dungeons of Castle Clogwyn had apparently been wishful thinking. This time, I at least wasn't chained to the walls, though my wrists had been skillfully bound. With the freedom to move about the dingy, dark cell, I soon found myself pacing in a vain attempt to get rid of some of my fractious, furious energy.

Worries for Seren, for the entire castle and the village of Gefell with Alannah and a shadow creature on the loose, along with my growing fury at Cadfael, consumed me. I needed to know that Seren would survive and that Clogwyn and those in Gefell would be safe. Instead, I was locked in the dark due to Cadfael's ridiculous pride and his insulting accusations.

How dare he even imply that I would seek to harm Seren? I loved her with everything that I was. I would *never* harm her. Oh, I was well aware of his rule that I was not to step foot outside of Clogwyn without Drystan or Cadfael's permission, but if I hadn't been with Seren tonight, she would have died.

As I reached one end of my cell, I came to a stop and slammed my hands against the wall before dropping my forehead against the hard stone, squeezing my eyes shut. It was killing me being locked away. Not only did the oppressive darkness bring back memories of the night I'd spent locked in a cellar years ago, waiting for the warriors of Blaidd to come kill me, but I needed to act in this moment. I needed to bring an end to all of this. If Drystan and Cadfael would simply turn me loose, I would hunt Lorcan down and destroy him. No matter what his intentions were or the past we shared, he was Fianna's servant, doing Fianna's bidding. There was hope for Blaidd with Seren as its eventual Ri; there would be no hope for it if Lorcan filled that same role.

The clang of the cell door pulled me out of my dark thoughts and I tensed, turning around to face whoever was entering, all the while wondering if Cadfael had decided to inflict more punishment upon me. Three warriors walked in, one of them carrying a torch. I could make out a few more shadowy figures standing out in the narrow hallway, just outside the barred door. Two of the warriors roughly took me by the arms and shoved me out of the cell. I tried to school my expression at the sight of Laoise, flanked by two more warriors, waiting for me. It seemed that she was indeed perhaps a stronger ally than I'd previously given her credit for.

"I will take the shifter from here," Laoise said.

The warriors holding me released me, though they didn't unbind my hands. Laoise motioned for me to follow her and I did so. It was either her or the dungeons, an easy choice. She was silent as she led the way up the stairway to the tower above, then out into the castle hallways. One look out the windows told me that it was still night. Torches guided our way as Laoise continued to lead me on.

"Has the festival continued?" I asked as I followed just behind her. "Were there any more attacks?"

"There have been no more attacks, though the festival did continue," she answered, though I caught the disapproval in her tone. "It ended hours ago."

She offered no further information and silence fell between the two of us again. Eventually, we came to a set of rooms on the opposite side of the castle. Laoise ushered me inside ahead of her into a common room, leaving me to assume that we had come to her chambers. She closed the door behind me before walking over to a table and picking up a small dagger. I couldn't help but tense as she unsheathed the blade before walking behind me, but a few seconds later, the rope binding me fell away. I rubbed my sore wrists as she walked back around in front of me and put the dagger away.

"Your little discovery did put quite a damper on the evening," she said, motioning for me to take a seat in one of the tall wooden chairs near the hearth. "Though Cadfael, as always, wanted to put on a good front. Still, he was most displeased."

"Do you know how Seren fares?" I asked.

"Stable, the last I heard, thanks to Cian. Though from what I understand, Drystan's warriors did not find your attackers, though Lewella is confident they found the scene of the fight and is holding that to Drystan and Cadfael as proof of what happened."

"It *is* what happened." I forced myself to take in a deep breath, even as my jaw tightened and I fought not to completely lose my temper. I was so weary of being doubted. "How did you free me from the dungeons? And why?"

"I still have my own influence within these walls and as I have said to you before," she said, clasping her hands in her lap, "I am an ally. A clan cannot survive if it is nothing more than a desolate wasteland. Tell me of this shifter that was seen with the shadow creature tonight."

"She's the same shifter that broke through the castle defenses a little over a week ago," I answered, Laoise's mouth turning down at the words. "She's worked with Lorcan for some time now. He uses her primarily as a scout, but she's a formidable fighter as well."

"And the shadow creature itself? Was there any indication as to why it was here?"

"A shadow creature has one purpose and one purpose only: to sow destruction and death wherever it goes. They're dangerous beings. Lorcan knows this. It's why he uses them to start his fires and why he's been a difficult foe for Drystan to get the upper hand on. No mortal can kill them. I only wounded the one tonight and only because of my gifting." I paused, running a hand down my pant leg and taking a deep breath before continuing. "I think that creature had every intention of killing Seren."

"I suspect such a creature would have gladly killed all of you," Laoise said, raising her brows. "How do you know for certain that it was after her specifically?"

"I know those creatures. The way it acted; I believe its ultimate goal tonight was to kill her."

She pursed her lips. "Would Lorcan not have learned that Seren is not the way to get to Cadfael after his failed kidnapping of her?"

"I can only tell you what I saw. If Seren dies, Cadfael has no successor. Not one that he has named, at least. Lorcan is no fool, and neither is Fianna. They will exploit whatever they can. Regardless, Castle Clogwyn is far more at risk than Cadfael or Drystan believe. A shifter has already broken through its defenses. If a shadow creature were to get inside the keep..."

"It would undoubtably be a disaster. In that, you and I agree. I can assure you that such concerns will be brought before the council with the utmost urgency. And if there is anything else you witness or hear, I will always be willing to listen."

I nodded, feeling a bit of the tension in my muscles ease. No matter my previous feelings about Laoise, I couldn't deny what she'd done tonight. Or what she'd been doing to try and aid Seren these last few weeks, including advocating for the recent refugees.

"You're no doubt exhausted after your long night." She got up from her seat and I did the same. "You can see yourself back to your room, I assume?"

"Yes," I replied. "Thank you... for my release. And for listening."

"As I've said, consider me an ally."

I gave her a respectful nod before leaving the room. Once I stepped out into the hallway, I barely stifled a yawn before scrubbing a hand over my face. I was beyond exhausted and my ribs in particular ached fiercely. If I wanted to keep myself out of yet more trouble, it would probably be wisest to go back to my room, but I wouldn't be able to rest; I was too worried about Seren.

Squaring my shoulders, I turned instead and walked off in the direction of the infirmary. I didn't want to land myself back in the dungeons, but I had to see her, Cadfael be damned. I'd come far too close to losing her tonight.

CHAPTER 18

LESS LIKE DEATH

Seren

WHEN I WOKE, MY body no longer felt like it was on fire, though there was a dull, throbbing pain in my leg. I groggily tried to throw back the blankets and sit up, but a wave of dizziness overtook me. I winced, bringing a hand to my forehead.

"You're not going anywhere just yet."

Mother's voice startled me and I looked over to see her seated in a chair beside my bed. A quick glance around the room told me that I was in the infirmary, in one of the private rooms. I didn't remember getting here, my last memory being of sprawling onto Ceol's neck in excruciating pain. A shiver passed down my spine as I remembered the shadow creature and I felt a sharp, burning tingle in my leg, as if I could still feel the beast's fangs sinking into my skin.

"We've been so worried," Mother said, taking my hand. "I'm so relieved you're still with us."

I saw the tears shimmering in her eyes as she gave my hand a squeeze, and my own throat thickened. Having her at my bedside was strange, for I could never recall her doing such a thing before, even when I'd been a small child. And yet having her here in this moment felt like it was another piece bridging the distance that had grown between us.

"The others?" I asked. "Were they badly wounded?"

"Cian has seen to them," Mother replied, blinking rapidly and clearing her throat. "He felt their injuries were minor in comparison. Here; he wanted you to take this when you woke up."

Her movements were stiff, as if it pained her to get up and walk, but she went over to the nearby table and began mixing up some sort of brew. Once she was finished, she returned to my bed and helped me sit up before passing me the drink. I made a face when I took my first sip of the strong, earthy concoction. It was less than palatable, but I managed to get it down, despite the nausea in my belly.

"Where are the others? And Cryfder and Awyr?" I handed Mother the mug back and slumped back against the pillows. My body no longer felt like it was on fire, but my head ached, my stomach was unsettled, and there was still a dull throb in my injured leg.

"Sioned went back to her chambers to rest for a bit," Mother replied. "She sat with you for the last few hours. Your wolves are fine; they're with the rest of the pack. Cian sent Mair off to get some rest and Sioned and I eventually convinced him to go do the same. Your father..." Mother's expression darkened, her mouth turning down. "Your father took it upon himself to oversee the festival and claimed to be overly weary afterward. He has promised me that he will come check on you sometime tomorrow."

My stomach clenched. The festival. The people would have been extremely vulnerable during such an event.

"The creature," I said, my fear making my heart race as I tried to sit back up. "Did the creature return? Was there another attack?"

"No one has seen any signs of it," Mother answered, gently pushing me back down. "Lewella took a handful of warriors out to scour the forest. She found the... scene of your attack, but nothing more. Drystan has put the castle on full alert. The warriors know to be looking for any signs of danger."

I took in and released a long breath. It made me uneasy that Alannah and the creature had gotten away, but at the same time, I was relieved that no other lives had been lost.

"And Bran?" I asked. "Where is Bran?"

Mother wouldn't meet my gaze, dropping her chin and shifting in her seat. "Bran is..."

She trailed off and my chest tightened. I hadn't thought him that badly wounded after his fight with the shadow creature, but honestly, I couldn't remember much after I had been bitten. I braced myself for the worst, all the while desperately hoping that I hadn't lost the man I loved, when the jiggling of the door handle caused both Mother and me to start.

Mother got to her feet, wincing as she tried to move quickly, just as the door was pushed open. My heart hammered in my ears but the tension fled from my body when Bran stepped inside. I could see the rips in his shirt and the partially healed wounds on his arm, along with the dirt and bloodstains on his clothes, but he was here and whole. I let out a sigh of relief, Bran's eyes widening as his gaze locked on Mother. He came to a sudden stop, swallowing hard.

"Banrion Esyllt," he said, giving her a low, respectful nod. "I... was hoping to see Seren."

"I see that Laoise was successful," Mother replied and I swore I saw a hint of a smile tug at her lips.

"Yes." Bran ducked his chin. "It seems I have more friends within these walls than I first thought."

My gaze flitted between the two of them as I struggled to piece together their cryptic conversation. I had quite obviously missed something.

"I could use a drink and something to eat," Mother said. "I think it best if Seren has someone here with her while I'm gone. I assume you would be up to that task?"

"Yes, Banrion Esyllt. Thank you," Bran replied.

Mother came back over to my bed and pressed a brief kiss to my forehead before bidding me goodbye, the uncharacteristic show of affection leaving my throat thick. As she latched the door behind her, Bran hurried over to my bedside.

"How are you feeling?" he asked, taking my hand.

"Less like death," I answered, squeezing his hand in return. We'd come far too close to losing one another tonight. "Do you know what time it is?"

I could see that it was still dark outside the room's one small window, but Spirits only knew how long I had been out of it.

"Well past midnight," he replied.

"Cian has seen to you?" I inclined my head toward the wounds on his arm.

He nodded. "My wounds were minor. I'm more worried about you."

He brushed back a few loose strands of my hair, tucking them behind my ear, and I briefly closed my eyes, soaking in his touch. I would never forget the horror I'd felt as I'd watched him launch himself at the shadow creature, or the fear of those moments being his last.

"I'll live," I told him as I opened my eyes. "Why was my mother talking about Laoise?"

He grimaced. "Your father sent me to the dungeons. Laoise had me released."

"The dungeons?" I abruptly went to sit up in bed, outrage flooding me, but a shooting pain down my leg left me wincing and slumping back down.

"Easy, Ren," Bran said, placing a hand on my shoulder. "I'm not happy about it, but I wasn't in there for long."

"How dare he," I said, anger threading my voice and my jaw tightening. "After everything you did to save my life; to save all of us."

My agitation caused me to jostle my leg and another wave of pain coursed through me. I bit down hard on my lower lip, letting out a low hiss of pain.

"Do you need me to go get Cian? Or your mother?" Bran asked, worry clouding his eyes and wrinkling his brow.

I shook my head. "I'll manage. It's fading now."

I could feel the pain decreasing, but I could also feel myself growing drowsy. Whatever concoction Cian had left for me was most likely to blame. I knew I had slurred my last few words and Bran frowned.

"Brew Cian left," I said, fighting the urge to let my eyes flutter shut. "For the pain."

"You need your rest." He leaned over and gave me a soft kiss, but before he stepped back from the bed, I managed to catch a hold of his wrist.

"Stay," I told him, patting the space next to me on the bed. "Mother said to keep me company."

The words didn't come out entirely clear, judging from the rueful half-smile on his face, but I was fairly confident he'd gotten the gist of it.

"She did say to keep you company, but she might not be too pleased if she comes back and finds me in your bed."

"I'm almost one and twenty. I can have a man in my bed if I please."

He laughed, shaking his head before climbing into the bed beside me. I fought to stay awake as I felt him press up against me, careful of my injured leg, but Cian had quite clearly intended for me to sleep. As one of Bran's arms came around me, I rested my head on his chest.

"I love you," I murmured.

"And I love you, Ren." He kissed me on the top of the head. "I always will."

As he stroked my hair, my eyes fluttered shut. Alannah and the creature might have gotten away, but Fianna hadn't won this time. And as far as I was concerned, it was never going to. Not while I still had breath left in my body.

CHAPTER 19

GAMES AT PLAY

Bran

ONCE AGAIN, I HADN'T intended to spend the entire night with Seren, but my exhaustion had won over and I'd been lulled to sleep while lying with her and holding her in my arms. Esyllt had woken me just as dawn had begun to break and to my surprise and relief, the Banrion of Blaidd hadn't seemed the least bit upset or alarmed to find me in bed with her daughter. Instead, she had warned me that she'd gotten word that Cadfael was coming to check on Seren before breakfast and while she herself was not upset, it might be best if he didn't find me in his daughter's bed. I didn't disagree.

As much as I didn't want to leave Seren, I did. Despite never thinking particularly highly of Esyllt in my youth, she did seem to be showing a significant level of concern and care for her daughter these last few weeks. Seren had been mentioning changes in her mother since her kidnapping and this morning, I'd seen them for myself. I believed she would be in good hands with Esyllt watching over her, and Cian, I knew, would be seeing to her as well.

Upon leaving the infirmary, I made my way back to the warriors' quarters. I needed to change and clean up after last night's fight and trip to the dungeons. I should have time to do that before breakfast, as after I ate, I knew I'd be expected in the training yard. When I eventually reached my room, I found a warrior standing outside my door with a particularly disgruntled expression. I slowed my steps and the warrior turned to face me, her scowl deepening.

"Pennathe Drystan expects you in the stable and ready to ride out in three hours," she said. "He will be traveling north with a group of warriors and you will be traveling with them. Cian will be sent to make certain you're in good enough shape to do so."

I couldn't stop myself from jerking my head back, thrown by the news, but I didn't have the chance to ask any more questions, as the warrior turned on her heel and stalked off. Last night I had been in the dungeons and today I was being sent north as part of the war band? Something I'd been denied for months? I could barely keep up with Cadfael and Drystan's erratic behavior. *At least they're doing something,* I thought. I could only hope last night's attack had scared some sense into them. Erratic behavior aside, this would be my chance to end Lorcan once and for all—and I would take it.

Squaring my shoulders, I pushed open the door to my room. While part of me worried over leaving Seren after the events of last night, this was my opportunity to do my part to set things to rights. Ridding the clan of Lorcan and Fianna was the best way to keep Seren, and the people, safe. I turned my attention to packing my things. At times like this, I supposed it was a good thing my belongings were meager. I walked over to the wooden chest that held my clothes and other items, stifling a yawn. I'd no doubt have a long ride ahead of me. The few hours of sleep I'd caught with Seren would help, but it wouldn't be enough.

I pulled out a large canvas bag and began packing clothes and other items, including the one small dagger I'd hidden away since I'd first arrived. I worked as quickly as I could, knowing I still needed to get cleaned up, eat, and apparently get seen by Cian. On top of that, I needed to tell Seren goodbye as well. I had no intentions of just disappearing on her. I'd also need to let my father know I was leaving these walls. I knew how much it had hurt him to lose me during the Purge and I didn't want to inflict that kind of pain on him again by just up and vanishing.

I was stuffing the last of my clothes into the bag when there came a harried knock at the door. I frowned, glancing out the window. Judging by the sun, I still had time before I was expected at the stable. *Of course, not that I would put it past Drystan to change his mind on a whim,* I thought. I grumbled under my breath as I strode over to the door, but when I opened it, I found my father, not a warrior, on the other side.

"Thank the Spirits," Father said as I let him in. "I tried to find you last night after I heard about the attack, but they'd told me you'd been taken to the infirmary and were in no state for visitors. I told that dolt Seachnall that he was being ridiculous, but he wouldn't listen to a word I said. All these years I've lived here and no one has ever kept me out of the infirmary before."

I couldn't hold back a snort of disgust, my anger at Cadfael and his lackeys growing. It would be just like them to cause my father more distress and pain. "You were likely told that because I spent the night in the dungeons. Not the infirmary."

"The dungeons?" Father repeated, his eyes widening with alarm. "Why in the blazes were you there?"

"Because Cadfael in his misguided arrogance decided that I was responsible for the attack. As if I would even dream of causing such harm to come to Seren."

"Were you harmed?"

"Not badly, but Seren..."

I trailed off, biting my lower lip. I could still vividly remember the moment the creature had latched onto her leg. It would always stay with me, I suspected, along with the memories of the fear, horror, and anger that had streaked through me.

"I did hear about that," Father said. "Though the word is that she's recovering under Cian's care."

"I'm leaving this morning," I replied, deciding it was better to just spit it out. "With Drystan and a band of warriors. We're headed north."

Father swallowed hard, his brow furrowing as he seemed to finally take in the partially filled bag sitting on my bed. "I suppose it's to be expected. You're one of the warriors now. You'll be careful?"

I resisted the urge to correct him that I was not one of the warriors of Blaidd and I never would be, but it was clear he was already struggling with my abrupt departure. "Always."

I resumed packing, but I could see the pain in Father's expression. He didn't want me to go, and I could understand why. He had just gotten me back, after all, but this was something I had to do. I knew Lorcan better than anyone else at Clogwyn. If anyone was going to be successful at hunting him down, between my knowledge of him and my gifting, I had the best odds. An uncomfortable silence fell between us as I buckled the bag shut. I glanced over my shoulder to see that Father had crossed his arms and was staring down at the ground. He rocked his weight back onto his heels, pursing his lips as if he were weighing his thoughts.

"I don't mean to tell you what to do and I know that you and Seren care for one another," he said slowly.

I couldn't help but tense, his tone telling me that there was a *but* coming. "We love each other."

"Cadfael is a dangerous man. His opinion of you hasn't improved since you returned here, Bran. Perhaps it is wise if you don't get tangled up with his daughter."

"If I hadn't been there last night, she would have died." The words came out far sharper than I intended, but I was so weary of being questioned about what Seren and I felt for one another. "I love her. I would give my life to keep her safe. I almost have, on more than one occasion. The only reason I would *ever* willingly give her up would be if it would save her."

Father pinched the bridge of his nose, letting out a low breath. When he looked up at me, I could see the glimmer of moisture in his eyes. "I just do not want to lose my son."

His voice cracked and my frustration and anger softened. He'd already lost my mother and for years, he had lost me too.

"I know," I told him, "but I cannot lose her."

Another knock came at the door and I cursed under my breath. The Spirits only knew who it was now. Father took a step back and I strode over to the door, hopeful that perhaps it was only Cian. I was certainly ready for him to tend to the persistent dull ache in my injured arm. Unfortunately, it was not Cian who awaited me in the hallway. Instead, it was one of the last people I wanted to see: Domhnall. I tightened my grip on the door, resisting the urge to slam it in his face. I wasn't in the head space to deal with his arrogance or his taunts.

"Is there something I can do for you?" I asked, fighting to keep my tone civil.

"A word, if you please," he replied, giving a pleasant smile that only served to put me more on edge. He'd hated me as long as I'd known him and I doubted he'd had some sudden change of heart.

"I'm afraid I already have company," I told him.

"I have to get back to the stable," Father said, coming up behind us. "I won't keep you from speaking with Domhnall."

My jaw tightened but I nodded. I knew what Father was doing, understood it, even. Domhnall was one of the Ri's advisors, not the sort of man to be turned away, no matter how much I wanted to. And Father was going to keep to the protocol that was expected of him as a castle servant. Father embraced me and I swallowed against the tightness in my throat as we stepped back from one another.

"Travel safely," Father said.

"I will."

Father gave Domhnall a respectful nod before leaving the room, and I begrudgingly stepped back to let him inside. He lazily looked about the space, perusing it with almost a bored expression and I worked my jaw as I watched him. Some days, I struggled to understand what it was Seren saw in him, though I couldn't deny that he at least seemed to understand the gravity of the situation with Fianna and Lorcan. It was perhaps his only saving grace, at least as far as I was concerned.

"You needed to speak?" I said, crossing my arms.

"Yes." He faced me, clasping his hands behind his back. "I spoke with Laoise this morning regarding last night's... events. She has pushed Ri Cadfael to act and it seems that after last night, he has agreed. Drystan will be taking a very large band of warriors north. I assume the two of us aren't wrong in our hopes that you will do your part to see to this problem now that it seems you are heading north as well?"

"Believe me," I said, holding his gaze, "when I find Lorcan, I will kill him."

"Laoise will be pleased to hear it." He gave a slow nod before ducking his chin for a brief moment and lightly clearing his throat. "As for the other matter I wished to discuss with you, I'm afraid it is more of a personal nature."

I stiffened, my shoulders bunching, but Domhnall held up a hand.

"I'm aware that you and I have not always seen eye to eye," he said, "but I think we can both agree that Seren's safety is of considerable concern after last night."

I was uncertain of where he was trying to take this, but I gave a stiff nod. Seren was far from incapable, but Fianna was a formidable foe and that shadow creature had clearly been after her.

"I want you to know that I will do everything I can to keep Seren safe during your absence from these walls. I swear that to you."

I averted my gaze, working my jaw again. I didn't trust him and I didn't want to be beholden to him in any way. And at the same time, I *was* worried. Alannah had breached these walls once and a shadow creature had gotten far too close to the castle grounds. Seren was vulnerable here.

"Why are you telling me this?" I finally asked.

"Because I am aware of how close Seren came to death," he answered. "And because I believe two grown men should be able to put aside their distaste for one another in the interest of keeping someone else safe."

I studied him for a long moment, still struggling with the long-held feelings of distrust I'd had for him, and battling with the knowledge that soon, I would be far away from here. Clogwyn wasn't safe anymore—last night had proven that, just as it had proven that Seren was in danger. Spirits knew Cadfael wasn't going to be trying to keep anyone safe, not even his own daughter. I knew Fianna had been speaking to her of the blood of the line of Blaidd. If vengeance against the Wolf Spirit's line was what it wanted, she was in grave danger indeed.

"I would appreciate it if you would be willing to look out for her," I said, despite how bitter the words tasted on my tongue. "So long as any feelings you may or may not have for her are kept in check."

I noticed the way his shoulders tensed and even though I'd most likely crossed a line with my bold statement, I didn't regret it. I'd long suspected some of his hatred of me might stem from jealousy. Even though I knew Seren didn't care for him in that way, I'd seen the way he looked at her.

"If there is one thing I excel at, it is self-control." There was something in his tone that niggled at me, but I made myself shrug it off.

He was right. We were grown men. We ought to be able to put aside our differences for the greater good. He *had* been helping Seren and looking out for her of late, just like Laoise. I would have to trust that they would continue to do so in my absence.

"I'll let you get back to preparing for your journey." To my utter shock, he gave me a low nod of acknowledgement before turning and letting himself out of my room.

As the door closed behind him, I let out a low groan and ran a hand through my hair. There were games at play here, games of humans and games of Spirits, and navigating them felt close to impossible. *Lorcan,* I told myself as I turned my attention back to my pack. *That's your focus. Lorcan.* The sooner I killed him, the sooner Blaidd, and Seren, would be safe.

CHAPTER 20

FIVE HUNDRED YEARS OF SILENCE

Seren

IF IT WASN'T FOR Mother and Cian, I doubted I would have even seen Bran before he was sent north with Drystan. As it was, Cian had passed on a message to Bran to meet me in the gardens near the castle kitchen while Mother had helped Mair slip me out of the infirmary. I still wasn't completely healed from the attack, but I would be damned if that kept me from saying goodbye to Bran. My leg in particular still pained me when I walked and despite Cian's best efforts, I would bear scars on my skin from the creature's bite. Still, such scars were a small price to pay compared to my very life.

My emotions were torn as Mair helped me navigate the castle hallways, my pace slow with my aching leg. This was the opportunity we had been waiting for, Bran having the chance to hunt down Lorcan. If anyone could kill the dangerous mind-speaker, it would be him. And while I knew it would be a difficult task to take the life of the man who had once saved his own, I knew he would not falter when the time came. Bran knew what was at stake: the very future of the clan and the people who called it home.

And at the same time, I worried for him. He would be in the thick of the danger, pitted against a formidable foe, and from what I had gathered, Drystan's band that he was taking north was still too small to stand against a powerful foe such as Fianna. Father had still insisted that most of the warriors remain at Clogwyn. While I could understand wanting to protect the castle after the events of last night, his actions weren't going to defeat the true trouble. Father needed to strike against Fianna and Lorcan, direct and hard, not keep hiding away in his keep.

"Thank you again for coming with me," I told Mair as the two of us rounded a corner. She'd truly been a far better friend than I had ever hoped for and she had taken a risk in helping me sneak out.

"I was happy to," she replied.

The two of us stepped out of one of the doors on the back side of the castle and onto the crushed shell path that would lead us to the garden. The morning air was cool, but the fog that danced across the ground and slightly obscured the path told of a warmer day ahead. Mair and I continued our slow trek undisturbed, but just as the stone wall of the garden came into view, I felt my body go rigid, my vision blurring before completely blackening—

The smoke that filled the air left me choking and gagging. The forest was desolate, nothing more than burned trees and scorched earth. I heard the shadow creature's otherworldly growl before I saw it. It emerged from the smoky haze, its amber eyes flickering brightly as it stalked toward me, its body low to the ground and its teeth bared.

I pedaled backward, slamming into the tree behind me. The trunk was hot and the bark disintegrated under my touch. The creature continued to stalk toward me and my heart pounded in my ears. Suddenly, the trunk of the tree became smooth and firm. Something long and slender pushed against my spine and I reached around to grab it, still keeping a close eye on the creature.

The feel of a smooth wooden longbow made me start. I pulled it around in front of me to see it strung and ready to use, but I found I could only stare at the weapon in confusion. I knew the intricately carved running wolves and crashing waves that had been etched into the wood. The bow I held in my hands was no ordinary one. The cry of a hawk raised the hair on the back of my neck and I felt the rush of wings as the bird swooped down and fought to snatch the bow out of my hands—

"Seren?"

Worry tinged Mair's tone and tremors wracked my body as I was thrust back into the Mortal Realm. Mair had never witnessed one of my visions before and I knew how alarming they were for those watching. My whole body would go as rigid as stone, my pupils would enlarge, and the breath would leave my lungs as my soul traveled to the Spirit Realm. While I was used to feeling short of breath and briefly disoriented after my visions, I wasn't used to the fiery pain that coursed up and down my leg where the shadow creature's fangs had sunk into my skin.

"I'm alright," I said, fighting to take deep breaths as I rubbed my hand down my aching thigh. "I just need a moment."

Mair pursed her lips. "If you're sure..."

"I'm sure." I wasn't missing saying goodbye to Bran. Not for anything.

After a few moments, the shaking in my body ceased and my breathing became deep and even. The fiery pain had left my leg, with only a dull throb remaining.

"I'm ready," I told Mair, squaring my shoulders.

The two of us began walking again, Mair keeping a close eye on me with her brow wrinkled. I gave her a reassuring smile, but my thoughts raced with what I had seen. Why had the Spirits been showing me Rhonwen's bow? I knew the story, knew of the power it had once held, but as far as I knew, no one had even taken the bow off its customary place on the wall in the Ri's study in over a century. It was an ordinary weapon now; that was how the story went. The Spirits hadn't wished another mortal to possess such power after Rhonwen's death. It had been kept as a symbol to our people, a piece of our history, and the very fabric of our clan, but it was nothing more than that. Wasn't it?

My thoughts flitted back to the day in the study weeks ago when I had heard the strange, unusual voice speaking of being forgotten. A slight shiver passed down my spine as those memories and the memories of the vision I'd just seen merged in my thoughts. The bow had come to the clan before when it was in great peril. Could something have awoken in it after five hundred years of silence? I pushed my speculations aside as Mair and I reached the garden gate. I would get to the bottom of this mystery, but in this fleeting moment, my focus was on Bran.

"I'll wait here," Mair said after we stepped through the gate. "Take your time."

"Thank you."

She offered me a smile, which I returned before walking off down the rows of blooming plants, searching for any sign of Bran. The sweet scents of flowers and pungent scents of herbs wafted through the air and soon, I spied Bran standing at the end of one of the narrow paths. He turned when he heard me, our gazes locking.

He was dressed to travel in a dark blue shirt and a pair of dark brown pants. A leather vest fit snugly over his shirt and his dark blue cloak, which bore the embroidered wolf's head seal of Blaidd, was customarily worn by the members of the war band. He looked the part, a fierce warrior striking out to defend our people. My chest hitched as I looked at him, trying to memorize every detail of his handsome features, soaking him in. Spirits only knew how long it would be before I saw him again.

We closed the distance between us and upon reaching me, he took me into his arms, holding me close. I rested my head on his chest, wrapping my arms around his waist, my throat thick. I knew he had to go—this was the moment we had been waiting for—and yet the very real possibility that he might not come back to me in the end left an ache in my chest. Squeezing my eyes shut, I listened to the steady thrum of his heartbeat, soaking in the sensation of his warm body pressed against mine.

"I'll be back, Ren," he murmured, kissing me on the top of the head before easing back, though he still kept his arms around me. "And when I'm back, he'll be dead."

I rested a hand on his chest, looking up at him. "Be careful. Promise me that."

"I will be," he replied, taking my hand in his own while his other remained loosely around my waist. "And you be careful as well. The castle isn't as safe as it once was."

"I will." I swallowed hard, averting my gaze as tears pricked my eyes.

"I *will* do my part to put an end to this and I will come home to you," he said, a fierceness in his tone that commanded me to meet his gaze. I knew, without any doubt, that so long as there was breath in his body, he would do as he said.

I blinked rapidly, a few tears coursing down my cheeks in spite of my attempts to hold them at bay, and pressed my lips against his. Our kiss was long and slow, as if it was its own sort of heart-wrenching goodbye. I knew he had to go, had known that at some point we would be saying a goodbye, and still my heart felt as if it were breaking. Last night had shown me a glimpse of the power he would encounter trying to put an end to Lorcan and I couldn't help but fear for him.

"I love you," I said when we broke apart. "I will always love you. No one else."

"Just as I will always love you."

He pulled me into one more close embrace, stroking my hair as I pressed my face into the hollow of his neck. For a moment we stood there, not needing words to express what we both so clearly felt, before he let out a heavy sigh.

"I cannot linger long," he said, stepping back from me. "Drystan is expecting me."

I nodded, letting out a shuddering breath and pulling my shoulders back. "Come back to me."

"I will."

He gave me one last brief kiss before turning away. A painful lump lodged in my throat as I watched him walk off, his dark blue cloak billowing behind him with the light breeze that had picked up on the air. *You will see him again,* I told myself as he disappeared from view. He had his role to play and I had mine. I would not waste this time apart. I had my own plans, ones that involved discerning why in the blazes the Spirits had shown me Rhonwen's bow.

CHAPTER 21

MAKE HIM YOURS
Alannah

FIANNA HEALED ITS SHADOW creature, but it did not heal me. That was my punishment for failing it. I had been forced to make the long journey back to Ioliare with an ugly gash on my side that ran from my rib cage down to my hip. Cadfael's wretch had had regrettably good aim with her blade and I had been forced to suffer the consequences. The journey back north had pushed me to my breaking point and by the time I finally reached the camp, I'd barely had the energy left to shift back into my human form.

I was left crumpled on the ground after I did so, my body in agony as cold chills coursed through me. I feared my wound was infected. I'd hardly been able to treat it or keep it clean in my present state. The shadow creature that had traveled with me ran off the second I was human once more, leaving me alone in the tall grass as it loped into the camp. Somehow, I forced myself to my hands and knees, managing to crawl through the darkness of night to the edge of the camp, one arm wrapped around my side and my teeth clenched. The mercenaries standing guard began shouting when they saw me, but I was only barely aware of them because of my excruciating pain.

"Alannah!"

I started at Dara's fractious shout, throwing myself off balance. The worry in his voice left me confused. Our relationship was supposed to have been one of convenience, nothing more. A wave of dizziness crashed over me when he reached me, causing my eyes to flutter.

He lifted me up onto my feet, supporting me as I swayed. The furrow in his brow was deep as he inspected my injured side, further confirmation that the wound was as bad as I feared. My shirt was ripped where the sword had sliced through it, the wound itself covered in dried blood and dirt.

"Come," Dara said, slipping an arm around my shoulders. "Aengus is waiting."

"Aengus?" I shook my head in confusion as I shuffled along beside him, barely able to keep myself upright. What was Aengus doing here? Lorcan never called him without reason. Had some other ill befallen our band while I'd been absent?

"Lorcan's... abilities informed him that you would be in need of Aengus' gift when you returned." Dara's gaze was straight ahead, but the light of the fires still burning in the camp's center, despite the late hour, illuminated the tightness in his jaw.

He'd always been leery of Fianna and its creatures, though he was too prideful of a man to admit it. He cared little for the uncanny; Dara's devotion was to coin and his own desires, nothing more. But it appeared that while Fianna had made me suffer, it would spare my life.

By the time we reached our hut, I was worried I was going to faint. Black spots danced at the edges of my vision and the pain in my side was unbearable. Dara helped me through the front door and I barely managed to stumble to my bed with his assistance.

"I'll be right back," he said, "with Aengus."

I managed a weak nod and he strode out of the room as if Fianna itself were on his heels. I stared blankly up at the poorly thatched roof, my skin slick with sweat. I didn't know how much time passed, but eventually I heard the steady footfalls of people entering my tiny room.

"How long has she been like this?" Aengus asked.

His voice was calm and measured and I found that just hearing it soothed me. I turned my head toward the door just in time to see him kneel at my bedside.

"The blazes if I know," Lorcan snapped, he and Dara having remained in the doorway.

"Almost three days," I said before another wave of pain left me squeezing my eyes shut and grinding my teeth.

Aengus frowned, setting a bag of healing supplies down on the floor beside him before taking my wrist. His touch was gentle but firm as he took my pulse, yet when he began to probe my wound, I couldn't hold back my whimpers.

"How bad is it?" Lorcan asked, his tone sharp as he impatiently tapped his foot.

"Even with my gift, she will need a few days to recover," Aengus replied. "Infection has set in."

"I need it handled swiftly," Lorcan said. "I have work for her to do." He paused, his voice dropping low, but not so low that I could not hear him. "If she's going to keep being so useless and failing at her tasks, she could have simply gotten herself killed and done us all a favor."

Aengus had taken hold of my wrist again and his grip tightened. I cracked my eyes open to see that he had pinned Lorcan with a disparaging look, his brows drawn in and his mouth turned down. I wouldn't deny that hearing Lorcan's words hurt, but I had long known of his cruel streak and I *had* failed. Not just him, but Fianna as well.

"I will work best if I'm undisturbed," Aengus said, an edge to his voice.

"Then I suppose we'll leave you." Lorcan sent me one last glower before turning and stalking off with a sharp word to Dara to join him. Dara hesitated, glancing back over at me, but only for a moment before following behind Lorcan.

Aengus watched the two of them go. As soon as they disappeared, he let out a deep breath, flexing his free hand.

"I am sorry you were spoken to in such a manner," he said, looking back at me.

The unexpected show of kindness left me momentarily speechless and an odd warmth flooded me. I wanted him so badly in moments like this.

He will be yours.

Fianna's voice made me start, the sudden movement causing a sharp pain in my side that left me releasing a cry of agony.

"Easy," Aengus murmured, soothingly rubbing my shoulder. "I know it's hard, but I need you to lie still so I can tend to this."

I closed my eyes and released a shuddering breath, doing my best to do as he instructed. He began to clean my wound as Fianna's darkness drifted into the air, murky and enticing. If Aengus noticed the Stag Spirit's presence, he didn't show it, continuing to work in silence. Though he was gentle, I had to fight to not shrink away from him as his hands traveled down my side. The pain was intense, but soon it was replaced by a strong warmth that began to radiate from his body to mine.

I failed you, I told Fianna, the Spirit's darkness still lingering.

You are mortal, Fianna replied. *I can expect nothing less. But you have shown the strength to bear the consequences. Continue to aid me, help draw him to my side, and he and the place of Banrion will be yours.*

As the Spirit's presence dissipated, I felt Aengus remove his hands from my body. My pain had considerably lessened and my head was much clearer. I opened my eyes to see him running a hand through his hair, his shoulders slightly drooped. It was clear that using his gift had drained him, but it did nothing to change the strong pull I felt toward him. I wanted him, and I would have him. Fianna had promised.

"That's all I can do for now, I'm afraid," he said. "The infection is at least gone. You will need to rest. I'm going to leave the wound open to the air for the time being, but I'll come check on you again in a few hours."

I nodded and he rummaged through his bag, pulling out a salve that he applied to my side. Once he was finished, he buckled the bag closed and slung it over his shoulder before getting to his feet. He went to leave, but I grabbed a hold of his wrist, pulling him to a stop. He looked down at me with a slight wrinkle in his brow.

"Thank you," I told him, holding his gaze.

A faint smile crossed his face, one that left my heart fluttering. "You are most welcome."

An ache settled in my chest as departed the room. *He'll be back,* I reminded myself as the canvas flap swung shut behind him. I closed my eyes and settled more comfortably into my bed, my thoughts returning to the smile he'd given me and the feelings it had stirred within me. He would be mine. Fianna would make it so, and the two of us would rule Blaidd side by side, ushering in the Stag Spirit's new era. There was much I could bear for the promise of that future.

Aengus stayed at the camp for two days, tending to my injury, before returning to Beag. Those stolen hours with him alone in my room were something I ached for in his absence, though I did my best to hide my longing from Dara and Lorcan. Both had been considerably temperamental of late and I didn't wish to get on the wrong side of either them. Lorcan wanted me focused on the tasks he gave me and Dara had become strangely possessive of me. Fianna insisted I had its protection, but I still saw no need to tempt fate.

A few days after Aengus left, misfortune fell on our small band. Four of Dara's fighters made the mistake of eating tainted meat from a store of supplies that had been stolen, leaving them violently ill. We could not afford to be down four fighters, especially with news that Drystan traveled north from Castle Clogwyn with another band of fresh warriors ready to fight. And so I found myself gliding through the air above the village of Beag, on my way to fetch Aengus for Lorcan. It was a task I'd been happy to perform.

As I soared over the village, my keen vision allowed me to easily find Aengus' home on the village outskirts. I was careful to land in the shadows near the small barn belonging to his neighbor, making sure I wasn't in full view of anyone when I transformed back into my human body. It was early enough in the morning that the village was largely quiet, but one could not be too careful with the gift of shapeshifting in the Clan of Blaidd.

I waited a few moments before stepping out of the shadows, making certain no one else was nearby, but outside of a couple of crows and a few sheep milling about in a pen, this part of the village was vacant. I walked around to Aengus' back door. As I knocked, I tried to ignore the slight flutter in my chest.

During my convalescence, I'd seen hints that perhaps Aengus too was feeling the attraction between us: his gentle touches, lingering gazes, and the large amounts of time he spent with me, time that went far beyond a healer merely tending to his patient. I still wondered how exactly it was that Fianna intended to turn Aengus to its side, as he had always been a man to avoid violence, but it had not shared such details with me yet. Still, I knew better than to doubt it.

After waiting a few moments with no answer, I knocked a second and third time. Eventually, the door was flung open, revealing Aengus. He still looked half asleep, his blond hair mussed and his clothing rumpled. He blinked rapidly before dropping his chin and massaging his forehead.

"Alannah," he said with a heavy sigh.

"Is that the way to greet a girl who just flew miles to see you?" I gave him a smile, keeping my tone light.

"Forgive me," he said, his voice softening as he stepped back from the door, motioning me inside. "It was a long night. Come in, please."

The doorway was narrow and my body brushed against his as I passed him. My heartbeat sped up in response and I noticed a faint flush come to his cheeks. Just that brief moment was enough to flame my desire. I wanted him more than I'd ever wanted any man, even Bran.

"Lorcan has fighters who are ill," I told him as we walked into the great room and I took a seat in front of the hearth. "Dara believes they ate tainted meat."

Aengus walked over and leaned against the stone mantle above the hearth, his lips pressed into a thin line. I studied his features, the tension in his shoulders and the heavy circles under his eyes. Something had him troubled. A loud thump from farther back in the house made him tense and me jump. My gaze flew to the narrow hallway that led to the bedrooms.

"You have company?" I asked, arching a brow.

"My father," he replied with a slight grimace. "He arrived from Cnoc last night."

I tilted my head, my curiosity piqued. That was certainly an interesting development. I was aware that Aengus had aged parents living in the village near Castle Clogwyn, but what would draw one of them here? Especially with the battleground the northern part of the clan had become in recent months.

"If you tell me the symptoms of those who are ill, I can send treatments," Aengus said.

"Lorcan wants more than that." I shook my head. "He cannot afford to lose more fighters and he needs them well as soon as possible. He wants your gift."

More noise came from the back of the house and Aengus anxiously looked over his shoulder. "I'm needed here. I can't just up and travel right now."

"If you make time, he'll make it worth your while."

"And if I don't?"

"You know what he'll do."

His jaw tightened and he stared down hard at the wood floor. I didn't exactly like threatening him like this, but I had no other choice. Lorcan got what he wanted or there was a price to pay. That was the way it had always been, and Aengus knew that as well as I did.

Aengus swallowed hard, looking back up, though he still didn't meet my gaze. I could see the indecision on his face and I highly suspected it had something to do with his father. His hedging since I'd arrived told me he didn't wish to speak of it, but I couldn't help him if he wouldn't tell me what had him so on edge.

I got up and walked over to him, placing a hand on his shoulder as I came to stand beside him. "What troubles you?"

"I..." He pinched the bridge of his nose and I could feel the muscles in his shoulder tense under my hand. How a healer stayed in such excellent shape was a mystery to me, but I certainly wasn't going to complain.

"Tell me," I murmured, soothingly rubbing his shoulder. "Maybe I can help."

"My mother has passed." His voice cracked and he let out a long, shaky breath before continuing. "And in the wake of her passing, I... learned things from my father that I was not previously aware of. He has burdens he bears, difficult ones. He needs me right now."

The pain in his voice affected me more than I expected. I knew the loss of one's parents. I'd lost both of mine to an illness, after all, at far too young an age. I had loved them and I knew they had loved me. Sometimes, I wondered what path my life would have taken if they had lived and I'd never been sent to live with my wretched sister.

"I am sorry for your loss," I said, giving his shoulder a gentle squeeze. "If you ever wish to speak with someone, I'm afraid I am all too familiar with the loss of a parent."

He finally looked at me, holding my gaze as he reached up and covered my hand with one of his own. A fiery warmth coursed through me at his touch, bringing another wave of wanting.

"Thank you," he said.

"If I could allow you time to sit with your grief..." I trailed off, licking my lips. "But Lorcan is neither a patient or understanding man."

"No." Aengus gave a bitter laugh, the dark cloud that had come over his features leaving me wondering if he was remembering the last time he had defied Lorcan. "No, he is not. I will let my father know I've been called away for a brief time and get my things. He should be able to manage well enough on his own for a few days."

"I could check on him. If you wished. It is an easy enough thing for me, flying to Beag."

He searched my face before giving a slow nod. "I would be appreciative of such a thing."

"Then I shall do it."

I flashed him a smile that he returned. When he straightened, I reluctantly let my hand fall away from him. If I wanted him to choose me as his Banrion, I needed him to want me, to need me. Luckily for me, that was a game I knew how to play.

Which is why you will do what Lorcan cannot.

Fianna's voice drifted into my thoughts as Aengus disappeared into the back of the house. Its voice was faint, almost as if I was hearing it in a fog, but the cold chill that briefly filled the room left no mistaking its presence. An eagerness settled within me while I waited for Aengus to return. I could see it, the pieces of Fianna's plan falling into place, and I would choose wisely. Lorcan had had my loyalty once, but Aengus would have it now. It would be a grand future we would create, a Blaidd that defied anything the Wolf Spirit and its ilk had ever wrought.

A new era was coming, and I would be ready for it.

Chapter 22

A Shifter's Task

Bran

THE JOURNEY NORTH HAD been long, exhausting, and far from pleasant. Rain and storms had plagued us almost the entire three days' ride to the village of Dearg, making travel miserable. We'd finally made camp along the banks of the Weindio River, a few miles outside the village. To the west, the Coed mountains loomed and to the east were the mountains of Ioliare. Despite Drystan's refusal to listen to me, I knew Ioliare was where Lorcan was hiding. The mountains were untamed, often treacherous, and strong with the Spirits—including Dark ones.

Since we'd made camp outside Dearg almost a week ago, I'd been sent on a number of scouting missions, but none had allowed me to step foot into Ioliare. There had been fires in the Coed in recent weeks, as well as one near Dearg, that made Drystan suspect that Lorcan was nearby. I was itching to venture into Ioliare to hunt Lorcan down, but thus far, Drystan had refused. Instead, I'd been sent into the Coed with warriors to assist and watch me, each of them there to make certain I did exactly what I was told. The warriors resented being made to watch my every move as much as I did, but Drystan was insistent.

My irritation at his ridiculous rules and restrictions grated on me. To help ease my frustration, I was currently taking my pent-up resentment out on the dagger I was sharpening. The activity perhaps wasn't the wisest choice in my current state, as I'd already almost cut my hand twice, but I needed some way to deal with my building tension. Outside my tent, I could hear the constant noise of the camp, even as dusk began to fall. A place like this was never truly quiet and at times over the last few days, it had brought back memories of being a part of Lorcan's band. I wasn't proud of all I had done during that time in my life and I knew Lorcan needed to be destroyed, but it was difficult at times to forget how he had saved my life. How I had, at times, felt like I had perhaps found the family I had lost when I had been first brought into his circle. But, in the end, all of that had been tainted by Fianna's darkness.

I was so deep in my thoughts that when the tent flap opened, I started and almost sliced my finger on my dagger. Cursing under my breath, I looked up. Emer was peering in at me. She was dressed in the customary dark blue and brown clothing of the warriors of Blaidd, with her dark hair pulled back into a tight braid. I had been particularly glad that she and Lewella had both made the journey north with Drystan, as it often felt like they were the only two warriors in the camp who didn't act as if I were moments away from attacking them.

"Drystan wants to see you," she told me.

I nodded, putting my whetstone and dagger away before getting to my feet. Spirits only knew what the warrior chief was going to demand of me now, but he wasn't a man to be kept waiting. I joined Emer outside my tent and the two of us made our way through the tents supporting the forty-some-odd warriors Drystan had traveling with him.

The Weindio flowed down from the mountains to our left, barely visible by the light of the torches and fires that had been lit as night had fallen. The smell of wood smoke and roasting meat was in the air, many of the warriors gathered around small fires outside their tents, sharing a meal. They all cast us dark looks as we passed them.

"Did Drystan give any hints as to what he wants?" I asked Emer, keeping my voice low in an attempt not to draw any more undue attention.

"No," Emer replied with a shake of her head.

I sighed. Hopefully whatever Drystan wanted would be quick. I'd already spent a better part of the day scouting to the east, though I'd been hemmed in by the warriors who'd been forced to come with me. Still, the terrain had been rough and I was ready for a decent night's sleep. For all I knew, Drystan had another plan to send me out. *Though if he does it under cover of night, it might be easier to slip away on my own,* I thought.

Emer and I walked the rest of the way to Drystan's tent in silence and I tried to ignore the uneasy feeling in the pit of my stomach. I couldn't say any of my interactions with the warrior chief had ever been particularly pleasant. When we reached Drystan's large tent, the warriors standing guard stated that only I was to enter and Emer hung back as I ducked through the canvas flap.

Drystan stood over a small table, using candlelight to study a large map that had been spread across it and was spilling over the edges. There was no one else in the tent save for the two of us. Apparently, whatever it was he wanted of me was not for the eyes and ears of others. I cleared my throat as I walked up to him, clasping my hands behind my back.

"Ah, good," Drystan said, turning to face me. "I have another task for you tonight, shifter."

The blatant refusal to use my name made me grind my teeth as I came to stand next to him, my shoulders bunching. I was so weary of his callous treatment. I was more than ready for the day Seren took her place as Ri, for I had no doubts that replacing Drystan would be one of the first things she would do.

"Word has come from Dearg that men suspected of being in league with Lorcan have been spotted here." Drystan pointed to a place on the map, a mile upriver. "These men have been consistently seen in this area over the last few days and just yesterday, the villagers spied something that looked like a crude shelter. I want you to go see what you can find, but I think it is vital that we don't spook these men if they're lurking nearby."

"So you'll be sending me on my own then?" I asked.

"Don't make me regret it," he answered, his eyes narrowing.

"I wouldn't dream of it."

"If these men are Lorcan's, we will plan to capture them and interrogate them. I want them alive."

I nodded, though I was unable to keep my mouth from turning down as I listened to him. Lorcan would never be so foolish as to set up even a temporary camp so close to Dearg. Still, I was being granted the opportunity to go out on my own. There would be no one there to watch my every move and report it back to Drystan, and no one to force me to walk into the trap I was fairly confident Lorcan was laying. Tonight could be my chance to get one step closer to ending all of this. I could slip away into Ioliare in my wolf form and hopefully have Drystan be none the wiser.

"I want the area scouted tonight and a full report in the morning," Drystan said. "And not a word said to anyone else in this war band. Are we clear?"

"Yes, Pennathe Drystan," I replied, giving him a respectful nod despite the sour taste in my mouth as I did so. He was hardly deserving of the respect he demanded, as far as I was concerned, but for now, I had a part to play.

He sent me off with a dismissive wave and I left the tent. The warriors outside cast me uneasy looks, but I ignored them and kept my head down as I walked back to my tent. Emer was already gone. I would make ready and leave this place as quickly as I could. Drystan and Cadfael were never going to put an end to this darkness at this rate, but I would. Tonight, I would bring the Clan of Blaidd one step closer to extinguishing Fianna's flames.

CHAPTER 23

WHAT A TRAITOR
DESERVES

Alannah

NIGHT HAD FALLEN AS I soared over the rushing dark water of the Weindio River, waiting for Drystan to take the bait that Lorcan had laid for him. Tonight, Lorcan would strike, but not where Drystan suspected. Our band would not come from the north, where we'd led Drystan to believe we were hiding. Instead, we would strike from the east.

My task tonight was simple enough: destroy whoever walked into the little trap Dara had laid while he and the others attacked the camp. Lorcan had once again come with us to command the shadow creatures, an oddity that had become more and more common of late.

I dipped lower in the sky and soon, movement along one bank of the river caught my attention. I altered my course, flying up onto the branch of a nearby birch tree, its foliage obscuring me from the view of whatever shadowy being was creeping along the river.

As I folded my wings, my breath caught at the sight of a large grey wolf slinking along the rocks at the water's edge. There had been rumors that Drystan had brought Cadfael's precious shifter scout with him and as I stared at the wolf, I knew that rumor to be true. The wolf was Bran. I knew him far too well to be fooled otherwise.

My heartbeat quickened as Bran drew closer with cautious, slow steps. His ears flicked back and forth as he listened to the noises around him and I was careful to hold perfectly still so as to not alert him to my presence. Strangely enough, he wasn't headed in the direction of the crude shelter Dara's men had built. No, Bran was headed in the direction of Ioliare. I didn't know what his game was, but it couldn't be good.

Bran is here, I told Lorcan, tapping into the connection we shared with our blood bond. *He's alone and he is traveling in the direction of Ioliare.*

Destroy him, Lorcan replied. *He has betrayed us and we will deliver two significant blows to Cadfael this night. He will lose his warriors and his shifter.*

Bran continued to creep down the riverbank in my direction, easily scaling the slick, wet rocks. Suddenly he stopped, his body growing rigid as he lifted his nose and sniffed the wind. I didn't hesitate, swooping down from the tree with a loud shriek as I stretched out my talons. I raked my talons across his back, causing him to snarl. He snapped at me with his fangs in retaliation, barely missing my right wing. I flew out of his reach, my wings giving me the ability to dodge and avoid his powerful jaws.

I didn't stay away for long, however, circling around him at a rapid speed to throw him off before diving down near his side and striking at his neck with my beak. He yelped, pulling feathers from my side as he ripped me off him. We were both bloodied and breathing heavily, but the fight wasn't done; I could see his anger still burning strong in his glowing golden eyes. I had almost forgotten what a formidable foe he was and we continued to attack one another, a wild mass of feathers and fur.

The longer our battle raged, the more my fatigue grew, causing me to make a costly mistake. I flew too low, too focused on his teeth and forgetting to be equally wary of his giant paws and sharp claws. I was able to strike at his neck again, seeking his jugular, but he batted me away with his front paws. The force of his strike knocked me to the ground and before I could get back into the air again, he closed his jaws around one of my wings.

I shrieked as he began to shake me, his teeth sinking into my flesh and crunching my bones. He sought to pin me to the ground with his paws and for one horrifying moment, I thought I would feel him biting into my throat, but I was able to maneuver and swipe one of my feet across his face, my talons drawing blood.

He yipped, jerking his head back as blood dripped down into his eyes. It was enough to get his grip on me to loosen and I fought free of him, awkwardly flapping back up into the sky. Every time I moved my wing, fiery, excruciating pain erupted in my body, but I forced myself to ignore it. I had no hope of surviving if I could not fly.

I couldn't get as high in the sky as I would have liked, but the blood dripping into Bran's face blinded him enough to keep him from pursuing me. His sides heaved and blood ran from his open wounds. He stumbled after me, but only made it a few steps before collapsing to the ground. Out here, alone, with no one to aid him, he was as good as dead.

As I will be if I don't get out of here, I reminded myself, forcing my wounded wing to move. I had to get back to the others.

I needed a healer and I would be damned if I would die out here alone in the woods. I cast one last look at Bran's unmoving body. He was nothing more than a large grey lump bleeding out over the rocks, but that was the death he deserved. The death of a traitor. Pushing against the pain, I began to follow the river south. I would not meet the same end, no matter what it cost me.

CHAPTER 24

DEATH'S DOOR

Bran

I KNEW I NEEDED to shift, and soon. I could feel my strength waning as I half-dragged myself across the forest floor. Everything hurt and I knew I had lost too much blood. The gashes across my face made it difficult to see, but still, I stumbled on through the dark forest, knowing that I had to make it back to camp. I was far too close to death's door and I was in desperate need of a healer.

Each time I thought back to the fight with Alannah, a fresh rage would flush through me. It was that anger that kept me moving. I would get back to camp, get healed, and then I would find Lorcan and I would kill him. I repeated that mantra to myself over and over again as I crawled through the dark.

In my pain-induced haze, I misjudged the ground and went tumbling over a small grouping of rocks. The pain as I hit the ground left me gasping. I fought to stay conscious as I lay in the underbrush, feeling myself growing weaker by the moment. I couldn't wait any longer. If I didn't shift now, I would be stuck in my wolf form until I was fully healed.

Squeezing my eyes shut, I called on the last of my strength to shift back into my human form. Doing so almost made me lose consciousness, but I hung on, grinding my teeth against the pain. Once I was human again, I pushed myself onto my hands and knees. Everything hurt, but somehow, I got to my feet. I stumbled forward at a halting pace, not getting far before tripping again, this time over a large tree root.

I couldn't bring myself to rise, instead staring blankly up at the dark canopy of trees above. The realization that I might not even make it back to camp settled over me, leaving a deep ache in my chest. If I died here, I would fail to bring about Lorcan and Fianna's end. If I died here, I would fail Seren. I would lose her.

We hadn't had enough time, she and I, and at the same time, I wondered if a lifetime would have even been long enough. Her beauty, her heart, her desire to care for her people; all of it made me love her. I wanted the rest of whatever life I had to be at her side. I wanted to marry her.

The thought rang in my mind, startling me with the clarity with which it came to me, despite my pain-induced haze. Cadfael had passed decrees at the start of his Purge that didn't allow shifters to wed, I knew that, but I wouldn't let that stop us if marriage to me was what Seren wanted. I knew she wouldn't let it stop her as well. *First, however,* I reminded myself, *you have to make it out of here alive.* There would be no future for us at all if I perished here in the wilderness. No future for any of us if Fianna won.

I fought to get back on my feet once more, gritting my teeth as I pulled myself up off the ground. If I lived through this, I would ask her to marry me. There was no one else in this life for me but her and I would do everything that I could to support her and make certain she knew the depth of my love for her.

As I stumbled on, I tried to pay close attention to my surroundings, but soon I began to feel disoriented. It was harder to focus and the swelling on my face, combined with the dried blood, made seeing almost impossible. A large fallen limb tripped me and I fell forward, collapsing a third time.

The hoot of an owl echoed through the forest from somewhere nearby, the only noise save for my shallow, rasping breathing. Was this how I would die? Alone in the woods? I made another attempt to rally myself, only to slump back down onto the ground. At some point, the trees above me began to spin and I let my eyes flutter shut.

How long I lay there, drifting in and out of consciousness, I didn't know, but at some point, distant shouts broke through my foggy haze. I thought I heard my name. Groaning, I managed to roll over onto my side, though I couldn't get my feet under me. Someone, or something, was crashing through the brush and a few moments later, I could feel someone shaking my shoulder. I cracked my eyes open to see Emer crouched down in front of me. In the moonlight, I could tell that bits of soot and ash covered her clothes and face and she smelled strongly of smoke.

"Bran," she said, shaking my shoulder again. "What happened? How badly are you hurt?"

"Bad enough," I mumbled. "Alannah. Lorcan's shifter. Waiting for me."

I wanted to ask her what had happened to her, and yet somehow, I already knew. Lorcan and Fianna had been at work while I had been lured away to tangle with Alannah.

Emer looked over her shoulder and I followed her gaze to the shadowy forms of other warriors standing behind her.

"We need to get him back to camp," she said to the others. "He needs a healer. We'll have to carry him. Tegan, Culwch, you get his feet."

I couldn't hold back a yelp of pain when I was lifted off the ground. My head lolled to the side as those carrying me began to walk. I let my eyes shut again and I drifted off into the blackness that beckoned me, my last thoughts of Seren and the world we so desperately wanted to create.

CHAPTER 25

DESIRES OF THE FUTURE

Alannah

My arm was likely broken in two places. Dara had at least discerned that, though it was beyond his skill to heal. Lorcan had sent him to find me after I had confessed to him the severity of my injuries through our blood bond. Dara had stumbled across me a few miles out from our temporary camp within the bounds of Ioliare. I'd fainted the moment I'd seen him, thankfully already in my human form, and woken on the back of his horse.

We were riding with haste to Beag at Lorcan's command. We were close enough to the village, and my injuries required Aengus' skills. I'd barely maintained consciousness as Dara's grey gelding galloped through the forest and only his strong arm around my waist was keeping me in the saddle. It was still dark, though I suspected dawn could not be far off. I could smell the smoke on Dara, a reminder of the ambush he and Lorcan had orchestrated on Drystan's camp. According to Dara, our little band had come out the victors once again, thanks to Fianna's creatures.

By the time Beag came into view, it took everything in me to hold back my tears. The jostling of the horse had made me want to scream with agony. Dara guided our mount to Aengus' cottage, the hint of light on the horizon warning that dawn was not far off. He dismounted and then pulled me off the horse as well, carrying me in his arms as he made for the back door.

"Just hold on a little longer," he told me quietly as he climbed the back steps.

He banged on the back door and we only had to wait a moment before Aengus answered. He was still in his sleeping clothes, but his eyes widened as he looked down at me, his face paling.

"Bring her in," he told Dara, stepping back and motioning the other man inside.

Aengus had Dara bring me to the back room, instructing him to lay me on the bed while he ran to change and gather his healing supplies. I hissed, gritting my teeth as Dara eased me onto the narrow mattress.

"I can't believe Bran did this," Dara said, stroking a few strands of my bloodstained hair back from my face before letting out a low growl. "After everything Lorcan did for him and everything Cadfael did to your kind." He had been fuming from the moment I had told him who had wounded me so gravely.

"Cadfael's daughter has bewitched him," I said, clutching the blankets as another wave of pain hit me, "but if the Spirits will it, he will have died the death he deserves."

"If he has not already met such an end, I will make certain he meets it myself."

Dara's tone was cold with a tinge of something that made his words sound like more of a vow than a threat. Bran had made a fatal mistake in turning against us, one he would pay for. It was disgusting how easily he could give his loyalty to the man who had tried to see him killed instead of the one who had saved him.

The door to the room opened and I turned my head to see Aengus step inside room. He instructed Dara to light a few more candles as he came over to my bedside. As Aengus knelt down beside me, our gazes locked, and as I took in the concern in his eyes, some of my own fears eased. Aengus would not let me slip from this Realm to the next. He would save me.

Dara cleared his throat and my gaze flitted to him. He looked between Aengus and me with a frown.

"I need to take a look at this and see how bad things are," Aengus said, his tone soothing as he gently took hold of my arm. "I'm afraid it will hurt."

I clenched my jaw, managing a slight nod. He probed my arm and I couldn't hold back my whimpers of pain as he did so. The tears that pricked my eyes left me feeling ashamed of my weakness and I blinked them back, willing them not to fall.

"Can you fix her?" Dara asked, coming to stand at the foot of the bed. "Lorcan will pay handsomely. She's far too valuable for him to lose."

"I can, but it will not be quick," Aengus replied. "Three days, perhaps four. It will be best if she stays here so that I can tend to her."

"I suppose do what you must," Dara said, pressing his lips together. "I will stay here with her. For now, at least."

I raised my brows, doubting that Lorcan would be willing to spare him for a full four days. "I will be fine here on my own in Aengus' care. Lorcan will have need of you."

"We'll worry about such things later," Dara said, waving his hand before looking back over at Aengus. "Just heal her."

"I will work best without interruptions." Aengus inclined his head toward the door, giving Dara a pointed look.

Dara scowled and for a moment, I thought he would argue, but he stiffly turned and strode out of the room.

You will use this time with him to your advantage, Fianna said, its voice drifting into my thoughts as Aengus began to pull out an assortment of items from a leather bag. *You will draw him to you and by drawing him to you, you will draw him to our cause.*

The Stag Spirit's faint presence vanished almost as quickly as it appeared, but a warmth filled me as I watched Aengus out of the corner of my eye. While I would certainly rather not be in the current state I was in, I would have no qualms about spending more time with Aengus.

He once again placed his hands on my arm. "This will hurt at first. The mending of bones is not a simple thing, especially when they are broken in more than one place."

I took a deep breath, nodding and bracing myself for what was to come. At first, I felt nothing more than the usual heat that came with his gift, but then that erupted into a fiery pain that left tears streaming down my face. Aengus spoke quietly to me as he worked, promising me that it would be over soon as he used his gift to knit my bones back together. When he finally took his hands away, the pain had begun to dissipate, and I let a sigh of relief.

"That's enough of that for now," Aengus said, bracing himself with his hands on the edge of the bed, his weariness evident in his voice and his drooping shoulders.

I swallowed hard, taking in a few deep breaths. He then pulled out a basin of water and strips of cloth, cleaning my cuts and gashes before covering them with a salve. I let my eyes flutter shut as he bandaged my wounds and to my surprise, a few moments later, I felt him brush the hair back from my brow. His hand lingered along the side of my face and a pang of longing coursed through me. I opened my eyes to look up at him, holding his gaze.

"Get some rest," he murmured. "I'll be back to check on you later."

As his hand fell away, I felt the absence of his touch like a physical jolt. *But I will have days with him,* I reminded myself. Dara's presence had the potential to complicate matters, but I intended to use every moment of our time together to my advantage. I would make him want me. I would make him see what he could do with the blood that ran through his veins. We would dream of the future Fianna could help us create together.

I watched him as he gathered up his things, my thoughts racing with what that future could hold, but soon exhaustion overtook me. The last thing I felt as I drifted off to sleep was Aengus' hand stroking my hair. He would be mine soon and one day, Blaidd would be ours.

CHAPTER 26

DEFIANCE

Seren

THE FOREST WAS PITCH black and heavy mist obscured the narrow path in front of me. In the distance, I heard the clanging of blades and the thud of arrows hitting flesh. I pushed through the mist, trying to find my way to the battle that I could hear raging, but a wall of flames erupted in front of me, forcing me to skid to a stop.

The air grew thicker, leaving me gagging. The leg that bore the scars from Fianna's creature burned as the fire swirled and sparked in front of me. A shape began to form in the flames, a giant stag made of smoke and ash with flaming antlers. I stumbled backward, trying to dart away, but another wall of flames stopped me.

"Do not think that you are going to alter fate this time, little mortal," Fianna said, its voice making me cringe as it grated on my ears. "I will have your life; I will have your father and his war band's lives; and I will have the life of your little shifter."

The noises from the battle grew louder and I could see the tops of the trees going up in flames. An angry cry broke from my lips as I desperately looked for a way out, but a circle of flames rose up from the scorched earth and surrounded me, pinning me in place.

Fianna gave a rasping laugh before merging back into the flames from which it had come. The circle of fire around me grew even taller, trapping me where I was. Through the haze of flames and smoke, I could see shadowy figures fighting as the forest continued to become an inferno.

My stomach clenched and my heart pounded in my ears. The flames around me were so high, I had no hope of escaping the prison Fianna had locked me in. The cry of a hawk made my whole body tense and I ducked just in time to avoid the creature's talons as it swooped down on top of me.

The hawk careened around, only to fly back at me again. A ferocious growl came from behind me and I barely had time to look over my shoulder as a large grey wolf leapt through the flames. It snapped at the hawk, the two creatures engaging in a fierce battle.

I had no time to try and intervene on the wolf's behalf, however, as another being stepped through the circle of flames, this one far more sinister and deadly. The shadow creature stalked toward me, letting out eldritch shrieks and hisses that raised the hair on the back of my neck. My leg burned as if it were on fire as the creature bared its fangs. I remembered the pain of sharp teeth sinking into my flesh.

The wolf and hawk were still locked in their deadly battle, a blur of flapping feathers and snapping teeth. The shadow creature drew in close to me, its shoulders bunched. My heart was in my throat, the creature moments away from launching itself at me, but suddenly the ground rumbled and shook, throwing me off balance.

I tried to scramble back up onto my feet. As I did so, my hands brushed against smooth wood. A longbow, one etched with running wolves and raging rivers, lay on the ground at my feet. I didn't think. I grabbed the weapon and the quiver laying underneath it. Leaping up, I pulled an arrow from the quiver and nocked it. I centered my breathing, adjusted my stance, and loosed.

To my utter shock, the arrow dug deep into the creature's shoulder. It let out a shriek, shaking its head as black blood oozed from its wound, and then launched itself at me. My second arrow imbedded itself in the creature's neck and it stumbled to its knees. I loosed again, putting my third arrow right between its eyes. It slumped to the ground, unmoving, as it slowly disintegrated into a pile of ash.

Whirling around, I confronted the wolf and hawk still engaged in their deadly battle. Both of them were wounded, blood covering their bodies, but neither was willing to admit defeat. I nocked another arrow, focusing directly on the hawk's heart, but the creature dodged it. My arrow clipped its wing and it screeched in rage before flapping back high into the sky.

I raced to the wolf's side as it collapsed. I fell to my knees beside it, knowing without a doubt as I placed a hand on its bloodied back that it was Bran. His sides heaved and his eyes were only partially open. Tears streamed down my face as his blood stained my skin—

The first noise I heard as I was thrust back into the Mortal Realm was the loud crash of a goblet hitting the stone floor of the Great Hall. Ale spilled everywhere, splattering the skirt of my dress and my leather boots, but I barely registered it. My breathing was fast and uneven as I struggled with the usual disorientation. A fiery pain seared through my right leg, leaving my stomach churning, as if I were feeling the bite from Fianna's creature all over again.

"Seren?" Sioned placed a hand on my arm, making me start. "What did you see?"

I swallowed hard. "Darkness."

Cian, who was seated on the other side of me, had already begun to clean up the mess I'd made with my drink. I went to bend down to help him, but he waved me off.

"It's alright," he said. "I've got it. Just give yourself a minute."

I nodded, straightening and letting out a shaky breath as the memories of the haunting vision swirled around in my thoughts. I rubbed my right thigh with an unsteady hand. The pain was at least dissipating, now down to a dull ache. Few people survived a wound from a shadow creature and Cian had told me that they often never truly fully healed.

"Here," Sioned said, passing me a cloth napkin and angling her head toward my ale-covered dress.

I took it and did the best I could to soak up as much of the ale as possible. Hopefully the dress itself wasn't ruined. A servant had come over and helped Cian clean up what remained of my mess and I was given a fresh goblet of ale. Most everyone in the hall had at least gone back to eating their dinner. It wasn't the first time I'd had a vision in the middle of a meal. Across the table, Domhnall was watching me intently, his brow slightly wrinkled, and Laoise kept stealing glances my way as she spoke with Arwel.

"You're sure you're alright?" Cian asked.

"I'm sure," I replied, turning my attention back to my half-eaten plate of food.

I ate a bit more, but my stomach was too unsettled for me to make much of a dent in my meal. Father was in deep discussion with Ithel, the two of them apparently having tired of scowling at me after my initial disruption, and instead had returned to whatever they'd been talking about all night long. I needed to speak with him, but I also needed to him to listen to what I said and what I had seen. Interrupting him in the middle of a talk with one of his advisors would be a surefire way to start the conversation off on the wrong foot.

Still, I knew I couldn't wait long. That vision had been a warning, I had felt that clear in my bones, but it had also held answers as well. Rhonwen's bow had killed the shadow creature, just as it had done in the legends. Could it do so again? Ithel finally turned his attention away from Father, turning to talk with Arwel, and I seized my chance.

"Father," I said, "I need to speak with you. After the meal."

"Whatever it is can wait until morning." He waved one hand and shoveled a large spoonful of lamb stew into his mouth.

"I am afraid that this cannot wait." I held his gaze, my jaw tight, despite the glower he fixed me with.

"Yes, it can." He shoved his spoon into his bowl so hard that flecks of broth splattered onto the wooden table.

"I have concerns for Drystan and the war band." If nothing else would get his attention, perhaps that would.

"Do you think I chose that man as my warrior chief because he is incapable?" Father scoffed. "Whatever your concerns are, they are unwarranted."

"And yet Seren sees things that others do not," Mother said, sitting a bit straighter in her seat as she cut Father a sharp look. "It would not kill you to listen to her."

He snarled at her, his grip on his goblet so tight that his knuckles grew white, but Mother didn't wither under his gaze. She looked every inch the Banrion of Blaidd as she stared him down and I felt a slight bit of pride well within me. It had been good to see her taking her place more and more. And truth be told, I admired her greatly in moments like this one.

"Seren's judgement is obviously not to be trusted," Father snapped. "She has proven that over and over again."

"You are a fine one to speak of judgement." Mother arched a brow before taking a sip of her ale, her calm tone a contrast to Father's irate one.

His face reddened as he spluttered at her, letting out oaths I'd never heard him utter at her before. Mother ignored him, though I noticed tension creep into her shoulders. My own anger rose at the insults he hurled and beside me, Sioned's expression had turned hard. With one last curse, Father dug back into his soup with force, making a mess as he did so. Cian awkwardly moved a few peas around on his plate and Sioned swished her drink in her goblet, her movements stiff with agitation. An uncomfortable tension had come across the table. I picked at my stew, keeping an eye on Father. He was in a mood, that was clear, but the clan didn't have time to wait for him to get over his petulance. He needed to know what I had seen, and he needed to act.

I waited until he got up from the table before bidding the rest of the table goodnight and following behind him. No one stopped me. Warriors opened the double doors for him and he stormed out of them while I followed close behind on his heels. I caught up with him in the entryway, calling for him to stop, only to have him ignore me.

"Father!" I shouted again. "I need to speak with you. This matter cannot wait."

"I do not have time for this, Seren," he retorted, lengthening his stride.

I muttered an oath of my own in Old Pernish, jogging to catch up with him.

"You might not have time for this, but I assure you that Fianna does," I said as I reached him, fighting to match his swift pace. "What I saw tonight showed danger, but it also showed a way to perhaps stop this darkness. Drystan needs to be aware of—"

"Damn it, Seren, that is enough!" Father turned to me so abruptly that he almost knocked me over. His hands curled into fists and he narrowed his eyes. "Do you think I've forgotten the last time you demanded a need to act on a whim and warn Drystan of some perceived danger?"

"There *was* danger. Had I not done so, you might not even be aware of Lorcan. I know that I am not infallible, but this is not the first time the Spirits have shown me something that could put an end to all of this. A way to get the upper hand on Fianna and Lorcan both."

"And what is this mysterious solution that the Spirits have deemed to show you?" Father crossed his arms.

I took a deep breath, letting it out slowly and making myself hold his gaze. "I believe that Rhonwen's bow could be used against Fianna and its creatures. I saw it destroy one of them tonight in my vision. The creatures are how Fianna sets its fire. Take them away and you will have crippled it."

Father let out a mocking laugh, shaking his head. "It is a bow, Seren. An ancient one. Nothing more."

I jerked my head back, stunned at his blatant disrespect. And not just of me, but of the Spirits as well. He should have known better. He was Blaidd's Ri. He had made his own vows when he had taken that title, to protect the Wolf Spirit's people and follow its guidance and wisdom.

"At one time, it was more than just a bow," I said, lifting my chin. "It defeated Fianna before, along with Cigfran and Pysgod. It could do so again."

"You come to me with nothing more than stories of years long gone. I do not have time to waste on such foolishness."

"It is not foolishness," I said, my nostrils flaring. "It is an outrage for you to even speak of it as such."

"It is an outrage for you to think this conflict will be solved by an ancient relic!" He shook his head with disgust before swiftly walking off once more.

"I saw death!" I hurried after him, not willing to let it go. "I saw your warriors perish. I saw Bran die. How many more lives must be lost?"

Father let out a bitter laugh, curling his lip. "I should have known this was about your regrettable choice of a lover."

"This is about more than just him," I said through gritted teeth. "It is about this very clan and all of those who call it home. If Fianna controls Blaidd, there will be nothing left. How can you stand here and pretend to not see what is right in front of you? Find a way to use the bow, send the full strength of your warriors north to crush Lorcan and Fianna once and for all. You are supposed to care for this clan! Why won't you?"

"My caring for this clan cost me my son!" Father came to an abrupt stop, jabbing a finger at my chest. "You know *nothing* of sacrificing for Blaidd. Do not make such accusations when I have made the greatest sacrifice anyone should ever be forced to make. Fianna is none of your concern. The sooner you accept that, the better."

He turned, striding up the staircase and leaving me standing at the foot of it. He had never been more wrong. Fianna *was* my concern. Because of the blood that ran through my veins, it had always been my concern, but it was even more so now, after the vow I had made to the Wolf Spirit.

There would clearly be no reasoning with him, but I would not ignore what I had been shown. I would not lose our clan or the man I loved because of Father's blind arrogance. If defying him once again was my only option, so be it.

Chapter 27

Schemes and Relics

Seren

I DIDN'T SLEEP THAT night. Nor did I spend the long dark hours of night in my bed. Instead, I had retreated to the anteroom in my chamber, seeking the guidance of the Spirits, but as dawn broke over the Dail, I had little to show for my efforts other than what I had already been warned of. A heavy weariness engulfed me after my long night and I could see sunlight peeking through the drawn curtains.

Again and again, I had seen what I had been shown at dinner the night before. Again and again, I had seen Rhonwen's bow. And yet nothing I'd seen was certain. Sometimes the warriors appeared and sometimes they did not. Sometimes I was able to loose an arrow at the shadow creature before it devoured me; other times I wasn't. Sometimes Bran died and sometimes he was spared. The only things that had not changed had been Fianna and the presence of Rhonwen's bow.

There was a quiver in my stomach as I slowly got up off the floor. The brazier was still going strongly, filling the room with the scent of pungent herbs. I walked over to the table and put it out. I could feel the slight shake in my hands as I worked, a silent reminder that I had pushed my body close to its limits.

I knew I had to act, but I had hoped for some sort of direction, some hint as to what exactly I was supposed to do. Shaking my head, I stepped out of the antechamber. *Just give me something,* I thought, not even truly expecting an answer after a night of uncertainty, but then I felt it. A cool, gentle breeze brushing the back of my neck. I froze with my hands still on the door, my breath catching.

North, the Wolf Spirit whispered. *The bow must go north.*

I blew out a shaky breath as its presence vanished. North it was then. As I stepped back into my common room, Awyr and Cryfder both lifted their heads, the two of them sprawled out on the stone floor, soaking in a ray of early morning sun. They got up at the sight of me, trotting over to greet me. I rubbed the tops of both of their heads, my stomach growling. It would be time for breakfast in the Great Hall soon, but I had reason to linger in my own chambers for a while longer.

I had sent word to Cian last night, asking him to meet me in my chambers this morning before the morning meal. If anyone would be willing to aid me discreetly, it would be him, especially with the absence of Emer, Lewella, and Bran. I dressed and readied for the day, the familiar routine offering some distraction for my anxious feelings. I had just walked back out into the common room when I heard a knock at the door. Cryfder and Awyr both tensed, their ears pricking toward the noise, and they stayed right at my heels as I walked over to answer.

Cian stood on the other side, but when I caught a glimpse of the figure standing behind him, I sucked in a sharp breath. I certainly hadn't expected Domhnall. I shot Cian a questioning look, my grip on the door tightening. I had specifically asked him to come alone.

"Domhnall wished to speak with you as well," Cian said, clearing his throat before lowering his voice. "And after speaking with him, I believe he could be of help."

I hesitated, worrying my lower lip, but after a moment, I stepped back to allow them in. I had trusted Domhnall before, and he had proven that my trust was not misguided multiple times over the last few weeks. I could trust him now. The three of us sat in the chairs near my hearth, Awyr and Cryfder coming to lie at my feet.

"You said you have seen death?" Cian asked.

"I have seen many things," I answered as I rubbed my forehead, the slight remnant of a headache lingering after a long night of separating my soul from my body. "I fear that Drystan and those with him might be in considerable danger."

"Your father knows this?" Domhnall said.

"Yes, and he has made it clear he would rather continue to play ignorant and do nothing," I replied, unable to keep the bitterness from my voice.

"A council could be called if you see this as a big enough threat," he offered.

"There isn't time for that. And... there is more."

Domhnall raised his brows while Cian studied me thoughtfully. I took in another deep breath before continuing. I trusted Cian's connection with the Spirits enough that I didn't think he would scoff at me outright, but Domhnall was another matter entirely.

"I believe Rhonwen's bow has the power to play a role in defeating Fianna," I said. "Not only do I feel that Drystan needs to know of these growing threats, but I feel that the bow needs to be delivered to him as well."

"I know the stories, but..." Cian rubbed the back of his neck. "No one has even touched that bow in a hundred years. The power it once had is long gone."

"I know," I replied, "but I also know what I've seen."

"I don't mean to speak any disrespect toward the Spirits, but... it's just a bow." Domhnall shook his head. "There are many old relics from when the island was created, but their power has all faded."

My jaw tightened. So much for hoping they wouldn't doubt me. I knew how it sounded, but I also knew what I had seen. I knew what I had been told. Rhonwen's bow had a role to play in all of this, whether anyone else could see it or not.

"I'm taking the bow north, one way or another. Just as I am going to warn Drystan of what I have seen," I said, lifting my chin. "You can either help me or not."

"How are you planning on even getting a hold of it?" Cian asked. "I don't think Uncle is going to just let you just walk off with it."

"He won't," I answered. "Which is why I'll be taking it without him knowing."

"You're planning to steal it?" Domhnall jerked his head back.

"That bow belongs to the clan, not to my father." Even as I said the words, I felt a slight quiver in my belly. What I'd said was true, but I doubted Father was going to see it that way.

Cian massaged his temples, grimacing before dropping his chin. "You're deadly serious about this, aren't you?"

"Yes."

He heaved a heavy sigh before looking back up at me. "Then I guess I'm going to be helping you break into Uncle's study."

We both looked at Domhnall, who pursed his lips before letting out a long, low breath. "I suppose count me in as well. Fianna has to be stopped, through whatever means necessary, and..." He hesitated, holding my gaze as he continued. "I made

Bran a promise that I would look out for you and aid you while he was away from this place. And I don't make such promises lightly."

I blinked rapidly, my brow wrinkling at the unexpected mention of Bran. The two of them had always struggled with even being civil to one another, but perhaps they'd found a way to move beyond that and Domhnall had put aside some of his prejudice.

"We'll have to wait until nightfall to break into the study," I said. "After midnight. We can make everyone think we've gone to bed and then meet there. The castle will be asleep. We can get our hands on the bow and hopefully slip out before anyone realizes we, and it, are missing."

"Your father has resumed warriors standing guard outside his study since Fianna's return," Domhnall said. "Not to mention the warriors standing guard at the gates."

"Leave them to me," Cian said.

"You?" Domhnall's brows shot up and he looked over at Cian with disbelief.

"Just because I'm not a warrior doesn't mean I don't have my own ways of disabling someone," Cian replied.

Domhnall looked between the two of us. "Truly, sometimes your family frightens me with the lengths you're all willing to go to."

"I'm not going to kill anyone," Cian said with a wave of his hand. "And Seren is right, she's not taking something that belongs solely to Uncle Cadfael."

As we made our plans, I tried to ignore the unsettled feeling in the pit of my stomach. Father would be furious if we were discovered. I knew that we could trust Gruffudd to help us slip in and out of the stables without notice, and Cian expressed that with a little help from Mair, who he also felt was trustworthy enough to let in on our plans, he could come up with supplies for our journey.

Once our plotting was complete, the three of us left my chambers with the wolves in tow, heading to the Great Hall to partake in the morning meal. We would go about our days as normally as possible and hopefully Father and the rest of the castle would be none the wiser until we were well on our way from here.

Cian kept up small talk as we walked, but my thoughts were consumed with what lay ahead. I had clearly heard the Wolf Spirit tell me that the bow must go north, but what then? *You'll figure it out,* I told myself. I had to. Fianna would not rest until it controlled every inch of Blaidd and I could not let that happen. When we reached the hall, Cian stepped through the double doors first, but Domhnall placed a hand on my arm, gently tugging me to a stop. I turned toward him with a questioning look.

"There is one thing I want you to know," he said, his voice soft as he held my gaze. "No matter what happens, I would protect you with my life."

There was something in his voice, in his eyes, a longing that momentarily threw me. I knew at one point he had harbored deeper feelings for me than mere friendship, but since I had made my affections for Bran clear, I was almost ashamed to admit that I hadn't thought of such things. The look in his eyes, however, left me wondering if Domhnall had so easily put those feelings aside. Did he still care about me in that way? *He knows how I feel about Bran,* I reminded myself.

"I thank you for that," I said.

He took my hand in his, giving it a squeeze before offering me a respectful nod. "I'll see you tonight."

I remained where I was for a moment, watching him walk into the hall and make his way over to Laoise before squaring my shoulders and stepping into the hall, myself. I shoved aside any uncertain thoughts of where Domhnall and I stood. In this moment, my focus needed to be on my people. I would not fail them.

Despite knowing that I was doing what had to be done, my heart still pounded and my palms were sweaty as I rounded the corner of the hallway that led to the Ri's study. Stealing away from the castle in the dead of night was inviting its own trouble, I knew that from experience, but this time, I was going a step farther. I was stealing Rhonwen's bow. Whether or not it belonged to the clan and not Father wouldn't matter to him. My thievery would be yet another betrayal to add to the long list he kept tallied.

The people need this. Blaidd needs this, I reminded myself, shaking off my disturbing thoughts as I drew nearer to the study. The hallway itself was dark, only a few torches lit here and there since it was well past midnight and the rest of the castle was asleep in their beds. Thankfully, I knew the castle well enough to navigate with ease in the dark. The small pack that was slung across my back was light enough that it didn't make any extra noise, but I still moved cautiously. The last thing I needed was to be discovered.

As I approached the study door, I saw three shadowy figures. Two of them were slumped on the ground, leaning up against the wall. Cian hovered over them. I let out a quiet sigh of relief when I reached him. His plans for sedating the guards had gone off without issue. He was taking the pulse of one of the warriors and while the man's head was lolled to the side, his chest rose and fell with a steady, even rhythm.

"They're going to have a splitting headache in a few hours," Cian said quietly, dropping the man's wrist and straightening. "But other than that, they should be no worse for the wear."

"Have you seen—"

I didn't get to finish the question, cut off by a loudly whispered curse in Old Pernish. I whirled around to see that Domhnall had crept up on us, his eyes wide as he looked down at the unconscious warriors.

"By the Spirits," Domhnall said. "I hope you didn't kill them."

"They're fine," Cian replied. "The key?"

"Here." Domhnall pulled it from his pocket and Cian and I stepped back to give him access to the door.

Because of his position as advisor, Domhnall had been the one with the easiest access to the key to the study. He opened the door and ushered Cian and me inside ahead of him. The room itself was eerily empty, only the faint light of the moon shining in through the windows and allowing us to see.

The bow was mounted on the wall over the stone hearth. I made my way over to it, my pulse racing. We didn't have much time to do this and we couldn't afford any mistakes. Cian and Domhnall were right behind me and when we reached the bow, I turned to my cousin.

"You're the tallest," I said. "I'll get a chair."

"I've got it," Domhnall said, holding up a hand.

He strode over to the table at the room's center, picking up one of the wooden chairs and carrying it back over to place in front of the hearth. Cian climbed up onto it, but even with his height and the added boost from the chair, he still struggled to get leverage on the bow. It was no small weapon and as Cian tried to lift it up off the wall, it thumped loudly against the stone. I held my breath as the noise reverberated through the empty room and Domhnall let out another curse under his breath.

"I could lose my place on the council for this," he muttered with a huff.

I cast him a sharp look. "Your place on the council won't matter if this clan is under Fianna's control."

"Seren," Cian said, "grab me a few books. I just need a little more height."

I left Domhnall to help Cian off the chair while I hurried over to one of the shelves carved into the stone walls. Grabbing the largest of the leather-bound volumes that I could find, I raced back over to Cian and Domhnall. We stacked them up on the chair but I bit my lip when we finished. It wasn't going to be the sturdiest of perches for Cian to balance on.

"We'll try and steady you," I said, motioning for Domhnall to go to Cian's other side.

Between the two of us, we helped Cian as he climbed back onto the chair. The tension in my muscles mounted as Cian once again grappled with the bow, but soon, the weapon came free. Cian scrambled back down and passed me the bow. As I took it in my hands, my fingers running over the ancient carvings etched into the wood, an odd sensation jolted through me. I blinked rapidly as I looked down at it, remembering the day I could have sworn I heard it speak. Had the power that had disappeared in the wake of Rhonwen's death truly returned to it?

"Let's get out of here," Cian said, breaking me out of my thoughts.

"And what about all of this?" Domhnall said, gesturing to the chair and the haphazard stack of books.

"It won't matter so long as we're away from here before the break of first light," I said, striding toward the door.

Cian and Domhnall followed behind me and we once again stepped out into the hallway. I released a long breath, trying to quell the quiver in my stomach as we passed the still unconscious warriors. Domhnall paused and shoved the key into the pocket of one of the warriors and I felt a twinge of guilt over the blame the man would take. *Remember what's at stake here,* I told myself as we took off into a jog.

The castle remained dead quiet as we darted down the hallways, but my chest was still tight and my mouth was dry. When we eventually burst through one of the servant's doors and out into the back courtyard, I felt like I could finally draw a deep breath. We were one step closer to our goal.

We continued on at a jog to the stables. The horses were turned out for the night in the small paddocks, which made it easier for us to access them without drawing too much attention. Domhnall and Cian left me to fetch our mounts while the two of them went to sneak into the tack room and gather our tack and the rest of our gear. Gruffudd had promised to make certain it would all be in a place that would be easy to get to without being seen.

It took a bit longer than I would have wanted, but I managed to catch all three of our horses, tying them up along a paddock fence, my anxiety mounting as I waited for Cian and Domhnall's return. When the two of them finally reemerged in the darkness, I hurried over to help them carry the horses' gear.

"Were you seen?" I asked as I knocked the worst of the dirt off Ceol before throwing his saddlecloth onto his back.

"I don't think so," Cian replied as he saw to his mare. "No one was watching the tack room, though there were plenty of warriors in the rest of the stable."

Tense silence fell between us as we finished tacking up our mounts. I was careful as I lashed Rhonwen's bow to Ceol's saddle, a niggle of doubt making me hope I'd done the right thing in taking the weapon. There would be no way of escaping the consequences of such actions.

As soon as the horses were ready, we swung up onto their backs.

I forced myself to take a few deep breaths as I settled into the saddle and Cian led the way to the nearest side gate. The moonlight lit our way down the shell stone path we were following and I listened hard for any signs of pursuers, though I heard nothing. When we reached the gate, I was relieved to see it already open. Two warriors, who I assumed had been the guards for the night, were slumped on the ground, leaning up against the stone outer wall, while a third hooded and cloaked figure motioned for us to ride through. I recognized Mair as we rode past and my heart twisted to know just how involved she was in our scheme. I hoped she didn't pay the price for it in our absence.

I had no time to even thank her, unfortunately, for Domhnall urged his stallion into a gallop as soon as we were through the gate, and Cian and I were forced to follow suit. We raced through the darkness, the stone walls of Clogwyn fading from view behind us as we headed for the shelter of the forest. As soon as we burst through the thick wall of trees, the underbrush forced us to slow our mounts.

"I think we should avoid the main trails," I said as I brought Ceol abreast beside Domhnall's stallion. "Those will be the first places someone looks. There's a deer path that leads to the river. It lets out farther downstream. If we follow the river west, we'll avoid Gefell and from there, we can head into the Dail."

"So long as you're sure you know where you're going," Domhnall said, pursing his lips as he glanced back at the castle.

"You forget that I grew up in these woods," I replied, urging Ceol forward to take the lead of our trio.

As my stallion trotted through the dense forest, I squared my shoulders, my worries slowly being replaced by confidence the farther we got from the castle. We'd done it. We'd defied Father and stolen the bow. Now I just had to see this all the way through to Fianna's defeat, no matter what.

CHAPTER 28

FESTERING DARKNESS

Seren

THE STORM AT LEAST waited to hit once we were out of the mountains. We were almost a full day out from the castle, a few miles from the village of Cawl, when the black sky that had been threatening rain all day erupted into a torrential downpour. The horses were on edge with the loud rumbles of thunder and the frequent flashes of lightning, and it took all of my effort to keep Ceol under control. The stallion didn't want to be out in the middle of the raging storm any more than I did.

Domhnall rode beside me, while Cian brought up the rear. The rain fell so hard, it was almost impossible to see the rough muddy road we were following. All of us were soaked through, the horses included, and a chill had settled in the air, causing me to shiver. Another flash of lightning snaked to the ground, making the hair on the back of my neck rise and causing the horses to shy when it struck nearby, entirely too close for comfort.

"We can't stay out in this!" I shouted as soon as we all had our mounts back under some semblance of control. "We have to find shelter."

"The first thing we see," Cian called back, his jaw set and his expression grim.

Despite Ceol's reluctance, I encouraged him forward. We were in an open, hilly stretch of land, following a road that wasn't often traveled. We had remained leery of being on the main roads, despite them offering a more direct route north, not knowing whether or not Father had sent warriors to drag us back to Clogwyn.

The wind blew the rain in sheets and Ceol lowered his head, flicking his ears back as the pelting rain began to sting my exposed skin. I pulled my cloak more tightly around me, shivering again with the damp chill in the air. Even something as simple as a rock ledge or a copse of trees would do at a time like this, something to shield us from the heavy rain and constant lightning.

I had just begun to worry that there would be no shelter to be found when I caught a glimpse of a small cottage nestled on top of the hill we were climbing. It was just off the road and I could see smoke rising from the chimney. I didn't particularly want to expose us to strangers, but we couldn't stay out in this storm. I called to Domhnall and Cian, fighting to be heard over the crashing thunder as I pointed up at the cottage. They both nodded in return and we urged our horses up the muddy hill, diverting off the road when we reached the top of it.

Wood fencing surrounded one side of the cottage, filled with sheep who were huddled under a large lean-to. On the other side of the cottage, there was a small barn and a decent-sized garden. The homestead belonged to herders, from the look of it, and I prayed to the Spirits that they would at least be willing to let us ride out the storm in the barn.

We swung off our horses, Cian offering to stay with our mounts while Domhnall and I sought out whoever lived here. Rain streamed off the hood of my cloak and I tried to ignore the squishing of my soggy boots as we walked to the front door. I didn't think I'd ever been so soaked. Domhnall knocked and I started as another crack of lighting lit the sky behind us, followed by a booming roll of thunder. I anxiously looked over my shoulder, relieved to see that despite the increasing storm, Cian had managed to keep control of the horses.

The door to the cottage creaked open and I saw a wide-eyed woman, not much older than myself, standing on the other side. She didn't open the door fully, but I could tell that she was dressed in the simple clothing of a herder, her shirt and pants made of dark-colored, earth-toned cloth that was well-worn but equally well mended. Her brown hair was pulled back and there was clear skepticism in her brown eyes as she looked up at Domhnall and me. We'd all dressed as plainly as possible when we left Clogwyn, but despite currently resembling drowned mice, I knew our attire spoke of us being more than just herders or farmers. From somewhere deeper in the house, I heard the loud laughter of a young child and the woman's shoulders visibly tensed.

"We're travelers seeking shelter from the storm," I said. "If we could perhaps take shelter in your barn, we'll leave as soon as the storm passes."

"We can pay," Domhnall added. "Handsomely."

I cast him a sidelong glance, wondering just how much coin he'd brought with him on our little venture. I knew his mother had made certain he'd come to Clogwyn well off, but I didn't need him flaunting such wealth and making us the target for robbers and thieves. Not that the woman in front of us looked like anything of the sort, but it wasn't unwise to be cautious in a situation such as this one. The woman pressed her lips together, glancing over her shoulder as a tall, blond-haired man came to stand just behind her. His stance was wide and his expression far from friendly as he stared down at us.

"You'll have to find shelter elsewhere," he said, crossing his arms.

"If we can just stay in your barn," I replied, allowing a bit of the desperation I felt inside to color my tone. Spirits only knew how long it would take to find some other shelter in this open stretch of land and we couldn't risk staying out in the storm. "We won't be any trouble and we'll be gone the moment the weather clears."

"These parts are too troubled of late to be taking in any strangers." The man shook his head.

"You would turn away the Ri's daughter?" Domhnall's cheeks were flushed, his eyes narrowing. "*Your* future Ri."

I silently cursed both his temper and his carelessness. I hadn't wanted to go around telling anyone and everyone who we were. I didn't believe for a moment that Father wouldn't send warriors after us, and we didn't need to make it any easier for them to find us. The woman paled at Domhnall's words, her grip on the door tightening while the man's stance grew even more rigid.

"Please," I said, softening my tone. I didn't want to intimidate them and I didn't appreciate Domhnall's attempts to try to. It was too much like what my father would have done. "We mean you no harm. We only seek shelter from the storm."

The man began to speak but the woman cut him off, holding up her hand.

"You swear you mean no harm?" she asked.

"Yes," I answered, holding her gaze.

She let out a shaky breath before stepping back and fully opening the door. The man began to protest again but she stopped him with a few sharply muttered words.

"You can put your horses in the barn," she said, focusing back on me. "We have space for you and your friends inside the house."

"Thank you," I replied, unable to hold back a soft sigh of relief.

Domhnall went and told Cian the news, my cousin offering to see the horses to the stable for us. I was tempted to go with him, but I also didn't like the thought of letting Domhnall go into a stranger's home on his own, especially after our initial chilly welcome and his show of temper. The woman ushered the two of us into the cottage, water dripping from our cloaks and boots onto the wood floor as we entered.

"You can hang your cloaks in front of the fire," she said. "The great room should fit the three of you comfortably. I'm Betrys and this is my husband, Eurig."

With Domhnall having already blown any chance at anonymity we would have had, I decided to stick as close to the truth as possible without offering much in the way of details.

"Seren," I replied before motioning to Domhnall. "And my companion, Domhnall. My cousin, Cian, will be joining us shortly."

As Domhnall and I shed our wet cloaks, Eurig and Betrys shared a hushed conversation before he hurried off to what I assumed was the great room. Betrys gave us a nervous smile, then motioned for Domhnall and me to follow her. She escorted us into a decent-sized room, one that would be considered large compared to the rest of the house, from what I could tell. There were three wooden chairs in front of a large hearth, and two hide windows let in the faintest of light. Across the hallway, I spied what looked like a kitchen of sorts, but it wasn't the trappings of the house that drew my focus and piqued my curiosity.

A young girl was seated on the floor in front of the hearth, playing with a well-loved stuffed wolf and a few hand-carved

wooden blocks. From her dark hair, brown eyes, and facial features, I suspected her to be Eurig and Betrys' child. Eurig had
knelt down beside her and was coaxing her into gathering up
her toys. When he heard Domhnall and me come into the room,
he tensed, looking up at us with a wary expression.

I felt a slight twist in my stomach at his reaction. There was
clearly something off here and yet at the same time, I didn't feel
as if Betrys and Eurig necessarily meant us harm. If anything,
I'd begun to wonder if they were afraid of us. Betrys showed us
where to lay our wet cloaks out so that they would dry while
Eurig helped his daughter finish picking up her toys before
ushering her out of the room.

"I can get you something to drink to help warm you up,"
Betrys said, a note of forced cheer in her voice. "Please, have a
seat."

"Something to drink would be wonderful," I replied. "Thank
you."

She gave me a tight smile before walking off into the kitchen.
I settled into a chair in front of the fire while Domhnall pulled
another one close and took a seat.

"I'm not so sure we should be drinking anything they offer,"
he said, casting a dark look in the direction of the kitchen.

"I don't think they mean us any harm," I replied. "Honestly, I
think they might be more worried we mean them harm."

He scoffed. "If they've nothing sinister to hide, they have
nothing to be worried for."

My thoughts flitted back to the child and the way that Eurig
had almost seemed to shield her from us as he had hurried her
out of the room. She looked to be around the age that most
children began to show signs of their giftings, if they had them
at all. I shook my head, pushing the speculative thoughts aside.
Giftings were not so common. What would the odds be that we
had stumbled across a child that had one?

There was a knock at the front door and Eurig strode down the hallway. I heard Cian's low voice drift into the cottage and a few moments later, he joined us in the great room. After discarding his own cloak by the fire, he took a seat in the last empty chair.

"The horses are settled," he said, leaning back in his seat and stretching his legs out in front of him. "Storm is still raging."

"I think we'll be safe enough here until it passes." I bit my lower lip as I heard slightly raised voices come from the kitchen.

Domhnall frowned, glancing across the hallway. The voices stopped, but the loud bang of a slamming door followed. I shifted in my seat, Domhnall and Cian exchanging an uneasy look. By the Spirits, I hoped I hadn't made a mistake in insisting we take shelter in this place. A few moments later, Betrys walked into the great room carrying three steaming mugs. Her smile was still forced and her hands weren't quite steady as she passed us our drinks.

"I hope I didn't make it too warm," she said as I took my mug of what appeared to be some sort of cider.

"I'm sure it will be fine," Cian said, giving her a gracious smile. "Thank you."

"Of course," she replied. "Is there anything else I can get you?"

"No, thank you," I told her. "We appreciate the shelter. As soon as the storm is over, we'll be on our way."

Betrys nodded, her nervous smile crossing her face again. "I have some work do in the kitchen. I'll be in there if you need me. Eurig has gone out to check on the flock."

She bid us farewell and I took a quick sniff of my cider after she left the room. Not smelling anything suspect and half-heartedly scolding myself for being paranoid, I took a sip. It was more flavorful than I was expecting and I wrapped my hands around the outside of the mug, letting its heat warm my chilled skin. The storm continued to rail outside, the sky growing even darker as evening slowly settled. We didn't have time to be delayed, but none of us had control over the weather and traveling in a storm like this posed too many risks.

"We're still alive, you know," Cian said, drawing me out of my thoughts. He was speaking to Domhnall, who was still staring into his drink with a scrunched-up brow and a suspicious expression. "It's not poisoned."

Domhnall let out a huff before taking a tiny sip of the cider.

"Well, not with anything fast-acting, at least." Cian shrugged one shoulder.

Domhnall spit his drink back out into the mug, half choking on it as he cleared his throat. I attempted a half glare at Cian, who gave me a wry look in return, but really, I was fighting to suppress a chuckle.

"Very funny," Domhnall grumbled, wiping the back of his mouth with his sleeve.

A crash of thunder rumbled so loudly that it made me wince. If anything, the storm outside seemed to be getting worse, not better, which was the last thing we needed. Who knew what actions Fianna had already taken in the north? A shiver passed down my spine as my thoughts flitted to Bran, the raging forest fire, and the deadly fighting I had seen in my vision.

My grip on my mug tightened and I let out a long breath, trying to calm my growing fears. There had been multiple outcomes in all of the visions I'd seen, reminders that the future was ever changing. It was not set in stone that Bran would die or that the warriors of Blaidd would be slaughtered by Fianna's ilk. I had to keep reminding myself of that. When the three of us finished our drinks, I offered to take our empty mugs back to Betrys in the kitchen.

"Are you sure you should be going in there on your own?" Domhnall asked with a frown.

"If Betrys means me any harm, it isn't as if I'm not armed," I replied, motioning to the dagger strapped to my waist.

He tightly pressed his lips together but gave a stiff nod, passing me his empty mug. Cian passed me his mug as well, and I left the great room behind, crossing the hallway into the kitchen. It was a simple space, with a large hearth for cooking, a few chairs, and a long table. Betrys stood over the table, scrubbing a dirty pot in a basin of water. She turned when she heard me enter, starting slightly.

"Thank you, for the cider," I told her, holding up the mugs. "Where would you like these?"

"Right here is fine," she said, nodding to a spot on the table next to her. "I'll get to them next."

An awkward silence filled the room as I went and set the mugs down where she had indicated. I stepped back from the table and had started to turn and leave when Betrys cleared her throat. I paused, turning back toward her. She fidgeted with the pot, splashing a bit of dirty water onto the table before taking a deep breath.

"You will have to forgive Eurig," she said, not quite meeting my gaze. "He... worries. About our daughter."

An uncomfortable feeling settled in the pit of my stomach and I gave a slow nod. "These are difficult and dangerous times."

"One day," Betrys said, her voice wavering as her hands began to shake, "she was out playing with Eurig. She loves to play in the mud near the sheep pens; she always has. We only turned our backs for a moment, but when we looked back at her, we knew." She paused, a sheen of tears coming to her eyes. "And in that moment, I knew what it was to live with the fear that someday, someone would come and take my child away from me."

My throat tightened as her words settled over me. I knew what she wasn't saying. Her daughter was a shifter and by my father's decree, she would be sentenced to death if anyone learned the truth of what she was. Part of me was stunned that Betrys had even confessed it; and to me, of all people. And yet even as my heart broke for her, anger coursed through me as well. This was the world my father had created. This was the darkness he had allowed to fester and grow in every corner of Blaidd. No parent should have to live in fear of losing their child. That was not the kind of future I wished for my people.

"I swear to you that I will cause no harm to befall your daughter," I said, holding Betrys' gaze. "None of us will."

She blinked rapidly, dropping the pot into the basin of water with a splash. Swallowing hard, she rubbed at her eyes with her arm.

"Thank you," she said. "I have heard the stories... of what you did during the Purge. And I've heard the rumors that you have shown the shifter that is said to be at Castle Clogwyn your favor. Eurig is too afraid to hope after these last few years. We have been spared here, but there have been so many who have lost everything with the fires and there have been patrols that have come through looking for any shifters they could find. I fear for my child. I fear that she won't have a future."

A painful lump settled in my throat. There were people like Betrys all over Blaidd. People, children, just like her daughter, just like Bran, who lived in fear for their very lives. Others still who had lost everything to Fianna's flames. An ache settled in my chest, as if I could feel the physical weight that I would one day carry, but as Betrys stared at me with tears in her eyes, I knew I could do no less than what I had promised.

"I know it is hard to hope," I told her. "But I promise you that the day I become Ri, not only will I make certain Fianna is banished from this land, I will also make certain that Blaidd is a safe place for *all* who call it home."

A few tears spilled down Betrys' cheeks, ones that made me blink back my own, but the smile she gave me was free of the fear that had previously engulfed her. "And I will thank you for that. From the very depths of my heart."

She wiped at her face again before turning back to the table and resuming scrubbing the pot. I quietly left the kitchen, giving her the time to grapple with her emotions in private and halfway wishing I could do the same myself, my own emotions warring within me.

How many stories like Betrys' were across Blaidd? My father had claimed he had purged all the shifters from the land, but Bran and Betrys' daughter were proof that that was false. How many people had lost everything, including those they loved? Could the people truly wait for the role of Ri to pass to me, and what if Father did try and defy the hymddeol? The questions swirled around in my thoughts as I stepped back into the great room. I was so lost in them, I hardly noticed Domhnall speaking to me when I resumed my seat. He placed a hand on my arm, causing me to start.

"Is everything alright?" he asked, his brow furrowed.

"It's fine," I replied, mustering up a smile that I hoped was convincing. I understood Betrys' fears and I would not betray her confidence. I knew beyond a shadow of a doubt that I trusted Cian, but even though I hated to admit it, my trust in Domhnall, especially as far as shifters were concerned, was less certain. "It sounds like the storm is letting up."

The rain had slowed and the thunder was becoming more distant. Before too long, only a drizzle remained. Dusk was settling, but we needed to make it at least a few more miles before stopping for the night. We'd already lost too much precious time waiting for the storm to pass. Cian gathered up our cloaks, which were still damp, though at least not dripping wet, and I returned to the kitchen to let Betrys know we would be on our way. She saw us to the door, composed once more.

"Thank you for your hospitality," I told her.

"Of course," she replied.

Cian and Domhnall stepped out of the cottage and I went to follow them, but Betrys placed a hand on my arm, stopping me.

"Thank you," she said quietly. "For your promise."

"I meant every word," I told her.

She gently squeezed my arm, hope in her eyes, and I made myself tear my own gaze away from her, stepping out into the light rain. By the Spirits, I would put an end to all of this. I pulled the hood of my cloak up over my head, averting my gaze from Cian and Domhnall as I did so, my throat thick.

"Let's get moving. We have more ground to cover before we stop for the night," I said, striding across the muddy ground toward the stable.

The two of them followed behind me. I *would* see an end brought to the heartbreak and darkness Father and Fianna had brought to our land. The Stag Spirit's hold was deep, but it was not so deep that I could not uproot it.

CHAPTER 29

WEAPON OF THE WOLF

Seren

I'D BEEN DISTRACTED ALL day. We'd been following a less traveled trail along the banks of the Weindio, heading north toward the village of Dearg. Though it had been a full day since my conversation with Betrys, I couldn't get her words, or the look on her face when she'd told me about her daughter, out of my thoughts.

People were suffering. Lives were being destroyed. The world outside Clogwyn was so vastly different from the one Father tried to paint and control within the stone walls of the granite keep. I feared that the clan could not wait for him to step down. Even more than that, I feared he would never do so willingly. Laoise had hinted that we might need to take more decisive and direct action against him and in my heart, I knew she was right.

The thoughts left a quiver in my belly and I let out a long breath, trying to focus on the trail in front of me. The sun was setting after another day of heavy riding, the trees on either side of the river casting long shadows as the day drew to an end. Domhnall and Cian rode in front of me, our horses traveling at a slow trot. They both looked as weary as I felt, but we still needed to make it a few more miles if we intended to reach Drystan's camp tomorrow.

My jaw tightened as my thoughts flitted to the warrior chief. Most of the time, he was no more reasonable than Father, but surely, he wouldn't want his warriors' lives at risk. He had to remember the price he'd paid the last time I'd forewarned him of danger and he'd ignored me. And Lewella was there. I knew she would believe me and my warnings and if she felt the situation warranted it, I had seen her speak out against Drystan before. He had to grasp how dire the situation was. The scorched, dead earth, ruined forests, and destroyed homes were growing across Blaidd.

We pressed our horses onward, finally agreeing to call a stop for the night. There was an open break in the trees right along the river, and that was where we eventually made camp. Cian saw to the fire and Domhnall set up our sleeping pallets for the night while I tended to the horses.

Once our mounts were untacked, I walked them down one by one to the river to allow them to get a drink. As I stood next to Ceol, my stallion greedily guzzled down the cold mountain water. I scratched his neck, my gaze drawn to the opposite bank. Had it only been almost two months ago that Bran and I had been following this very same river south, fleeing Lorcan? Somehow, it felt like a lifetime had passed.

The thoughts of Bran made my throat tighten and I swallowed hard. The fear that some ill had already befallen him had haunted me ever since we had left Clogwyn. It had been so tempting to risk venturing into the Spirit Realm to see if I could glean more of his future, but I didn't dare take that risk right now. It would make me far too vulnerable and we didn't have time to be slowed down by the aftereffects of my visions.

Ceol took one last long drink, water dribbling from his black muzzle as he raised his head, and I walked him back over to the trees where I'd picketed the other horses. I retied the stallion, giving him one last scratch before joining Domhnall and Cian around the fire.

Cian had pulled out a bit of dried meat and was using that, along with some freshly foraged greens and river water to make a soup of some sort. I settled down next to Domhnall, the weariness of the day catching up to me as I tried get comfortable on the hard, uneven ground. We'd been pushing ourselves ever since we'd left Clogwyn and I would be ready for a bit of rest once we reached Drystan's camp.

"You've seen nothing else since we left?" Domhnall asked while Cian busied himself stirring and sampling his soup concoction.

"No," I replied with a shake of my head.

"Perhaps that's a good thing," Domhnall said, giving me a half-smile.

"Perhaps." I returned his smile. I'd been hoping the same.

His gaze returned to the fire and I studied him for a moment in the fading light. He could exasperate me at times, but I couldn't deny the support he'd offered me over the years, especially these last few weeks. He was risking much, coming on this journey with me, and he hadn't turned back, despite the difficulties. Even if my feelings for him didn't run any deeper, I was still grateful to call him a friend.

Cian continued stirring the soup, mumbling to himself as he tossed more ingredients into the pot. I'd just leaned back on my hands, starting to allow myself to relax a little, when I caught the first whiff of strong smoke in the air. At first, I told myself it was just a shift in the breeze making the campfire smell stronger to me, but something about the odor was off. I frowned, my muscles tensing as I sat up straighter, scanning the surrounding forest. I saw nothing and began to chastise myself for spooking at my own imagination, but then I caught a flash of something hazy and grey darting between the trees.

"I think I saw something," I said, grabbing the hilt of my dagger. I scooted over to the saddlebags, which had been dumped on the ground nearby. My sword leaned against the pile of leather bags, along with Rhonwen's bow.

"I don't see anything," Domhnall said, his mouth turning down as he sat up and surveyed the forest.

Cian was still occupied with the soup, but he too had glanced warily over his shoulder at my pronouncement. The forest was growing even darker as the sun set and I couldn't shake the sense of foreboding that had come over me. This would be the ideal time for any number of creatures to be hunting. I tried to hope that whatever it was had wandered off, but moments later, a suffocating darkness crept into the air. Cian dropped his wooden spoon into the pot with a clang, his shoulders tensing, and I knew that he too felt the Stag Spirit's presence.

The horses had begun to stamp their feet, their necks arched and their nostrils flared as they tossed their heads in alarm. I grabbed my sword, unsheathing the blade, just as a circle of flames shot up out of the ground, encircling our small camp and trapping us in place.

An eldritch screech made me want to cover my ears and a shadow creature burst out of the trees. Domhnall let out a slew of curses, the creature only mere feet from me. I took a firmer hold of the hilt of my sword, my mouth going dry as the creature fixed me with its flickering amber gaze. Smoke billowed from its nostrils and sparks flew from its mouth as it bared its fangs. Once again, I felt the phantom pain in my leg from my last tangle with such a being.

The shadow creature lunged at me and I darted out of its path, swinging my blade even though I knew it would do little good. My blade brushed across the creature's smoky hide, leaving not even a scratch behind. The creature shrieked and leapt at me again, but Domhnall intervened, shoving me behind him as he pulled me out of the creature's path and swung at it with his own sword. The creature let out a low hiss, backing off slightly, but it never took its gaze off me. Domhnall and Cian kept me stuck behind them, both of them wielding their swords as they sought to stay between me and the creature.

I almost tripped over the saddlebags as the two of them crowded me and I muttered a soft curse. I was no warrior, but I was arguably the best fighter of the three of us. The shadow creature let out another shriek, its fangs bared, and my stomach clenched. We had nothing with which to even wound it, much less defeat it. Our weapons would do us no good against such a foe.

"Watch out!" Domhnall shouted as the creature lunged again, barely missing Cian with its sharp claws.

My palms had begun to sweat and I could feel the heat of the flames as they grew even closer to us. We were running out of time.

Use me, Daughter of Blaidd.

I started at the strange voice and my gaze fell on Rhonwen's bow, the weapon practically on top of my feet. It shouldn't work any better than our swords and yet I remembered what I had seen in my visions. The shadow creature shrieked again and my decision was made. I threw down my sword and snatched up the bow, yanking an arrow from the quiver. I nocked the arrow and loosed.

The creature let out a cry that made me wince, jerking away from us. It snarled and snapped at the arrow, which had dug into its shoulder. Unlike our swords, which hadn't even pierced its smoky body, the arrow was in deep, and black blood oozed from the wound. I grabbed another arrow, loosing again. It embedded itself into the creature's neck, causing more black blood to stain its body.

It thrashed and shrieked, trying to attack us still, but its movements were uncoordinated. I loosed a third arrow, aiming for where I assumed the creature's heart to be. When my arrow struck, the creature dropped to the ground. For a few seconds, it struggled, fighting to get back up and letting out rage-filled cries that made my ears ring, but then it went completely still. The fire encircling us vanished, leaving behind nothing more than a faint circle of blackened earth and a few wisps of smoke.

"Is it... dead?" Domhnall asked, still holding his sword defensively as we all stared at the unmoving creature.

"I don't know," I said, my heart still pounding.

We stood in tense silence, watching the creature for any signs of movement, but nothing happened. After a moment, Cian took a tentative step toward it.

"Wait," I said, pulling out another arrow. "I'm coming with you."

Cian nodded and Domhnall was quick to follow us, grumbling about not letting the two of us risk our necks without him. I kept the arrow ready to nock as we crept over to the creature. It still didn't move and as we got closer, I could see that its ember eyes were now nothing more than black coals. Cian went to poke at it with the tip of his sword, but the body suddenly disintegrated into a pile of soot and ash. A strong wind blew through the trees, seemingly out of nowhere, picking up the remains of the creature and carrying them off into an odd sort of spiral until the remains vanished into the air. The arrows had remained, though they were covered in black blood. I picked them up, grimacing at the way the blood clung to my hands. Later, I would clean them and return them to the quiver.

"How in the blazes did you know that bow would do that?" Domhnall asked, staring wide eyed at the bow.

"I saw it," I answered. "In a vision. I'm telling you, it's more than an old relic. It has a role to play in all of this."

"Apparently," Domhnall said with a slight frown.

Cian let out a heavy sigh and I followed his gaze to the pot of soup that had been left over the fire. The charred remains of the spoon could be seen sticking up out of it and the pot itself was smoking.

"So much for dinner," he said.

"Better dinner ruined than our lives," Domhnall replied. "I think it would be wise to find someplace else to camp for the night. In case there are more of those... things lurking nearby."

"I agree," I said. "We'll find someplace upriver. I don't know exactly how many of those creatures have been unleashed in Blaidd, but I know it's more than one."

Domhnall and I set to packing up once more while Cian discarded our ruined dinner. Night had fully fallen over the forest by the time we were done, and combined with the adrenaline coursing through me, I was jumpy. I kept Rhonwen's bow close to me, not wanting to risk being parted from it if there were more shadow creatures lurking about.

It was no ordinary weapon, that was for certain. Tonight's fight had proven that. Just as it had proven that the bow was the key to defeating Fianna. Surely even Drystan couldn't deny a weapon that killed a shadow creature.

CHAPTER 30

SOMETHING NEW

Alannah

FOR FOUR DAYS, I had shared Aengus' home. He had tended my wounds, had seen to my every need, and had left me dreading the day I would have to return to Lorcan's camp. Dara had been called back to Lorcan's side three days ago and he had obeyed that command, despite showing marked disapproval at leaving me alone in Aengus' care. For now, Lorcan had been content to let Aengus work his gift on me, emphasizing that he needed me alive and well to perform my tasks for him. Whether or not Fianna had anything to do with my extended stay in Beag, I certainly wasn't going to argue about more time in Aengus' presence.

As my days with Aengus had passed, I'd begun to suspect that I wasn't the only one feeling the sparks between us. I noticed the way his gaze was continually drawn to me, the softness in his voice, and the way his touches would linger. Still, despite feeling like the two of us were growing closer, I'd noticed that

Aengus hadn't been entirely himself. Something had him unsettled. Whether it was something to do with me, or Lorcan, or something else, I wasn't certain, but I was determined to find out.

Today, Aengus had finally deemed me well enough to get out of the house, and I was looking forward to a short stroll through the nearby forest. I was still sore and had lost some of my strength, but I ignored the discomfort as I dressed and pulled my hair back into braids. I needed to take whatever time alone with Aengus that I could get; Spirits only knew how long it would last. I hadn't forgotten Fianna's ultimate goal. Aengus needed to be won over to the Stag Spirit's side if he was to one day take his place as Ri of Blaidd.

After pulling on my boots, I stepped out of my room and walked down the hallway to the great room, where Aengus awaited me. He stood staring pensively out a small window, the sun catching his blond hair and causing it to glint gold. When he heard me, he turned, and the unease on his face vanished, replaced by a soft smile.

"Ready?" he asked.

I nodded and he offered me his arm. I took it, in part because of the support it offered but also for any excuse to be close to him. We left the house, passing by a small sheep pen, and then strolled into the woods. The sky was a brilliant blue, filled with white puffy clouds, and the forest was bursting with all manner of shades of green. Birdsong and the rustle of leaves created a soft chorus of song as we walked and I turned my face to the sun, basking in its warmth and the beauty of the day.

We took our time following a slightly cleared trail, the edges of the village still visible through the trees. Aengus moved slowly, something I appreciated, given the state of my sore body. As we walked, I studied him, not bothering to hide my obvious interest. He was sporting a few days' worth of stubble, but there was something about the light scruff that made him more handsome. For a man who was no warrior or farmer, he was surprisingly fit and well-muscled, with broad shoulders that slimmed into a tapered waist. Every now and then, sunlight would filter down through the trees and give his blond hair that alluring golden sheen. I wanted him to be mine. He should be mine.

He will be, Fianna said, its voice seeming to whisper on the breeze that blew through the trees. *I will grant you both more than you have ever dreamed. Just help me convince him. Help him see the grand future that awaits you.*

A shiver of anticipation passed down my spine. *Banrion.* I was inching closer and closer to such a future. Aengus glanced over at me, a slight furrow in his brow, and I flashed him a smile to put him at ease. He didn't need to know of my deal with Fianna just yet.

"How arc you feeling?" he asked. "Just tell me when you're ready to head back and we will."

"I'm feeling fine," I replied. "Being out here... it lets my thoughts not dwell on what happened."

"Do thoughts of the attack still trouble you?"

I averted my gaze, not wanting to admit what he already knew. He'd been there when my memories had haunted me in the night. When I had felt Bran's teeth digging into my skin all over again, shattering the bone. It was a weakness, one I loathed, despite Aengus' insistence that such things happened.

"No," I told him.

"I'm happy to make you another tincture," he said. "Dark thoughts are not easy things to bear."

Somehow, with his last words, I knew we were no longer just talking about me. It was the perfect opening to pry a little deeper.

"Something has troubled you these last few days," I said, careful to keep my tone and expression soft as I slowed my steps, bringing us to a stop.

"I have had many things to consider since my mother passed," he replied with a slight grimace.

Silence fell between us as I weighed my next words. I knew his father had returned to Cnoc almost a week ago, but Aengus had been tight-lipped about what all had transpired before he left.

"I take it these things you have had to consider have not been pleasant?" I asked.

At first, he did not answer and I feared that perhaps I had pushed too soon, but then he let out a heavy sigh, coming to a stop as his shoulders slumped.

"I have not told anyone this," he said, his gaze on the village, barely visible through the trees. "But perhaps speaking of it will ease my mind." He glanced over at me, his brow wrinkled. "I must ask that you do not repeat this to anyone."

I took his hand in mine and gave it a squeeze. "I promise."

He looked back at the trees again. "My father confessed a truth to me. One that my mother, on her deathbed, made him promise to tell me. My parents were not my true parents by blood. My father was Ri Cadfael's brother, Fionn, and my mother was a castle servant. I was born to her, at Castle Clogwyn, but she and Fionn were not together in any sort of formal way. My presence within the castle walls apparently made Cadfael furious. He had become Ri shortly before I was born and he forced my mother to get rid of me or lose her place at Clogwyn. She gave me up. It was only by luck she was friends with my adoptive family and they were willing to take and raise me."

I did my best to look surprised, as if I had never heard any of his story before this moment, but inside, I could feel both pleasure and anticipation building. He knew the blood that ran through his veins, the blood of the line of Blaidd, and I'd heard the resentment in his voice when he'd spoken Cadfael's name.

"I have wondered," he said, dropping his chin and running his thumb along the back of my palm, "why it is you, Lorcan, and the others do what you do. And I think, perhaps, I am beginning to understand. Cadfael is a man who ruins everything he touches."

"He stole everything from me." I paused, waiting for Aengus to look up and meet my gaze before continuing. "He stole my family, my home, and any hope I had for a future. Blaidd needs change. It needs a Ri who will usher in a new era."

His breath caught and he looked away. "I cannot disagree with you, but..." He shook his head, working his jaw. He was uncertain. I could feel the tension radiating from his body into mine through our clasped hands.

"It's time for something new in Blaidd," I said softly. "*Someone* new."

I gently brought my free hand up to the side of his face, turning it toward me. The rush of emotions he was feeling was written all over his face and I brushed my thumb over the stubble along his jaw.

"These last few days have been more perfect than I could have ever imagined," I told him. "I didn't think I would ever have such happiness again. I will miss you when I leave this place."

His gaze dropped to my lips, his breathing growing slightly unsteady. "I find that I will miss you as well."

I was the one who kissed him, but he was the one who pulled me tightly to him with a passion I had not anticipated. I'd kissed my fair share of men, but none of them compared to Aengus. He was confident, firm, and heat surged through my body as I opened my mouth to him. A low groan tore from his throat as he deepened our kiss and pushed me up against the trunk of a tree. I didn't even care about the rough bark digging into my back as his muscular body pressed up against mine. He was mine and I was going to keep it that way.

A shout broke us apart, both of us breathing raggedly as Aengus used the tree trunk to brace his hands on either side of my head. The shout came again and I frowned when I was able to discern my name. Aengus looked over his shoulder, his body tensing as Dara's voice drifted through the trees, getting louder with each shout. I swallowed hard as a dull ache settled in my chest. I wasn't ready for this to come to an end.

This is no ending, Fianna said, its words soothing me. *You have not lost him. But the game must be carefully played.*

"He's waiting," Aengus said, unsteadily taking a few steps away from me.

I nodded, Dara's unwelcome presence a silent reminder of all that stood between us, and Aengus offered his arm again. Our walk out of the forest was much quicker than our walk into it had been. Dara was pacing at the back of the house, his horse tied and waiting, the beast looking as if it had been ridden hard. Aengus called a greeting and Dara whirled around, his eyes narrowing as he looked between the two of us.

"It's time to go, Alannah," Dara said, motioning for me to come to his side before looking over at Aengus, his brows drawn in. "Lorcan has need of her and he hopes you've done a decent job, healer."

I stiffened at his rude tone but Aengus offered an easy smile.

"She's healed well," he replied. "She should be ready."

"I've gathered your things," Dara said to me. "Lorcan wants you to ride back instead of shifting, to save your strength. Let's go."

He brusquely motioned for me to follow him before turning on his heel. A bitter taste filled my mouth and I scowled at his retreating back. There was no good reason for him to be in such a snit.

"I know you must go," Aengus murmured and as he looked down at me, I saw the longing in his green eyes. "I will not try and stop you, but I..."

Our kiss had meant something. I could hear it in his voice and feel it in the sparks that crackled in the air between us. I couldn't defy Dara and Lorcan right now, but something had been forged here these last few days between Aengus and me. Something Fianna and I both could use to our advantage, knowing that Aengus knew the truth of who he was.

"I'll come back to you as soon as I can," I said, holding his gaze. "I promise."

He nodded, stealing a glance at Dara, who still had his back to us. Before releasing his hold on me, he brushed a brief kiss over my lips. I hated walking away from him. Lifting my chin, I strode up to Dara, who had already untied and mounted his horse. He pulled me up into the saddle with him, barely giving me time to get settled before urging the horse into a gallop. This was only a setback. I would have forever with Aengus. Fianna would make sure of it.

CHAPTER 31

IN SHAMBLES

Seren

IT WAS LATE AFTERNOON by the time we reached where Drystan's camp should have been, but what we found a few miles from the river left me sick to my stomach. There was no encampment awaiting us, only the scene of a fire and a battle that was now over. I reined Ceol to a quick halt, my heart thudding in my chest as I surveyed the ghastly sight before me: the blackened grass, the dead trees, and the hints here and there of what had once been a tent or a weapon. Though I saw no bodies, I could see where a large fresh grave had been dug away from the river.

"We were too late," I said, swallowing hard.

"The bodies have been buried." Cian's voice was tight as he pointed to the grave. "There must have been survivors of some sort."

"Shall we see if they have fled to the village?" Domhnall asked.

North, Daughter of Blaidd. You must go north. The Wolf Spirit's voice whispered to me, a breeze ruffling the loose strands of my hair.

"I think we should check the surrounding areas first," I said, casting Cian a sidelong glance, hoping that he had felt the Wolf Spirit's presence as well.

Domhnall frowned. "And what if whoever attacked them is still lurking?"

"I agree with Seren," Cian said. "We check the surrounding areas first and then we head to Dearg."

I urged Ceol into a trot, pointing the stallion north, while Cian and Domhnall fell in behind me, Domhnall doing so with a huff. I ignored his grumbling as we skirted the site of the battle. As we passed the grave, I sent up a silent prayer to the Spirits to help guide the souls of the lost from this realm to the next, all the while hoping that Bran was not among the dead.

My stomach churned as we continued following the river. I didn't want to think of the consequences if my visions had indeed become reality. We rode for roughly a half mile more before we caught the first glimpse of canvas tents. I let out a long sigh of relief, the tension in my shoulders easing. There had been an attack, but it hadn't ended in annihilation.

I urged Ceol into a faster pace, Cian and Domhnall coming to ride abreast with me as we approached the edge of the camp. Warriors stood guard, their numbers and stances making it clear that they were on high alert. I heard shouts break out when they spotted us, and by the time we reached them and brought our horses to a halt, the five warriors standing guard had been joined by six more companions.

"I must speak with Pennathe Drystan," I said as I swung from Ceol's back.

There was a shuffling among the crowd of warriors and they parted for Lewella to push her way through. She tilted her head at the sight of me, blinking rapidly. When I caught sight of the bandages wrapped around her upper arms, my chest tightened. I hoped the war band hadn't suffered too greatly.

"Seren," she said, her brows slightly raised. "We weren't expecting you."

"I must speak with Pennathe Drystan," I told her. "The matter is urgent."

She nodded slowly before calling for warriors to see to our horses. I unlashed Rhonwen's bow and quiver from Ceol's saddle before the stallion was led away. Lewella motioned for us to follow her and I fell in step with her, Cian and Domhnall sticking close behind us. We made our way through the rows of tents toward the camp's center and my sense of unease grew as we passed more and more injured warriors.

"What happened?" I asked Lewella, keeping my voice low as we walked. "We passed the burn site a half mile back."

Lewella pressed her lips together into a grimace. "We were attacked—ambushed, rather. It caught Drystan by surprise, but luckily for him, we managed to keep from being overwhelmed."

"Did it catch you by surprise?" I asked, noticing her carefully chosen wording.

"Drystan and I have not been in agreement of late regarding this foe we fight," she replied, casting me a sidelong glance.

I knew Father and Drystan both expected loyalty from those around them—demanded it, even—but I couldn't help but see the cracks that were forming. Cracks like Laoise and Domhnall being bold enough to question Father's capability. *And perhaps Lewella is another,* I thought as Drystan's large canvas tent came into view.

Lewella spoke to the warriors standing guard outside and in moments, we were let in. Drystan was in deep discussion with three of his warriors, the embroidery on their shirts denoting their high rank. Lewella motioned for us to stay where we were. She walked over and spoke to Drystan and though I couldn't hear what she said, he looked over at us with a scowl. He waved Lewella off and she rejoined us.

"He'll speak with you in a moment," she said. "I'm afraid I'm needed elsewhere."

"Of course," I replied. "Thank you for seeing us here."

She gave me a respectful nod before stepping close and dropping her voice once more. "Don't let him intimidate you."

I held her gaze and gave a nod before she saw her way out of the tent. A churning settled in my stomach as we waited for Drystan and I shifted my weight, my grip on the bow tightening. I didn't have any reason to believe that he would be more open to my knowledge than Father, but I had to try. Especially after the recent attack that had transpired here. Fianna was not going to rest until it had destroyed all of Blaidd.

"We saw what it did too," Domhnall said quietly, resting a hand on my shoulder. "We will tell him as much."

I glanced over at him, giving him a weak smile as he gently squeezed my shoulder. His hand lingered before dropping away, but I didn't have the time to dwell on it, as Drystan finally dismissed his warriors and turned his attention to us.

"Dare I ask what has drawn the three of you here?" Drystan asked, crossing his arms as he faced us.

"The Spirits have shown me something that has the power to potentially change the tide of this fight," I answered, lifting my chin as I addressed him, refusing to shrink back under his glower.

"Does your father know you're here?" Drystan raised his brows.

"I came of my own accord," I replied. "But only because of—"

"I do not have time to listen to the whims of a girl who understands neither war or strategy." Drystan picked a map up off a table and turned his back to us. "Go home, Seren. You are not needed here."

I could feel my face flush at the dismissive response, my shoulders tensing with fury.

"You do not wish to listen to the wisdom of a seer?" Cian said. "Or have you decided to deem yourself so above the Spirits that you do not need their guidance?"

"Being a seer does not necessarily make one wise," Drystan snapped.

"Neither does being a warrior chief," Domhnall said. "By refusing to listen to Seren, you refuse the Wolf Spirit as well."

Drystan whirled around, his face reddening as he narrowed his eyes at Domhnall. "One of these days, boy, you are going to overstep your bounds one time too many and then Cadfael is going to send you back to Seabhac with your tail tucked between your legs, like he should have done years ago."

Domhnall stiffened, one of his hands clenching into a fist. He started to take an angry step toward Drystan but I put an arm out and stopped him. The last thing we needed was some sort of fistfight between Domhnall and Drystan, even if Drystan deserved it.

"The Spirits have shown me Rhonwen's bow," I said, holding the weapon out in front of me, "and they have shown me that it has the power to kill Fianna's shadow creatures."

Drystan turned slowly, pressing his lips together before he let out a short laugh. "It's a bow, Seren. A relic of a time past. Nothing more."

"You dare insult the Spirits thus?" I said, heat flushing my body. "You dare doubt them?"

"I find it difficult to believe that the Spirits would make such an outlandish suggestion," Drystan said with a sneer. "That bow has been sitting in the Ri's study at Castle Clogwyn for five hundred years. You think you are the first to try and use it? It is an ordinary weapon of ordinary means. Whatever power it once held is long gone."

"We saw it kill a shadow creature with our own eyes," Cian said, his jaw tight. "We were attacked on our way here and if it hadn't been for Seren wielding that bow, we would all be dead."

"A story is not proof." Drystan's tone was sharp, his brows narrowed.

"You discount the word of two witnesses and the woman who wielded the weapon herself?" Domhnall drew back his shoulders, a clear challenge in his voice.

Drystan let out a low growl and snatched the bow from my hands before yanking an arrow from the quiver. He nocked the arrow on the bow but as he went to draw it, the bowstring snapped and the arrow dropped to the ground. Drystan grimaced, shaking his arm where the string had popped him before giving the weapon a disgruntled look and thrusting it back at me. My stomach clenched as I took it from him. Our one chance at defeating Fianna and he had ruined it.

"Clearly a simple bow," he said. "And an ancient one at that, that has quite obviously seen too much age. Nothing more. Fianna will not be defeated by wild imaginings. I suggest you go home to Castle Clogwyn, Seren, where you belong. Domhnall, I would hope you would be capable of seeing her back, though Cian, I must request that you remain here for at least a few days."

"It is more than a simple bow," I said, my voice shaking with fury. "It *did* kill that shadow creature. I know what I saw."

"I am done discussing it," Drystan retorted before turning his gaze to Cian. "My healers have been working long hours and with the number of injuries from Fianna's creatures, many of my wounded are in need of someone more skilled. In particular the shifter. He ran afoul of Lorcan's scout the night of the battle."

Bran. The images of what I had seen in my vision returned to me and I felt like someone had punched me in the gut. Bran battered and wounded. Bran bleeding out on the forest floor. *But at least he's not among the dead,* I thought, releasing a shaky breath.

"I will not shirk my duty to the wounded if I can help them," Cian replied, though his rigid spine and his carefully chosen words made it clear that he would be doing so for the wounded, not Drystan.

"Good," Drystan said with a stiff nod. "Have one of the warriors outside see you to the healer's tent and have another sent to fetch Domhnall and Seren's horses."

He waved us off, putting his back to us once more. It took Cian steering me by the shoulders to get me to leave. Rage and fear bubbled inside of me and I clutched the bow so tightly, my knuckles turned white.

"I'm not going to let them force you to leave here without you seeing Bran first," Cian whispered into my ear after we ducked through the tent flap.

Different warriors now stood guard outside, but when I recognized one of them as Emer, some of my fear and frustration eased. I wondered if Lewella had sent her, but regardless, I was glad she was here, alive and unharmed.

"Domhnall would like to let the horses have time to recover before making the return journey," Cian said, addressing Emer. "If you could perhaps find him someplace to rest as well, we've had a hard last few days' ride. I'm afraid from the sounds of it, I will need to take advantage of Seren's skills in assisting me in the healer's tent; while she's here, at least."

"Of course," Emer replied. "Culwch, go with Domhnall, please. Make sure he gets whatever he needs. I'll see Seren and Cian to the healer's tent."

Culwch gave a slight frown but motioned for Domhnall to follow him. Domhnall glanced over at me, his brow wrinkled as he hesitated. I placed a hand on his arm in reassurance.

"I'll come find you when I'm done helping Cian," I said. I glanced down at the bow, reluctant to let it out of my sight after what had happened with Drystan, but knowing it would only get in my way if I had to help Cian care for Bran. "Take this, will you? Keep it safe."

Domhnall pressed his lips together but took it and the quiver from me with a nod. "I will watch over it."

He followed Culwch off to another part of the camp. I watched him disappear before Cian slipped an arm around my shoulders, guiding me along with him and Emer to the healer's tent. My legs felt laden with stones as we walked and by the time we reached the long, narrow tent, a painful lump had settled in my throat. I feared for Bran, unable to forget the images I'd seen in my visions.

A few words from Emer granted us entry and she led the way through the tent toward the back of it. My heart ached as we walked past the rows of wounded warriors all laid out on the ground on pallets. The smell of sickness was in the air and their haggard, drawn faces spoke of their pain. How long would Fianna's terror drag on? So many of the wounded bore hideous burns, along with injuries from arrows and swords. Our people had already suffered too much. I was not content to sit back and let them suffer more. One way or another, I would fix the bow. Our people couldn't afford for me not to.

"They've been keeping him off on his own because of the complaints others have made about his presence," Emer said as we walked to the far corner of the tent. "He was in poor shape when we found him. The healers have kept him stable, but it will be good that you're here, Cian."

I took a deep breath, trying to steady my nerves and the knots in my belly, but when I finally laid eyes on Bran, tears pricked my eyes. He was lying on a bedroll, shirtless, with his chest and shoulders wrapped in numerous cream-colored bandages, a few of them showing signs of being stained with dried blood. His left leg partially poked out from the blankets that covered him and I could see that it was bandaged as well. His face and neck were an assortment of colorful bruises and the long gash across his nose and down the right side of his face left it clear that it had been Alannah who had wounded him so.

Cian wasted no time going straight to Bran's side and beginning to assess the extent of his injuries. Emer hung back while I went to Bran's other side, kneeling down next to him and gently taking his hand in mine.

"Spirits, Bran," I murmured, my voice hoarse as a few tears trickled down my cheek.

"Ren?" His voice was rough from lack of use and he blearily blinked his eyes open, turning his head toward me with a low hiss.

"I'm here," I said, brushing his hair back from his brow. "And so is Cian. He's going to heal you."

Bran gave an almost imperceptible nod before closing his eyes once more. I furiously wiped at my tears with the back of my hand. I couldn't lose him. Not like this. Not because of Fianna's wretched darkness. I clutched Bran's hand in mine, forcing myself to draw in a few deep breaths to help get control of my swirling emotions. I would need to be focused if I was to help Cian.

"This will take more than one day," Cian said, looking over at me as he inspected Bran's leg. "I don't think there will be any permanent damage, thankfully. Maybe some scarring. I will tell the healers and Drystan that I need your assistance to get him back on his feet."

"Thank you," I told him, holding his gaze.

He set me to the task of first helping him remove Bran's bandages so that he could have better access to the wounds. There were more long, deep gashes from Alannah's talons all over his body, along with a few puncture wounds that had mostly like come from her beak. It was clear that the healers had done what they could, but none of them had Cian's gift. I cleaned each injury, Cian coming behind me and using his gift to begin knitting the marred flesh back together. Once he'd done as much as he could, Cian took a step back from Bran's pallet. He was pale and his hands shook with fatigue.

"I'll rebandage his wounds," I said. "You take a moment."

He didn't argue with me, nodding before slumping down onto the ground. Emer brought me fresh bandages and I set to work. Cian had at least already almost fully healed the wounds on Bran's face with only the faintest of scars remaining along the right side of his nose as evidence of his brush with death.

"I'll have to wait until tomorrow to continue," Cian said, scrubbing a hand over his face as I tied off the bandage on Bran's leg. "His body needs rest anyway."

"As do you," I said, giving him a pointed look.

"Trust me, I know," he replied with a weak, wry smile.

"I'd like to sit with him for a while," I said, covering Bran's legs with a blanket once more.

"I had a feeling that would be the case. I'll let the healers know."

"I'll see about getting you something to sit on, Seren," Emer said, having gone to stand in the shadows a few feet away.

"Thank you," I told her.

I settled down on the ground beside Bran's bedroll for the time being, taking his hand again. Cian got to his feet and walked over. He gently placed a hand on my shoulder, causing me to look up at him.

"He's going to be alright," he said. "His body just needs time to heal."

I nodded and Cian gave my shoulder a squeeze before leaving with Emer. I rubbed at my aching chest after they left, gazing down at Bran. I worried how much time we truly had. How long would it be before Fianna struck again? Its power only seemed to be growing.

And now the one weapon we did have is in shambles, I thought, my jaw clenching as I thought back to Drystan ruining Rhonwen's bow. In theory, at least, it could be re-strung like any other bow. I knew how to do that, though part of me worried it might be more of a challenge with Rhonwen's otherworldly weapon. Releasing a long, low breath, I rolled my shoulders, trying to rid myself of the ache that had settled in them from holding them so tightly. One thing I knew for certain: I wasn't going back home to Clogwyn. The Spirits had sent me here for a purpose. Nothing, and no one, would keep me from it.

CHAPTER 32

HOPE AND DESIRE

Bran

I HAD DANCED FAR too close to death after my fight with Alannah. Thanks to Cian's treatment, my injuries had greatly improved, though I had been left with a few scars, and I had been able to leave the healing tent last night. At Seren's insistence, I'd joined her in her tent, her quarters much larger than mine had been.

The two of us were sprawled out on a pair of joined sleeping pallets, one of my arms wrapped around her while she slept with her head on my shoulder, our legs tangled together under the blankets. Having her in my arms was something I vowed to never take for granted again. Outside, I could see the first hints of light through the small slits around the edge of the tent flap, a sure sign that dawn was breaking and the camp would be bustling with activity soon.

I shifted some and tried not to wake Seren in the process. She needed her rest; her dreams and her visions had been especially troubled these last few days. According to Cian, I should be ready to return to my duties in another day or two. While I was more than ready to resume my hunt for Lorcan, I was also uncomfortably aware that Seren would not be in this place for much longer.

Drystan wanted her out of his camp. Though I knew she had no intention of returning to the castle—she'd told me that much when she had told me about Rhonwen's bow—Drystan had made it clear she wouldn't be tolerated here a moment longer than was necessary. For now, Cian had been able to argue that he needed her assistance with the large number of wounded, but that argument wouldn't hold forever. Regardless of where Seren went, we would be separated once more. She had her promises to keep to the Spirits and I had servants of Fianna to hunt. Letting out a quiet sigh, I noticed she was beginning to stir.

"Good morning," I murmured, pressing a kiss to her cheek.

"Good morning." She brushed a few strands of tangled hair back behind her ear as she stifled a yawn.

"How did you sleep?"

"Better than last night." She paused, biting her lower lip as her gaze flitted to Rhonwen's bow laying on the ground a few feet away. "I just wish I could fix it. I have to."

"You will," I told her, cupping the side of her face. "I know you will."

I had heard the story of how Drystan had doubted her words and broken the weapon. Seren had been relentless in trying to re-string it, something that should have been a simple enough task, but thus far, every attempt had failed. I believed her and the claims she made regarding the bow, no matter how far-fetched it all seemed. Seren had more of a direct connection to the Spirits than any of us because of her gift, and Domhnall and Cian had both borne witness to her killing a shadow creature with the bow. Drystan was blinded by his arrogance and his pride, as always.

"How are *you* feeling?" Seren asked, tilting her head as she searched my face.

"Considerably better after Cian's treatment last night," I answered.

"Good. I came far too close to losing you."

Her voice caught on the last word and I pulled her to me. It had been too close. We'd already lost each other once because of the Purge. I couldn't bear to lose her again. The longer I held her, the more that thought resonated in me. What I wanted more than anything else was a life with her. I didn't want to rush or push her, but I loved her. There would never be anyone else for me. Not after her.

"Ren," I said, taking a deep breath before putting enough distance between us so that I could look down at her. "Marry me."

Her breath hitched, her lips slightly parting as she stared up at me. I winced, the gravity of what I had just blurted out rushing over me. There would be obstacles before us if we were to enter such a union, considerable ones. Ones that she might not want to have to face.

"Not that you have to," I added. "I know the decree your father passed during the Purge. I just..." I cleared my throat, the back of my neck heating. "That night when I was lying in the forest, thinking that I would die there, I couldn't stop thinking about the life I wanted to share with you. And about how much I love you. I know everything has gone so fast but I—"

She cut me off with a kiss, wrapping an arm around my neck and pulling me close. I let out a groan as I opened my mouth to hers, working a hand into her hair. We didn't need words in a moment like this one and as my mouth moved over hers, I tried to tell her with everything that I was just how much she meant to me. I tried to express to her the hope and desire she ignited inside me. When we were forced to part for air, she rested her forehead against mine, her eyes fluttering shut as the softest of smiles played across her face.

"Yes," she whispered before opening her eyes to meet my gaze. "And while I don't give a damn about my father's ridiculous decree, I know he'll do everything in his power to stop us. He'll say it's too dangerous, try and make it about the safety of the clan. I don't want to give him that opportunity."

I pressed my lips together, hating the bitter taste in my mouth. It would be against the laws of the clan for us to wed. Seren could wind up in the dungeons, or worse, and as for me, I could be executed on the spot. The law against shifters marrying was one of the first Cadfael had put forth at the start of the Purge and as far as I knew, he'd never repealed it.

"We marry in secret," she said. "Away from the castle. We tell no one. Not until I'm Ri and I can change things."

I swallowed hard, knowing the wisdom of her plan, even with the slight twinge of regret squeezing my chest. It would hurt to not have my father present and I hated for Seren that those she loved, such as her mother and Sioned, wouldn't be present at such a joyous occasion. But she was right. We couldn't risk anything else. Not until she was Ri of Blaidd.

"You're sure you want to do this?" I asked. There was a gravity, and a deep danger, to the choice we were making. I didn't want her to feel coerced or trapped in any way.

"Yes. So long as you're willing."

I kissed her again, my touch firm and sure. I would marry her no matter what stood against us. My devotion to her was something I never wanted her to doubt.

"I suppose we should get planning, then," I said, pressing a featherlight kiss to her forehead before easing away from her.

"We'll need a village elder, someone we can trust. Preferably someone who doesn't know you or me, although I know that part might be more difficult." She paused, worrying her lower lip. "I know it's a risk to involve anyone else, but I believe we can trust Cian. He'll keep our secret and he's been in the north enough with the war band over the last few years; he's bound to know some of the nearby elders reasonably well."

"I agree." I knew she trusted Cian explicitly and he'd given me no reason to doubt him since my return to Clogwyn. "Whatever the future holds, we're going to face it together. I love you."

"And I love you," she said. "With everything that I am."

Our lips met again and in moments, I was lost to her touch and her kisses. The rest of the clan could think what they wished, but I knew in the depths of my soul that I was hers and she was mine. We were a part of each other, connected in a way that was as old as time itself. My future was with her. It always would be.

CHAPTER 33

A NEW FUTURE

Seren

I HAD SAID YES to marrying Bran. A year ago, I never would have believed such a thing would come to pass, and yet nothing had ever felt more right. As the two of us stepped out of my tent, I couldn't keep the smile off my face. We'd had a late breakfast this morning, finding ourselves a bit distracted in bed after Bran's unexpected proposal, not that I had any complaints. Our morning of bliss, however, had come to an abrupt end when Emer had shown up at my tent, telling us that Lewella wished to speak to the both of us.

There was a slight quiver in my stomach as Bran and I walked through the camp. I held Bran's hand as we walked, wondering if Drystan had finally decided to force me out of this place. He had certainly made no efforts to hide how much he resented my presence. As we went deeper into the camp, my sense of unease grew, leaving me worrying that more was wrong than merely Drystan's current vendetta against me. There were noticeably less tents, horses, and warriors, as if half the camp had up and left in the middle of the night.

"Do you think another attack?" I asked, my grip on Bran's hand tightening. "One that caused Drystan to split up the warriors?"

"I don't know," Bran said, his mouth turning down as he, too, surveyed the scene. "But Lewella should know more."

We continued on our way to Lewella's tent and I tried to ignore the growing quiver in my belly. Fianna was still out there, as was Lorcan. When we reached Lewella's quarters, she ushered us inside and to my surprise, Cian and Domhnall were both already present. Cian wore a grim expression and Domhnall looked as unnerved as I felt, causing my stomach to twist itself into more knots.

"I'm sure you've noticed the changes in the camp this morning," Lewella said. "Drystan felt he had a lead on Lorcan and he's split the warriors. He's taken half of them south toward Beag and left the rest under my command to stay put here for the time being."

"What lead does he think he's found?" Bran asked, skepticism coloring his tone as his brow furrowed.

"A mercenary was taken captive by a farmer outside of Beag and claims to have been working for Lorcan," Lewella replied, pressing her lips together, her tone flat.

"You think it's too convenient." Bran cocked his head.

"Don't you?" Lewella said, raising her brows before letting out a frustrated sigh. "What we need more than anything else is reinforcements, but Ri Cadfael will not send them."

"My father seems to believe he has already won," I said, unable to keep the disgust from my tone. "I do not wish to say this, but I greatly question what aid, if any, will come from Castle Clogwyn."

"The council still does not press him?" Lewella asked, her gaze flitting from me to Domhnall.

"There are only two of us on the council willing to do so," Domhnall replied. "And Drystan's blind loyalty is a considerable obstacle. The Ri and the warrior chief of Blaidd have always exerted the most influence over the war band and right now, the two of them are of the same accord."

"I fear that from what I have heard from Drystan of late, he also shares the ridiculous belief that this battle is already won." Lewella rubbed her temples.

"Would numbers truly make that big of a difference?" Domhnall asked.

"It is one of the few things that might make any difference at all," Lewella answered. "Lorcan has advantages over us; advantages like those damn shadow creatures. One of them is worth two dozen warriors, at least. Still, if we were able to overwhelm him to the point of crushing him, we might be able to get the upper hand."

"And what if you had something to destroy the creatures?" Cian said, casting me a sidelong glance.

"I'm not as much of a skeptic as Drystan, as far as that is concerned," Lewella replied. "Which is why I am more than willing for you to stay here for the time being, Seren. We might just have use for that bow."

My stomach clenched, a strange mixture of relief and dread filling me. More time here without the threat of being cast out would be a reprieve, but I still hadn't fixed the bow. I had tried everything I knew to re-string it, but nothing had worked. I had even pleaded to the Spirits for guidance but had been met with silence. Still, I wasn't giving up just yet.

"I have no intentions of returning to Clogwyn anytime soon," I said.

Bran reassuringly squeezed my hand while Domhnall shifted his weight before clearing his throat.

"If you truly believe that numbers would help this cause," he said, focusing on Lewella. "While I can make no promises, as her feelings toward Cadfael markedly shifted in the wake of the Purge, I would be willing to ride north and speak to my mother. I doubt a being like Fianna will stop at seizing control of just Blaidd, and if there is one thing Mother does care about, it is protecting her borders. Blaidd can't risk this fight becoming some sort of stalemate, much less losing it."

I couldn't stop my sharp intake of breath and Lewella and Emer's eyes both widened. It was a considerable offer that Domhnall had put forth, and a potentially powerful one.

"If you would be willing, I would not say no to warriors from Seabhac," Lewella replied. "And while Drystan will most likely be insulted by such a force, he also is not going to dare jeopardize our good relationship with Ri Muireann by turning them away."

"Then I will ride north," Domhnall replied, "and see if I can sway my mother to concern herself with Blaidd's troubles."

Bran and I excused ourselves while Lewella and Domhnall began to discuss the details of involving Ri Muireann and her warriors. Cian left the tent just behind us and after he ducked through the tent flap, I placed a hand on his arm to stop him.

"If we can speak with you," I said, lowering my voice. "Privately."

Cian arched a brow but nodded, the three of us walking off to the camp's outskirts. We eventually came to a stop by an isolated line of trees, mere feet away from the river. For a moment, as we stood by the gently flowing water with the chirps of birdsong filling the air and the sun's warm rays beaming down on my skin, I could almost begin to hope again. If Domhnall could gain his mother's aid, if we weren't reliant on my father doing what was right, if I could fix the bow, perhaps peace *could* return to Blaidd. The clan could move toward a new future and Bran and I could be a part of that by tying ourselves together through marriage.

First, however, we had to actually wed. I took a deep breath, focusing on Cian. "We wish to marry."

To my relief, Cian grinned. "I had a feeling that was coming."

"And we wish to do so here," I said. "In secret. Away from Father."

Cian pursed his lips but gave a slow nod. "Because of the decree?"

"Yes," I answered, hesitating slightly. Father's decree could mean trouble for Cian if he was found to have aided us. Bran's grip on my hand tightened, as if he too picked up on my tension. "Can you help?"

"Of course," Cian replied. "I would be happy to. And I mean that wholeheartedly. Though I hate to say it, I think the trouble will be finding someone willing to wed the two of you, what with the punishments Uncle Cadfael has put forth for such things. I've heard Lewella speak of the village elder in Dearg, that she's a woman who is willing to look the other way at times, for the right reasons. I could ask Lewella to help me get in contact with her. That is, if you would be alright with Lewella being involved?"

I glanced over at Bran. "I trust her. And Emer."

"I would be also," Bran said with a nod. "How soon do you think you could speak to this elder?"

"By tonight, perhaps," Cian replied. "The village isn't far. Not that I think either of you are incapable of planning this, but I'd like to see it to it for you." He paused and smiled again. "You can consider it my unofficial wedding gift."

I pulled him into a hug, a slight thickness settling in my throat. He had always been more like a brother to me, especially since losing Eamon. To have him offer to do such a thing, to have his support, meant much.

"Thank you," I told him as I stepped back.

"And thank you from me as well," Bran said, the two of them embracing and clasping each other's shoulders.

Cian bid us farewell, promising to speak to Lewella and Emer in private about the matter, and as he strode back into the camp, Bran took both of my hands in his, gently turning me toward him.

"You're certain you wish to do this?" he asked.

"Yes," I answered, holding his gaze. "I've never been more certain about anything."

He leaned down and kissed me and I closed my eyes, savoring both the blissful moment and his touch. I didn't want a life without him, and I wanted no one but him. Blaidd would have a new future, and that future would start with us.

CHAPTER 34

AS OLD AS TIME ITSELF
Seven

IN THE END, CIAN, with a little help from Lewella, came through for us far faster than I would have ever imagined. The night after Bran proposed, the two of us found ourselves standing outside the home of the village elder of Dearg, the darkness of the night and our cloaks hopefully hiding us from any prying eyes. I held tightly to Bran's hand, trying to quell my nerves as we stood at the back door of the elder's home. I wanted to do this—I loved Bran—but there was a part of me that still feared someone would try and stop us. Not that I would let them.

Bran gave my hand a gentle squeeze and I loosened my grip some, releasing a long breath. It was late and we'd seen no one when we'd ridden in on our borrowed mount, my beloved Ceol, with his distinctive dun coat, left behind in an effort not to draw too much attention to ourselves. Bran had knocked twice on the door already, but there had yet to be an answer. I hoped the elder hadn't had a change of heart. I knew that Cian had given the elder, Ceridwen, scant details regarding us and our situation, but with the risks to her, he'd felt it only fair to inform her that she would be handfasting a shifter.

"You can change your mind, you know," Bran said softly. "I don't want you to feel forced into this."

I shook my head, looking up and holding his gaze.

"I want you," I told him. "I want this."

The back door suddenly opened, causing the two of us to start. An older woman stood on the other side, dressed in a dark grey gown. The smile she gave us, along with the friendly sparkle in her green eyes, did much to put me at ease.

"Come inside," she said, stepping back and motioning for us to enter. "My apologies if you had to wait. I'm afraid these ears don't hear as well as they used to. I'm Ceridwen. You are Lewella's friends, yes?"

"Yes," I replied as we stepped through the door. "Thank you for being willing to do this."

"I'm always happy to join two people in love," Ceridwen replied. "No matter who they might be. This way, if you will."

She led us down a narrow hallway and into a great room. Candles had been lit, giving the space a dim but intimate light. Ceridwen gathered the thin cord that would be used to bind our hands in the handfasting before walking back over to us.

"Shall we begin?" she asked.

Bran and I voiced our agreement, the two of us holding out our right arms at her instruction. Ceridwen began to speak the familiar words of the handfasting, binding our souls and bodies as our mortal selves were bound to the land and our spirit selves to the Spirit Realm, and a sense of rightness settled over me. I held Bran's gaze as Ceridwen bound our hands together with the cord. As we were tied together in the most intimate of ways, the cord took on an odd golden glow. The moment was so brief, I almost wondered if I'd imagined it, but still I clung to what I'd seen, hoping it was the Spirits' way of giving their own approval of our union. My voice didn't waver when it was my time to pledge my part of our bond, and neither did Bran's when he did so in return. I didn't care what my father, or anyone else, thought. I loved Bran, and he was no monster. He had my heart completely and he always would.

"I wish the two of you many years of happiness together," Ceridwen said as she unbound our hands, the handfasting complete.

"Thank you," I replied, unable to keep the smile off my face.

"It was my pleasure." She smiled in return. "It is clear the Spirits meant for the two of you to be bound together in such a way."

Bran took my hand in his and Ceridwen saw us out, the two of us thanking her again before we stepped back out into the darkness. Though part of me wished to, I knew we couldn't linger. We needed to get back to camp if we wished to keep what we had done a secret. I tugged Bran along back toward our mount, tied in the woods behind Ceridwen's home, but before we reached the mare, Bran gently pulled me to a stop. I looked up at him expectantly, the moonlight that drifted down through the breaks in the trees highlighting his features.

"Ren, I..." He ducked his chin, roughly clearing his throat before he looked back up again, a glimmer of moisture in his eyes. "I'd always hoped for the chance to have a family of my own. Even after the Purge, even when I threw my lot in with Lorcan. To have one with you, that's a gift I thought I would never get."

I claimed his lips with my own, my heart swelling with love for him as I wrapped my arms around his neck and he pulled me close. He kissed me in a way that left me aching for more. How I wished we had more than a few stolen moments tonight.

"I love you," I said, slightly out of breath as we parted for air. "There's no one else I would want to share this life with."

He trailed kisses down my neck, the touch of his lips on my skin igniting a warmth inside me and causing a shiver of anticipation to trail down my spine. I couldn't help but silently curse that tonight we would have to spend most of our night traveling back to the camp in order to arrive before dawn.

"We should get going," I said, unable to hold back a sigh. "We have a long ride back."

"We do," he replied, flashing me a mischievous smile. "One that can wait until morning."

"Morning?" My brow wrinkled as I tilted my head.

"Cian arranged a little surprise for us."

"What sort of surprise?"

"A good one." He gave me one more lingering kiss before walking over to the mare and untying her. "Shall we?"

Though he'd untied the horse, he didn't mount, instead motioning for me to come walk along beside him.

I frowned. "Are we riding?"

"We're walking."

Thoroughly perplexed but willing to trust him, I joined him and took his offered hand. We walked back onto the dirt road that went through the main part of the village, the moon lighting our way. My confusion deepened when we came to a stop outside a tavern. Candlelight glowed in one of the windows, but the place looked closed up for the night. To my surprise, an older man came from around the back. Upon getting Bran's name, he took our horse and informed Bran that the tavern owner awaited us inside.

"What is all of this?" I asked as I followed Bran up the steps.

"A little arrangement from Cian, with a little help from Ceridwen, from what I understand. We have a room for the night; we just have to be back by a little after sunrise."

My breath caught, gratitude for our friends overwhelming me and leaving tears stinging my eyes. Bran slipped an arm around my shoulder as we stepped into the tavern and my pulse raced with the thoughts of what a night of privacy with my now husband could entail. The tavern owner awaited us just inside the door, Bran giving his name again before the red-haired woman passed us a key. She gave us a room number and motioned toward a small staircase before leaving us on our own.

Bran and I climbed the short flight of steps, wandering down a narrow hallway before coming to a room. He unlocked the door, ushering me inside ahead of him, and I took in the space that was to be ours for the next few hours. It was a simple room, with one bed wedged up against the far wall. A window gave a view of the distant Ioliare mountains, barely visible as looming shadows in the darkness of night. A few candles had been lit, letting me also make out a small chair and table shoved in one corner. Simple quarters, but clean and well cared for.

"I know it isn't much," Bran said as he came up beside me.

"It has a bed," I replied, smiling as I cast him a sidelong glance. "And privacy. I would say that's more than enough. Of course, in the past, you *have* proven to be a bit more creative than I've perhaps given you credit for."

The grin he gave me as he closed the space between us sent my heart racing all over again.

"Perhaps you would like to see just how creative I can be?" he said, taking my face in his hands.

"I can't think of a better way to spend the night," I whispered before his lips covered mine.

His touch consumed me and I gave in to my desire for him, my hands sliding up his back underneath his shirt. His hands were in my hair, his kisses taking my breath away. We broke apart long enough to tug his shirt off and as soon as it hit the floor, his mouth was on mine once more. I pressed my body against his, feeling more alive than I had ever felt in my twenty years, the two of us giving into a dance that was as old as time itself. Tonight was a gift that was not meant to be wasted.

CHAPTER 35

A Storm Ahead

Alannah

I MISSED AENGUS. IT was strange, this feeling of want and aching, so similar and yet different than what I'd felt when I'd lost my parents. It had been almost five days since I'd last seen him and I found that he invaded my thoughts at every turn. I hadn't wanted to leave him and as I stood in my hovel in the middle of the Spirit-forsaken Ioliare mountains, I couldn't help but think of the comforts of Aengus' home in Beag.

As if there is even such a thing as comfort here, I thought, stirring the pot over the hearth with a bit too much force. I'd caught a rabbit on my return from scouting for Lorcan and was using the meat along with a few scrounged plants to make a semblance of a soup. It was pathetic compared to the hearty meals I'd enjoyed with Aengus.

You will have those comforts soon. Patience. Fianna's words whispered into my thoughts and I let out a low breath, slowing my movements. Though it had not divulged the details to me,

I knew the Stag Spirit had plans. Something big was coming, something bigger than anything it had done before.

For now, however, I had to follow along with Lorcan's plotting, biding my time until Fianna was ready to make its move and I was reunited with Aengus. I'd spent all day watching and following Drystan and his warriors, as I'd done for the last three days. The man Dara had planted had lured the warrior chief into splitting his forces and had then led Drystan and his warriors on a chase into Ioliare. The past few months of fighting had already weakened Drystan, and the treacherous mountains would weaken him further. I had already seen glimpses of it. Lorcan would soon catch himself a captive more prizeworthy than even Cadfael's daughter. As much of a bastard as Cadfael was, I didn't see him sitting idly when I swooped into Castle Clogwyn with word that Lorcan had captured the clan's warrior chief.

I knew that once Cadfael was dead, Lorcan intended to seat himself as Ri in Castle Clogwyn, but I also knew that was not the end game Fianna had planned. It would be Aengus who would become Ri of Blaidd, one way or another, and it would be me who became his Banrion.

That particular thought soothed me and I took a deep breath. My few moments of calm, however, were short lived. Dara stalked into the hut, the canvas flap swinging behind him with the force with which he'd pushed through it. His jaw was clenched and his shoulders were taut as he broodily threw himself down in a nearby chair.

"Some sort of problem?" I asked him, glancing over my shoulder and raising a brow.

"Just a disagreement with Lorcan," he replied. "Damn idiot always thinks his little *connection* with the Spirits somehow outweighs my years of tactical experience."

I made a noncommittal noise, turning back to the soup. This was a long-standing fight between the two men. I certainly wasn't interested in getting in the middle of it. An awkward silence fell between us and I focused on the pot of bubbling liquid. It at least didn't smell completely vile. Behind me, I heard Dara shift in his seat.

"You've been avoiding me," he said.

The edge in his tone made me stiffen. I *had* been avoiding his bed, but I'd been hoping he'd been so busy with Lorcan that he wouldn't notice. It was Aengus' kisses and touch I wanted, not Dara's, but I wasn't quite ready to give up my more convenient lover. Not until Aengus was fully mine.

"Ever since you got back from the healer's." He paused, the tension in the air thick. "Did you think I wouldn't notice?"

I shrugged. "I've been busy. You know how Lorcan has been making me watch Drystan's every move."

"That never stopped you before."

I shrugged again, hoping he'd drop the conversation, and tasted the soup. As I did so, I made a slight face. Bland, again. Not even the rabbit had been able to bring the flavor I'd hoped for.

"What does a pathetic little healer have that I don't?" Dara got up from the chair and my muscles tensed in response as he came up behind me. I refused to acknowledge him. Refused to admit that he unnerved me tonight. He was often more brawn than brains, but his brawn was formidable.

"I think," he said, bringing his lips close to my ear as he took a hold of my shoulder, his grip tight enough to make me wince, "that you are playing games you shouldn't be playing. I was going to offer to take care of you, you know. When this was all over. But now..."

He made his last words sound like a threat, but I refused to be baited by him, continuing to stir the soup even as his fingers dug into my skin.

"You assume that I need someone to take care of me."

"Lorcan knows you've been up to things you shouldn't," he said, his tone cold. "You should think about who can protect you and provide for you once he takes his place as Ri."

"Maybe I already have."

He went to yank me back toward him, but a sizzling hiss popped in the air, along with the swirl of Fianna's darkness. Dara yanked his hand away as if he'd been burned, cradling it as he muttered a string of curses under his breath. My heart raced and my palms had grown sweaty, but I knew Fianna was here, protecting me from his wrath; I could feel it. Letting out a low growl, he turned on his heel and stalked off to his room.

I released a low breath after he disappeared, rubbing my stinging shoulder. I hadn't pegged him for one to get posses- sive. Our arrangement had been one of convenience, nothing more. In truth, he had no right to demand more. Even worse to assume that I would ever agree to be beholden to him. *What does Aengus have that he doesn't?* I thought with disgusted snort. *Easily ten years or less in age, for starters. Not to mention a far superior temperament.*

And Aengus will be Ri, I reminded myself. *Not Lorcan.* De- spite my silent reassurance, a quiver still settled in the pit of my stomach. I didn't know how Fianna planned to bring that about. Would I be forced to contend with Lorcan's vengeance and Dara's jealousy before that came to pass? Worst of all, was Lorcan onto my strange new connection with the Stag Spirit, despite my lack of blood oath?

Lorcan is nothing compared to me. Fianna's rasping voice filled my thoughts, easing some of the tension in my stomach. *There is a storm ahead, but you will weather it. As will Fionn's bastard.*

I breathed in deeply before letting my breath out slowly, pulling the soup off the fire. I *would* be Banrion one day and when I was, I would make Dara, and Lorcan, regret their threats.

CHAPTER 36

ILL TIDINGS

Bran

I WOKE BEFORE SEREN, hints of dawn's light just starting to show through our room's one small window. We hadn't slept much last night, but I didn't regret a moment of it, even when I yawned hard enough to pop my jaw. Seren was curled up next to me, nestled under the blankets with her blond hair splayed out across a pillow. I knew we needed to get back to camp, but I wasn't ready to leave behind the bliss we had found in this place.

For a few precious moments, it was like I could almost forget the looming threats and darkness. As I looked at Seren, I found myself trying to memorize every inch of her. *My wife.* Those words still felt strange even as they filled me with contentment. The future I had dreamed of, the one we'd both longed for, was finally within our grasp.

But you do not have it quite yet, I reminded myself. *Not while Fianna roams unchecked.* Fianna and Lorcan were still out there, none of us could afford to forget that. I gently rubbed Seren's back, pressing a kiss to her bare shoulder. She stirred, letting out a quiet grumble as she opened her eyes and rolled over to face me. She'd never been a morning person, something I'd always found oddly endearing.

"Morning already?" she asked with a frown.

"Unfortunately," I answered, brushing another kiss across her brow.

Letting out a sigh of her own, she moved closer to me, resting her head on my chest as her body pressed up against mine. Her closeness was almost enough to make me ignore the reality awaiting us outside, especially when she lightly traced one of the scars I bore from my fight with Alannah.

"Keep that up and we're never going to get out of here," I said, briefly closing my eyes as a shiver of pleasure coursed through me.

"If only." Her tone was wistful and she released another long sigh. "We do have to get back though."

"I know."

We reluctantly disentangled ourselves from one another and rolled out of bed. My gaze lingered on her as we dressed. We were one step closer to the future we'd dreamed of. The obstacles that still stood in our way—mainly Fianna, Lorcan, and Cadfael—were formidable, but I wouldn't give up now. And I knew she wouldn't either.

Once we were ready, we made our way out of the tavern hand in hand. It was early enough that most of the guests hadn't yet begun to stir and to my relief, no questions were asked of us by the tavern owner when we departed.

The sun had fully broken on the horizon when we reached the stable. We worked together to ready our mount and soon we were riding off down the dirt road that led out of the village. I let Seren take control of the horse, since she was the more skilled rider of the two of us, and as soon as we were back out on the main road, Seren urged the mare into a gallop.

We passed through open fields and patches of forest as we traveled, not seeing another soul as the sun continued its ascent in the sky. The temperature was warming after the coolness of the night before and the light fog blanketing the ground hinted at a warmer day ahead. As the horse galloped on, my thoughts kept flitting to the current state of the war band. I shared Lewella's unease over what Drystan had done and I wasn't entirely sure how much warriors from Seabhac would truly help, if Domhnall were even successful in gaining his mother's agreement. Fianna still had its shadow creatures and without Rhonwen's bow, we had no way to defeat them.

Suddenly, Seren's body went rigid, jerking me out of my thoughts, and my stomach clenched at the realization that she was having a vision. I released one arm from around her waist and grabbed the mare's reins. I wasn't able to pry them out of Seren's hands, her body stiff as stone, but I was able to bring the mare down to an abrupt halt.

The horse tossed her head, not appreciating my lack of softness, and I murmured an apology to the creature as I struggled to keep Seren steady in the saddle. A few agonizing minutes passed before the Spirits released their grip on her. When she came to, she was gasping for breath, tremors wracking her body as she slumped against me.

"Easy, Ren," I murmured, holding her waist firmly to keep her from sliding out of the saddle as the horse shifted underneath us.

She let out a shuddering breath, her voice wavering as she spoke. "My father..." She choked, swallowing hard before continuing. "I think he's in danger. I think Fianna is planning something, something greater than what it's done before."

Her foreboding words made my stomach clench.

"Do you want me to take control of the horse?" I asked.

Taking a deep breath, she straightened and squared her shoulders. "I'll manage, but thank you."

I didn't argue with her, releasing my hold on the reins. If she said she could manage, she could. Once again, she urged the mare into a gallop, the horse carrying us onward through the woods, the trees a green blur as we raced past them. Whatever Seren had seen had been enough to frighten her, and she didn't scare easily. If whatever she'd seen in the Spirit Realm had shaken her, it didn't bode well for the rest of us.

By the time we arrived at the gnarled old oak where we'd agreed to meet Cian, the mare was breathing hard. He was awaiting us underneath the boughs of the old tree, having earlier agreed to help us slip back into the camp unnoticed. He greeted us with a smile as Seren brought the mare to a halt. There was something forced about his cheerful expression, however, and I couldn't help but notice the heavy dark circles under his eyes and the paleness of his features.

"Everything go well?" Cian asked as he joined us.

"It did," I answered, slipping out of the saddle behind Seren.

"Thank you," she said as she pulled Cian into a hug. "All of you. Especially for last night."

"We were happy to do it," Cian replied but the smile on his face faded as the two of them eased apart. "I'm afraid Lewella needs to speak to the two of you at once, though. And I do not think that it is good news."

Seren pressed her lips together into a thin line. "I feared as much."

Cian raised his brows, fixing her with an expectant look.

"I had a vision," she said, visibly swallowing. "Early this morning. Fianna is on the move. I fear there is no time to waste."

Cian led the way back to the camp with Seren and me trailing behind him. My thoughts raced as we stepped out of the trees and back into the rows of canvas tents, countless dangerous and deadly scenarios coming to mind. The camp at least didn't appear to have been through any sort of battle or fire, but that didn't mean an attack hadn't already happened somewhere else. *All the more reason to take advantage of Drystan's absence,* I thought. I would push Lewella to let me go out on my own to hunt Lorcan. Spirits knew she was far more reasonable than the warrior chief was.

When we reached Lewella's tent, we were immediately ushered in. She stood inside with four other warriors that I recognized as other high-ranking members of the war band. The five of them were in deep conversation and I could hear the tension in their voices as well as feel it in the very air. Seren's jaw was clenched as she stood next to me, her features slightly pale. I thought back to her vision. Whatever she had seen had unnerved her and I deeply worried it could spell disaster for us all. Once Lewella had finished talking with the warriors, she sent them on their way before turning to us, grimacing slightly as she walked over.

"The handfasting went well?" she asked, the forced cheer in her voice noticeable, along with the deep wrinkle in her brow.

"It did," Seren answered. "Thank you all for what you did for us last night."

"I was happy to," Lewella said, her smile strained. "I'm only sorry to be the bearer of bad news in what should be a happy moment. Three warriors arrived back here last night. They're in poor shape, badly wounded by shadow creatures. Cian has stabilized them enough that they can speak and they have said that they are all that remains of the band Drystan took with him into Ioliare. The rest were slaughtered and Drystan was captured. They were spared to deliver Lorcan's message."

Lewella paused, pulling a folded and bloodstained piece of parchment out of her pocket and holding it out to me. "I was hoping you could perhaps confirm that Lorcan is indeed the one behind this."

I took it from her, my chest tight as I unfolded it. I scanned the hastily scrawled words, pressing my lips into a thin line as I read.

"It's not Lorcan's handwriting," I told Lewella as I handed it back to her. "But it is Dara's."

"The mercenary captain?" Lewella asked.

"Yes," I replied. "And I don't think it's a bluff."

"As I feared, then." Lewella grimaced again, putting away the note. "I've sent word to Ri Cadfael, but I cannot leave the warrior chief of Blaidd in the hands of a servant of Fianna."

"Has Domhnall ridden for Seabhac?" Seren asked.

"He has," Lewella answered. "He left yesterday evening. We're close enough to the border that he should be to Castle Ciall by now, but we have no way of knowing if Ri Muireann will even agree to send warriors back with him."

"How many days do you think you can you wait for him?" I asked. Personal feelings against Domhnall aside, Lewella was going to need more fighters, especially if almost half of the warriors posted outside Castle Clogwyn had been killed.

"No more than a day," Lewella replied. "I can't risk Drystan's life any longer than that."

"You've sent word to my father at Clogwyn?" Seren asked.

"I have," Lewella answered. "But I'm hesitant to wait for Ri Cadfael's response. From what the survivors have said, I worry that Lorcan will kill Drystan if he decides that it suits him." She paused, rubbing her brow before turning her attention to Seren. "What is the state of Rhonwen's bow? I have concerns about walking into an inescapable trap with the number of shadow creatures Lorcan was said to have at his disposal."

"Still broken." Seren grimaced. "If you wait a day, it will give me more time."

Lewella pursed her lips. "Will a day be long enough?"

"It will have to be," Seren replied, lifting her chin.

"Whatever resources you need will be at your disposal," Lewella said with a slow nod before looking back over at me. "I want you to go out ahead of the warriors. The survivors claim that Lorcan has specified a place where Drystan can be retrieved if I surrender, but I want his exact location and I want to know exactly what it is we're up against. I assume you will travel quickest if you go on your own, unimpeded?"

"You assume correctly," I answered.

"Good. You'll leave at once."

"Understood," I replied.

She would get no arguments from me. Not only was it a wise move, but it would allow me to do my own snooping and spying as far as Lorcan was concerned. When Lewella and her warriors fought to save their warrior chief, I had every intention to bring about Lorcan's death once and for all.

"Take a few moments with Seren," Lewella said to me. "Then get on your way."

The two of us murmured our thanks before ducking back out of the tent. We walked a little ways away, seeking privacy. The camp was busier now than it had been when we'd first returned, but we found a quiet spot between two nearby tents. As we came to a stop, I took her hands in mine, looking down and holding her gaze. I had to go, and I knew she knew it as much as I did, but part of me still hated parting from her under such circumstances. We hadn't even been married a full day.

"You'll be careful?" she said, a slight catch in her voice.

"I will. I promise." I squeezed her hands. "And you'll fix that bow, Ren. I know it."

"I have to." Her shoulders slumped before she hitched them up again. "We don't have any other choice. We have to have something to defeat those creatures."

I cupped the side of her face, pulling her in for a kiss and pouring as much of my passion and love for her into it as I could, hoping she felt what I didn't have all the words for. That I loved her, I believed in her, and I would do whatever I could to help her and our people.

"I'll come back to you," I said softly as we eased apart. "And we'll keep working toward creating a new future in Blaidd."

"You had better," she said, visibly trying to bring levity to her voice, "especially after I went through all this trouble to marry you."

I chuckled quietly before brushing another kiss over her lips. "I love you."

"And I love you. Come home to me, Bran."

"Always."

She pulled me in for one last kiss, my heart aching as I reluctantly let her go. I took no joy in walking away from her, but I had a servant of Fianna to hunt.

CHAPTER 37

NO MORTAL HANDS

Seren

WE WERE RUNNING OUT of time. If Domhnall did not arrive back to the camp at daybreak tomorrow, Lewella intended to ride out to Ioliare without him. My personal feelings toward Drystan aside, the clan losing its warrior chief would be a deep blow. That wasn't something Blaidd could afford and still, I had not been able to re-string Rhonwen's bow.

I'd tried every material imaginable, even taken the weapon to the bowyer who had been traveling with this part of the war band. Nothing had worked; every bowstring had snapped the moment it was strung. By the time evening began to fall, I was beginning to feel more than a little hopeless.

I worried for Bran, traversing the wilds of Ioliare with Fianna and its creatures on the loose, and I couldn't shake the vision I'd seen earlier in the morning. The one where my father had died, slaughtered by Fianna and its creatures. Whether that future was set in stone or not, I wasn't certain. As far as I knew, Father was still holed up in Clogwyn, but what I had seen had been far too gruesome and horrific to ignore.

In my desperation, I'd taken the bow down to the banks of the Weindio as dusk had begun to fall. It was the Wolf Spirit, after all, who had dug the rivers and lakes of Pern Coen. It had long been tied to water and I hoped that perhaps the rolling waters of the Weindio would help me glean the answers I sought.

Emer stood among the trees a few feet away, leaning up against a tall poplar tree with her longbow in hand and her sword on her hip. Lewella hadn't wanted anyone leaving the camp on their own with the most recent turn of events and Emer had offered to come stand watch while I was down at the river.

As I tried to get comfortable seated on the rocky bank, I was unable to suppress a slight wince. I'd been at this all day with nothing to show for it. The light in the sky continued to dim as the sun slowly set, its strong evening rays glinting off the water. The bow lay beside me, carefully propped up on a grouping of smooth mossy boulders and I allowed myself a soft sigh as I placed my hands over it.

Taking in a deep breath, I closed my eyes, focusing on slowing my breathing. *Please,* I thought. *Just show me something. Some way to fix this.* I was met with nothing but silence, and it was growing more and more difficult to tamp down my mounting frustration. I worked to block out the noises of the outside world, the gurgling of the river and faint chirps of birds, as I sought to separate my soul from my mortal body, seeking my way into the Spirit Realm. A splash broke my concentration and I bit my lip, biting back a curse.

Another splash came from nearby, this one louder than the first. By the time of the third splash, one that doused one of my pant legs with water, I couldn't hold back a muttered oath as my eyes flew open. What I saw in front of me, however, was not at all what I was expecting. A watery paw broke up out of the river. My eyes widened as I scrambled backward, instinctively grabbing the hilt of my dagger as a giant wolf made of swirling water surged out of the river. Behind me, I heard Emer gasp, followed by the thud of an arrow hitting the grass; hers, I presumed. Even though I had seen the Wolf Spirit like this before, my heart still pounded rapidly as it stared down at me with its gleaming blue eyes.

"Please," I said, getting to my feet and holding out the bow. "Tell me what I must do to fix this."

The Wolf Spirit cocked its head, its lips curling back into what almost looked like an amused grin. "Fixing such a weapon is not within your power, Daughter of Blaidd. For it was no mortal hands that made that bow."

I swallowed hard, my stomach churning. There had to be a way to fix it. How were we to stop Fianna without it? Hadn't that been what the Spirits had been telling me?

"You must see the bow to battle," it continued, its gravelly voice rumbling from its chest like thunder. "Its power has been entrusted to you for a purpose."

I nodded, watching the Spirit intensely. It extended one paw and bared its teeth, biting into its front leg before pulling out a strange, glimmering gold cord. My heart continued to pound as the Spirit dropped the cord at my feet. I bent down and picked it up, my mouth going dry as I grasped it in my hands. The sinewy cord glinted gold in the fading sunlight, an object that was strangely familiar to any other sinew used to create bowstrings, and yet also clearly something of the uncanny.

"See it done, Daughter of Blaidd," the Wolf Spirit said, drawing my attention back to it.

It collapsed back into the water and once again, there was nothing more before me than a gently flowing river. I felt heat in my hands, my gaze dropping to the strange golden sinew as its luster and color faded and it became nothing more than an ordinary looking bowstring.

"Spirits," Emer said, her voice coming out strangled as she strode up behind me. "I almost loosed a damn arrow at it. Have you seen it like that before?"

"Once," I said, rubbing the bowstring between my fingers. "When Bran and I were fleeing Lorcan and Fianna." I paused, casting her a sidelong glance with the hint of a smile tugging at my lips. "Can't say I'm even remotely used to it though."

Emer shakily laughed. "At least we'll have that bow on our side."

Pulling out the bow stringer I'd brought with me, I re-strung the bow, sending up a prayer of thanks to the Spirits when the string didn't snap. We wasted no time leaving the river and hurrying back to the camp, both of us eager to let Lewella know that Rhonwen's bow was useable once more. Even though night had fully fallen, I noticed an uptick of activity around the camp and hoped we weren't about to be met with more ill news when we arrived at Lewella's tent.

To my relief, however, it seemed that perhaps, for once, fate was in our favor. Lewella wasn't alone in her tent; she had been joined by Domhnall and what appeared to be two warriors of Seabhac. While the sight of Domhnall and his warrior companions was welcome, it was the sight of Bran standing with them that flooded me with relief. He bore the signs of his no doubt harrowing journey in the stains and streaks on his clothing and the light scruff covering his face, but he had returned to me. Lewella's expression brightened when Emer and I entered, her gaze fixed on the bow.

"It's fixed then?" she asked, gesturing.

"It is," I replied before turning my attention to Domhnall. "Your mother has agreed to lend Blaidd aid?"

"Yes," he said. "She was willing to send a score of warriors."

Hope filled me at the news and the bow gave its strange hum of energy, leaving my hands tingling. The tide was slowly beginning to turn in our favor.

"We'll leave in the morning," Lewella said. "Before dawn. Bran has confirmed that Lorcan does indeed have Drystan and that he is amassing some sort of host, one of more than mere mortals. I fear there's no time to waste."

"I intend to come as well." A wrinkle settled in Lewella's brow at my pronouncement and Domhnall's mouth turned down.

"That's hardly safe," Domhnall said. "It would be wisest for you to remain in one of the villages, perhaps with a warrior to guard you."

"I won't be staying back." I lifted my chin, focusing on Lewella instead of him. She was who I had to convince. Domhnall, nor anyone else for that matter, would have the power to overrule her in Drystan's absence. "I have to go."

"I don't mean to discount you with this," Lewella said, pressing her lips together. "But you *are* the next in line to be Rí of Blaidd and I fear this battle will be a particularly bloody one."

"I'm not staying back." I shook my head. "I can't."

"Seren, you cannot be serious," Domhnall said, letting out an exasperated breath.

"I think that this is Seren's choice, not yours," Bran told him, a steeliness to his tone as he narrowed his eyes at Domhnall.

Domhnall gave a frustrated growl, glowering at Bran in return. "It is far too dangerous and she is no warrior."

I stiffened, my grip on the bow tightening. "Are *you* going?"

"Well, I..." He spluttered, his face slightly reddening. "Of course I'm going."

"And are *you* a warrior?" I pointedly arched a brow, pointing the tip of the bow at him.

"That's entirely different!" he snapped. "My mother expects me to go with the warriors of Seabhac."

"And the Wolf Spirit expects me to go with the warriors of Blaidd," I retorted.

"I heard the Wolf Spirit say that Seren must be the one to take the bow into battle," Emer said, looking pointedly at Lewella. "It's dangerous, true, but I don't think now is the time to be defying the Spirits."

Domhnall's nostrils flared. "The risk involved—"

Lewella held up a hand, clearing her throat and cutting him off. His face flushed even redder and he folded his arms, his scowl deepening.

"Seren will come with us," Lewella said, giving me a slow nod. "This clan has done too much ignoring of the Spirits these last few years. I won't be continuing that."

Domhnall muttered something under his breath but otherwise stayed quiet, and some of my tension dissipated. I didn't wish ill on Drystan, but it was clear that Lewella would be ten times the leader of the war band than he was. I would make certain she got such an opportunity the day I became Ri.

Emer, Bran, and one of the warriors from Seabhac stayed with Lewella while the rest of us were excused from the tent. Domhnall still wore a perturbed expression as we stepped back out into the darkness of night, the camp now lit by various fires and torches. A few of the warriors from Seabhac wandered off with Domhnall's permission, the others going to linger by a nearby fire with what looked like the rest of their small band, while I remained outside Lewella's tent to wait for Bran. I expected Domhnall to go with the warriors, but he didn't, instead staying close to me. He angled himself toward me, laying a hand on my arm.

"Please, Seren," he said, his tone softening. "I beg you to reconsider this."

"This isn't a choice," I told him with a frustrated sigh. "This is something I have to do. Believe me, I am well aware of the kind of danger we will be facing, but I *must* do this. You must understand that."

"I do not want to lose you," He held my gaze as he spoke and there was something in his tone, something in his eyes, that left me wondering if I had perhaps misjudged the depths of his feelings for me.

You're making too much out of nothing, I told myself, shaking off the niggling thoughts. Domhnall had to know the two of us would never be together in such a way. I had affection for him, but not what I shared with Bran; not the impossibly strong sense of rightness that we belonged to each other that welled up from the depths of my soul.

"You won't lose me," I said, placing my hand over his and giving it a squeeze. "I won't be going into this carelessly, I can promise you that."

He opened his mouth to speak again, but one of the lingering warriors from Seabhac called for him. His brows drew in, his features cast in shadows, and he let out a quiet huff.

"I'll be watching out for you every moment," he said. "I swear that to you."

The warrior called for him again and he dropped his hand from my arm before striding off to the crackling fire. I watched him disappear into the shadows, trying to ignore the unsettled feeling that had taken root in the pit of my stomach. His concern, though perhaps borne of good intent, felt smothering. In some ways, it reminded me too much of the overbearingness he had shown after he had first found me with Bran months ago. *But he isn't going to stop me,* I thought, squaring my shoulders and taking in a deep breath. No one would.

The tent flap opened behind me, drawing me out of my thoughts, and I looked over my shoulder. It was Bran. He pulled me into his arms and I buried my face in his chest, soaking up every bit of his presence and his touch.

"I'll be there with you every step of the way," he said, lightly holding onto my upper arms as we eased back slightly from one another. "If the Wolf Spirit has told you that you must go, I won't try and stop you."

I kissed him, my heart swelling with love for him. *This* was why I had married him. This was why I wanted him to forever be at my side.

"I know," I said, holding his gaze. "And I love you for it."

"We should get some rest while we can," he said. "I fear Lewella is right in anticipating an ugly battle ahead. Fianna's power is only growing, as are Lorcan's forces."

There was a quiver in my belly at his words, but there was no turning back from this now. We struck across the camp hand in hand, headed for our tent, the firmness of Bran's grasp reminding me that I would not be alone in this fight. Fianna was the one who needed to take heed, for I was coming for it, with a weapon it should well remember. Rhonwen's bow had defeated the Stag Spirit and its ilk once before. It was time for it to do so again.

CHAPTER 38

DARK DEMANDS

Alannah

CADFAEL WAS COMING. THE sun was setting over the craggy peaks of Ioliare as I swooped down among the green foliage of the tree canopy. My sharp eyesight easily let me spot the horses and riders awaiting me underneath the boughs of the trees and I spread out my wings, extending my feet as I came to land on the soft forest floor.

In seconds, I shifted back into my human form, taking a moment to shake off the hints of wildness that still lingered after my long flight. The horses tossed their heads but didn't spook; they had largely become accustomed to my shifts of form. Lorcan and Dara were seated on the mounts, both men looking at me expectantly.

"What news?" Lorcan asked, his tone impatient as he fidgeted with his reins.

"He is coming," I answered. "Cadfael has left his keep—with his entire war band, from the looks of it. He was a day out, maybe two, the last I saw him."

Lorcan gave a cold smile while Dara shifted in his saddle. Dara didn't carry Lorcan's confident air upon hearing the news. Not that I could blame him. The full war band of Blaidd was a formidable force and Cadfael had clearly been holding back. We'd chipped away at his numbers the last few months and we'd delivered a considerable blow when we'd captured Drystan, but the war band still outnumbered us greatly. *But we have something they don't,* I reminded myself. *We have Fianna.*

"Very good, then," Lorcan said before turning his attention to Dara. "When we return, you will ready the fighters. And make certain that the prisoner is set out as bait."

Dara pressed his lips together, not meeting Lorcan's gaze as his grip on his reins tightened.

"You disagree?" Lorcan's face contorted into a scowl.

"I think it unwise to discount that we're outnumbered," Dara replied, his jaw clenched.

"We are not outnumbered where it counts," Lorcan snapped. "Fifteen shadow creatures is easily the equivalent of a full war band. Perhaps more. You dare doubt Fianna's power?"

Dara didn't answer and I felt the swirling darkness of the Stag Spirit as Lorcan stared intently at the other man. As Dara's face paled and his knuckles grew white, I knew Lorcan was using his gifting, a gifting that could grow even stronger and more persuasive with Fianna's aid when it came to the bending and twisting of minds. After a few tense moments, Dara let out a gasping breath before giving a terse nod.

"Good." Lorcan smirked. "I'm glad we have an accord." He picked up his reins, backing his horse up and wheeling the creature around. "Come. There is no time to waste."

As the two horses took off deeper into the forest, I was forced to quickly shift back into my hawk form, flying back up through the trees until I was high in the sky above them. I wasn't so foolish as to voice them, but I too had my doubts about this plan Lorcan had concocted. Yes, capturing Drystan and taunting Cadfael with his precious warrior chief had finally lured the Ri from his castle, but we would be woefully outnumbered in this battle Lorcan had planned, shadow creatures or not.

You wish to doubt me as well, little mortal? Have I not proven myself to you enough?

The edge in Fianna's voice left a shiver snaking down my spine. I didn't *want* to doubt it, but I had my uncertainties; ones that included how Aengus, not Lorcan, would become Ri of Blaidd. For if Cadfael was killed, I saw nothing stopping Lorcan from trying to make that claim himself. *And then there is no telling what he will do to me,* I thought, my stomach tightening. I hadn't forgotten Dara's warnings that Lorcan was quite possibly onto my connection with Fianna.

Those are not questions for you to concern yourself with, Fianna snarled, a strong, frigid wind almost blowing me off course. *Do not think that I have not orchestrated every step that Lorcan takes.*

And if Lorcan seeks to extract his vengeance on me?

You think I will allow it? It let out a strangled laugh. *Your obedience is all that is required here, little mortal. Do not question things that your kind will never understand.*

If that is what you wish, I replied, trying to tamp down my own frustration at the Spirit's continual vagueness.

It is what I demand. Especially if you wish to become the future Banrion of Blaidd.

Its presence faded, but its words, and its warnings, still rang in my ears. I would have to trust that its plans would come to pass and hope that no ills would befall me in the process.

CHAPTER 39

NOTHING SPARED

Alannah

THE SMOKE WAS SO thick in the air, it should have choked me. Flames raced across the ground, surrounding me on every side, burning everything, and everyone, in their path. But I was untouched, able to breathe and move as freely as if the raging inferno scorching the mountainside of Ioliare wasn't even there. The warriors of Blaidd, however, were not so lucky.

Their screams filled the air over the crackle and roar of the fire, each of them falling to their death whether it be by a mercenary's blade, Fianna's dark flames, or a shadow creature's bite. I gutted another warrior with my blade, preventing the woman from striking Dara's unprotected back as he tangled with another attacker. Blood and soot splattered my clothes and my exposed skin, sweat dripping down my back from the exertion and the heat of the surrounding flames. Cadfael had walked right into our little trap and Fianna was going to make certain we were victorious.

I cut down another warrior, ending the man's rage-filled battle cry by bringing my sword across his throat. He fell at my feet, revealing another warrior being mauled by a shadow creature behind him. The creatures had been in a frenzy since the moment the fire had begun, slaughtering warriors and devouring souls as they went. Another warrior ran up behind me, the man almost getting the upper hand on me until Dara dispatched him.

Come to me at once. Lorcan's voice, angry and harsh, made me start as the now dead warrior dropped to the ground. Lorcan followed his impatient words with images as well to guide me to him through the thick of the battle, showing me that he had cornered Cadfael and was ready to finish him. Dara grabbed me by the arm, yanking me along with him as we barreled through the warriors surrounding us, leaving me assuming that he had received the same instructions from Lorcan.

We battled warrior after warrior as we ran down the smoke-filled mountainside, flames engulfing every single tree, every inch of brush, and every blade of grass we passed. Lorcan continued to guide us using his gift and when we finally reached him, a euphoric feeling sang through my blood.

Cadfael was on his knees, cornered and pinned against a grouping of boulders by two shadow creatures. Blood dripped from their fangs, flames bursting forth from their mouths as they gave keening snarls. They looked more than ready to rip Cadfael apart from limb to limb before feeding on his wretched soul. Lorcan and Cadfael were surrounded by a giant ring of fire, keeping the warriors that so desperately wished to come to their Ri's aid at bay. Dara and I dispatched the ones who tried to get in our way before the two of us passed through the fire completely unscathed.

"So we find the great Cadfael of Blaidd," I said as we joined Lorcan. "Not the conquering hero now, are we?"

Cadfael let out a growl, his eyes blazing with hatred as he went to lurch to his feet, but one of his legs buckled beneath him and a lunging shadow creature sent him scrambling to press his back up against the stones.

"Hold him still," Lorcan said to Dara and me. "I do not want him escaping the ending that he has earned."

I couldn't suppress a cold smile as Dara and I strode over to Cadfael's side. I roughly latched onto one of Cadfael's arms, anticipation flooding me. How long had I waited for this moment? This was the man who had ruined my life and ruined my future. It was his edicts that had made my gifting a crime. It was him who had given my sister the opportunity to betray me for coin. It was high time he paid for the lives he had ruined.

Dara and I took a firm hold of Cadfael and I could feel Fianna's darkness swirling in the air as Lorcan fixed Cadfael with a steely gaze. Cadfael's expression contorted, his pain evident in his features as he gasped and hung his head. I had no doubt Lorcan was using his mind-speaking abilities, especially as Cadfael tried to jerk away from us, but Dara and I held the wretched Ri still, the creatures hissing and screeching as their bloodlust grew.

"You did not spare others." Lorcan spoke aloud, his eyes narrowed and his voice dripping with unsuppressed hatred. "And therefore, I will not spare you."

The shadow creatures both took a few steps toward Cadfael, the Ri of Blaidd shaking as his face paled. Lorcan began to speak in Old Pernish, the creatures lowering their heads to the ground and opening their mouths. Flames shot forth, racing across the ground to Cadfael. He bellowed with fury, fighting to free himself, but the injuries he'd sustained made him weak.

"Fight all you want," I hissed as I yanked him back. "It will not stop you from paying for what you have done."

Fianna's flames engulfed his body while not even touching myself or Dara. Cadfael screamed in agony as the flames devoured him, the disturbing sight enough to raise the hairs on even the back of my neck as Fianna's fire ate him alive. Cadfael's body grew limper and his screams became hoarser until he became such dead weight that Dara and I could hold him no longer. He collapsed onto the ground, the flames continuing to rage until they left behind nothing more than a husk.

Lorcan called the creatures off and then walked over to the singed body. A feral gleam lit his eyes as he yanked the clan ring of Blaidd off Cadfael's charred hand, the piece of jewelry somehow untouched by Fianna's flames. Lorcan held the ring up in front of him, a maniacal grin twisting his features as he slipped it onto his own finger. Once the ring was in place, he turned to face me, the coldness that suddenly filled his eyes making my stomach clench.

"I'm afraid the game is up for you," he said, unsheathing his blade.

"What in the blazes are you talking about?" I retorted, my heart hammering in my chest.

I went to pull out my own sword, only to have my arms wrenched behind my back by Dara. I fought his hold, kicking and screaming at him, but he held fast.

"I know you've been plotting against me," Lorcan said, baring his teeth. "I know how you have sought to twist Fianna to your side to overthrow me, but I will not have it!"

He raised his blade, swinging it at me, but an eldritch shriek that was loud enough to leave a ringing in my ears caused him to falter. The creature screamed in rage and the fire surrounding us vanished, allowing the warriors who had been so desperate to break in and avenge their Ri to race toward us.

Lorcan cursed. "Do not lose her!" he shouted to Dara as the warriors swarmed him.

Dara darted behind the nearby boulders with me in tow. I screamed, fighting him still, biting and clawing at him to try and free myself from his grasp. I wasn't going to let him kill me. Fianna had promised me the future of my dreams; it had promised me the place of Banrion with Aengus at my side. Dara wasn't going to take that from me.

"You're not getting away," Dara growled as he brought a knife to my throat. "Lorcan wants you dead and I will make sure it comes to pass."

I swallowed hard against the cold steel at my throat, my body trembling with rage. He had the upper hand and he knew it. My thoughts raced as I tried to think of a way to break his hold without risking my own neck, but a high-pitched hiss startled me, drawing my attention. A shadow creature slunk around the boulder, its gaze fixed on the two of us as smoke billowed from its nostrils and its ember eyes gleamed.

"Away with you, you foul beast," Dara shouted, kicking at the creature.

I cursed as he did so. His foolish actions would only antagonize the creature further. We might be immune to Fianna's fire, but we weren't immune to attacks from the beasts. The creature screeched, lunging at us with its fangs bared. Dara released me to defend himself, flinging me against the boulder in the process. The side of my head hit the stone so hard, my teeth rattled. I scrambled to my feet as the creature bit into Dara's leg. He let out a painful cry and I turned on my heel, ready to bolt.

For one moment, I thought I would be free of him, but a hand on my wrist yanked me backward. Dara staggered with his injured leg, but he held firm to me, raising his blade. I kicked at his wound, my blow landing true and causing him to slightly loosen his grip, but it wasn't enough. I still couldn't break away from him. He raised his dagger, but out of the corner of my eye, I saw that the creature wasn't done with him yet. It lunged at Dara's back, latching onto his shoulders with its massive claws. He let out a bloodcurdling scream, releasing me at once. I stumbled backward, thrown off balance, only to slam into the rocks again. The back of my head hit the hard stone and the next thing I knew, the world went black.

CHAPTER 40

INTO THE FLAMES

Seren

FROM THE MOMENT WE had ridden out of Dearg, the bow began humming, and by the time we first saw the curling smoke rising up from the trees on the edges of Ioliare, the weapon was vibrating with energy. I gripped it tightly as Ceol trotted through the dense forest, Bran keeping pace at my stallion's shoulder in his wolf form. We were circled by warriors of Blaidd and Seabhac, with Lewella riding just in front of me to lead the way. The smoke left me worrying we had arrived far too late, but there was little to be done for that now.

The air around us grew hotter and a dull roar could be heard as the smoke grew even thicker. Fianna's darkness slithered through the air, making the horses tense and snort. The forest around us, however, remained free of flames—until it didn't. We came around a bend, only to be confronted with a wall of fire, the roaring, sizzling inferno causing the horses to shy in alarm. I fought to keep control of Ceol as Lewella called for us to halt. She cursed, wheeling her stallion around before calling for her commanding warriors and the commanding warrior from Seabhac, Gwydion.

"We'll move forward on foot," she instructed. "The fire will make it too difficult with the horses." She paused, lowering her voice as she looked down at Bran. "Stay with Seren, no matter what."

He barked in response. I fought to ignore the jittery feeling in my chest as I dismounted Ceol, the stallion tossing his head and letting out a loud snort as he warily eyed the raging flames. I stroked his neck, doing my best to calm him. Lewella instructed a small handful of warriors to stay behind with the horses and I handed Ceol off to a warrior who led him away. I took a deep breath as we began to move forward into the flames, Bran practically glued to my side.

The smoke was suffocating and the heat from the flames was almost unbearable. It didn't take long for my eyes to water and I was forced to dodge flaming falling limbs and leaves. In the distance, I could hear the din of fighters and for one horrifying moment, I felt myself freeze. The images around me merged with the images the Spirits had shown me, the fight that had cost the war band of Blaidd, and my father, their lives.

An eldritch screech forced me back to the present and I tensed as a shadow creature came barreling out from between two burning trees. Two warriors loosed arrows at it, but they did nothing to penetrate the creature's smoky hide. I yanked an arrow from Rhonwen's quiver, nocking it on the bow. The creature paid me no heed as I loosed, too focused on attacking the warriors.

My arrow found its mark, digging in deep to the creature's hide and causing it to let out a shriek of pain as it faltered. I grabbed another arrow, loosing again, and as my arrow embedded itself in the creature's chest, it collapsed to the ground. We pressed onward, in moments reaching the fight that Fianna's fire was concealing.

Mercenaries tangled with warriors of Blaidd, warriors that, from the sheer number of them, I knew could have only come from Castle Clogwyn. The churning in my stomach deepened. I knew what I had seen. Father was here and this fight could cost him his life. I had no deep love for him, but I still did not wish him to die at Fianna's hands, nor did I wish to see the entire war band slaughtered. While it was easy to see how outnumbered the mercenaries were, they had something far more powerful than the warriors of Blaidd on their side: shadow creatures.

"Find as many of those things as you can and kill them!" Lewella shouted at me as I felled another one of the creatures with an arrow.

It wasn't nearly as difficult as I would have thought. Killing the creatures with Rhonwen's bow seemed to only draw the rest of them. Another shadow creature barreled toward me with a mercenary at its side. Bran lunged at the mercenary. He latched onto the man's leg with his powerful jaws, throwing him off balance before knocking him to the ground. I hurriedly nocked an arrow, loosing at the shadow creature, my arrow digging into its flank and buying me enough time to dodge out of its way. I loosed a second time, this time driving my arrow into the creature's forehead. It stumbled face-first to the ground, black blood oozing from its injuries as it lay unmoving.

The mercenary that had attacked Bran was also splayed out on the ground, his neck contorted at an awkward angle. Blood marred Bran's grey muzzle, a stark reminder of the toll a day of killing like this would take. Another mercenary came at me, blade swinging, but it was Emer who blocked him this time with her own blade. Bran came to her aid, leaping up to bite into the man's arm. The two of them efficiently dispatched the mercenary and Emer motioned for me to go ahead of her.

"The two of us will cover you," she shouted. "We can't end this without ending those creatures."

I nodded and we pushed our way deeper into the fighting, the creatures seemingly drawn to me as if pulled by some invisible string. But each time my arrows struck, they struck true. Two more creatures fell to my arrows, though one of them had almost latched onto my leg before Bran intervened. Through the smoky haze, I made out three large boulders, surrounded by warriors clamoring to get to them, only to be kept at bay by two shadow creatures. But it was the man on top of the stones, not the creatures, who ultimately drew my focus.

I knew his tall build and half-scarred face. Lorcan stood on top of the boulders, loosing arrows at the warriors beneath while his shadow creatures kept anyone from reaching him. A deep, vicious growl ripped from Bran's throat and my blood heated. Lorcan *would* die today.

I pulled out an arrow, ready to loose it at the creatures, but I stopped short, my gaze drawn to a body crumpled at the foot of the boulders. It was badly burned, but from a distance, the build of what remained of the burned form reminded me too much of my father. I froze, a coldness sweeping over me at the realization that the death the Spirits had shown me might have already come to pass. Father had died by fire in my visions and bile rose in my throat as I found myself unable to look away from the burned body.

A bone-chilling scream, however, broke me from my shock as one of the shadow creatures ripped into a warrior of Blaidd who had tried to breach the boulders. I nocked my arrow and raised the bow, my jaw set as I loosed the arrow at the creature. Lorcan and Fianna were not winning this fight. Not so long as I drew breath. The arrow flew true, hitting the creature in the neck. It screeched, releasing its hold on the warrior as blood spurted from its arrow wound.

Bran slammed into me, knocking me aside. I fell down on one knee just as an arrow dug into the dirt where we had been standing. I glanced over at Emer, relieved to see that she had gotten out of the way as well. When I looked back up at the boulders, Lorcan had his gaze on me and from the hatred gleaming in his eyes, I knew he had seen me and what I had done to his precious monsters.

Something in me snapped as our gazes locked. I was done with this. It was ending today. I took off into the fray of warriors, intent on the last creature. Emer shouted something behind me and Bran let out a series of sharp barks, but I ignored them, my focus solely on Lorcan and his remaining dark beast.

The second I saw my opening to shoot at the creature, I took it. Lorcan saw me, however, forcing me to duck at the last moment to avoid an arrow of his own, which caused my arrow to only graze the creature's side. It was enough to distract it and make it bleed, but hardly enough to kill it. The beast was quick to turn its attention to me, barreling at me with its fangs bared. I fumbled with another arrow, knowing that I wouldn't be able to release it in time, but Bran slammed into the creature's side.

My heart was in my throat as he pinned the creature to the ground, biting into its neck, only to have it lurch back up and fling him aside. I nocked my arrow, my heart pounding as I loosed again. My arrow struck the creature's chest, close enough to its heart to bring it down.

I yanked out another arrow, intent on turning my focus to Lorcan, only to hear a yelp from Bran. An arrow stuck out of one of his shoulders and judging by the vengeful grin Lorcan wore as he stared down at us, he was responsible for Bran's injury. My fury deepened and I loosed my arrow right into Lorcan's own shoulder.

It shouldn't have been a killing blow—it shouldn't have even been a particularly disabling one for a skilled fighter—and yet

Lorcan let out an anguished cry, swaying on his feet before tumbling down off the rocks. He didn't move after he hit the ground and from my position, I could see an unusually large amount of blood soaking his shirt. Bran came over to my side, limping on his injured shoulder, the arrow still protruding from it.

"Stay here," I told him, moving toward Lorcan's fallen form. He shook his head, letting out an irritated growl.

"You're not going over to the likes of him on your own," Emer said, startling me as she came up behind me, slightly out of breath.

There was no time for arguing with either of them. Cautiously, we crept over to Lorcan, his body sprawled out on the charred, bloodstained ground. Blood soaked his shirt, coming from the wound at his shoulder as if someone had cut his jugular. It dribbled from his mouth and he choked and coughed, struggling to breathe. Still, even in his dying moments, he hung onto his hatred, weakly spitting at us as we came to loom over him. His hand began to inch toward his waist and Emer slammed down on it with her foot, just in time for me to realize he'd been reaching for a dagger hanging there.

"I don't think so," she said, narrowing her eyes at him.

"You've lost," he said, his worlds barely discernable as he choked on his own blood. "Cadfael is dead. You're too weak to rule. Fianna knows it and so do you."

"And you're dying," I retorted.

"It's not done..." He trailed off, his eyes rolling to the back of his head as he gave one last gasping breath.

The fire all around us vanished, leaving behind nothing but smoke. I heard the dying cries of lingering shadow creatures, and the few remaining mercenaries began to cease their fighting as they realized how woefully outnumbered they were without Fianna's dark power to aid them. My gaze dropped to

Lorcan's right hand, disgust filling me at the sight of the clan ring of Blaidd on his finger. I reached down and yanked it off, slipping it onto my own.

As I straightened, Bran shifted back into his human form, the arrow from Lorcan still protruding from his shoulder. Blood stained his shirt and he was entirely too pale as he slumped back against the rocks.

"Spirits, Bran," I said as I hurried over to him, my chest tight. "You need a healer."

"I'll manage," he replied, though I could tell that he was gritting his teeth.

"Seren..."

My gaze flitted to Emer and she gestured behind me. I turned, feeling as if a heavy stone had settled in my middle as I looked more closely at the husk of a body splayed out on the burned ground. Part of me wanted to deny it, but even with the horrific burns, I knew that it was my father. Lorcan had admitted as much and deep in my gut, I knew it to be true.

I walked over to him, feeling as if I were in a fog as I dropped to my knees. I had spent most of my life resenting him, the latter years hating who he had become, and yet I still felt an odd sense of grief at the realization that he was gone from this Realm. Lorcan had not spared him and I did not want to dwell on the horrific death that must have come to him. He had finally acted, but he had acted far too late.

"Ren," Bran murmured, placing a hand on my shoulder.

At his touch, I felt moisture sting my eyes and I blinked my tears back, almost furious with myself for feeling such strong emotion. Father had been no hero—he had turned into little more than a monster in the wake of Fionn's death—and yet my chest still ached. After all these years, I apparently still felt something. I took in a deep breath, letting it out shakily as I swallowed against the lump in my throat. Bran squeezed my shoulder and I could feel his hand trembling, reminding me of how close I'd once again come to losing him.

"Take Bran to Cian," I told Emer, forcing myself to rise to my feet. "I will find Lewella. The remaining mercenaries need to be dealt with and we must prepare to take my father's body back to Clogwyn."

"I don't need to see Cian right now," Bran said, shaking his head. "I can wait."

"I cannot lose you as well." The words came out harsher than I intended but as I held Bran's gaze, I knew he saw every broken, anguished emotion swirling around inside of me. Emer came up and gently took his good arm.

"Yes, Ri Seren," she said, slightly inclining her head.

She wasn't wrong in saying it. My place was not confirmed by the council just yet, but in Father's passing, the title would be assumed to pass to me. And still, a sense of overwhelming grief that threatened to make me fall back down on my knees washed over me, my gaze falling to the dead bodies that littered the scorched ground. This had not been how I had wanted to become Ri of Blaidd.

Emer ushered Bran off and I glanced back at my father's body, a cool breeze brushing the back of my neck. *You will take your place as Ri of Blaidd, no matter what.* My jaw tightened at the Wolf Spirit's whispered reminder. I'd made a vow, one that I had promised to see through. Squaring my shoulders, I stepped away from the boulders, navigating the dead bodies covering the ground as the warriors who still lived continued restraining and capturing the handful of Lorcan's forces who had survived the fight. The weight of the clan ring felt heavy on my hand, but it was weight I would bear. It was time to set Blaidd to rights.

CHAPTER 41

THE STAG'S FAVOR

Alannah

I COULD FEEL MYSELF sliding across the ground, my limbs catching on tree roots and rocks, sending more agonizing waves of pain crashing through my body. My head throbbed, my mouth was dry, and my eyes were gritty as I squinted them open. I was in the forest, being pulled through dirt, brush, and bramble. Above me, I could see that the sun was setting, casting the forest floor in shadow.

There was another harsh jerk that caused a whimper of pain to escape my lips, followed by an all too recognizable low hiss. My spine went rigid, my breathing growing even more shallow as I realized it was a shadow creature that held me in its powerful jaws. It was what was dragging me by the shoulder across the forest floor.

My memory was fragmented. I recalled the fighting, the fire, and Cadfael's death. I remembered Lorcan and Dara turning on me, but I had no memory of how I'd gotten away from the battle. I could only surmise that the creature and Fianna had had something to do with it. Though, for all I knew, the creature had dragged me into the forest to make me its next meal.

I gasped and cried out as it pulled me over more rocks, feeling as if my arm were certain to be ripped from the rest of my body. The smoke that rolled off the creature made it difficult to breathe and its fangs digging into my flesh were like pins of fire sinking inside me. An instinctual part of me knew I should flee, but I was also well aware that I was in no condition to do so. If the creature were to kill me and devour my soul, I could only hope it would be quick about it.

The shadow creature continued on through the forest despite the fading light, not once loosening its hold on me. It was difficult to get my bearings in my pain-filled haze, but it appeared I was still within the safety of Ioliare. Blackness began to dance at the edges of my vision once more and just when I thought I could bear the pain no longer, the shadow creature stopped, releasing its hold on me and dropping me to the ground.

The jarring jolt left me whimpering and I pushed myself to roll onto my side. My attempt at getting to my feet was short-lived, as I soon discovered my right leg would bear no weight. Blood covered what I could see of my body; open wounds crisscrossed my arms, legs, and right side. My chest felt heavy as I fought for breath, the shadow creature standing over me. I wanted to run away from it, but I couldn't.

Turning my head, I struggled to take in my surroundings, listening to the gurgle of nearby water. The creature had deposited me a few feet from a flowing river. Smooth stones ran along the riverbank, covered in bright green moss, and ancient, gnarled trees surrounded me on all sides. The bubbling of the water tempted me, my parched throat making me desperate for a drink.

I rolled onto my belly and crawled to the edge of the water, fighting my way over the slippery, moss-covered rocks. To my relief, the shadow creature didn't try to stop me, remaining where it was as it watched me with its unnerving ember eyes.

By the time I reached the edge of the bank, I was shaking. I cupped a hand, dunking it into the river, only to yank it back out as the water burned my skin. I cursed; my hand was as red as if I had stuck it into open flames. The water began to bubble and hiss, steam rising off it. I fought to scramble away from the bank, my stomach churning and my hand throbbing, but I didn't make it far before the shadow creature stalked up behind me, snarling as it pinned me in place.

The bubbling water began to swirl and the shadow creature crowded me, fangs bared, until I crawled back over to the river's edge. An image began to form on the water, one that I knew all too well. Like its creatures, the Stag Spirit's body was made of smoke and ash, its antlers formed from burning flames, and its eyes blazed with scorching embers.

"What do you want from me?" I asked, my voice so hoarse, it was barely above a whisper. "If you have had your creature bring me here to kill me, have it be done with it."

But I have so many more uses for you if you're alive, little mortal. Fianna laughed. *Though even now, I know you feel the life leaving you.*

I gritted my teeth, my breathing shallow and weak.

You won't last much longer, but your future, Fionn's bastard's future, is not done yet. It paused, the rippling image of the Spirit on the water angling its head as smoke burst forth from its nostrils. *Not if you are willing to make a bargain to ensure it.*

"Of what bargain do you speak?"

Your soul, it said, pulling back its lips to reveal grotesquely sharp teeth. *I will save you and you will give me your soul in return.*

Aengus will be yours, Blaidd will be yours. So long as you become my servant.

The water rippled again, new images filling it, ones that left my heart aching. I saw Aengus' smiling face, I saw him kissing me passionately, taking me to his bed. I saw my sister thrown in Castle Clogwyn's dungeons at Aengus' command, forced to pay for what she had done to me. I saw myself standing by Aengus' side in the Great Hall, the clan ring of Blaidd sparkling on his hand as the people of Blaidd bowed before us. The water bubbled again and Fianna's form returned as a hacking cough ripped from my lungs, causing blood to trickle out of the side of my mouth. It was right. I could feel the life leaving me, and in the end, I was not ready to die.

I will do it, I said. *I will bind my soul to you.*

Fianna's lips curled back once more in what looked like a grotesque smile. Behind me, the shadow creature stepped toward me, letting out a low, rumbling hiss. I stiffened, my heart pounding as the creature reached me and lowered its head. It opened its mouth and flames burst forth, engulfing me. I cried out, expecting pain, but to my astonishment, none followed.

Instead, the flames wrapped around my body, healing the gaping wounds that covered me. Slowly, my pain vanished and my breathing deepened, the flames eventually morphing into smoke that blew away on the breeze. I was whole once more.

I sat up, staring at the pristine skin on my hands, my eyes wide. There was no sign of the battle that had almost cost me my life, save for one small place on the inside of my left wrist. A scar lingered there, one that looked like flaming antlers. Much like the small mark I had received after swearing my bond to Lorcan, it had a strange glimmer, but on this mark, I could feel the darkness that was imbued into it.

You have much to learn, little mortal, Fianna said. *You are not yet ready to take Castle Clogwyn, but soon you will be.*

I crawled up onto my knees, readying to get to my feet. I was going to need to find shelter and food. Otherwise, I wasn't going to last long in the middle of the wilderness.

Oh, not so fast, I'm afraid. Fianna let out a harsh laugh. *We need to make sure Fionn's bastard knows that he cannot live without you. Let's make that easy, shall we?*

Before I could even react, the shadow creature barreled into me from behind, shoving me over the edge of the bank and into the water. It had returned to its ice-cold temperature, no longer bubbling and boiling, but the once gentle water had become a raging current that threatened to drag me under. I fought it, grasping and flailing as I tried to keep my head above water, all the while being forced downstream at an alarming pace. Rage and panic filled me as I choked on water. Why in the blazes had Fianna saved me if all it was going to do was drown me?

Fear began to grip me as I continued to be pulled and tossed down the icy river, my heart feeling as if it would beat out of my chest, until I finally managed to latch on to a downed tree hanging over the water. I clutched the rotting trunk with everything I had to keep from being pulled back under. As I gasped for breath, I swore I heard a faint voice, but it was followed by nothing but the rushing of the river. I clawed at the trunk, trying to ease my way toward the riverbank, only to half slip and almost plunge back into the water in the process.

"Alannah!"

For a moment I thought I had surely lost my mind, for how could Aengus be here, but I turned my head toward his voice to see him crashing through the trees and racing for the river.

"Hold on!" he shouted as he reached the downed tree.

My heart was in my throat as he climbed onto it, carefully crawling down the length of the half-rotted trunk. The water roared beneath him, still trying to pull me away from my lifeline. My arms were shaking, my fingers struggling to maintain their hold on the wet, crumbling bark. Aengus was only a foot from me when one of my hands slipped and he uttered a string of curses, scrambling closer. I clung harder, trying to ignore the numbness that was setting into my body. Finally, he reached me. He wrapped one arm under my shoulders and hauled me up onto the tree trunk with him, almost rolling the both of us off in the process.

"Hold onto me," he said. "I won't let go. I promise."

I nodded, my teeth starting to chatter as I clung to him. He was breathing hard as he inched us back down the tree, holding me close. The moments were agonizing, the river still angrily raging below. When he finally hauled the two of us off the log, my shoulders sagged with relief. He kept an arm firmly around my shoulders, supporting me as I leaned against him, shivers overtaking my body.

"My horse isn't far," he said. "Can you walk?"

"I'll manage," I replied. "How... how did you find me?"

He looked away, not quite meeting my gaze. "I was asked to come treat a sick child in Sruth. When I was riding back... something told me to come this way."

It was the way he said *something*, along with Fianna's lingering words that left me highly suspicious of just what that something was. I wouldn't put it past Fianna to have planned all of this and regrettably, I also wouldn't put it past the Stag Spirit to have risked my life to suit its purposes. I had sworn my soul to it, but I would not go into this blind. I wouldn't make Lorcan's mistake of thinking I was indispensable.

"Come," Aengus said as more shivers continued to wrack my soaking wet body. "Let's get you back to my horse. We need to get you dry and warm, but I'd rather make camp for the night a bit farther away from here."

He kept an arm around me to support me as we walked and I breathed in his fresh scent. Earth and pine. Fitting for a healer and I needed the comfort it gave me. I was freezing cold, my fingers and toes feeling close to numb, but I still relished the feel of his warm body pressing against mine. I might not have agreed with Fianna's tactics, but I would not waste this opportunity. Aengus *would* know how much he needed me; I would make sure of it.

As I stumbled along through the forest next to him, he murmured encouraging words, gently rubbing my shoulder with his thumb. He didn't ask me how I'd come to be half-drowning in a river, though I suspected he soon would. His current focus, at least, seemed to be on getting me back to his horse as quickly as possible. It would give me time to come up with some story to spin for him as to how I'd ended up half-drowned in a river. The forest continued to grow darker and by the time we reached his mare, tied to the trunk of an oak tree, night had fallen.

Aengus pulled blankets out of his saddlebags, wrapping me up in them before helping me onto his mount. Once I was settled in the saddle, he swung up behind me, holding me by the waist as he took control of the mare. He guided her through the trees and to my surprise, the road was only a mere few feet away.

I recognized where we were, on the boundary of the southern part of Ioliare; the road the mare was walking down being one of the main roads that led north. We were miles away from what had become the battle with Cadfael and his warriors. A shiver passed down my spine as I wondered just how intricately Fianna might have planned all of this.

"We'll stop soon and I'll get a fire going to help you get warmer," Aengus said, pulling me a bit closer to him.

"Thank you," I murmured, pressing my back up against his broad chest.

"I wouldn't have left you to drown."

His words and the emotion that were imbued in them brought a smile to my lips, one that was hidden from him by the dark as the mare ambled on. I turned my head to get more comfortable in the saddle and my gaze fell on the shadowy trees lining one side of the road. My breath momentarily caught the briefest glimpse of glowing, ember eyes peeking through the trees before they vanished into the night, leaving nothing but darkness behind. A slight tingle came from my wrist, where the antler-shaped mark now marred my skin, subtle reminders of how cautiously I would now have to tread to keep myself in Fianna's favor. This was not over yet.

CHAPTER 42

FEARS AND BURDENS

Bran

THERE WERE CERTAIN MEMORIES that stayed with you. Images that wouldn't ever leave. I knew that seeing to the dead after the battle in Ioliare was something that would be forever emblazoned on my memory. I scrubbed at the dirt, grime, and dried blood that covered my hands, trying to rid myself of it before returning to the tent Seren and I were sharing. Cian had healed the wound in my shoulder the previous night and like the rest of the able-bodied warriors, I'd been pulled into dealing with the aftermath of the battle. I'd spent all afternoon helping see to the dead, along with helping Lewella identify as many of the bodies as possible.

We'd found Drystans's body along with Lorcan's and Dara's. There were countless bodies of both warriors and mercenaries, but the bodies of the warriors were the hardest for me to bear. For so many, I knew the names and faces of their families who would be left to grieve them. The one body that had eluded us thus far, however, was the one that haunted me the most. There had been no sign of Alannah and no proof that she had perished along with the others. Lewella had reminded me repeatedly that a fair number of the bodies had been burned beyond recognition and there was no reason to think that Alannah could have survived such a bloodbath, but still, I couldn't shake my unease.

By the time I was finished scrubbing my hands and arms, my skin was red, but at least it was clean. I tossed the dirty rag back in the small bucket of water and straightened, stepping aside to allow another warrior the opportunity to wash. I was largely ignored when I left, heading deeper into the camp. Though I was still far from accepted among the war band of Blaidd, both Seren and Lewella had made it clear that I was to be treated respectfully, something Drystan and Cadfael had never cared to demand, much less enforce. I suspected there was some resentment around that, but no one had defied it outright; not yet, at least.

Though Lewella hadn't set up camp on the battlefield itself, the edge of the burned forest could still be seen from the camp, the line of blackened trees and sooty ground a silent reminder of what had taken place yesterday. Upon reaching Seren's tent, I ducked inside, unsurprised to see her speaking with Lewella. In a far corner, Rhonwen's bow and quiver had been propped up with care. There was a connection between Seren and the weapon, one that I didn't know how anyone could deny after the battle. The Wolf Spirit had chosen her to wield it and to defeat Lorcan. If that was not enough to convince the clan that she was the one who should be the next Ri of Blaidd, I wasn't sure what would be.

I stood just inside the tent's entrance, giving her and Lewella space while they continued speaking. I was proud of Seren for how she had sought to fill her new role in the wake of Cadfael's death. It was a heavy burden she bore, with so much loss and destruction, but she was handling it admirably. Lewella, too, had proven herself these last few days. With Drystan's passing, I knew Seren intended to make Lewella Blaidd's new warrior chief, and there was no doubt in my mind that she was well suited to the task.

The two of them soon finished their quiet conversation, Lewella giving Seren a respectful nod before leaving the tent. As soon as the tent flap closed behind the other woman, Seren rubbed her forehead, her shoulders drooping slightly. I strode over to her, slipping my arms around her before lightly kissing the top of her head. She was strong—she had always been so—but I knew that didn't mean she didn't feel the weight of all that had transpired. I was determined to support her in every way that I could.

"Lewella estimates that we've lost almost half the war band," Seren said, her weariness evident in her voice. "And from what she's gathered, my father left only a small number of warriors behind to protect Clogwyn." She paused, scrubbing her hand over her face. "I suppose at least the worst of the threat is behind us now."

"There will be time to rebuild," I said, rubbing her shoulder. "And Lewella is a good leader."

She nodded, pressing her lips together as her gaze drifted to the tent flap. "I'm worried about the land. I would have expected to see it starting to heal by now if Fianna was truly defeated."

"It's only been one day; it may just need more time. And the burns in this part of the mountains are fresh. Perhaps it's started to heal at the older burn sites first."

"Perhaps." She let out another sigh. "I suppose we'll find out one way or another on the ride back to Clogwyn."

She tensed in my arms when she mentioned the castle.

"You're still worried about the council?" I asked.

"As far as I know, Father never named a successor," she answered, worrying her lower lip. "That means that the council will have the final say. I doubt it will be unanimous."

"You've handled things incredibly well here. I've seen it, Lewella has seen it, and we're not the only ones. You were right about Fianna. You were right about everything. They'd be fools to ignore that."

"We'll have to tell them." She angled her head toward me, finally meeting my gaze. "About us. That's not a secret I can keep from the people as Ri."

My stomach clenched even as I knew she was right. The council, and the clan, would have to know the truth of our marriage. I only hoped no one sought to use it against her.

"They will have to accept it, one way or another," she said, setting her jaw. "Things will change when I am Ri, and the attitudes and laws regarding the shifters will be one of them."

"And that is one of the many reasons you will make a good Ri for Blaidd."

She moved closer to me, resting her head on my chest. Some of my own tension eased as I held her. We would face all of this together, just as we had done in every moment leading up to now. Tomorrow, we would leave this place, and I was more than ready to leave any remnants of Fianna and its darkness in the past. It was time for the Stag Spirit to become nothing more than memory on this land.

"I hope the clan can move on from this," Seren said softly. "I hope we can find peace."

"We will," I told her, rubbing her back. "Together."

I held her tight, resting my chin on top of her head. I'd be lying if I said I wasn't nervous about what all would await us when we returned to Clogwyn, but we had each other. Fianna was gone, its hold broken and its servants defeated. Lorcan could no longer sow the Stag Spirit's darkness and do its bidding. And if Alannah had somehow managed to cheat fate and survive Fianna and Lorcan's demise, she would soon find out what a formidable enemy I was. This clan was only moving forward, not backward. Seren and I would ensure that.

CHAPTER 43

THE START OF SOMETHING NEW

Seren

THERE WAS A STRANGE numbness to grief. Though it had been four days since the battle in Ioliare, I found the odd fog of grief still lingered. I felt the loss of my father, but in the end, I grieved more for the clan than for him. For the warriors who lost their lives to Fianna's flames and Father's pride. For the blood-stained, ash-laden land that carried the weight of so much death and loss.

It weighed heavily on me, but I was determined to feel it. Every soul-crushing moment of it. This was not my first walk with grief. It had been a heavy companion during the Purge and after losing Eamon, but I would feel every moment of it now so that I would remember, so that I would not repeat my father's mistakes.

As the tall granite walls of Clogwyn came into view, I drew in a deep breath, squaring my shoulders. It had been a long ride from Ioliare, and now it was time to face my next challenge. Lewella had sent a messenger to Clogwyn ahead of us, informing those at the castle of the battle and of Father and Drystan's deaths, but I knew such news would be a heavy, devastating blow to many.

Bran rode beside me, at my insistence, with Domhnall at my other side as our horses ambled down the wide dirt road. Since we'd started the journey back to Clogwyn, Domhnall hadn't been far from my side. The warriors he'd brought from Seabhac had departed for Castle Ciall the same day we had left for Clogwyn, bearing a message for Ri Muireann expressing my gratitude for her aid. The clan of Blaidd owed her a great debt for what she had done in our time of need.

I was pleased that over the last few days of travel, Bran and Domhnall had maintained their unspoken truce. There was no lost love between them, but I would need both once we were back inside the castle walls. Once the council officially named me Ri, Bran would be my consort, the clan's Tiarna, and I would need Domhnall's support in particular in the coming days, as I didn't anticipate the council taking such news well. I hoped Laoise would support me as well, both in my claim as Ri and in my marriage, but I didn't envision Arwel and Ithel doing so. Not after witnessing their undying loyalty to my father.

Lewella rode in front of us, and we were surrounded by a score of warriors she had hand-picked as my personal guard for the time being. She had taken her role as my protector seriously, and she had my complete trust as warrior chief. Behind us rode Cian, followed by a small cart that bore my father's body. He would be given a pyre at the castle, an honor given to every Ri of Blaidd to allow their body to return to the land. Over the last few days, I had caught myself wondering how my mother would react to the news of Father's death and if she would grieve him. They were questions I had no answer for and ones that felt more pressing as we rode up to the portcullis.

I'll find out soon enough, I thought as the castle gate lifted, creaking and groaning as it went. I squared my shoulders as our horses trotted into the courtyard. I was not surprised to see Sioned standing on the castle steps with Ithel and a handful of warriors, but my throat still thickened at the sight of her. So much had irrevocably changed.

I brought Ceol to a halt, swinging from his back as Bran and Domhnall dismounted as well. Warriors descended the steps to see to our horses, Sioned and Ithel following behind them. I removed Rhonwen's bow from the saddle, having kept it close to me the last few days, now handing it off to Lewella for safekeeping. Sioned immediately embraced Cian upon reaching him, hugging him tightly. Domhnall lingered at my side while Bran came up behind me, placing a hand on the small of my back. I leaned in to his touch, grateful for his solid, strong presence. The last few days had been no easier for him than for me, but we had leaned on and found solace in one another. I would need him now more than ever as we faced our next challenges.

"It is true then?" Sioned asked as she walked over to me, her gaze falling on the cart and the bundled body inside. "He is gone?"

"Yes," I replied, swallowing hard before pressing my lips together.

"And Pennathe Drystan as well?" Ithel asked, his tone sharp.

"Yes," I answered. "Though I am afraid that Pennathe Drystan's body was in no condition to be brought back to Clogwyn."

"There is much for the council to see to with all of this ill news," Ithel said, his brow furrowing as he motioned to Domhnall to follow him. "There is no time to delay."

Domhnall nodded, placing a hand on my shoulder. "I'll come check on you later."

"Thank you," I told him. He gave my shoulder a squeeze before letting his hand fall away.

He followed after Ithel and I tried to ignore the slight quiver in my stomach as the two of them strode up the castle steps. Without Father having named a successor, the council would have the final say on who would become the next Ri of Blaidd, a power I knew they were all well aware they wielded. *You have Domhnall,* I reminded myself. *And perhaps Laoise, as well.* Domhnall, I at least knew, would speak on my behalf.

"Is Mother well?" I asked Sioned, my chest tightening at the thought of something ill having befallen her as well in my absence. There was no sign of her, but at the same time, that could simply be due to her illness keeping her abed.

"She wanted to be here to greet you," Sioned replied, "but her pain was bad enough today that she could barely walk. I insisted that she rest inside; she could barely make it down the steps."

"I can go up and see to her," Cian said.

"I'll go with you," I said.

"She would appreciate that." Sioned paused, taking a deep breath before letting it out slowly. "I know there will be arrangements to be made for Cadfael's pyre. I've already told Esyllt that I am more than willing to help see to those so that she does not have to bear that burden alone."

"I will help as well," I said, looking back over my shoulder at the cart that bore Father's body. "You're right: It's far more than Mother should have to bear on her own."

"I'll handle things here for now." Sioned placed a gentle hand on my arm. "Go see your mother."

"Do you want me to come with you?" Bran asked me.

"Always." I took his hand in mine and Cian led the way up the steps, a warrior standing guard at the door letting us inside.

There was a noticeably tense air in the castle as we walked through the entryway and up the staircase that led to the second level, passing various servants as we went. A few gave me skeptical looks, but no one said a word. Father's death would come as a shock to those who called Clogwyn home, especially after all the years he'd spent crafting his band of loyalists inside the castle walls. Even if the council did not oppose me outright, I expected I would be in for a battle after officially becoming Ri.

I kept a hold of Bran's hand as we made our way to the Ri's chambers, another wave of grief washing over me when we reached the tall oak door with its wolf's head carving. One day, this would be my chamber to share with him, and yet right now, I still could only see it as a space belonging to my parents.

As Cian pushed open the door, I pushed such thoughts aside. In this moment, my focus needed to be on Mother. She was seated on a fur-covered bench in the common room, her face a bit paler than usual, but her eyes were bright as she took in the three of us. I was relieved to see her in at least somewhat good spirits, though even from the doorway, I could see how swollen her hands were. With Sioned expressing that she could barely walk, I could only imagine the pain she was enduring in her legs and feet.

"Seren," she said, half-choking on my name. "Thank the Spirits."

I hurried over to her and as I sat down beside her, she pulled me into a tight embrace, causing tears to prick my eyes. Truly, things had changed between us—for the better.

"I am so sorry," Mother said, her voice wavering. "I am so sorry you have had to bear such burdens, but I am so relieved you've come home."

My tears came in earnest at her words; there was no holding them back. My whole life, I had yearned for her to show me such love and comfort, and in the presence of it, in the wake of so much loss and death, it both brought me to tears and soothed something deep inside me. When we finally eased back from one another, tears stained Mother's face as well, and she wiped at them with the back of her hand. She cleared her throat, turning her attention to Bran and Cian, who both hung back by the door. Their expressions were somber and I could have sworn I saw a sheen of moisture in the eyes of both of them.

"I would welcome any relief you can offer, Cian," Mother said. "And I am relieved to see that the two of you have returned alive and whole as well."

At that, Bran blinked rapidly before briefly ducking his head, my own heart warming at Mother's inclusion of him. I wanted to break the news of our marriage to her and Sioned first before it was announced to the rest of the castle and clan, and Mother's acknowledgement of him bolstered my hope that she would take the news well.

Cian walked over to Mother, kneeling down on the floor in front of her, while Bran came and stood beside me. He placed a hand on my shoulder, giving it a squeeze, and I smiled up at him, briefly covering his hand with my own. Cian saw to the worst of Mother's pains, her hands noticeably less swollen and the line in her brow softening by the time he was finished using his gifting.

"I'm afraid I need to see to the infirmary," he said as he straightened. "Mair is going to have a lot on her hands with the influx of injured warriors who came back with us."

"Of course," Mother said. "Thank you, Cian, as always."

He hugged her, as well as Bran and me, before departing, closing the door softly behind him.

"The council has been spreading the word that your father never officially named a successor," Mother said, angling herself toward me. "I'm afraid I was never able to get him to speak of such things to me, but I believe they are correct in this."

"I don't have any reason to doubt them either." I bit my lip, Bran rubbing my shoulder as my body tensed. "I know Father did not wish his successor to be me."

"Your father's wishes aside, you are the next in line for the place of Ri and from the stories I am hearing regarding you and Rhonwen's bow, it seems clear that you are the Wolf Spirit's chosen."

I ducked my chin, a slight flush tinging my cheeks. I was aware of the stories that had already started spreading regarding me and the bow. In truth, I was somewhat uncomfortable with the way those stories were starting to embellish and grow. I felt a connection to the weapon, that was true, but all I had done was what was necessary and what was right.

"I just want to do what's best for Blaidd," I said, lightly shrugging one shoulder. "For our people. They've had enough death and devastation to last a lifetime."

"And that is why you *should* be taking the role of Ri." Mother placed a hand on my knee. "There will be those who will grieve your father and will be inclined to think as he did, but that doesn't make you any less suited for the task."

I fidgeted with my sleeve as silence fell between us. There was a question I deeply wanted to ask, but at the same time, I wasn't sure if I should dare voice it.

"Do you..." I trailed off, clearing my throat before starting again. "Do you grieve him?"

She released a heavy sigh, her gaze drifting to one of the windows, the rays of morning sun it let in dancing on the granite floor. "Perhaps not as I should. Your father could be a cruel and difficult man and I am afraid that colors my years with him."

Her confession did not shock me. Instead, it offered me an odd sense of relief. "I fear I do not grieve him as I should either. Only... what could have been. If he had been different."

"I know." She leaned over and hugged me again. "That is what I grieve as well. It isn't wrong, Seren. Not with the man he was and the man he became."

"Why did you marry him?" I blurted it out before I could stop myself. It was something I had wondered more and more since Father's passing.

Mother took in a sharp breath, a pained expression crossing her face.

"I was young when I wed your father," she said slowly, "and from an entirely different world. I'd only just turned eighteen. Too young, perhaps, to fully grasp the situation I'd found myself in. I'm afraid that in the end, I let myself be blinded by his title, his words, and his promises. I listened more to what I wanted to hear and the opinions of others instead of following my own heart. I won't lie to you and say that I have not regretted my choice to marry your father over the years. I have, but I do not regret being gifted my children."

Tears stung my eyes once more, a few of them trailing down my cheeks before I wiped them away.

"There are many things I wish for you in this life," she said, her gaze flitting to Bran before settling on me once more. "But one of them is for you to marry someone you truly love. A lifetime is a long time. Do not settle for anything less than that."

It was the perfect opportunity to confess the truth to her and her words assured me that she, unlike many others, would not judge us so harshly.

"Bran and I wed," I said, taking his hand as I sat a little straighter on the bench. "In Dearg. It wasn't that we didn't want you there, it was just, with Father's decrees..."

"I understand," Mother said, as she gave the two of us a broad smile. "I am happy, for the both of you."

"We haven't, ah, told everyone just yet," I said, biting my lip.

"When you do, I will make sure this castle knows I support you both," Mother replied. "Just as I will make sure that the castle knows I support you taking the role of Ri. I still have some weight as Banrion and I too will have a say in who leads this clan, along with the council."

I hugged her again. "Thank you."

"Come here, you," she said, motioning Bran over as we eased apart. "You're a part of this family now too."

I saw the sheen in his eyes before Mother embraced him. How long had Bran wished for that? For a family? *This will be the start of new beginnings for all of us,* I thought, a sense of determination settling over me. *For the entire clan.*

The shadows Father and Fianna had cast would fade and we would be free to create a better Blaidd. I would see to it.

CHAPTER 44

A SAFE PLACE

Bran

AFTER LEAVING SEREN WITH Sioned and Esyllt, I found Father in the stables, tending to the many horses that had returned with us from Ioliare. The familiar smells of horses, hay, and leather, were soothing to me as I strode down the stable aisle. I'd grown up in the Ri's stables and I had many fond memories of the old oak and stone buildings. The moment Father got a glimpse of me, he released an audible sigh of relief, half-tripping as he let himself out of one of the stalls in his rush to get to me.

"Thank the Spirits!" he said as he embraced me.

I hugged him tight, trying to rein in the raw emotions my exchange with Esyllt had brought up. For the first time in a long time, it felt safe to hope for what could be.

"You're alright?" Father asked as he stepped back, giving me a once-over. "You're unharmed?"

"Thanks to Cian," I replied.

His face paled and I winced, slightly regretting my words. Spirits only knew how worried he'd been since I'd left. I didn't need to worry him further.

"What happened?" he asked.

"An arrow to the shoulder," I answered. "It was minor. Completely healed now."

"Is it true what they say about Ri Cadfael?" Father asked, lowering his voice as two other stablehands, leading yet more travel-weary horses, walked past us.

"It is," I replied.

Father cast a sidelong glance toward the other stablehands, waiting until they were out of earshot before speaking again. "I know it is not wise to speak ill of the dead, but Cadfael has reaped what he has sown."

"I can't say I disagree with you."

I did not grieve the Ri of Blaidd, not after he had made my life a living horror, and I doubted I ever would. *Of course, even his daughter and his wife do not fully grieve him,* I thought, thinking back on Seren and Esyllt's earlier conversation.

"You must be careful in the wake of all of this," Father said, his expression grim.

My brow furrowed. "Careful?"

"A hatred like what Cadfael spewed forth does not die with one man. No one was expecting him to die, certainly not in this way. There will be those who wish to continue on like he did, for nothing to change, and plenty more who are afraid of what the future will bring. Fear changes people, even good ones."

"Cadfael had many loyal to him, yes, but surely they will realize that the clan cannot live in the past. It must move forward."

"There are plenty within these walls who *will* want to continue to live in the past, no matter how bloody and tragic it was, simply because it gave them power."

A quiver settled in my stomach. I wanted to deny his words, but I had spent years with Lorcan. I had seen firsthand what a lust for power could do and I knew there were still many at Castle Clogwyn who, like Cadfael, desired power and control above all else.

"Just be careful, is all," Father said, clasping me on the shoulder. "Maybe lay low for a bit until all of this passes and Seren is able to get the clan under control."

I shook my head. "I'm afraid there won't be any laying low for me."

"And why is that?" Father raised his brows.

"Seren and I married while we were in Dearg."

Father's eyes widened. "I know you love her, but Bran, I... You could be killed with Cadfael's laws."

"Seren is going to change things," I said, holding his gaze. "The moment she becomes Ri, she will get rid of Cadfael's edicts against shifters. She's going to make this clan a safe place for us again."

Father rubbed the back of his neck and I could see the doubt in his eyes. "Grand plans are good and well, Bran, but she may see such things differently when she is faced with the challenges of leading this clan."

I bristled. I knew Seren. She would stay true to her word.

"She's not going to change her mind on this. She means it," I said.

"It's not her I question." Father sighed. "I fear it isn't going to be as simple as her making a few decrees to get this clan to accept shifters again. Not with the terror that Fianna and Cadfael stirred up, and not with the way Cadfael died."

"Cadfael died because of his own pride," I said, my jaw tight. "It's a start. We're not foolish; we know it won't be that simple, but neither of us is going to rest until things in Blaidd have changed—for the better. Banrion Esyllt will be behind us as well. We'll have support."

"Just... promise me you'll be careful."

Even as my frustration at him grew, I could see the fear plainly written in his features. Fear that I understood. He'd already lost me once. That wasn't a trauma so easily forgotten, for either of us.

"I will," I told him. "I promise. Have you stopped for the midday meal yet?"

"I did earlier," he replied, "and they need me here with all these horses to tend to. I'll find you at dinner tonight."

I bid him farewell, somewhat reluctantly leaving him so that he could return to his duties. I'd wanted him to show more happiness at the news of my marriage to Seren, but at the same time, I also understood his worries. *We'll manage,* I told myself as I stepped out of the stable and walked back across the courtyard. *We've faced Fianna, for Spirit's sake. Surely, we can face this.*

Once inside the castle, I made my way to the Great Hall to get something to eat. Like breakfast, the midday meal was an informal affair, with food laid out in the hall for a few hours and the castle inhabitants able to come and eat when it suited them. Seren would be tied up with Sioned and Esyllt for the next few hours, seeing to the details of Cadfael's funeral pyre, but after that was done, I would rejoin her. We'd both wanted to go ahead and move my things to her chambers. Word was that the council would meet tomorrow regarding the future of the clan and it was at that meeting that we planned to formally announce our marriage.

A few curious, and some unfriendly, looks were thrown my way as I entered the hall and got my food. I offered a pleasant smile here and there, knowing that whether I liked it or not, I would need to convince the people of Clogwyn to trust me if I wanted to be of any help to Seren. Once I'd filled my plate and gotten a mug of ale, I took a seat at a far table, near one of the tall, narrow windows that looked out onto the castle gardens. I was halfway through my meal when I spied Mair threading her way through the tables toward me. She looked a bit harried and a slight feeling of unease settled over me as she slipped into the seat across from me.

"I'm sorry to bother you," she said, glancing over her shoulder before looking back at me, keeping her voice low. "Cian wanted me to pass this on to Seren, but she's apparently not to be disturbed right now and I have to get back to the infirmary soon."

"I'll make sure she hears it," I replied, tilting my chin in a motion for her to continue.

Mair took a deep breath, briefly glancing around us once more. "Ithel takes treatments for an illness he has with his skin. He was due another batch today and I told Cian I'd take it to him."

My food felt rock hard in my stomach at the mention of the advisor. Ithel had been one of Cadfael's staunchest allies and one of Seren's greatest detractors.

"Go on," I said.

"I heard yelling when I reached the door. Him and what sounded like Laoise. They were talking about Fianna and the role it played in Cadfael's death, along with its ties to the shifters. And then Ithel started ranting about Seren being an unacceptable choice as Ri, that she would undo everything Cadfael had ever worked for, and that he would never allow her to take the title. And it sounded like Laoise agreed with him."

Ithel wasn't wrong, Seren *would* undo everything Cadfael had done, but that was what the clan needed. Though we'd all known the council was unlikely to easily accept Seren as Ri, my chest had still tightened as I listened to Mair's story. Were they already plotting against her?

"That can't be." I shook my head. "Laoise knew the danger Cadfael posed. That's why she was helping us. She's been Seren's ally; why would she suddenly change her mind now?"

"I don't know, and I'll admit, I didn't hear it all clearly, but Ithel wouldn't let me inside and when I passed him his treatment at the door, I saw Laoise in there with him. I don't know if they're actually up to anything or not, but Cian felt that Seren should know."

"I'll be certain to tell her," I said. "Thank you."

"I have to get back to the infirmary," Mair said as she got to her feet, "but for what it's worth, I think Seren is exactly who this clan needs."

Even with her vocal support, my unease remained as she walked off. As Banrion, Esyllt could make it harder for the council to work against Seren, but there would still be plenty of opportunity for Ithel and others like him to plot and scheme. As much as I'd distrusted Laoise initially, I found it hard to believe she would betray us after all she'd done to aid us in opposing Cadfael.

I grimaced at the thought, Father's warnings ringing in my ears and leaving me without much of an appetite. Seren and I had known this wouldn't be easy, but I had thought that for certain, after the truth of what had happened in Ioliare came to light, the people would have to recognize the pivotal role Seren had played in saving the clan. They would have to see her as the best choice for Blaidd's future. Now, I worried we might have more of a fight on our hands than either of us had anticipated.

CHAPTER 45

LED ASTRAY

Alannah

ALMOST A WEEK HAD passed since my near drowning, and I had made no move to leave Aengus' home in Beag. Neither had he even once indicated that he did not wish me to stay. I had told him the first night what had become of Lorcan and I had concocted a half-truth as to how I had not met a similar fate, telling him that I had managed to get away from the battle after Dara had turned on me and tried to kill me. We had not spoken of it since. Those memories weren't ones I wanted to revisit and Aengus had been kind enough not to press me.

The two of us had settled into an oddly comfortable sort of rhythm. The first few days, he had kept me confined to the bed in his spare room, insisting my body needed time to heal from the cuts and scrapes I picked up during my brush with death in the river, along with my slight hypothermia. Once he'd deemed me healed enough, I'd begun taking over simple tasks for him while he was off seeing to his patients: tending to his horse and his small flock of chickens, along with fixing our meals.

I suspected the novelty of domestic life with Aengus would wear off soon, but thus far, I had heard nothing from Fianna, and I wasn't so unwise as to try and make my next move without it. I carefully stirred the pot of stew I had cooking over the hearth, glancing over my shoulder at the common room. Aengus had spent a better part of the day tending to a sick woman in the village and had told me he expected to be home late. Night had since fallen and I hoped he'd return soon. If he didn't, I'd be eating without him and setting his dinner aside. There was no sense in letting the food grow cold.

It hadn't taken me long to realize the oddity of the hours Aengus kept. I'd wondered how much it had to grate on him, being at everyone's beck and call, expected to tend to their every whim, but he'd brushed the question off when I'd asked. I'd just removed the stew from the hearth, the meat and vegetables inside now fully cooked, when I heard the door open. I couldn't hide my smile as I ladled up bowls for the two of us. Aengus' days, and the occasional night, were for those who demanded his healing abilities, but everything else was for me. He hadn't ventured into my bed yet, but we'd had our fair share of kisses and touches in the darkness of night.

"That smells excellent," Aengus said as he came up behind me, slipping his arms around my waist.

I smiled, leaning into him and pressing my back up against his broad chest. "I bartered with Trefor this afternoon, a few eggs for some of his summer squash. Hopefully it will add a bit of flavor."

"I'm sure it will be wonderful." He kissed the top of my head before backing away and picking up the two bowls.

He took them into the common room, the two of us taking a seat beside one another at the small table. The candles I'd lit earlier brightened the space, despite the darkness that had descended, and a comfortable silence fell between us as we ate. We'd grown accustomed to one another surprisingly quickly. To me, it was another sign that we were meant for each another.

"I heard that news has come from the south," he said when we were halfway through our meal.

"Oh?" I asked, tilting my head as I looked over at him.

"It seems Seren does intend to take the place of Ri."

I stiffened, fighting to keep the scowl off my face. This was not how this was supposed to go. Aengus was supposed to be Ri, not Cadfael's wretched daughter, and I was supposed to be his Banrion.

Patience, Fianna hissed, the scar on the inside of my wrist tingling with a short, sharp pain. *Seren will not steal what is meant to be his, but her demise is one that must be carefully orchestrated.*

I bit down hard on my lower lip to hide my wince, rubbing my stinging wrist against my thigh under the table. I hadn't been able to hide the mark from Aengus, and I could tell he was curious about it, but I didn't want to draw any more attention to it than necessary. Not yet.

"Of course, it's not decided yet." Aengus lightly shrugged one shoulder. "Seems the council has to weigh in on the matter before it's all said and done."

Some of the tension in my shoulders eased. All my months of spying at Clogwyn for Lorcan had shown me that Seren had no real allies within the castle walls.

"Hopefully the matter will be settled soon," I said, focusing on my stew as I tried to school my features. "Spirits know the clan needs stability."

Aengus nodded, making a noise of agreement before focusing once more on his meal. Silence fell between us again and soon we finished our food. Aengus gathered the bowls to take them back to the kitchen, but he froze when a scratching noise came at the door. I furrowed my brow, the scratching coming a second time, followed by an eldritch hiss I knew all too well.

I leapt to my feet before Aengus could react, hurrying over to the door as if I were pulled by some sort of invisible string. I knew the creature that was outside, and I was drawn to it. Aengus shouted my name, racing up behind me, but I'd already flung open the door and stepped out into the night. There, at the bottom step, a shadow creature paced, barely visible in the darkness save for its glowing ember eyes. The creature whipped its head around, stopping its pacing the moment it saw me.

"Alannah!" Aengus grabbed me by the arm, moving to push me behind him, but I threw him off.

"It won't hurt me," I told him.

"Do you know what in the blazes that is?" he said, his eyes wide as he shook his head in disbelief.

"I know exactly what it is and I'm telling you, it won't hurt me."

He reached for me again but I easily evaded him, descending the steps to the creature. It stalked over to me, letting out a strange purring noise as it rubbed against my legs, little puffs of smoke coming from its nostrils.

They will answer to you now. I felt a rush of Fianna's power as the Spirit whispered into my thoughts. *I will teach you to control them and they will learn to obey you.*

The creature let out another eerie purr, its eyes flashing with flickering flames as it looked up at me. I stroked the top of its head, my hand growing hot, as if I could physically feel the otherworldly connection between me and it.

"Alannah." Aengus' voice was wary as he spoke, still staring down at me from the safety of the top step.

Fionn's bastard is ready to know the truth, Fianna said. *Convince him of what must be done. The creatures will not be far. All you need do is call them.*

The creature nudged my legs with an odd sort of affection before loping off into the night. I watched it until it disappeared into the forest behind Aengus' home. A strange thrill coursing through me, I turned my attention back to Aengus. I could see the paleness of his features in the light of the moon, his expression somewhere between admiration and horror.

"Come inside," he said, shakily motioning for me to do so. "Before someone sees."

I cast one last look at the shadowy forest before doing as he bade. He wasn't unwise to not want to linger. The people of Beag would hardly know what to make of one of Fianna's creatures being here. I walked back into the common room and took a seat in the closest chair, Aengus trailing behind me. He jerkily ran a hand through his hair, swallowing hard as he came to a stop a few feet away. He didn't take a seat, instead staring me down with haunted eyes.

"How did you... what just happened?" he asked, his voice slightly strangled.

"I am connected to them," I answered, relaxing in my seat in a languid manner. He needed my confidence right now. He needed to know there was nothing to fear. "Fianna has seen the plight of the people of Blaidd. It has seen how the Wolf Spirit has failed them. It knows it is time for a new era."

Aengus averted his gaze, working his jaw as the Stag Spirit's intoxicating darkness filled the room. It was here; I could feel it, like a lover's caress brushing against the back of my neck.

"Blaidd will have its new era," Aengus finally said, still not meeting my gaze. "Cadfael is dead. Seren is the next Ri."

"Seren is Cadfael's own blood." I couldn't hold back a scoff. "Surely you do not expect her to end what he began?"

"She is different than he is."

"She is weaker, that is for certain."

Aengus stiffly shook his head. "I have met her. She is not her father. The people of Blaidd have suffered, but I do not see that for their future."

"You hold her in such high esteem," I said, disdain tinging my voice. "But she will be no different than her father in the end."

"Neither of us knows that." He finally looked at me, holding my gaze. "And even if she isn't, Fianna is no being to be trusted. Look at Lorcan's fate."

"Lorcan brought his fate upon himself." My spine stiffened and one of my hands curled into a fist. "I would not be here without Fianna. I would be dead on a battlefield. For I assure you, if Fianna had not spirited me away and Seren had found me instead, she would have taken no mercy on me."

His eyes widened and he swallowed hard. I had told him nothing of Fianna saving me, but he needed to know that truth; he needed to know that Fianna was not what he had been taught to fear.

"Alannah," he said, softening his tone, "don't you want something different? Different than the life you had with Lorcan? Has it been so bad these last few days?"

He doesn't want this, I told Fianna, biting my tongue in frustration. *Listen to him defending her as if she is even worth defending.*

He needs to know that she is not to be trusted, Fianna said. *He needs to know the truth about his precious blood kin. That she cares nothing for him. That she knows who he is, knows the blood they share, and has left him here in this pathetic village in order to make certain she keeps her power for herself, just like her father. Do not forget what it is you gave me in exchange for your life.*

I took a deep breath, the sharp tingle returning to my wrist as I once more held Aengus' gaze. "I want a new future for Blaidd and I know that cannot happen under Seren. I know that Fianna saved my life, that I would be dead without it. You say you met her. Did she even acknowledge who you were?"

"She didn't know," he replied, but I could hear the hint of doubt in his tone as he pressed his lips together.

"She *did* know. She knew and she refused to acknowledge it. She knew and yet she has left you here alone in this isolated village, never acknowledging the connection between you."

"And you would know this how?" Aengus' brow furrowed, his shoulders tensing as he took in a sharp breath.

"Because Fianna knows. Because it sees far more than you and me." I paused, letting the words settle, feeling the Spirit's presence in the room growing. The tingle in my wrist was growing too. I had to convince him, had to bring him to our cause; it was my soul that was on the line if I didn't.

"She knows who you are, Aengus. She doesn't acknowledge it because she is no different than her father. She wants power, power that she doesn't have to share, and you are an obstacle to that. So she leaves you here. Ignores you. You're no threat to her that way. She doesn't care about you; she never has. That's the kind of person she is. Do not think for a moment that she is cut from a different cloth than her father. Whatever façade she has put forth, she was raised on his hatred. Not once did she try to stop him, not even when he was murdering my kind."

His jaw clenched and he crossed his arms, dropping his chin.

"She isn't what Blaidd needs," I said. "You are."

"And what do you suggest I do?" he snapped, showing the first sign of temper as he jerked his head up. "Ride up to Castle Clogwyn and beg them to believe the truth of my parentage?"

"Of course not. We look to Fianna. It wants what is best for Blaidd. We let it guide us."

"Fianna burned half of this clan with its fires. It ruined the lives of many."

"Because it was provoked. Because the Wolf Spirit left it no choice. It was not Fianna who was murdering the shapeshifters of this clan. That was Cadfael, the Wolf Spirit's precious chosen."

He fell silent, his shoulders drawn in as he stared hard at the empty hearth. Fianna's presence was so strong in the room, I swore I could almost taste it, and despite whatever Aengus might put forth, I could see the cracks forming in him. What I had told him of Seren had hit its mark. He was torn—torn between the world he knew and what he could be.

I slowly rose to my feet, training my gaze on him as I closed the distance between us. When I reached him, I ran a finger along his jaw before gently turning his head back to me.

"You can do this, Aengus," I said softly, caressing the line of his jaw again. "You can lead Blaidd, let its people start anew. All Fianna asks is that you trust it and that when the day comes, you step into the role that has come to you by blood."

"How can I trust it?" he asked, briefly closing his eyes as a wrinkle settled in his brow.

"How can you trust the Wolf Spirit after all that has happened? After what Cadfael wrought? Not once did it seek to remove him."

He let out a shuddering breath and I cupped the side of his face. "It saved me, Aengus. If it was nothing but darkness and evil, why would it have done such a thing? Its creature did not harm either of us tonight; it merely paid its respects. Is it not possible that the stories you were told, the ones I was told, were exaggerations? That Fianna might not be as evil as we were taught to believe?"

"You trust it?" He barely breathed, our faces mere inches apart.

"How could I not after what it has done for me? I would not lead you astray," I whispered. "I care about you too much."

His chest hitched and I kissed him, wrapping my arms around his neck and pressing my body against his. He kissed me in return, holding nothing back. As his mouth moved over mine, I pushed even closer to him, backing him up against the wall. A groan escaped his lips as I parted them with my tongue. I had never wanted a man like I wanted him and I needed him to know it. Needed him to be willing to follow me down the path Fianna had chosen for us.

When we were forced to part for air, he hoarsely whispered my name, putting slight space between us so that he could look down at me. His eyes were dark with desire and I knew he felt what I did: the want and the heat between us.

"I do not know if I have what it takes to lead," he said, breathing hard. "But I do know that I want what is best for Blaidd and... for us."

"As does Fianna," I said, giving him a soft smile. "You have greatness in you, Aengus. I have seen it."

I brought my lips to his neck, kissing him slowly under his jaw before trailing kisses down toward his chest. He shivered, his pulse jumping in his neck at my touch.

"Stay with me tonight," I murmured as I pulled away from him.

He took my face in his hands, bringing his lips crashing back down onto mine, leaving me no doubts as to how the night would end. A euphoric feeling filled me as he guided me toward the back of the house, his lips barely leaving mine. Fianna would have its Ri, I would have him, and soon we would have the entire clan of Blaidd at our feet.

CHAPTER 46

WILLING TO SERVE

Seren

MY STOMACH WAS IN knots as I walked the long hallway to the Ri's study, my leather boots softly clacking on the granite floor. Today, the future of the Clan of Blaidd would be decided. In moments, I would be the one on trial before the advisory council as they decided whether or not I was fit to be Ri.

And we'll already be starting off on the wrong foot, I thought, casting Bran a sidelong glance as he walked beside me. He was wearing a new set of clothes, looking particularly handsome in his charcoal grey shirt with its silver threaded embroidery, his black pants and black boots. His expression was solemn, but the line in his forehead betrayed his own unease.

The council would not be pleased with his presence. I suspected that displeasure would grow even deeper when they learned he was more than just my lover; he was my husband. Mother walked on my other side, her chin lifted high and her shoulders back in a seemingly uncharacteristic display of confidence. Something in her had shifted since Father's passing, as if a great shadow had been lifted from over her. She still had her struggles, both with her past and her ailing body, but whatever hold Father had had over her was now gone.

As Banrion, I knew her words would weigh heavily today, and I was glad she would be on our side. She and I were dressed similarly, both of us wearing dresses of the same dark blue hue. I had taken care with my hair and the rest of my appearance, knowing that the council would be looking for any reason to disparage me and not wanting to give them any opportunity to. And, if I were honest, taking such care with my appearance had helped bolster my own flagging confidence.

As we neared the door to the study, Mother slowed her steps, placing a hand on my shoulder before pulling me to a stop. I angled myself toward her, looking up at her with a questioning gaze.

"No matter what they say in there," she said, "you deserve this role. You have always deserved it."

My throat tightened painfully and I ducked my chin, blinking rapidly at the tears that stung my eyes. I had wanted my whole life to hear such words from her and it soothed some deep, aching part of me to finally hear them. She squeezed my shoulder and began walking again, Bran placing a reassuring hand on the small of my back. I sent him a quick smile as we reached the study door.

The warriors standing guard gave Mother a respectful nod before letting us in. Arwel, Ithel, and Lewella already awaited us. Though she would make no official choice, as the current stand-in warrior chief, Lewella would be present for today's affair. It was something I was grateful for, as I knew I could count on her to show support for both Bran and me. We were, however, noticeably missing Laoise and Domhnall.

Domhnall's absence in particular made my stomach twist into more knots as Mother, Bran, and I took a seat at the table. He and Laoise had both been avoiding me since I'd returned home, leaving me even more worried that the council was plotting something behind my back. I wanted to think I could count on both of them to support me—I *should* have been able to count on them after all that had happened over the last few weeks—but a part of me wasn't so sure. Especially after hearing of Laoise's potential scheming with Ithel.

The door opened again and Laoise and Domhnall strolled in, Laoise looking particularly at ease as they joined the rest of us at the table. Domhnall gave me a reassuring smile as he settled in his seat and I felt some of the tension in my shoulders ease. Even if Laoise wasn't keen to support me as Ri, there was no reason to doubt my ability to count on Domhnall.

"That is all of us then," Ithel said, taking on a commanding tone as he glanced around the table. "I believe this meeting may begin. And I believe I must begin it by asking why exactly the shifter is present." He paused, scowling at Bran. "I fail to see what business he has being here."

I took in a deep breath, meeting Ithel's perturbed gaze. "He has business being here because he is my husband."

Gasps and muttered oaths broke out around the table, but it was Domhnall more than any of the others who drew my focus. He had gone perfectly still, his shoulders bunched, and yet I clearly saw the pain in his eyes. My chest tightened as I took in his wounded expression. Should I have taken him aside and told him the truth instead of letting him find out like this? I still remembered our kiss in the stables months ago and yet I thought he had understood the truth; that Bran was the one who held my heart. *But that still might not mean that the truth doesn't hurt,* I thought with a wince.

"It is *entirely* unacceptable for a shifter to be Tiarna of Blaidd," Ithel said, narrowing his eyes at Bran. "For that reason alone, Seren should not even be considered for the role of Ri."

"Since when is a shifter unable to be Tiarna?" Mother asked, raising her brows. "There is certainly precedence for it. Bran would be far from the first."

"Have you forgotten the Purge, Banrion Esyllt?" Ithel scoffed. "The very fight your husband gave his life for."

I bit my tongue to stay silent, knowing that I was not to speak unless they directed a question at me. That was the way such meetings had always been held when it came to choosing the next Ri, but I wanted nothing more than to defend myself and Bran. He placed a hand on my thigh under the table, sensing my tension, and I slipped my own hand over his, lacing our fingers. It would grate on me to be forced to listen to them accuse us and squabble, but it would be no easier for him. At least we were here together.

"My husband's choices these last few years have been misguided," Mother said. "That should not be difficult to understand after these last few weeks. I fail to see where Bran has done anything but prove his loyalty to this clan and to Seren since returning to Castle Clogwyn."

"Pennathe Lewella," Arwel said, his level tone a sharp contrast to Ithel's fury. "What has been your experience with the shifter?"

"Bran has given me no reason to doubt his loyalty or his character," Lewella answered. "Despite the often poor treatment he has received from others, he has done nothing untoward, underhanded, or aggressive since serving the war band."

Ithel let out a disgusted snort, muttering under his breath, but Arwel studied Bran with a thoughtful expression, lighting a flicker of hope within me. I looked expectantly at Domhnall, hoping that he too would vouch for Bran's character, but his gaze had grown cold and his jaw was clenched as he stared at the two of us.

"I believe," Laoise said, clearing her throat, "that we are here to discuss Seren's suitability as the next Ri of Blaidd. Not the shifter."

"Her choice to marry such a person clearly reflects on her poor judgement," Ithel replied. "A vital quality one should have if they are to be Ri."

"And yet a quality that Cadfael was so sorely lacking," Mother said pointedly.

"Ri Cadfael made regrettable choices in his later years." Arwel held up a hand. "But that was not always so. Though I must say that I agree with you, Banrion Esyllt. We are here to discuss Seren, not her choice of husband."

"Ri Cadfael did not wish his daughter as his successor," Ithel said. "He made that perfectly clear."

"And yet, unfortunately, he never chose another heir," Arwel replied. "The law would dictate that the title would pass to the next of blood kin."

"Unless," Ithel said, "that blood kin is deemed unsuitable. Which I would argue is the case here."

"That is your opinion," Mother said. "I feel it should be noted the favor that the Wolf Spirit has shown Seren. Rhonwen's bow has not been wielded in such a way in five hundred years and yet she used that very weapon to drive Fianna from this land. Such a thing cannot go ignored."

"I witnessed Seren's connection with the bow," Lewella said, sending me an encouraging glance. "There was no doubt in my mind that the Wolf Spirit meant for her to be the one to wield the weapon. When Pennathe Drystan tried to do the same, he failed."

"The ability to wield a relic does mean one should become Ri," Ithel retorted. "A Ri is more than a warrior. It is a person who is responsible for an entire clan. What dealings has she had with politics, with trade, or with handling law?"

"Her lack of experience on those matters is not for lack of want," Mother said. "Seren cares for the people. Is that not the most important quality to be found in a Ri of Pern Coen?"

"And yet the people do not care for her," Ithel said. "They do not trust her, and with good reason."

"The people have been fed lies about her, by her own father, no less." Mother's tone was hard, her spine rigid.

"Seren's lack of experience is notable," Arwel said. "Though I do feel Banrion Esyllt raises a valid point when she speaks of the bow. We should not ignore such clear signs from the Spirits."

"I would hardly call what has transpired a clear sign." Ithel sneered. "It is hardly enough to base the very future of the clan on. Ri Cadfael had his doubts about her abilities, with good reason."

"There is another option here," Laoise said, raising her voice to draw everyone's attention as she made a placating motion with her hand. "One that could perhaps be more of a compromise."

"Which is?" Ithel crossed his arms.

"Cadfael did not choose his successor," Laoise replied. "He was short-sighted in planning for the future, a regrettable mistake on his part. I agree that Seren does not have the necessary experience and I question if she will have the support of the people, especially considering her marriage. The people of Blaidd have not forgotten the Purge and what all they lost at the hands of the shifters."

"What they lost at the hands of Fianna. Not the shifters," I snapped, unable to keep my mouth shut any longer. Her words of doubt hit me like a punch to the gut. I had trusted her and this was how she was going to repay me?

Laoise gave me a quelling look before continuing. "I will choose to ignore that uncalled for statement. I propose that the title of Ri be given to Domhnall. He has the experience with politics, trade, and law after his years on the council and exposure to it while growing up in his mother's hall. He is well liked by the people of Blaidd. I believe they would accept him willingly."

Bran's grip on my hand tightened as a bitter taste filled my mouth, my chest hitching. My gaze shot to Domhnall and I didn't even try to hide the hurt and anger in my expression. How could they? They had been allies. *Domhnall* had been an ally. Even if I could not count on Laoise, I was supposed to have been able to count on him.

"And how exactly is that a compromise?" Mother asked, shaking her head. "You would give the role of Ri of Blaidd to a son of the Ri of Seabhac?"

"There would be concern, of course, about the role of Ri going to Ri Muireann's son," Laoise answered. "And it would be understandable concern. But, if Seren and Domhnall were to wed, the line of Blaidd would continue through their inevitable children."

"Except that I am already married," I said, my body flooding with anger.

"If you truly care for the people of Blaidd," Laoise said with irritating calm, "then surely an annulment is not too much to ask?"

I stared at her in shock for a split second, my mouth falling open, as I tried to grapple with the audacity of what she had just said. How *dare* she even suggest such a thing?

I shoved my seat back from the table, abruptly getting to my feet, my heart pounding and my body hot with fury. "I will not just sit here and—"

"Seren." Mother firmly took me by the arm, casting me a warning look, though it was clear that she was no more thrilled with the direction of conversation than I was.

"I hardly think it fair or acceptable to ask such a thing of Seren," Mother said, looking back at Laoise. "She should not be forced to wed in order to lead the people of Blaidd, much less leave her husband."

Mother gently pushed me to sit and somehow, I managed to do so, though my body still shook with barely concealed rage. Bran took my hand again under the table, holding it tightly, and I could feel the tension radiating from him as well. His jaw was clenched and his face had flushed.

"I find that I agree with Banrion Esyllt," Arwel said. "That hardly seems like a compromise and as much as I question if the people of Blaidd would fully accept Seren, I question even more if they would accept the son of the Ri of Seabhac."

"You have been oddly silent on this matter, Domhnall," Ithel said, gesturing to him.

Domhnall pressed his lips together, his gaze darting around the table as he seemed to take each one of us in. He shifted in his seat, fidgeting with one of the rings on his hand before clearing his throat. "My aim since coming to Castle Clogwyn has always been to serve the people of Blaidd. Whatever form that may take."

Bran grumbled something under his breath and I narrowed my eyes at Domhnall. It was a vague response, leaving me feeling that he was more interested in covering his own hide than anything else.

"I believe that the Wolf Spirit has been clear in who it has shown its favor to," Mother said. "Seren may have things to learn, but she can learn them. She has what matters most: a willingness to care for the people of Blaidd."

"I am afraid I cannot agree with your confidence, Banrion Esyllt," Laoise said. "Seren is not my choice for the next Ri of Blaidd. I believe that role should go to Domhnall."

"Though it would be irregular and not without its troubles, I am inclined to agree," Ithel replied.

Two against one, I thought, my stomach churning as I waited for Arwel and Domhnall to voice their choices—if they would even allow Domhnall to do so. If they didn't, it would come down to Arwel. He had never been an ally of mine and to my knowledge, he rarely sided against Ithel on council matters.

"I do not think it wise for Domhnall to voice a choice in this matter," Arwel said. "It would be a conflict of interest. And as I find myself inclined to support Seren, we find ourselves at an impasse."

My breath caught. That was a development I wouldn't have anticipated in a hundred years.

"I think everyone here trusts Pennathe Lewella's judgment," Mother said.

"Pennathe Lewella is hardly an unbiased choice," Laoise snapped.

"One could argue the same regarding you and young Domhnall," Arwel replied. "Do not think we have all not noticed the way you have taken him under your wing of late, Laoise. Pennathe Lewella, your choice?"

"After the events of what happened in the wilderness of Ioliare and seeing Seren's devotion to saving this land and its people from Fianna, while I do not deny Domhnall's own fine qualities, I believe Seren to be the best choice for Blaidd," Lewella answered.

Laoise's nostrils flared, her hands clenching into fists on the table, while Ithel's neck corded and a vein popped up under the skin.

"Then I suppose it is decided," Ithel said, his voice tinged with barely disguised bitterness. "Seren will be the next Ri of Blaidd and I will be leaving this council effective immediately."

He stood from the table, shoving his chair back in place with a loud thump. He gave me no nod of respect, not even an acknowledgement, before storming out of the room, the door to the study banging shut behind him. It was childish and uncalled for, and even more ridiculous after all the things he had accused me of.

"Would anyone else like to abdicate their position?" I asked. "For I would far rather know of your unwillingness sooner rather than later."

I was met with silence, though I noticed Domhnall would not quite meet me gaze, his lips still pressed together into a thin line.

"I believe that everyone at this table is willing to serve you, Ri Seren," Arwel answered. "Any personal misgivings aside."

Mother smiled, giving me a respectful nod that Arwel copied. Though Laoise still wore a scowl, she did the same, followed by Domhnall and Lewella. There would still be an official ceremony to come, but as each of them nodded to me in return, I was struck by the gravity of what had taken place. It had happened. I was now Ri of Blaidd.

"The announcement will be made to the castle tonight at the evening meal in the Great Hall," Arwel continued. "I assume, Banrion Esyllt, that you will wish to oversee the Enwi ceremony?"

"Yes," Mother replied.

"Then I think we have covered what we must for today," Arwel said. "Though I would advise the matters of making an official selection of warrior chief and finding a replacement for Ithel be a priority."

"They will be," I replied.

"Congratulations, Ri Seren." He gave me another respectful nod before getting up from his seat.

The others followed his lead, gathering their things as they rose. Mother pulled me into a hug as soon as we got to our feet.

"You will be good leaders for the people of Blaidd," she said, looking over at Bran as we eased back from one another.

"Thank you, Banrion Esyllt," Bran replied, a hint of a smile tugging at his lips.

Lewella came over to offer her congratulations as well, and I promised her that I would confirm her as warrior chief as soon as possible. There was no one else I wanted for the task. Arwel and Laoise had left the study, the latter in a huff, but Domhnall lingered near the door, his expression unreadable as he stared at us. Our gazes locked and he dropped his chin, slipping out into the hallway. I immediately excused myself from the others, following after him.

Guilt left my throat thick, but there was a sense of betrayal that simmered in me as well, leaving behind an ache in my chest. I should have perhaps told him privately about my marriage, but what in the blazes had gone on with him and Laoise to get her to push for him to be Ri? How could he pretend to be my ally and then go behind my back? I called his name as I caught up to him and he stopped, waiting as I closed the distance between us.

"When did you marry him?" he asked, his hurt bleeding through into his voice.

"When we were outside Dearg. Before the battle. I should have told you. That's what a friend would have done."

"Right." The quiet chuckle he let out as he crossed his arms held a trace of bitterness. "A friend."

"And what of the stunt you just pulled with Laoise?" I asked, my anger flaring once more with his show of petulance. "Is that why you've been avoiding me? So you could plot with her behind my back? I was counting on you to support me."

"Seren..." He dropped his gaze to the floor, rocking his weight back onto his heels for a moment before looking back up at me. "I had no idea she was going to do that. She sprung it on me as much as she did on everyone else. And I haven't been avoiding you. I was worried that she was going to work with Ithel to undermine you and I was trying to talk her out of it, but I swear to you, she said nothing to me of becoming Ri."

I shook my head, still feeling the hurt of his betrayal. "Then why did you not speak up in my defense?"

He sighed, running a hand through his hair. "It's not an excuse, but I was trying not to provoke Laoise. With as close as we've become these last few months, she knows certain things, things she could use against me. She's crafty, conniving. You know this."

I worried my lower lip. I couldn't exactly disagree with his assessment. Had I not seen just how conniving Laoise was just now?

"If she has threatened you," I said, "I will not stand for any sort of blackmail on the advisory council."

"It hasn't come to that," he said, his tone soothing as he placed a hand on my arm. "And I don't think it will. I can handle Laoise."

"You will tell me though?" I asked, my brow furrowing. "If she threatens you. I mean it when I say that I won't tolerate such behavior on the council, even if my father did."

"I will, if it comes to that. I promise. Forgive me for not speaking out more. The news of your marriage, it threw me, and then Laoise stunned me even more with her outlandish idea of me becoming Ri. Believe me, I want to keep my place here and my place on your council."

"I want you to stay on the council as well," I said, biting my lip. "I just need to know that I will have your support when I need it."

"You will." The smile he gave me was weak, but he held my gaze.

"Thank you." I glanced over my shoulder at the study door. "I probably need to get back in there. There's much to plan."

"Of course," he replied, gently squeezing my arm.

A niggling part of me felt that there was still something off with him as he flashed me another half-smile, but I shrugged it off. As he'd said, he'd had a number of unexpected things thrown at him today. *Not to mention whatever Laoise is holding over him,* I thought. I had every intention of getting to the bottom of that. Shaking my head, I returned to the study. I would have to deal with that later. Right now, I needed to focus on bringing stability and peace to my people. It was time for change.

CHAPTER 47

THE OPPORTUNE MOMENT

Alannah

I WORRIED I'D LEFT Aengus too soon, that with time away from me, he would be tempted to give in to his fears, but Fianna had been insistent that I travel to the village of Gefell. While my flight south had been uneventful, I had been met with disturbing and infuriating news when I reached the village outside Castle Clogwyn. Seren had been chosen as the clan's next Ri and Bran was to be her Tiarna.

From the moment I'd heard the news, I'd been seething, though Fianna had had little patience for my anger. At least with each passing day, Aengus' uncertainties had begun to lessen, as he too had begun to hear Fianna's voice. He was slowly changing his views and every night I spent in his bed had me longing more and more for the future Fianna had promised.

It was a future I was especially eager for tonight as I sat in in the raucous, crowded tavern in the heart of Gefell. Fianna had guided me here and I'd managed to get one of the last tables the Golden Ram had. The meal had been better than I'd expected, a delicious plate of roasted lamb smothered in sauce and goat cheese, and the ale was decent. For the most part, I'd been ignored by the rest of the tavern's inhabitants, most of them well into their ale for the night and occupied by the rowdy musicians performing in one corner of the room. A place like the Golden Ram was an easy enough place to disappear in plain sight, and that was exactly what I needed tonight.

I washed down another bite of lamb with a swig of ale as the musicians played a particularly lively tune. What exactly I was waiting here for, I wasn't entirely certain, but Fianna had made it clear to me that the Golden Ram was where I was to stay, and the Stag Spirit could be quite persuasive. I absently rubbed the mark on the inside of my wrist, recalling the fiery pain that had erupted from it when I had challenged Fianna earlier, telling it that my time would be best spent flying to Castle Clogwyn and slitting Seren's throat.

He is here, Fianna said as the door to the tavern banged open. I sat a bit straighter in my seat, searching the crowded room for the newcomer. My gaze fell on one Cadfael's advisors. Domhnall was his name, if I recalled correctly from the snippets of conversation I'd overheard while lurking around the castle for Lorcan. His height and fine clothes made him stick out in the crowd, and my brow furrowed. This pathetic whelp was who Fianna wanted to help us sow its darkness?

Yes, Fianna replied. *He will serve his purpose.*

I went to get up from my seat, but a sharp pain in my wrist had me plopping right back down.

Wait, Fianna hissed. *Appear too eager and you will cost us this opportunity.*

Domhnall pushed his way through the crowded room, taking a seat at a table mere feet away from me. His cloak and hair were damp from the steady rain outside and there was a noticeable droop in his shoulders as he leaned forward and rested his elbows on the scarred and worn wood table.

I watched him, continuing to sip on my drink while doing my best not to make it too obvious that he had drawn my eye. He ordered a pint of ale, finishing it quickly and calling for another as soon as he was done. Two pints turned into three and the more he drank, the more it took hold of him. His face began to grow flushed and every so often, he would sway in his seat, but he continued to throw coin down on the table and throw back drink, seemingly oblivious to his inebriated state.

Now, Fianna said. *When he is at his weakest.*

I got up from my seat, Domhnall so deep in his ale that he didn't notice me approach his table.

"Mind if I join you?" I asked, pulling out the chair across from him and flashing him my most flirtatious smile.

He blinked slowly as he looked up at me, then gave me a drunken grin.

"By all means," he said, his words slightly slurred and his movements uncoordinated as he motioned for me to take a seat.

"Forgive my forwardness," I said as I settled in the chair, "but do you by chance hail from Castle Clogwyn?"

"I do," he answered, puffing out his chest before downing another large gulp of ale. "I'm a member of the advisory council."

"What an honor to meet someone so important." I brought a hand to my chest, my eyes widening as I feigned a sense of awe that I most certainly did not feel. I'd spied on Clogwyn enough to know that the man across from me was nothing more than an opportunistic idiot.

"I've been serving at Clogwyn for a number of years now. My mother is Ri Muireann of Seabhac."

I resisted the urge to roll my eyes. Was it possible for a man to have a more overblown ego?

"Truly, it is an honor," I said. "If it isn't too bold of me to ask, have you met the new Ri? I'm visiting from Dearg and there has been much talk about her of late."

His expression darkened and he briefly fell silent, staring hard at his mug. "Yes, I am well acquainted with her."

"Do you think she will do well for the people?"

His scowl deepened and he swished the ale in his mug. "Not as well as another might have done." He took another long drink but then suddenly slammed the mug down, causing ale to slosh over the edges of it, splattering the table. "I was going to be Ri. Did you know that? We had planned it all. I would marry Seren and take the title. I loved her. I was going to rescue her. But then she ruined it all and went and married that bastard."

I softened my expression. Jealousy was certainly something I could work with. "The new Tiarna, you mean? Are the rumors about him true? Is he really a shapeshifter?"

He clenched his jaw, giving a jerky nod. "She made a mistake, throwing her lot in with him. He'll only bring this clan to ruin. His kind aren't fit to rule. And now she's cost me everything."

I inwardly bristled at his hateful words, working hard to keep my expression neutral. This was the prejudice that had almost cost me my life.

It will come back to him tenfold in the end. Tell him he can have what he wants, Fianna said. *So long as he aids us.*

Aids us how?

We will break her and we will start by taking away what she holds most dear: her precious shifter. Once he has been lured away from her side and destroyed, she will be one step closer to being brought to heel.

Domhnall was broodily swishing the ale in his mug again and I rested my chin in my hands, tilting my head.

"It sounds like you don't think this shifter should have the place of Tiarna," I said.

"He shouldn't," Domhnall spat, his face becoming redder. "He'll turn on her. Betray her. Betray us all. She should know better, especially after what happened to her father and brother. If that shifter isn't a servant of the Dark Spirits now, he soon will be. They're all the same in the end."

Anger rose in me again and I gritted my teeth. He was a pawn in this game. I had to keep reminding myself of that, and when Aengus took his place one day, Domhnall and those like him would learn to regret such words.

"What if," I said, trailing my fingers along the table as I took on a more demure, seductive tone, "I told you I knew a way to lure the shifter away from Castle Clogwyn? Surely, once Seren is out from under his spell, she will see that she has been misguided in her decision to trust him. More than that, once she sees proof that he *is* a danger to the clan, surely she would not wish him to stay."

He grabbed a hold of my arm, his erratic movement almost knocking over his mug. I steadied it with my free hand, barely saving myself from having its contents spilled all over me.

"You can do that?" he asked, his eyes wide.

I gave him a slow smile. "I can do that and more. But I would need your help, of course. A lowly villager like me can't exactly enter Castle Clogwyn with ease."

"You'll get rid of him?" His grip tightened. "Make sure he never comes back?"

"I can promise that you will never lay eyes on him again," I replied.

Because I will kill him, I added inwardly, my pulse thrumming. Bran's demise would be a particularly enjoyable one to bring about.

"What must I do?" Domhnall released his hold on me but gripped the edge of the table so hard, his knuckles grew white. His eyes glittered with anticipation and too much ale as he eagerly awaited my response.

He will meet you in this place again tomorrow night, Fianna said. *If he is earnest in giving his aid, he will come and ask for you by the name of Alis.*

"If you truly wish to aid me, you will meet me here again tomorrow night," I told Domhnall. "That will give me time to see to the business I have here."

He frowned, his eyes unfocused. "Tomorrow? You swear it?"

"I swear it," I replied.

He gave a slow nod, taking another sloppy swig of his drink. "Tomorrow then."

"In the evening, just after sunset. Ask for Alis."

"I will." He drained his mug, wiping his mouth with his sleeve, only to miss half the ale that still dribbled from his mouth.

I gave him a broad smile, even as disgust for him curled within me. "I will forever be indebted to you. Ri Seren will be a fool indeed if she does not see what she could have in you."

He grinned, calling for more ale, his obnoxiously loud voice making me wince. How could I even trust that he wouldn't completely forget this whole conversation in his drunk stupor? Even worse, what if he decided to report back to the castle what I had said once he became sober once more?

He won't, Fianna said. *His ambition and jealousy run deep. He will be a useful pawn to twist, you will see. Your work here is done.*

The Spirit's words were followed by a tingling pain in my wrist that made me bite my tongue. Turning my attention back to Domhnall, I flashed him another smile before rising.

"Until tomorrow night," I said.

"Tomorrow," he echoed.

I went back to my own table, tossing down a handful of coin to pay for my meal before throwing my cloak back over my shoulders and seeing my way out of the tavern. As I stepped back into the drizzle outside, I threw my hood over my head, both protecting myself from the rain and obscuring my features from any who dared to look at me too closely. I would spend my night in the forest, seeking Fianna's guidance, and tomorrow I would put into motion the downfall of Seren of Blaidd.

CHAPTER 48

MAKE IT SO

Seren

THE WHOLE OF CASTLE Clogwyn and the entire village of Gefell had gathered to watch me make my oath to the Wolf Spirit and to our clan. The gravity of what I was about to do weighed heavily on me as I stood on the top of the castle steps and looked out over the sea of people. I'd never seen the courtyard so full, the crowd watching me with what felt like a mix of anticipation, uncertainty, and wariness.

Mother stood in front of me, with Cian at her side. Bran was just behind me while Awyr and Cryfder obediently sat at my feet. The rest of the pack was gathered on the other side of the landing, corralled by the Nead Mathair and her assistants. The wolves were just as much a part of the Enwi, or naming ceremony, as any other member of the castle. The council of advisors stood near the wolf pack, overseeing the ceremony. Laoise had fixed me with a scowl, though Domhnall and Arwel at least appeared to look on with some manner of approval.

Tonight, once the oaths were spoken and the clan ring of Blaidd was slid onto my hand, I would be the Ri of Blaidd, in name and in blood. Bran would follow, making his own vows as Tiarna, and as the people watched us in the fading evening light, I silently pleaded with the Spirits to allow them to accept us.

Mother had already spoken the story of the first Ri of Blaidd, Iowerth, and how he had been chosen by the Wolf Spirit to lead the clan. Even though I had heard the story since I was a child, it resonated differently with me tonight. It was no small matter I was embarking on, no small oath I was taking. It would be up to me to guide Blaidd's people and care for the land that had been gifted to us. It was not a responsibility to be taken lightly.

"Your hand, Seren," Mother said, holding out her own.

I took a deep breath before placing my hand in hers, palm up. Cian pulled out a long dagger, its hilt made from bone and decorated with intricate carvings of wolves, unsheathing the blade and passing it to Mother. It had belonged to Iowerth and had been used in every Enwi ceremony for generations. Mother held my gaze as she brought the dagger to hover over my palm, the pride in her eyes making my throat thicken.

She brought the blade to my skin, slicing a small line across my palm. As my blood oozed to the surface, Cian took the blade and passed Mother the clan ring. She placed it on my bleeding palm, wrapping my fingers around it as she held my hand in both of her own.

"Do you vow to protect, care for, and honor the land and its people?" Mother asked.

"I do," I answered, projecting my voice so that it was clearly heard by the gathered crowd.

"May the Wolf Spirit show you its favor and may the clan of Blaidd prosper." Mother smiled.

As she uncurled my fingers, I felt a breeze brush the back of my neck and I knew the Wolf Spirit was near. The clan ring was streaked with my blood and once she'd removed it from my palm, Mother slipped it onto my right hand. She then motioned for Bran to step forward. I moved back slightly to give him space and he too placed his hand in Mother's. She took the blade from Cian once more, slicing an identical line across Bran's palm. At her instructions, the two of us joined hands, our blood intermingling as Mother held our hands together with her own.

"Do you vow to protect, care for, and honor the land and its people, as well as pledge your loyalty to Ri Seren?" Mother said to Bran.

"I do," he answered, his voice clear and strong.

Mother raised our joined hands as the three of us turned to face our people.

"Ri Seren and Tiarna Bran of Blaidd," she called.

The response was subdued, but at least no one openly protested against us. It gave me some hope that perhaps, with time, we could show them that we were to be trusted, even with Bran's gift. Arwel stepped forward with Mother, inviting those who had attended the ceremony to join us on the back side of the castle for a celebration feast, and the people began to disperse, escorted by warriors.

"Cian will see to the two of you before you join us," Mother said, placing a hand on my shoulder and giving it a squeeze. "I am proud of you. The both of you."

"Thank you," I told her, kissing her cheek before Cian ushered Bran and me inside the castle.

"This will only take a moment," Cian said as we stood in the entryway.

He took our hands one at a time, using his gift to heal the small wounds before passing us clean damp cloths to wipe away the remnants of blood.

"Thank you," I said as I wiped specks of blood off the clan ring before placing it back on my hand. "And thank you for standing in tonight."

"It was my pleasure," he replied with a smile.

The role of carrying Iowerth's blade was usually given to the castle seer, but Cian had stepped up to perform the task. The three of us walked through the castle itself to reach the feast and I felt the nervous knots that had twisted up in my stomach at the start of the ceremony slowly unwinding. As Cian escorted us out to the feast, I took Bran's hand in mine. Tables of food and drink had been set up around a massive fire while musicians had already struck up a merry tune. Some dancing had even begun as the night's festivities commenced.

As I expected, Bran and I weren't given much peace when we joined the crowd, countless villagers and servants wanting to come and get a good look at the new Ri and Tiarna of Blaidd for themselves. Cian stuck close to us and soon we were shadowed by Lewella and Emer while we greeted our people. Bran was on the receiving end of most of the skepticism, but with Emer and Lewella flanking us, no one seemed inclined to cause trouble—not tonight, at least.

When Bran and I finally got a few moments to ourselves near a table of baked goods, I couldn't hold back my sigh of relief. Bran let out a soft chuckle, slipping his arm around my shoulders and pulling me to him.

"You're only a few hours into your new role, Ri Seren," he teased.

I smiled as I leaned against him, shaking my head. "Don't tell me you're not equally as exhausted."

"It is much to take in." He paused, bringing his lips close to my ear and dropping his voice. "Though I hope you won't be too exhausted later tonight."

My pulse quickened as I caught his insinuation and my smile broadened. "Oh, I think I'll find it in me to have a second wind."

Bran chuckled again, his breath caressing my ear, along with his sensuous tone, causing a shiver to course down my spine. "You look beautiful in that dress tonight, by the way."

"And here I was thinking that you were only thinking about taking it off."

"Oh, believe me," he said, leaning down and kissing just behind my ear, "I'm thinking about that as well."

Heat warmed my body as his lips pressed against my skin. I had the feeling we wouldn't be getting much sleep tonight, but I wouldn't be complaining. I might even have to pass my thanks on to Sioned for pulling the gown together so quickly. The dark blue dress with its off-the-shoulder sleeves and low back was flattering on me and I particularly loved the fierce-looking wolves that had been embroidered onto the bodice. Bran, quite clearly, approved as well.

I rested my head on his shoulder, watching a handful of couples dance to lively music by the light of the fire. It felt like it had been so long since Clogwyn had experienced such joy, I was determined to hold onto it. Next to us, Emer and Lewella looked to have relaxed as well. Lewella had wrapped her arms around Emer's waist, the two of them talking quietly to one another. I deeply hoped tonight was just the beginning of what would become a peaceful era for Blaidd.

Movement on the other side of the table caught my eye and I frowned as I watched Domhnall slip by us. It was too dark to see him perfectly clearly, but there was something in his movements that set me on edge. Almost as if he was creeping by and hoping not to be seen.

"What is it?" Bran asked.

He turned his head, following my gaze, but Domhnall had already slipped off into the darkness.

"Nothing," I said, shaking my head. "I just thought I saw something."

The smile I gave him seemed to put him at ease and I rested my head back on his shoulder while he traced circles on the exposed skin of my upper arm with his thumb, further turning my thoughts to what would await us tonight once we got to slip away ourselves. It had been a long day for all of us. For all I knew, Domhnall might have wanted some privacy of his own. He'd given me his promise that he was on my side. I'd have to trust him. *This is the start of peace,* I told myself as I once again watched my people enjoying the night. I would make it so.

CHAPTER 49

RID OF HIM
Alannah

I'D RETURNED TO THE Golden Ram after spending a night in the forest near Gefell. I'd purchased a room at the tavern for a few hours to wait for Domhnall and to my relief, the tavern owner hadn't questioned me too deeply when I'd paid for the room. From our brief conversation, he seemed to assume I'd requested the room for some sort of intimate liaison and was happy to take my coin leave me be. And with the Enwi ceremony tonight, there were plenty of folk coming and going from Gefell, which meant plenty of chaos for me to simply fade into the background.

I twirled the end of my braid, my frustration mounting as I stared out the window, looking out at the street on the front side of the tavern. Still no sign of Domhnall. I was ready to be away from this place, ready to return to Aengus, but I had a purpose to fulfil first. I fingered the smooth, folded piece of parchment that I'd carefully tucked into my pocket. The letter had come from Fianna itself, brought to me last night, deep in the forest. The Stag Spirit had created the parchment from smoke and ash. I'd watched in amazement as it had glowed with flickering flames and the words had been penned in a scrawling script.

The letter would carry weight, of that I had no doubt. Fianna had sworn that anyone who saw it would recognize Drystan's penmanship. The Stag Spirit had fabricated a compelling lie, that Bran had continued to serve Fianna even as he had served Cadfael, and Drystan had uncovered the truth just before he was captured by Lorcan. It would label Bran a traitor, something I suspected many in Blaidd, in particular many at Castle Clogwyn, would be more than willing to do.

The soft knock at the door made me start and I instinctively reached for the dagger that hung at my waist. I let out a long breath to calm my racing heart and got to my feet, still keeping a hand on the hilt as I opened the door. Domhnall awaited me on the other side. He was no longer the slobbering drunken mess he'd been the night before, his eyes sharp and wary and his jaw tight as I stepped back to let him into the room, releasing my hold on my blade.

"You know," he said as he came to stand near the window, folding his arms, "I'd begun to wonder if perhaps you were a figment of my imagination. If perhaps I had conjured you to help me deal with my troubles."

"I assure you," I replied, flashing him a cold smile, "I am quite real."

He cleared his throat, shifting his weight. "This thing you promised last night?" He dropped his gaze before looking back up again. "You can truly make it come to pass?"

"So long as you are willing to do your part."

"And it will get rid of him? For good?"

"It will."

"And no harm will come to Seren?"

There was a slight tightness in my chest, but I kept my expression carefully neutral. I could tell this particular lie would be important if I wanted to ensure his cooperation. "Of course not. It is not Seren who is the danger to Blaidd, after all."

"Swear it." A muscle in his jaw ticked and his shoulders tensed as he stared me down.

"I swear it," I replied, holding his gaze.

He studied me, a tense silence passing between us before he gave a slow nod, seemingly almost to himself. "Let's have it, then."

I pulled the letter out of my pocket. I'd crumpled it and stained it with dirt at Fianna's instructions to make it look all the more real. "This came into my possession after it was found at one of the war band's old camps outside of Dearg, shortly before the fire that took Ri Cadfael's life."

Domhnall took the letter from me, his brow furrowing as he unfolded it and began to read. His expression twisted the longer he read, a scowl soon marring his features as he gripped the parchment tightly.

"This is quite the accusation," he said, looking back up at me, his eyes slightly narrowed. "One that could get me into a great deal of trouble if it is not true."

"I have been told by others that the handwriting undoubtably belonged to Pennathe Drystan."

His gaze dropped to the letter again and he pursed his lips. "It does look like his hand. Though it is more than just me who will have to confirm it."

"If it is true, however, the current Tiarna cannot keep his place. It would be putting the clan in grave danger."

"And what am I to say when someone asks how I came to possess this?"

"Tell them the truth. That you were given it in confidence by a villager of Dearg who was concerned for the safety of the clan."

He stared hard at the letter for another long moment, running a thumb over the battered parchment. "I will make certain this gets into the right hands." He folded the letter again, shoving it into his pocket. "I cannot linger here, lest anyone from the castle notice me missing."

"Of course. I understand," I said, walking back over to the door to open it for him.

He followed me, bidding me a mumbled farewell before slipping out of the room. I closed the door behind him, giving him a few moments to be on his way before I made my own departure. I was eager to get back to Beag and back to Aengus, for we had much work to do. I could feel Fianna's pleasure like a visceral warmth. First, we would destroy Bran and then we would destroy Seren. Soon, there would be a far more worthy Ri sitting in the Great Hall of Castle Clogwyn. Fianna would see to it.

CHAPTER 50

UNTRUTHS

Bran

SEREN'S FIRST DECREE AS Ri was to end her father's cruel treatment of shapeshifters in the Clan of Blaidd. While I, and I was sure many others, felt immense relief at her edict, not all shared such feelings. The council in particular had been a source of trouble over the last few days.

Laoise had been staunchly opposed to Seren's new decrees, though at this point, I suspected that Laoise would oppose any-thing Seren did out of sheer spite. Even Arwel, who wasn't as opposed to Seren's rule as Laoise, had had his misgivings about what she had done regarding shifters. Domhnall, of course, had been leery as well, though he hadn't outright opposed her. I personally couldn't wrap my head around Seren's continual trust of him, but trust him she did, even going as far as to name him chief advisor with Ithel's departure.

At least there's Mair, I thought as I walked down the shell path that led to the cottages on the back side of the castle. *Even if her position is only temporary.* Seren had appointed her to fill the place on the council vacated by Ithel until she could find a more permanent solution. While Mair hadn't exactly been welcomed by the other council members who had questioned her lack of experience in such matters, she had been stalwart in her support of Seren. Spirits knew Seren needed that right now, especially with the growing undercurrent of discontent surrounding her new role as Ri.

Once I reached the small cluster of cottages outside the castle walls, I made my way to my father's home. We hadn't seen much of one another since the night of the Enwi and he'd invited me to join him in his cottage for a midday meal. With Seren wrapped up in a meeting with Lewella over the current state of the war band, I'd been more than happy to oblige. I walked up to the front door and knocked, Father soon answering and ushering me inside. The scent of roasted meat wafted through the cottage and my stomach grumbled in response.

"I just got everything all finished up," Father said, leading the way into the kitchen while I followed after him. "You had good timing."

We both took a seat at the small table, splitting the roasted chicken, fresh bread, and cooked greens Father had made.

"A part of me still almost can't believe it," Father said as he mixed a bit of cut-up chicken with his greens. "My son as Tiarna of Blaidd."

"To tell you the truth, I almost can't believe it myself," I replied with a half shrug. "I still don't know if I feel used to it yet."

I'd long hoped for a future with Seren, but I hadn't quite envisioned becoming Tiarna. It was a role I felt unready for, despite trying to do my best to fill it. Supporting Seren as Ri was easy, but getting others to trust me was much harder. The fears Cadfael had sown, especially at Castle Clogwyn, ran deep, and many still feared and resented me. I hadn't dared admit it aloud, not even to Seren, but there were times I wondered if I really was the right man to be Tiarna, times that I feared that maybe I was making Seren's role as Ri next to impossible.

"The council is certainly giving Seren a time." Father gave a slight scowl as he dug into more of his chicken.

"They don't like what she's doing, that she's changing things."

"Can't say I know many a person who takes well to change. They'll come around, I'm sure."

I certainly hoped so, though I didn't think it was going to be any time soon. A brief silence fell between us before Father stopped eating, looking back up at me with a hint of hesitance in his eyes.

"You're happy up there?" he asked. "With this new life of yours?"

I bit my lower lip, hating the feelings of uncertainty that welled up within me. It had been harder than I'd thought. Much harder.

"I'm happy to be in a position to enact change," I answered. "And I absolutely don't regret marrying Seren."

"I know you love her," Father said, his tone becoming a bit gruff with emotion. "Could hardly separate the two of you from one another from the moment you met. Even when you two were just children, she was always coming down to the stables, wanting to know where you were. Sometimes I—"

A loud, insistent knocking on the door kept him from finishing and we both frowned as we looked toward the common room. The knocking came again and I went to get up, but Father waved his hand, motioning for me to stay seated.

"I'll see who it is," he said, pushing back his chair.

An unsettled feeling came over me, but I pushed it off. Yes, Seren had her detractors at Clogwyn and in other parts of the clan, but that had been expected. Fianna, our greatest threat, was gone. There was no reason to jump to the worst conclusions. When Father returned, however, my sense of unease wasn't so easily vanquished. Emer was with him, her expression tight. Her posture was stiff, uneasy, with none of the friendliness I was used to seeing from her.

"I'm afraid I need you to come with me, Bran," she said. "At once."

"What is this about?" Father asked, gripping the back of his chair.

"I can't say," Emer replied with a hint of apology. "But hopefully it should be resolved quickly."

I got up from my seat, a churning in my stomach as I turned to my father.

"I'm sure it will be fine," I told him. "I'll find you after dinner tonight. The meal was excellent."

Father gave me a brief hug before I left the cottage with Emer. It was a beautiful late spring day, the sky a brilliant blue and the distant forest bursting with green, but I wasn't able to enjoy it like I had on my walk down from the castle. I cast Emer a sidelong glance as the two of us stepped through one of the castle gates. She'd been silent the entire walk, her expression still grim.

"What exactly is this about?" I asked.

She shook her head. "I've been asked not to speak of it. Once we get to the Ri's study, Seren and Lewella will tell you everything."

My stomach twisted at their names and I was left worrying what ills could have happened as we strode down the castle hallways to the study. The warriors standing guard let us in without question.

Seren and Lewella were seated at the circular table at the center of the room, both of them looking as grim as Emer. I spied a crumpled piece of parchment on the table in front of Seren, the parchment itself battered and stained. Tension filled the room as we approached, Seren continually twisted the clan ring on her finger. My gaze briefly flitted to Rhonwen's bow as I walked past it, the weapon once more hung back on the wall. Blaidd was supposed to be free of the darkness that had haunted it the last few years. What could have happened?

"Have a seat, Bran," Lewella said when I reached the table.

I did as instructed, Emer standing just behind me. Seren, I noticed, wouldn't meet my gaze, worrying her lower lip as she stared hard at the parchment. Lewella looked over at her as I settled in my seat, Seren giving her a slight nod before taking a deep breath and finally looking up at me.

"This was brought to Lewella this afternoon," Seren said, pushing the piece of parchment toward me. "I must know if it is true."

I pulled the paper the rest of the way to me. Despite its ragged state, I immediately recognized Drystan's handwriting. Confusion filled me as I began to read, but it was quickly replaced by shock and fury. The scrawling script accused me of conspiring with Lorcan and Fianna while serving Cadfael, even going as far as to say that Drystan had worried that I was involved in a potential plot that he had uncovered, centering around taking Cadfael's life. A hard knot grew in my belly and I clenched my jaw as I shoved the letter back at Seren.

"You know this isn't true," I told her, my tone hard.

"No one here is trying to unjustly accuse you," Lewella said, giving me a pointed look. "I'm the one who insisted you be brought here, without knowing why, and questioned about this. As warrior chief, I can't just shrug something like this off."

"When I left Lorcan, I left him for good," I said, my hands tightening into fists under the table. "I would *never* go back to Fianna. Not after what Seren did to free my soul."

"I knew you wouldn't," Seren said, the tension leaving her shoulders as she let out a deep breath. "And I could find no connection between you and Fianna in the Spirit Realm, but Lewella felt you needed to be questioned. And I..." She swallowed hard. "Things haven't exactly been clear to me of late in my visions. Lewella expressed concern over Fianna clouding my visions, twisting what I'm seeing and I'm Ri now. I had to know the truth. I had to put any doubts to rest."

I could tell by her expression and her tone that she'd taken no joy in what had just happened, but it still hurt. The knots in my belly remained clenched and an uncomfortable tension passed between us. Things *had* changed since she had become Ri, in ways I hadn't accounted for.

"Whatever Drystan thought he found, it wasn't true," I said, my gaze moving to Lewella, unable to so easily shake off my frustration with her either. From a purely defensive standpoint, I could understand what she'd done, but her lack of trust still cut. "You know how he felt about me. I'm not going to lie and say I had great fondness for either him or Cadfael, but I wasn't going back to the darkness I'd left behind."

"I know how much Drystan resented you," Lewella replied. "Believe me, I do. He was always ready to believe the worst and jump to conclusions where you were concerned. I'm willing to chock this up to Drystan making assumptions about things he didn't have any solid proof of and letting his prejudice get the better of him." She paused, getting to her feet. "Is that enough for you, Ri Seren?"

"Yes," Seren answered, letting out a long, low, breath. "Thank you, Pennathe Lewella."

"You're welcome, as always," Lewella replied. "We'll leave the two of you."

She walked over to Emer, the two of them giving both Seren and me respectful nods before departing the study. When the door shut behind them, Seren slumped in her seat, bringing a hand to her forehead.

"I'm sorry," she sighed. "I didn't want to accuse you of what Drystan did, much less believe it. But I have to think of the clan now, too."

"I wouldn't go back to Fianna," I said, my voice catching as my hurt bled through. "Not after what you did, after the price you paid for my soul. I swear that to you."

She got up and I stood as well. She came over and wrapped her arms around my waist, pressing her face into my chest and I held her tight.

"I hated that I had to do that," she said, her shoulders drooping. "Truly, I did."

"We'll get through this," I murmured, kissing the top of her head. "No matter what trouble gets thrown at us. Together."

"Together," she repeated, giving me a light squeeze.

She made no move to leave my arms and I continued to hold her, working to set my own hurt and doubts aside, even as residual anger swirled within me. I wanted to know just how that letter had come into Lewella's possession, for I could see no purpose for it other than someone wanting to cause trouble. I'd known people didn't care for me, but to spread such lies? To accuse me of being a traitor?

The thoughts left a bitter taste in my mouth and I swallowed hard, my hold on Seren tightening ever so slightly. We would get through this, and we'd do it together. At some point, people would have to see that what we were doing was for the good of the clan and they'd have to get tired of opposing us. I had to believe that, for the both of us.

CHAPTER 51

MEANT TO RULE

Seren

I BELIEVED BRAN. IT had hurt me as much as it had hurt him to call him before me and even remotely imply that he might have done what Drystan had accused him of. I'd hoped that confrontation would be the end of it, but the rest of Clogwyn, and a large part of the clan, didn't seem so easily convinced.

Laoise had brought me the letter, insisting that Bran couldn't trusted, which alone was suspect, as far as I was concerned. She had every reason to make up falsehoods; she'd been opposing us from the moment Bran and I had become Ri and Tiarna. My insistence, and Lewella's, that there was no truth to Drystan's accusations had meant nothing to her. At every turn, Laoise was sowing doubt and distrust, and nothing I did or said seemed to put a stop to it.

But Laoise wasn't my only trouble. My visions of late had, once again, grown dark and still the Spirits whispered of the blood of the line of Blaidd. Their whispers, and the glimpses of darkness and fire, only further confused me. I'd begged the Spirits for answers, but they'd only continued to keep the images in my visions shrouded in shadows, leaving me with nothing but frustration. They were capricious beings, they always had been, capable of sending great aid while also capable of leaving more questions than answers. Yet at the same time, I knew what I had borne witness to. Lorcan had died, the shadow creatures and Fianna's fire along with him. I'd seen that with my own two eyes. *Then why is the land still not healed?*

The intrusive thought left a sick feeling in the pit of my stomach and I shook my head, taking a deep breath and focusing between Ceol's ears. *Time,* I told myself as my stallion walked down the streets of Gefell. *It just needs more time.* But that excuse was starting to sound hollow, even to me, and far too much like my father.

Emer rode beside me, two more warriors close behind us. I'd just finished meeting with the village elder, Tesni, inquiring about the state of the village and any needs that those who called it home might have. While Tesni had been polite enough, I had still sensed an undercurrent of wariness from her. That distrust was something I'd seen play out far too often since becoming Ri and try as I might, I couldn't seem to shake it.

Ceol spooked as we rounded a corner, scooting forward and drawing me out of my thoughts as I fought to keep my balance on his back. A large group of villagers had gathered in the middle our path and the stallion tensed as he eyed them warily. I stroked his neck, keeping control of him as we brought our horses to an abrupt stop. The villagers advanced toward us with angry shouts, and my chest clenched. Their voices were jumbled, but I still picked out things from their angry cries: demands to denounce Bran and accusations about a fire somewhere in the north.

Ceol pranced in place, the villagers moving to surround us, the tension in the air palpable. I didn't know what fire they spoke of, but the mere mention of it was enough to make my stomach tie itself into knots and a cold chill wash over me. This couldn't be happening again. We had defeated Fianna with the power of the Wolf Spirit. It couldn't be back.

Emer moved her mare in front of Ceol in an attempt to block the villagers from reaching me. "Keep them at bay!" she called to the warriors behind us before turning to me. "We need to get you back to the castle. *Now.*"

She did her best to shield me as we pushed our horses through the crowd, breaking into a gallop as soon as we were clear of the villagers. My heart pounded as we raced back to Clogwyn, the sick feeling in the pit of my stomach growing with each step Ceol took. I had no idea if the fire the villagers were yelling about was real or nothing more than a rumor, but I would get to the bottom of it as soon as I could.

Emer pushed us hard and Ceol had broken into a lather by the time we reached the portcullis of the granite keep. Once we were through the gate, I handed Ceol off to a stablehand, who immediately promised me he would personally make sure the horse was fully cooled out before going back into his paddock after our hasty ride. Once we'd handed the horses off, Emer ushered me up the steps. We'd only just stepped through the heavy oak doors when we were met by Mair.

"Ithel arrived at the castle less than a half hour ago," she said, her shoulders tense and her expression troubled. "He demanded an audience with Seren. When he was told she wasn't here, he refused to leave, and Laoise and Arwel insisted he be allowed to wait in the Ri's study. He wouldn't say what he wanted."

"Then I suppose I shouldn't keep him waiting," I said, my heartbeat ticking up a notch at the unwelcome news.

I didn't know what Ithel was here for, but after the alarming encounter in Gefell, it made me feel even more on edge. I knew he'd retreated to Gefell after leaving his place at Clogwyn and as far as I knew, he was no more of a supporter of me now than he'd been the day he'd left the castle.

"I'm going with you," Emer said. "I don't trust him. Especially after what just happened."

"I can go as well, if you would like," Mair said. "I'm free for the rest of the afternoon; Cian doesn't need me."

Since I'd appointed her to the council, Mair had been splitting her duties between the council and the infirmary, something Laoise and Arwel had made it clear they found inappropriate from an advisor, but I had no issue with it. Honestly, I wondered that if the rest of my council had work outside of their advisory duties, maybe they'd have less time to plot and cause trouble. As a member of my current council, it wouldn't be a bad idea to have Mair with me, and the stubborn set of Emer's jaw told me she wouldn't be talked out of joining us.

"Let's go see what he wants then," I said, motioning for the both of them to follow me.

The three of us strode through the castle to the Ri's study and I tried not to dwell on the worst-case scenarios that would have drawn my former advisor—and unquestionable enemy—back to the castle, not that that was easy. When we reached the study, the warriors standing guard let us inside, where we found Ithel sitting comfortably at the table in the room's center. He barely acknowledged me with a respectful nod as we approached him, and his smug expression made my spine stiffen.

"And where is your husband, Ri Seren?" Ithel asked as the three of us took a seat.

"Helping Pennathe Lewella train the new members of the war band," I answered. "Is there something I can do for you, Ithel?"

"I've come to express my concerns," he said. "And it appears not a moment too soon if the shifter is involving himself with the war band."

"Bran was a part of the war band before becoming Tiarna," I replied, my jaw clenching at his refusal to use Bran's name or title. "What are these concerns you wish to raise?"

"Two things have come to my attention," Ithel said. "The first is that there was a fire not far from Beag a few days ago. A wildfire, admittedly, from what I have heard, but there are rumors that there were some oddities about the blaze."

I bit the inside of my cheek, trying to keep my expression neutral. I didn't want him to know I had not heard of such a thing yet, even if he was only here spreading falsehoods.

"The second," he continued, "involves the accusations against your Tiarna. I have been made aware that proof was found that he was still involved with Lorcan and Fianna all the while convincing Cadfael and the rest of us that he was loyal to the clan. I would certainly say that is highly suspicious, especially if taken into account with the recent reports from Beag. Who is to say that Bran has not fooled us all and is still Fianna's servant?"

"I would warn you to take care making such accusations of your Tiarna," I said, stiffening in my seat, anger leaving my body hot and my face flushed.

"Oh, believe me when I say that I do not make such accusations lightly. You father was, at times, misguided toward the end of his life, but he understood what it meant to rule. You, I fear, will lead us all to ruin following your heart instead of your head."

"What is this purpose of your visit, Ithel?" I retorted, my patience with him and his insults growing thin. "You are no longer a member of my council."

"To warn you." His eyes narrowed, his face twisting into a glower. "I will not sit back and watch you ruin your father's legacy. Rhonwen's bow or not, I do not believe for one moment that you are the Wolf Spirit's chosen to lead the Clan of Blaidd and each moment that passes, you prove that more and more true. Do not think I will go quietly, Ri Seren."

He got to his feet, the tension in the room thick as his threat settled over me, leaving me curling my hands into fists under the table. Emer and Mair both eyed him with distaste as he stepped around the table.

"I will make certain a warrior sees you back to Gefell," Emer said, getting up as well. "We wouldn't want any ill to befall you, especially with these dangerous times you have hinted at."

A look passed between Emer and me and I gave her a slight nod before she saw Ithel out. Sending an escort with him would be more about keeping him from causing trouble than his safety, but either way, it was a wise move. As the door closed behind them, my shoulders slumped and I rubbed my forehead, already feeling a headache forming. Would there be no end to this?

"I assume there is no news of this fire?" I asked Mair.

"Not that I'm aware of," she answered. "Unless—"

She was cut off by the door loudly banging open and we both started, turning in our seats to see Lewella and Bran stride into the room. Bran immediately hurried over to my side and Lewella wasn't far behind him.

"Are you alright?" he asked, coming up beside me and resting a hand on my shoulder as he leaned down, worriedly searching my face. "We just heard about what happened in Gefell."

"I'm fine," I answered, taking his hand and giving it a quick squeeze. "Emer got me back to the castle quickly."

"I'm afraid I have more troublesome news," Lewella said as she reached my other side. "A messenger just arrived from Beag."

My stomach dropped and I gripped the edge of my seat. "With what news?"

"It appears there was a fire three days ago, after storms blew through the village," Lewella replied. "From most of the accounts, it was a wildfire from a lightning strike, nothing more. It was out in the wilderness, wasn't large, and didn't spread far. There is, however, one of the villagers who claims to have seen an odd sort of creature near the fire."

"What kind of creature?" I asked, twisting the clan ring with my thumb as a tightness settled in my gut.

"As far as I know, he was light on the details." Lewella pressed her lips together. "Something not overly large, maybe no bigger than a large wolf, but the man claimed it was dark and he didn't get a good look."

"It could have easily just been a wild animal fleeing the blaze," Bran said.

"Certainly plausible." Lewella nodded. "I don't think there's any need to panic and I don't think it's wise to jump to conclusions. Wildfires aren't impossible; they happen, and with this one starting after a series of storms, it could have easily been started by lightning or something of that sort. That being said, the people are anxious."

"And hardly being helped by Ithel and those like him." I sighed, rubbing the clan ring on my finger with my thumb.

Lewella raised her brows, looking between me and Mair.

"He was just here," Mair said. "Threatening Seren and bringing up those baseless accusations against Bran."

Bran grew rigid, his mouth turning down as his hand on my shoulder tightened.

"I can have him watched," Lewella said. "With as tense as matters are right now, especially in Gefell and Clogwyn, the last thing anyone needs is him stirring up trouble."

"It might not be a bad idea to do so," I replied. "Though I think it should be done discreetly."

"I can manage that," Lewella said. "It might even be a task for Bran, if he's willing."

Her gaze flitted to him but before he could respond, Mair made an uneasy noise in the back of her throat. I looked over at her, gesturing for her to speak.

"I'm not trying to imply that Bran is incapable," she said, "but I have concerns that Bran being discovered spying on a former member of the council might add more fuel to this current fire. Especially now that he's Tiarna."

She was more right that I wanted to admit, and judging by Bran's clenched jaw, he was as frustrated as I was with the current predicament we found ourselves in.

"I can find someone else for the task," Lewella said. "Mair makes a valid point."

I nodded, unable to stop myself from releasing another sigh. "I agree that Ithel should be watched. And I want this fire in Beag looked into more closely as well. It can't hurt to be too cautious. I suppose it would also most likely be wise to call another council meeting soon with all this upheaval."

"I will see to Ithel and preparing a group of warriors to send to Beag." Lewella gave me a respectful nod before taking her leave with Emer.

Mair followed shortly after with the promise that she would get word to Domhnall that a council meeting needed to be called soon, as it would be the chief advisor's task to see to the arrangements. As the door closed behind Mair, my gaze drifted to Rhonwen's bow, hanging on the wall a few feet away.

"We saw it destroyed," I said, biting my lower lip. "Everyone who was there did."

"The fire could have been something as simple as a lightning strike," Bran replied, his tone gentle.

"I just want Blaidd to be safe," I said, hating the slight shake that crept into my voice. We'd won. How could this all be coming undone? "I want peace."

"There will be." Bran placed both of his hands on my shoulders before leaning down and lightly kissing the back of my neck. "We just have to stay the course."

He gently massaged my tense muscles and I briefly shut my eyes, leaning into his touch. I couldn't shake the feeling of dread that had washed over me since the encounter in the village, and I hated the doubts that circled and taunted me. I'd known this wouldn't be easy, but I hadn't expected things to be like this. *You promised,* I reminded myself, releasing an unsteady breath. *That was your vow.* At the time I'd sworn my oath to the Wolf Spirit, I had thought it had seemed deceptively easy; apparently, I hadn't been wrong in those suspicions. But it was a vow I had to keep. Even if I was confronted with more of a fight that I'd bargained for.

CHAPTER 52

TAINTED NAME

Bran

THINGS HARDLY GOT BETTER over the following days. If anything, they got worse. There had been another show of protest down in Gefell just yesterday, though thankfully Seren hadn't been present. Ithel, it seemed, was most likely behind the growing unrest, but according to Lewella, he wasn't an idiot. He was careful in what he did and how he did it. No one had managed to catch him in any overt betrayal just yet.

The worst part for me was knowing that the accusations surrounding me were doing nothing to help Seren. Things had gotten even more outlandish in the last few days, with rumors circulating that I was the creature, presumed to be a wolf, that had been seen at the fire in Beag. No matter what Seren said, it wasn't enough to squash such doubts, especially not when the likes of Laoise and Arwel were all too ready to give credence to them.

Domhnall irked me most of all. He had yet to speak out against Seren directly, but neither did he go out of his way to throw his support behind me. As far as the council went, Mair was my only vocal supporter, but her age and the newness of her position didn't lend her much credence, at least as far as the castle inhabitants and the villagers were concerned.

As I opened one of the servant's doors, Cryfder gave a short bark, bringing my attention back to the wolves at my feet. With the door open, the two wolves trotted off ahead of me and into the night, Cryfder momentarily distracted by a moth that came and flapped in his face. I let the wolves go, able to see them by the full light of the moon and the few torches lighting the back side of the castle, knowing they would come back when called.

Crossing my arms, I leaned against the light-colored bark of a nearby birch tree, watching over the two wolves while they did their business. The night air was cool and pleasant, especially after the warm day we'd had, and a light breeze ruffled my hair. I kept an eye on the wolves, but my thoughts inevitably drifted to Seren. It was wearing on her, the rumors and dissention. She was trying to bear it well, but I could see what it was doing to her.

She had thrown herself into trying to connect with the people of Blaidd, especially the village elders, and while not everyone in Blaidd was against her, the ones who were had the loudest voices. On top of that, she hadn't been sleeping well, waking up shaken from her visions. She had been closed-lipped about what she had seen of late and I'd tried not to press her, but whatever it was she was seeing, it wasn't any good.

The wolves soon trotted over to me, ready to go back inside. I rubbed the tops of both their heads with all the affection I felt for them before letting us back into the castle. Seren and I both relished Awyr and Cryfder's companionship these days. Even if no one else cared for us, the wolves were convinced the sun rose and set on us.

Once inside, we made our way up to the castle's second level to return to the Ri's chambers. It had been a bit strange to me, staying in a place I had long known but never envisioned myself inhabiting. Even for Seren, it had been an adjustment living in chambers she had always seen as belonging to her parents. I was just about to our quarters when someone called my name from behind. I stiffened as I recognized Domhnall's voice. He was the last person I wanted to speak to right now, but at the same time, I also couldn't afford to ignore him. He wielded power as chief advisor and I didn't need to give him any more reasons than he already had to oppose me. I stopped, instructing Awyr and Cryfder to stay at my side as I turned around.

"A moment, if you please," Domhnall said upon reaching me.

The torch light cast his features in shadow in the dark hallway, making it difficult to read his expression, but I still noticed him wrinkle his nose in disgust when he glanced at the wolves. Pressing my lips together, I gave a slight nod, despite the fact that what I really wanted to do was avoid him and rejoin my wife in bed.

"I have... concerns that Seren might not fully understand the severity of the current situation," Domhnall said. "Things are hardly getting better and the people are only growing more uneasy."

"And have you discussed this with her?"

"Of course I have." He held up a hand as if to placate me, the action only furthering my annoyance. The man was skilled at making his talking down to you seem polite, I'd give him that.

"This situation, however, is not entirely about her," he continued. "The rumors about you are making people uneasy, especially the recent ones placing you at the scene of the fire in

Beag. And uneasiness has the power to grow into something far more problematic."

"The rumors about me are untrue." My jaw clenched and my spine stiffened. I was so weary of that ridiculous letter from Drystan being brought up, especially after all I had done to save the people of Blaidd from Fianna's darkness.

"Be that as it may," Domhnall said, "there are plenty of people who believe them. And the more recent troubles in the north only add fuel to that fire."

"There has been nothing to tie that fire in the north to Fianna."

"Not yet," Domhnall said, drawing out the words. "But even if there never is, that's not the point. This is politics, Bran. This is about what people believe, not what is. I can understand that you can't grasp that, with your upbringing, but you'd be wise to learn it quickly if you intend to help Seren and not be a burden to her."

"If you're quite done insulting and berating me," I replied, practically snapping the words, "my wife is waiting for me."

He tensed when I said the word *wife*, and it didn't go unnoticed by me. Seren insisted that he had accepted our marriage, but I wasn't so sure. If anything, I suspected the feelings he harbored for Seren were still there, just hiding below the surface.

"I'm warning you," Domhnall said, an edge to his voice. "Your connection to Seren is adding to her troubles. What this clan needs is stability and to be able to trust those leading it. If you can't find some way to clear that tainted name of yours, you're going to ruin her and this clan."

One of my hands clenched into a fist and I took a deep breath to try and keep a rein on my temper. "Thank you for your entirely unsolicited advice."

I didn't let him respond, turning on my heel and calling for the wolves to come with me, the two of them happily obliging.

As I stalked into the Ri's chambers, my blood boiled. I was so over being doubted, tired of being accused of hindering Seren when all I wanted to do, all I had ever wanted to do, was help her.

Clearly reading my sour mood, the wolves left me to go curl up in bed as we stepped through the bedroom door. Seren was seated in front of the vanity, combing her hair, already dressed in a sleeping gown. She turned in her chair when she heard me enter and despite my attempt to school my features, her mouth turned down as she looked at me.

"What is it?" she asked, her brow furrowing.

I hesitated. I valued honesty and I didn't want a lack of it to come between us, but I knew the burdens she already bore, burdens she bore in part because of me. I didn't want to add to them.

"Nothing," I said, forcing myself to smile. "It's just been a long last few days, is all."

She gave a light tilt of her head, searching my face for a long moment before giving a small nod and resuming combing her hair.

I readied for bed myself while she finished with her hair, the two of us soon climbing into the ornate four-poster bed with the wolves. Seren had just pulled the covers up over her when she froze. I knew the tell-tale signs of her having a vision, from the rigidity of her body to her dilated eyes. I moved over to her, slipping an arm around her shoulders as I waited for it to pass.

The vision wasn't a long one, but when she came to, she was still gasping for breath and wracked with tremors. I tugged her to me, rubbing her shoulder as the two of us waited for the aftereffects of the vision to pass. Awyr had crawled over to us, the black wolf eying Seren intently as she nudged at her hand with her black nose. Seren gave a tremulous smile, rubbing the wolf behind the ears.

"Feeling better?" I asked Seren, kissing the top of her head as her shaking began to cease.

She nodded, pressing her lips together before letting out a heavy sigh. The droop in her shoulders and the way she wouldn't quite meet my gaze only added to my growing unease. I worried for her, for us, and for Blaidd.

"What did you see?" I asked her, despite knowing full well I might not get an answer. The ever-changing nature of the future meant that seers did not always share everything they'd seen, and I tried to respect that.

She rubbed her forehead, staring at her lap for a moment before finally looking back up. "I'm not entirely sure what I'm seeing. Not yet."

"But it worries you?"

Her gaze drifted to the window, a pained expression drifting across her face.

"Yes," she said, her voice strained.

As much as I wanted to press her, I could tell she didn't want to take the topic of conversation further tonight. I blew out the candles near the bed and we both curled up under the blankets, the wolves coming to sleep on our feet like they did every night.

Seren fell asleep quickly, no doubt exhausted from her vision. I, on the other hand, found that sleep would not come so easily. I tossed and turned, unable to get Seren's haunted voice and Domhnall's pointed words out of my thoughts, one phrase in particular that he had hurled at me staying with me more than any other. *If you can't find some way to clear your tainted name...*

My word meant something to only a few. What I needed was proof: proof that Drystan's letter was fabricated, solid proof that the fire in the north was nothing more than a wildfire and that we were all spooking at nothing because Fianna had truly been destroyed. I needed proof—the clan needed proof—that I was the right person to be Tiarna of Blaidd.

I rolled over again, staring at the dark outline of Seren's sleeping form. She wouldn't say it, but I knew how much harder our marriage was making things for her. I loathed to admit it, but Domhnall was right. She *needed* me to clear my name so that all these accusations, all this darkness, could finally be put to rest.

Before I lost my nerve, I slipped out of bed, careful not to wake her. I'd been locked up in the castle for weeks and if I was going to get to the bottom of this, I needed to get outside it. I was tired of the concerns over how things would look or what others would perceive. I had a gift. It was time I used it.

I worked quietly to pack only the smallest and most basic necessities onto my person, things that would stay with me when I shifted. As I straightened after slipping a dagger into my boot, my gaze fell back on Seren and my throat tightened. I was doing this for her, for our clan, but there was still a part of me that worried she wouldn't understand. I could have woken her, could have told her what I intended, but I was too afraid she'd try and stop me.

Swallowing against the lump in my throat, I walked over to a table near one of the windows where Seren usually handled her correspondence. I picked up a quill and carefully pulled out a small, empty piece of parchment. I dipped a quill in the ink but then hesitated. How much should I tell her? I wrestled with the question for a few long moments before finally jotting down a few sentences. I wouldn't be gone long, only a few weeks at the absolute most. As soon as I got to the bottom of this, I'd return and once my name was clear, no one would have any reason to doubt me. There was no need to involve Seren any more than necessary, not right now and not with the way the vultures of Clogwyn had been circling her, looking for any weakness or sign she wasn't fit for her role.

I folded the parchment and set the quill back in its holder, fingering the leather handfasting bracelet I wore on my wrist. I intended to travel predominantly in my wolf form, but I wouldn't be able to stay in it the entire time. The bracelet would be another clue as to who I was. I wanted, needed, to remain unnoticed and unseen while I was away. Ignoring the tightness in my belly, I unclasped the bracelet, laying it on top of the letter, a silent promise to Seren that I would return to her. When I walked back to the bed, Cryfder woke, pricking his ears toward me and looking as if he were ready to bolt up at any moment.

"Stay," I quietly told him, creeping over to Seren's side.

I leaned over and pressed the softest kiss I could to her cheek in an effort not to wake her. "I love you," I murmured as I eased away from her, knowing she wouldn't hear me, but also feeling like I had to leave her with those words.

She stirred slightly at my touch, grumbling something unintelligible under her breath before falling back into deep sleep. I couldn't suppress my smile, even as my chest ached. The little things, like how much she hated to have her rest interrupted, were the things I would miss being away from her. *But when I come back, we'll be one step closer to peace,* I told myself as I stepped back from the bed. Cryfder still eyed me where he lay, his golden eyes almost seeming to beg me to take him with me, wherever I was going, but he stayed put as I'd told him.

Tearing my gaze away from the things I loved the most in this life, my wife and our wolves, I squared my shoulders and strode over to the door. I let myself out into the bedroom and into the common room, trying to ignore the way my heart raced. It wouldn't be easy to get out of Clogwyn unseen; Lewella had kept the castle closely guarded since the trouble with Ithel, and with good reason, but there were benefits to being Tiarna. I knew where warriors would be and where they wouldn't.

Already formulating my plan, I crept out into the hallway. I hated that part of me felt like a traitor, sneaking away in the night like this, but I consoled myself with the reminder that I wouldn't be gone long. As soon as I'd handled this for Seren, I would return.

CHAPTER 53

VANISHED

Seren

CRYFDER WOKE ME, NUDGING my hand and letting out low whines as he stood over me in the bed. I rubbed my eyes and sat up halfway, glancing down at Awyr, who was at my feet but also looking at me expectantly.

"I'm coming," I told them, throwing back the covers. "Usually you wake Bran up when you need to..."

I trailed off when I looked over at the other side of the bed. Bran wasn't there. The covers were pulled up and only the slightly askew pillows were any sign he'd slept there the night before. I frowned, swinging my legs over the side of the bed. Perhaps he had gotten an early start to the day? Though for what, I didn't know.

Shaking my head, I got to my feet, Cryfder leaping down next to me and letting out another series of low whines. I rubbed the top of his head and grabbed a dressing robe to pull on over my sleeping gown. Normally, I would get at least mostly dressed before taking the wolves out, but I could tell that Cryfder's needs were rather urgent.

As I pulled a pair of my boots out of my wardrobe, something caught my eye. I straightened and my stomach lurched at the sight of Bran's handfasting bracelet laying on my desk. My pulse quickened as I walked over to it, my mouth growing dry. It lay on top of a folded piece of parchment that bore my name written in Bran's hasty scrawl. I picked the bracelet up, clutching it in my hand as I hastily unfolded the letter, scanning its contents:

I fear that you will not understand why I must do this, but I will be back. I promise you that. And when I return, we'll be one step closer to putting these troubles to rest.

All my love,

Bran

I blinked rapidly as I stared down at the page, my stomach churning as I tried to digest what I had just read. Even though I knew he wasn't here, I caught myself looking around the room, my grip on his handfasting bracelet so tight that the leather dug into my skin. How could he have just left? And sneaking out in the middle of the night?

My gaze dropped to the letter again as I hastily reread it. He was right. I *didn't* understand. Yes, we'd had our share of troubles of late, but why react this way? Why leave without a word? *And why leave his handfasting bracelet while at the same time promising to return?* I thought, swallowing against the lump in my throat. It didn't add up. It didn't make sense, and I was desperate for it to just turn out to be some sort of badly made joke.

I shoved the letter and the bracelet in the pocket of my dressing robe, almost ashamed at the shakiness of my hands, and pulled on my boots. Once I'd made sure my hair wasn't a complete fright, I called the wolves to me. When I strode out of our bedchamber into the common room, I hoped to perhaps find Bran there, ready to explain himself, but the room was empty. Letting out a shuddering breath, I stepped out into the hallway, the wolves trailing behind me. Since becoming Ri, I had fallen away from my father's insistence that the Ri chambers continually be guarded, thinking him nothing more than paranoid, but now I was wondering if there had been wisdom to that choice. It would have certainly made it harder for Bran to run away in the dead of night.

My insides still quivered as I navigated the winding hallways, descending the stairs and using one of the side doors to get the wolves out to the back of the castle. I managed to avoid any servants or warriors, something I was grateful for. I wasn't in a state where I was ready to run into anyone this morning. The castle grounds were blessedly quiet and I remained by the servants' door while Cryfder and Awyr trotted off to relive themselves.

The sun was breaking over the horizon and I could feel the warmth it would bring to the day, but the morning still bore a slight chill, causing me to pull my robe a little tighter around myself. I stuck my hand in my pocket and fidgeted with the bracelet, my throat tightening as I did so. I didn't care if he meant to return or not. What he had done had hurt.

We should have discussed it. Whatever it was that caused him to feel the need to leave, he could have told me. How many times had I defended him these last few months? I would have listened, tried to understand. He should have known that. Awyr and Cryfder finally rejoined me and I turned to go back inside, only to have the door swing open before I could get a hold of it.

"Spirits, Seren, my apologies," Domhnall said as I barely managed to get out of the way of the door. "Are you alright?"

"I'm fine," I replied, forcing a smile. If it were anyone else, I might have been suspicious as to what he was doing up and about at such an early hour, but I knew he often enjoyed taking his stallion out for a ride before breakfast.

"You're sure you're alright?" he asked, frowning as he searched my face.

The ache in my chest and in the back of my throat left me tempted to break down right there and tell him what all had transpired, but I knew how complex things had gotten at Clogwyn of late. I needed to know for certain about Bran before I spread such potentially troublesome news.

"I'm sure," I answered.

He pursed his lips but gave a slight nod, stepping aside so that I could pass through the door and back into the castle. I should have let him go, but as he went to step outside after me, I couldn't seem to stop myself.

"Have you seen Bran?" I asked, fighting to keep my tone casual.

"Can't say that I have," he said, stopping in the doorway and turning to face me. "Although..."

He ducked his chin and I tensed. "Although what?"

"I did see him last night, in passing," he said. "We spoke briefly and there were comments that he made, ones that, well... made it seem as if perhaps he were second-guessing his future here."

I felt like I had been punched in the gut and moisture stung my eyes, the note and bracelet in my pocket feeling as heavy as the granite stones that littered the mountainsides.

"I have to get ready for breakfast," I said, clearing my throat to try and rid myself of the unsteadiness in my voice. "Enjoy your ride."

I turned and left before he could press me further, Awyr and Cryfder following me obediently. I passed only a few servants as I hurried back to my chambers as quickly as I dared and somehow, I managed to keep it together until I was in the privacy of the Ri's chambers. Once I had closed the door behind me, however, the tears began to streak down my cheeks. I walked over to the closest chair, slumping down into it and yanking the note and bracelet from my pocket.

I read the note again, and again a second time, all while Domhnall's words rang in my ears. I didn't want to believe Bran had run off in secrecy, but the damning evidence was staring me in the face. I crumpled the note with one hand, the parchment now stained with my tears, making the ink run. My worst fears were ones I couldn't keep at bay: the fear that he would never come back and that maybe, in the end, he had betrayed me after all.

CHAPTER 54

NEVER COMING BACK

Seren

"They're waiting for you."

There was a deep part of me that wanted to ignore Mother. That didn't want to have to go sit down in front of the council and the village elders and admit the wrongness of my misplaced trust. It had been Domhnall's idea, and a valid one considering the shockwaves of unrest that had traveled through the clan with the news of Bran's disappearance. And even as that part of me bristled against what was ahead of me, I knew that I must follow through with it. I had made a vow, a promise to our people, and unlike the man I had called husband, I would not break such things lightly.

Taking in a deep breath and letting it out slowly, I turned away from the window in my common room to face Mother, somewhat surprised to see Cian with her. Not that I minded my cousin's intrusion. I had leaned on him heavily these last few days. This morning marked a full week since Bran's disappearance and it had been one of the longest weeks of my life. Lewella had investigated his sudden flight from Clogwyn, but had found no evidence of any foul play.

We had heard nothing; he had simply vanished into the night. For what purposes, Spirits only knew. In my heart, I still wanted to believe him innocent. It made me sick inside to think that he had gone back to Fianna, especially knowing the sacrifice I had made for his soul. Still, despite all the wantings of my heart, I fully recognized how his running off looked in light of the accusations made against him. Not to mention the Spirits' warnings and a second, albeit small, fire that had happened in the north.

The sight of Mother and Cian's worried expressions as they studied me had my throat thickening and my chest aching. I was so weary of crying. I had shed far too many tears for a man who had most likely shed none for me. Mother stepped forward and gently took hold of my upper arms, waiting for me to look up at her.

"You are not responsible for his actions," she said, holding my gaze. "I do not care what they say in there. He made his choices. Choices you had nothing to do with."

I knew she was right, but I would be lying if I said I hadn't struggled with guilt and doubts in Bran's absence. I worried I had failed my people. That in thinking Fianna defeated, I had missed its last remaining servant hiding right in front of me.

"I cannot help but feel a fool for trusting him," I said, dropping my chin and biting down hard on my lower lip.

"You are not the only one he fooled," Mother replied. "It was an honest mistake and you have enough humility to recognize it. The council and the elders cannot ask for more than that."

I swallowed hard, managing a nod.

"This will pass," Mother said as she pulled me into a hug. "It is his loss, Seren. It's nothing you did."

I clung to her in return, part of me still amazed that she was here, comforting me in the midst of all of my grief. I might have lost Bran, but I had gained my mother. When we eased back from one another, Cian pulled me into a hug as well, bringing tears to my eyes all over again.

"If I ever see him again," he said, "I'll beat him to a pulp."

"Not if I do it first," I replied, my voice muffled by his chest.

He let out a soft laugh as he stepped back. "I'll let you beat him to a pulp first and then I'll follow. How's that?"

"Acceptable," I said, managing a weak half-smile. One of the first I'd been able to muster up in days.

"I suppose there's no point in trying to put this off any longer," I said, letting out a long, low breath as my gaze drifted to the door.

There was no ignoring the quiver in my belly or the ache in my heart as we stepped out into the hallway. Despite wanting to curl up and hide with my grief and hurt, I did not have that option. I had to be strong for my people. I couldn't ignore what was happening around me and what I was seeing in my visions. Despite everything we'd done, everything we'd sacrificed, Fianna was still lurking. It was time to make it clear to my people that I would lead them through this building storm. It was time to label my husband a traitor.

Read More

Bran and Seren's story continues in The Seer!
Connect with Hannah E. Carey on her website at

www.hannahecarey.com

Want more adventures in the world of Pern Coen?

Tales of Pern Coen

The Hunter (Rhiannon & Conor's Story)

The Huntress (Rhiannon & Conor's Story)

The Successor (Briallen & Torin's Story)

The Betrayer (Ciara & Niall's Story)

The Ascendant (Ciara & Niall's Story)

Legends of Pern Coen

The Shifter (Bran & Seren's Story)

The Scout (Bran & Seren's Story)

The Seer (Bran & Seren's Story)

<u>Tales of Kelnore</u>

The Duchess (Faustina & Idris' Story)

About the Author

Hannah began writing stories from a young age and hasn't stopped since. She read her first romance novel as a young teen, quickly falling in love with the genre. She writes romantic fantasy with fierce heroines that is inspired by her love of mythology and contemporary romance that stars loveable four-legged companions. When she's not writing, you'll find her reading romance novels and spending time with her husband, horses, and dog on her small hobby farm.